"I don't laugh anymore at people when they say they have seen UFOs. I've seen one myself."

Former President Jimmy Carter
ABC News January 22, 1999

"I believe that these extraterrestrial vehicles and their crews are visiting this planet from other planets."

Major Gordon Cooper – Mercury Astronaut

"We can't deny that, and the evidence points to the fact that, Roswell was a real incident, and that indeed an alien craft did crash, and that material was recovered from that crash site..."

Astronaut Dr. Edgar Mitchell,
Apollo 14 Mission

"It is time for the truth to be brought out in open Congressional hearings. Behind the scenes, high-ranking Air Force officers are soberly concerned about the UFOs. But, through official secrecy and ridicule, many citizens are lead to believe the unknown flying objects are nonsense. To hide the facts, the Air Force has silenced its personnel."

Former Director of Central Intelligence,
Vice Admiral R.H. Hillenkoetter
The New York Times, Sunday,
February 28, 1960

HYBRID

THE TRILOGY

by

Louise Rose Aveni

ngel House Publishing

Sarasota, Florida

Disclaimer

This book was written as a work of fiction and, as such, any resemblance to persons living or dead is strictly the result of intertwining a compilation of personalities with the author's artistic creativity.

For information regarding permissions, write to:

Angel House Publishing
 8357 38th Street
Circle E #102
Sarasota, Florida 34243

Cover and Interior by George Cieszka
www.SRQwebdesigns.com

ISBN 13: 978-0-615-36366-0
Printed in the U.S.A.
Printed May 2010

Table of Contents

Book I

LUPO — Conversations With an E.T.

Book II

HYBRID–The Conversation Continues

Book III

KYRSTAL 2012–A New Beginning

*Why shouldn't truth be stranger than fiction?
Fiction, after all, has to make sense.*

– Mark Twain

Author's Notes

As we embrace the new dawning of the Age of Aquarius, taking another quantum leap into the acceptance of other beings, new dimensions, and spiritual realms, life on other planets holds the portent of an infinite number of possibilities.

No longer is this subject taboo. Quite the opposite. The human race, as we have come to perceive it, is not only reaching for the stars for answers but going inward on a parallel quest for truth.

You are about to embark on a literary journey into one of those infinite possibilities. The determination of its validity lies deep within the reader's soul. Only *you* can decide what rings as truth to you.

After all … what is unseen by some… is realty and experience for others.

Heartfelt Thanks

This has been such an amazing journey and one I have not had to travel alone. So it is then, that I take this opportunity to give thanks to those special spirits both in physical and non-physical, who have guided me and supported me by lending their talents and genuine inspiration in helping to make another dream come true.

Many thanks to:

My daughter Christine—Heartfelt thanks for your brilliant expertise in bringing your Mother's old ways into the technological now. Your persistence and diligence opened new avenues that proved to be invaluable. I am so proud of the woman you've become. I love you beyond words!

My daughter Vicki—How can I ever thank you enough for providing me with temporary safe haven and the magical space to write the majority of this epic. Love you to pieces!

Rosemary—Thank you for your unconditional love and friendship; your unwavering belief in me and encouragement to stick with it and see it through; but most of all, for providing the wherewithal for me to follow my passion. I am eternally grateful!

To my dear, dear family and friends from "A" to "Z" who

believe in me and have the uncanny ability to keep me grounded, yet let me fly and dream, all at the same time. Keep it up, as
I am nothing without you all! I am forever grateful and eternally
blessed to have you in my experience. Namaste!

Finally, to my "unseen"spiritual family — Your constant
inspiration and guidance keeps me forging ahead, even when I
lose my way. This is a story that needed to be told...and so, I do
this for you!

Peace to your journey
Love and light to your path
One in Spirit
Journey Well.

Foreword From
Stanton Friedman

As a nuclear physicist who has been interested in many different aspects of the UFO subject since 1958, I am very much aware of the enormous amount of information that has been processed via books, videos, TV programs, magazine articles, conference proceedings and radio talk shows. Unfortunately, through the veil of biased media, there has been a great variation in the accuracy and believability of this massive intrusion into our world. So many reported incidences, such as government attacks on flying saucers and various contactee scenarios are viewed as pure fabrication. However, the fact that the public-at-large continues to have a genuine interest and concern about this subject, is evidenced by some of the top grossing motion pictures of all time; such as **Close Encounters of the Third Kind**, **ET, Independence Day**, and the most recent movie blockbuster **Avatar**, which delves deeply into otherworldly possibilities. Many people have told me how impressed they were with the 1975 NBC dramatization, starring James Earl Jones, called "The UFO Incident of Betty and Barney Hill" that depicted their claims of an alien abduction.

The SETI Community (which *should* stand for Silly Effort to Investigate) has been consistently positive about the notion of there being perhaps as many as 10,000 civilizations in the galaxy and are able to transmit radio messages over interstellar distances, with Earth being one of these elite receptive groups. The problem is, SETI has appointed itself to handle this communication on behalf of the rest of the planet! SETI, of course, takes it as a given that there is no colonization, no migration, and no terra-forming, out in the vastness of space and so they unilaterally conclude that there is neither sensible nor scientific data in support of or relating to alien visitations. It's as if they've created a communication party line that deduced - NO UFOs!

Obviously, if aliens are visiting then there isn't much point in SETI, as that clearly indicates how they blatantly ignore all the large scale scientific studies that have been done. They conveniently and deliberately overlook the dozens of UFO related PhD theses and massive black budget programs. They arrogantly choose to disregard all the physical trace evidence cases, the hundreds of witnessed radar visual incidences, and the unambiguous confirmation that government agencies have, indeed, been withholding important evidence from the public. They don't seem to have any concern about the plausibility that alien spies may be living among us.

In HYBRID-The Trilogy, Louise Rose Aveni has created a fictional but fascinating inside look at what may really be happening and where we may be headed in the aftermath of 2012. With actual facts interwoven with creative storytelling, not surprisingly, she assumes that such avant-garde skills as long distance interpersonal communications are ever present and that interspecies planetary interaction has been going on for thousands of years. Hybridization, something quite new here on Earth, is an implicit tool for penetrating a society. It is comprehensible that if there has been colonization and migration, that our local galactic neighborhood may well be loaded with civilizations having rules about contact with such primitive newbies as us.

It's also highly possible that past civilizations came here to colonize the planet millions of years ago and that "WE" might be the result of that colonization. Judging by our hostile actions towards one another, Earth may very well have been chosen as a penal colony for those who committed galactic crimes. A little known fact is that Australia was originally settled by convicts, so it's not a far stretch to imagine our planet's original role in the solar system.

We now know that there are cataclysmic events that happen throughout our galaxy, such as meteor strikes, supernova explosions, and how depletion of resources, indeed, occur, making it all the more paramount to explore our local galactic neighborhood, for possible future colonization in the event of cosmic catastrophe.

One could confidently presume that every civilization is concerned with their own survival and security, which unquestionably translates into keeping tabs on the "primitives in its neighborhood"...such as us. I'm sure they're well versed on gamma bursts, polar shifts, earthquakes, tsunamis and other such potential cataclysms and any additional preordained cosmic anomalies.

As Earthlings, we take great pride in our accomplishments and our scientific advancements, however, some other nearby civilization may view us quite differently, thus considering us a threat to the cosmic neighborhood and are making a deliberate intent to prevent us from moving off the planet before we get our act together.

Anyone observing us from "out there" may be greatly disheartened by the simple fact that we're such a primitive society, one whose major activity has been that of tribal warfare. After all, during World War II we destroyed 1,700 of our own cities and killed 50 -Million of our own kind.

In 1938, humanity discovered nuclear fusion, the process that powers the stars. Within fourteen years thereafter, we exploded the first H-bomb, a fusion device with a three-mile wide fireball, releasing the energy of some 10 - million tons of TNT. Again, while considered innovative by humans, I'm sure that we're behind the times and rightly viewed as unruly juveniles by more advanced civilizations, who have long held this knowledge and so much more. So, it would not be unreasonable to assume that any civilization that understands the application of the fusion processes, would utilize it in connection with ultra-speed interstellar travel. It is impossible to believe that our local space-faring organizations would permit us to venture out with our brand of antagonistic friendship...which everybody else recognizes as out and out hostility.

So, as you consider who we are, where we're from and what our role is in the great scheme of things, I expect that you'll find HYBRID a contemplative and enjoyable read that inspirationally guides you through the realm of possibilities.

Stanton T. Friedman Nuclear Physicist
www.stantonfriedman.com

Book I

LUPO

CONVERSATIONS WITH AN E.T.

*To Mom and Dad and to all those in spirit
who know the truth*

Prologue

Somewhere in the foothills of the Matterhorn, just over the border of the Italian Alps, a small child races frantically into the cold, dark autumn night as the cries of wolves echo in the distance.

Stephan, barely three years old, cries out as, in haste, his delicate skin is pricked and scratched by low-lying brush that obstructs his flight. His ebony eyes are wide in full dilation to receive what little moonlight filters through the thicketed forest. All the while, his chest heaves to retain the breath that will lurch him forward even further into the night.

Distant voices call out to him, but he does not answer. Stopping only long enough to catch his breath, this desperate child of the night darts off in yet another random direction with no apparent course or destination.

The wolves' cries are ever closer while those of the humans are swallowed up in the abyss behind him.

Running harder now, he cannot stop, must not stop. He races blindly deeper into the forest in an attempt to secure safe haven, but from whom or from what? For all along, hasn't his course been deliberately set not in the direction of the voices that implore his response ... but away from them?

Growing weary, he slows his pace. Fatigue now betrays his young muscles as the terrain beneath his tender feet becomes mountainous.

Faltering at each effort of every step, he suddenly trips, falling in slow motion over a large unseen tree root. Before he can cry out in pain, the sounds of something moving in the nearby brush force him to cover his mouth, stifling the scream that waits within.

His concentration is now on the sound of breathing, albeit not his own. For he has all but stopped breathing in anticipation of what lurks nearby.

A twig snaps. He gasps another silent breath as his eyes train their focus on the immense yellow eyes that watch him from the surrounding brush.

Too young to gauge what would seem to others an eternity, he watches the creature slowly and stealthfully emerge from the darkness into the moonlight, where its identity is no longer a mystery.

Stephan shouts excitedly, "Lupo!" and as if returning the greeting, the large brown-and-gray wolf tilts its head as it approaches the boy.

Stephan

I was born in a Catholic hospital on February 10, 1957, in Varese, Italy, a little border town located between Italy and Switzerland.

Shortly after my birth, I was placed in an orphanage in Milan, Italy. My Earth name is Stephan (pronounced Ste-phan), last name, not important, as it changed later on, anyway. I never knew my mother or my father and was kept from any knowledge of them for my own protection, I was told. Why? I haven't a clue.

The first few years of my life were spent in foster homes. My earliest childhood recollections were around the age of three; I clearly remember having visitations with what I referred to as my "special friends", which, I later learned were E.T.'s (extraterrestrials). I had a blast traveling with them to amazing places in their magical ships and naively assumed everyone else did the same. Boy... was I wrong!

It all began when I was around three years old. I was taken to live with a foster family on a farm situated on a mountain plateau in the highlands, just outside of Milan. In those days, European farmhouses were structured literally like forts with the animals kept in stalls around the perimeter of a rectangular courtyard which featured the family living quarters on an upper level, accessed only by a surrounding catwalk. For centuries, this design was extremely successful in warding off any persons who might entertain thoughts of stealing livestock or causing harm to the residing families.

Oh, how I adored this place! For it was a natural playground for a three- year-old boy, with friendly trees to climb and soft, clay earth just right for making gooey mud pies to throw at my foster siblings. I can vividly recall riding on tractors, digging ditches with my plastic gardening tools and, best of all, not being scolded for getting dirty. Life was good then!

Even now, when I close my eyes I can totally recall the images and the fragrance of the rich brown earth, the brilliant cobalt blue skies with majestic snow-capped mountains off in the distance. For all intents and purposes, this was my heaven on Earth and one I never wanted to leave.

At a very early age, I began what my elders referred to as "sleepwalking"; in fact, I would even say it became one of my specialties, but these nightly excursions were so much more. Let me explain: One night, in particular, while taking one of my "evening strolls," I saw three unusual-looking childlike beings on the catwalk of our living quarters. One of the beings was taller than the other two and, strange as it may sound, I felt no fear and, more importantly, had an inexplicable sense of familiarity in their presence, as if We were connected somehow.

I don't recall actually speaking with them, at least not in the traditional way, but we did share a dialogue of sorts, an exchange of some kind that validated they were, indeed, there before me and meant me no harm. So, I continued to meet with them as often as I could and looked forward with great excitement to whatever new adventure they took me on. You'd think that was enough, wouldn't you… but there was more.

In Italy in the evening hours, the farmers were terrified of Lupo, which in Italian means "wolf." If one was spotted in the area, you could hear cries of "Lupo! Lupo!" – which was the equivalent of someone yelling, "Fire! Fire!" for it drew the same response from the other farmers and their families. My reaction, however, was enormously different, for I was, even at such a young age, an avid animal lover and the innocent child in me considered Lupo to be my friend, much to the dismay of my foster family.

Because I was so naïve, I threw caution to the wind and would *often wander away from the security of the hillside farm to run among the creatures of the forest. As a matter of fact, one night I found myself compelled to venture out into the darkness in search of Lupo. I had absolutely no fear, and so defiantly left the safe haven of the fortress in search of my "special friends" and Lupo. I have to tell you that was the defining moment that changed my life, as my action was viewed as careless and only the beginning of what would be conceived as chronic dysfunctional behavior.*

But I'll also tell you this, that night forever altered the way I looked at this illusion called life and in some strange, unexplainable way made me realize that I was different from everyone else and made me question where I was really from, for I knew deep in my heart I was not from this place called Italy. In fact, more often than not my gaze would drift skyward, searching and waiting. For what, you ask? I really didn't know at the time, but later it was made crystal clear to me.

Here's something else, years later I discovered through a casual reading of an article relating to UFO sightings in Italy, that E.T.'s (extraterrestrials) were referred to as "Lupo." In that moment, the pieces of my human puzzle began to take shape, as did the reasoning behind the magnetic draw toward Lupo and the unearthly visitors.

(Flashback)

Young Stephan bolts upright in his makeshift bed that's constructed on uneven slats of wood harvested from nearby trees surrounding his home - his *Castle in the Clouds,* as he would later refer to it.

His crude mattress, formed out of a combination of old blankets and hay, smells of the livestock housed in the courtyard fortress below; and yet, quite comfortable, at least for a small three-year-old body.

Stephan's bed, an addition to the three others that form the "dormitory" where he and his foster brothers sleep, is positioned nearest the bedroom door as reassurance for the toddler who derives great comfort being one step closer to his foster parents, he calls MaMa and PaPa.

Suddenly, something startles him out of his slumber? Was there a noise? Did anyone else hear it? He guesses not as the others remain deep asleep. The only sounds are the steady rhythmic inhales and exhales of the family, for they show no signs of acknowledgment that anything out of the ordinary is afoot.

Stephan remains alert as he cocks his head first, in one direction, and then in another. His tiny ears listening … listening. *There it is again!*

Now with intense curiosity and total abandon, Stephan throws back his coverlet in one long, effortless motion and then places his small bare feet onto the cold wooden floor.

Garbed only in a flannel nightshirt, even his slight frame causes the wooden floor planks to creak and moan as he pads his way across the dormitory but the sounds go unnoticed by his roommates as they continue their slumber.

With the stealth of a cat, Stephan silently works his way to the doorway of the living quarters, and then tiptoes through the kitchen until he finally spies the outline of the door that leads out onto the catwalk.

Making his way toward the front door, Stephan's focus is momentarily sidetracked, as an immense illumination spills through the kitchen window, giving the appearance of midday. The interruption is short lived and Stephan is, once again, totally engrossed in continuing his exploration of the puzzling sound that jolted him from his slumber.

Even on tiptoe, Stephan's small hands can barely reach the door latch and then…success! Carefully , he opens the door with a slow, deliberate intent so as not to wake the others.

Stepping out onto the catwalk, he's instantly blinded by a light so bright that he immediately covers his eyes with both hands, only peeking between his tiny fingers to allow his curious eyes to adjust. Now standing just outside the door, Stephan takes in a sharp, quick breath of crisp cold air and then releases a trembling shiver as he attempts to ignore the frigid outside temperature.

The illumination spotlights the courtyard below, exposing the livestock as they, too, remain undisturbed in their sleep. Stephan takes delightful notice of the fog that emits from his mouth as his warm breath hits the cold air and wonders if the bright light means it's morning and, if so, why isn't the rest of the family up yet? As his eyes make their final adjustment, Stephan scans the sky above, only to discover the twinkling mass of stars that tell him it is, indeed, still nighttime. Then he sees it! It is the brilliance from the full harvest moon that is the source of all this light.

There it is again! Startled by another noise that seems to come from close behind him, Stephan gasps another gulp of frigid air that's almost too painful to inhale. His eyes now in full expansion strain to bring into focus the shapes that are approaching. He wonders ... *is someone really there?* The question is no sooner thought, than answered — *Yes! Someone or something is there before him!*

First he sees one, then two ... no three! Three shapes coming ever closer to where he stands all alone on the catwalk. Two of the figures appear small — like him — while the third shape is much taller and appears to be standing behind the smaller ones as if introducing them to him, but without a sound. *Where are the words? I don't hear any words?*

They stand before him, their thin, barely there lips not moving; no audible words are exchanged; he only "hears" them in his head. *How do they do that?* he wonders.

For some unknown reason, Stephan has no fear of these strange beings, nor does he pay notice to the cold night air that only a moment before had him wishing he were warm and cozy in his dormitory bed.

A smile begins to form on Stephan's face as the trio moves

ever closer; all the while a low humming sound begins to swell from somewhere, its vibration permeating all that surrounds him, then — suddenly — there is nothing but complete dark silence.

The next thing Stephan realizes is that he's somehow now back in his bed, snuggled deep beneath his blankets. Lying still, eyes blinking furiously, he wonders ... *did that really happen? Was I having a dream?* His mind assures him that it *was* real — at least, to *this* three-year-old it was!

The crowing of the rooster in the courtyard far below officially announces the start of a new day. As the family rises one by one and begins moving about in preparation for breakfast and the daily chores ahead, Stephan bounds out of bed chattering in earnest all the while MaMa, his foster mother, attempts to remove his night clothing and dress him for the day.

As MaMa continues her struggle with this excited, wriggling toddler, Stephan continues to chatter on and on about how ... *first* there was a loud noise that woke him ... then there was the *big bright light* ... then how *very, very cold* the air was outside ... and then — the very best part that he has saved for last — there were those *three beings* coming toward him on the catwalk!

"What? What are you talking about, Stephan?" chirps Antonio, who at age nine is the eldest of the farmer's children and also one of his dormitory roommates. While MaMa pulls the warm crimson sweater she's knitted for Stephan over his head, his muffled reply is soon dismissed as nothing more than a toddler's ramblings about a dream he must have had last night. His other two roommates, Vincent, age seven, and Franco, age five, giggle openly as they tease Stephan about his wild imagination, all the while Stephan professes that this really, *really* did happen!

Overhearing this conversation, PaPa, who's in the nearby kitchen pouring himself his first container of hot coffee, seems disturbed by Stephan's reporting and begins to scold him about wandering about into the night. The giggles and the chiding directed at Stephan from the children continue until PaPa, who now stands obviously upset before them, bringing a halt to the morning chaos and immediate silence to their mocking as he beings to speak, his tone, more urgent.

The children freeze-frame to their spots and listen obediently as PaPa continues his lecture. He reminds all of them to *never* venture out into the dark without an adult and how there are hidden dangers that lurk in the nearby woods, in particular, Lupo!

"There will be no more of this foolishness, Stephan. Do you understand? The other children know better and now, so do you!" he finishes with complete command.

Lecture now over, the brood finds it safe to unglue themselves from their fixed positions and so scramble en mass to the kitchen table to devour the breakfast breads, whose sweet aromas have been wafting through the house since dawn.

As MaMa pours more hot coffee for PaPa and fresh goat's milk for the children, the talk soon turns to the day's chores ahead. There is no more mention of Stephan's wanderings. At least not today.

It is late fall and that means harvest time, even though the crop is barely large enough to accommodate the family's needs through the long, cold winter ahead. So life on the hillside farm continues as normal.

Normal. What an unusual word. What is normal anyway? Certainly what was thought of as normal no longer exists for young Stephan. He has a new normal as his nighttime visitations with his unusual friends continue in the weeks that follow. Only now, he no longer talks about these exciting encounters with anyone for fear of receiving another scolding. So they go on in silence.

He frolics with the farmer's children by day and his "other" playmates by night. Unlike most children at bedtime whose customary resistance is expected, Stephan has become unusually cooperative to bid all good night. His anticipation of playtime with his *friends* and all the new sights he'll see have him enthusiastically scurrying off to his bed without a fuss. Life on the hillside farm resumes as usual and all is back in order.

Then, one stormy afternoon - it all changes. An early approaching snowstorm keeps Stephan and the other children from their outside activities. The impending harsh weather forces them to stay indoors while PaPa hastens to finish his chores and prepare for the storm's arrival before nightfall.

While Antonio is off in a corner reading one of his favorite adventure books, young Vincent, Franco, and Stephan are all at the kitchen table quietly drawing and coloring, as they explore their individual imaginations on paper. Like most toddlers, Stephan can amuse himself for hours on end drawing on scraps of paper he's liberated from one source or another.

MaMa hums to herself as she stands at the stove preparing the evening meal, content that her family is warm and well. Curious about Stephan's concentrated focus on his doodling, she stops stirring dinner just long enough to glance over her shoulder and with sincere interest asks, "What's that you're drawing, Stephan?"

Vincent and Franco, totally immersed in their own creations, have not yet eyed Stephan's rendering. In typical childlike fashion, Stephan sees no need for description and proudly holds up the yet unfinished work of art.

Suddenly, the ladle once held in MaMa's hand crashes noisily to the floor, startling not only Stephan but Vincent and Franco, who shriek in surprise. With shaking knees, MaMa begins her slow, uncertain steps toward Stephan. Her mouth agape, eyes wide, not believing nor fully comprehending how a child as young as Stephan could create such an etching.

"What ...what's th.... what is this, Stephan?" MaMa pleads.

Hearing the commotion, Antonio enters the kitchen, open book still clutched in his hands and asks "What's all the noise about?" With unhesitant candor, Stephan spews out his description of the picture he's so carefully drawn. The other children begin to laugh and mock Stephan as he speaks but are quickly silenced when they note MaMa's reaction to the drawing.

Stephan wishes he hadn't been so eager to share these images as he unsteadily begins his explanation. "It's a ship ... It's the inside of one of the ships I ride in with my ... my friends ... you know, like the ones up in the sky ... like ..." he trails off barely audible.

Without warning, MaMa snatches the drawing from his small hands and, with quivering voice, orders Stephan to his room until summoned. Not understanding the reason for this scolding, Stephan tearfully jumps off the kitchen stool where, just moments before, he sketched in reverie and races tearfully to his bed.

Not long after being exiled to his room, Stephan hears PaPa enter the kitchen, loudly stomping the snow off his timeworn boots as he prattles on to anyone who will listen about his long, hard day's work. MaMa's still-hysterical voice begins to recount to PaPa the events as they unfolded just a few moments ago. Stephan clearly senses her disapproval and begins to fear what will happen next and so quickly retreats to the safe haven of the underside of his bed. Barely able to catch his breath in his hasty retreat, he hears the familiar creaking of the dormitory door as it opens wide.

There stands PaPa larger than life, Stephan's drawing clutched in his large hands that are still covered in earth from the day's labor. "Stephan? ... Stephan, it's all right. You can come out. Stephan, come to me," PaPa speaks without anger.

As Stephan's body involuntarily obeys the request, he emerges from underneath his bed with bowed head in slow approach, eyes fixed on the wooden floor, not daring to raise them up to meet PaPa's gaze.

PaPa gently takes Stephan's small hand in his and leads him back into the kitchen where MaMa and the other children stare at him in silent, wide-eyed confusion.

Lifting Stephan high upon the same stool he occupied

moments before, PaPa begins: "Stephan, what are these?"

Before answering, Stephan first glances at his foster mother then darts his eyes quickly back to PaPa, who now more urgently implores an explanation. Mumbling weakly at first, then, at PaPa's prompting, Stephan recites the exact same reply he provided MaMa a short while ago. To everyone's amazement, PaPa turns and, in silent disbelief, retreats out the front door out onto the catwalk, pauses for but a moment then heads down the stairs and into the courtyard below, Stephan's artwork still clutched in his hand.

MaMa, eyes red and swollen from her own tears, follows her husband's retreat leaving Stephan high upon his stool, with Antonio, Vincent, and Franco sitting around him, speechless.

So there he continues to sit listening intently, straining to understand the exchange of tones between his foster parents who are discussing what has just occurred. Vincent and Franco rush headlong to the kitchen window to watch and wait for their parents' next action, while Antonio stares blankly at Stephan who continues to struggle to process it all.

Stephan begins to quiver with anticipation of the punishment that's sure to follow. With all his might, he can't seem to wrap his young mind around the reason why his drawing has brought about such anger from the two people he's come to love and depend upon.

Then he hears their footsteps on the catwalk and is instantly engulfed with a renewed dread as the front door opens ever so slowly. Stephan braces himself for what is to follow. As his foster parents re-enter the kitchen together, heads held low, all four children hold their breath in anxious anticipation. Just when Stephan feels he's about to explode, PaPa calmly utters "Stephan... go wash up for dinner." *That's it? ... Go wash my hands?*

Without hesitation and before PaPa can change his mind, Stephan flies off of the stool and rushes to the sink in complete compliance. Much to his and the other children's amazement, there will be no punishment —just a genuine scolding from

PaPa to cease drawing these images, nor is he to ever speak of his nightly visitors again, for it will no longer be tolerated.

With mixed emotions, Stephan retreats to his room until he is called for dinner, grateful there will be no punishment, but the fact that his artwork has brought about such a powerful reprimand confuses Stephan all the more. Despite the fact that his *special friends* take him to magical places in strange soundless vehicles, and they do communicate without moving their lips - *How do they do that, anyway?* he still ponders - but they mean him, nor anyone else, any harm.

Although it doesn't seem fair to Stephan that he'll never be allowed to do this again, nonetheless, he does realize that he *must* obey his foster parents at all costs because he likes it here and doesn't wish to make PaPa or MaMa upset with him again. Enough said!

The sun has set and so PaPa lights a warm, inviting fire in the hearth. With dinner finally on the table, Stephan takes his seat but barely touches his food, all the while a single tear falls silently from his cheek onto his plate. The jeers and covered-mouth giggles from the other children are but another reminder of how different and separate he's beginning to feel from the others. He has yet to discover just how different he is and that he possess a higher-than-average intelligence far beyond his years, which will soon become an issue for those who don't understand.

Emotionally exhausted, Stephan takes himself to bed in grateful anticipation of sleep and the refuge he will most certainly find there. Sleep comes swift and deep. Deeper and deeper he goes as he is lulled by a soft, low hum that beckons him further into blissful slumber.

Not long after, Stephan finds himself running — no racing — through the freezing night, dressed only in his flannel nightshirt and warm woolen socks, grateful that his feet are protected from the rough terrain to some extent.

Voices call his name from a distance. Is he dreaming again? Is this real? Regardless of the answer, Stephan presses forward as fast as his small legs can manage.

Stopping only long enough to catch his breath, this desperate child of the night darts off in yet another random direction with no apparent course or destination.

The wolves' cries are ever closer while those of the humans are swallowed up in the abyss behind him.

Running harder now, he cannot stop, must not stop. He races blindly deeper and deeper into the forest in an attempt to secure safe haven, but from whom or from what? For all along, hasn't his course been deliberately set not in the direction of the voices that implore his response … but away from them?

Growing weary, his pace slows. Fatigue now betrays his young muscles as the terrain beneath his tender feet becomes mountainous.

Faltering at each effort of every step, he suddenly trips, falling in slow motion over a large unseen tree root. Before he can cry out in pain, the sounds of something moving in the nearby brush force him to cover his mouth, stifling the scream that waits within.

His concentration is now on the sound of breathing, albeit not his own. For he has all but stopped breathing in anticipation of what lurks nearby.

A twig snaps. He gasps another silent breath as his large ebony eyes train their focus on the immense yellow eyes that watch him from the surrounding brush.

For what seems an eternity, he watches the creature slowly and stealth fully emerge from the darkness into the moonlight, where its identity is no longer a mystery.

Stephan shouts excitedly, "Lupo!" and as if returning the greeting, the large brown-and-gray wolf tilts its head as it approaches the boy.

Chest heaving, tears flowing freely down his face, all Stephan can manage to blurt out is "Lupo! Lupo, I am so glad to see you!"

Lupo excitedly licks Stephan's tear-stained face as he prances about the boy's small body with gentle bumps and nudges in welcome. When Stephan finally calms a bit, Lupo indicates for the boy to follow him. He leads Stephan to a cave opening, deep within the thicket, where they'll be safe and a bit warmer, at least for a while.

Lupo's tongue is extended as he, too, reaches to catch his own panting breath. While stroking Lupo's thick fur, Stephan begins to stare into his friend's large yellow eyes. A low, barely audible humming vibrates all around them as they begin to exchange their unspoken thoughts.

Here they sit, this unlikely duo, caught up only in each other's gaze. Their breathing is now jointly paced at a remarkably slow rate. Not a sound is uttered as Stephan willingly becomes the receiver of unearthly knowledge and wisdom. For he has been chosen and must comply with the instructions being imprinted upon his young superior brain.

As the cold night air brings a shiver to Stephan's small body, his fixed gaze with Lupo is broken. Feeling that it is time to return home, Stephan reaches up to Lupo's thick, furry neck for one last embrace. A solitary tear falls from Stephan's eyes onto Lupo's extended paw in farewell ... at least for now.

As Stephan rises to start his journey home, he turns around to look back one more time upon his friend, but Lupo is gone.

Once again, Stephan becomes aware of the voices calling in the night. Only this time, instead of going away from them, he moves deliberately toward them.

Not long into his weary walk back, he is suddenly blinded by a single light that shines directly into his eyes and met with, "Here he is! I've found him!"

Before he can regain his vision from the blinding flashlight, Stephan is swept up into the billowing arms of PaPa, who speaks not a word as he firmly, yet gently, carries him back through the blackness of the forest to the warmth and comfort of their hillside farm.

Though the dim cast of light is barely enough to guide the searcher's' way home, it is enough to expose PaPa's grateful tears streaming down his otherwise rugged face. His breathing is quick and shallow as he trudges through the darkened forest, ducking barely visible tree limbs as he aims toward the light of the farm with Stephan cradled closely against his chest.

MaMa is perched anxiously atop the catwalk, wrapped only in a bed cloth, scanning the dark outline of the woods for any sign of PaPa and the others.

Then she spots them! The wavering beams from their searchlights broadcast their return. Silently, she prays they were successful in finding their tiny charge unharmed. Her heart all but stops when first she sees her husband emerge from the woods, as she squints to make out the form he holds close to him. As she spies the outline of Stephan's curly locks, she emits a loud cry of gratitude to God and the others for their unselfish efforts in bringing Stephan home safe.

MaMa races frantically down the catwalk, barely touching each tread. Armed with an extra blanket in her hands, she dashes to meet PaPa and Stephan as the other children watch and cheer from the kitchen window above.

Once inside, PaPa gingerly carries Stephan to his bed and lays the boy upon his pillow, gently stroking his head in silent thanks for his safe return. Stephan quickly falls into a deep, silent slumber despite MaMa's urgent efforts to remove his torn clothing and socks filled with earth and twigs. It feels good to be back in his Castle in the Clouds. He'll sleep well now.

Leaving Paradise

I was taken away from my mountain paradise after a year's residence, which I believed was an undeserved penalty for running off into the night to find Lupo. But the justification they used for this abrupt separation was to discourage long-term attachment between the families and the foster children for fear of traumatic repercussions for both when it came time to leave.

At any rate, I was moved into another foster home in the city of Milan. This was not a happy experience for me at all! This new family was using the welfare system to subsidize their income by taking in foster children. The allotments given to them for clothing and food for my benefit were redirected to their own four children.

I wasn't properly cared for, in fact, I was pretty much a non-entity to them, a ghostly figure who was forced to drink sour goat's milk and eat stale bread while their own children feasted on fresh eggs and meats. Like I said, not a good time for me...

But the ultimate abuse was of a more physical nature. In an effort to keep me from engaging in my nightly sleepwalking, I was tied up in a closet each and every night. I figured out that they did this as a way to ensure keeping their monthly subsidy, which would definitely cease, should I suddenly disappear and not return.

I was always being accused of trying to run away, when in reality what I believe to be true was that I was being taken by E.T.'s for programming, training, or scientific experiments. Because of my

21

young age, I wasn't always able to remember what was happening during those sleepwalks, or perhaps, most likely, programmed to forget.

Finally, at age four and a half, I was chosen by my adoptive parents, who were living in the United States.

Once earmarked for adoption, I was moved out of the foster home and placed back into the same orphanage until the adoption could be completed.

Unfortunately, I was to discover that this, too, was not a good place at all. Here I was, a little country boy thrown in with all these city children – not to mention my highly active psychic prowess and nighttime excursions; well, you can just imagine the level of disruption this produced.

I was beginning to learn that fear brings about many types of reactionary results. So, as a direct result of my sleepwalking, I would get daily beatings, mostly in the mornings, from some of the older children, as they were the ones who saw the evidence of my "relocation."

When I would have a visitation – I hesitate to use the word "abduction" here – I would be returned to the proximity of the area of my departure, to within eight to ten feet. This could sometimes mean the difference between being inside or outside a building. So if, for example, they found me in the courtyard when all the doors and windows had been secured the night before, it left them with no alternative but to deem me a clever escape artist.

When questioned by the nuns at the orphanage as to how I got outside, my emphatic explanation of E.T. or angel visitations was not met with any kind of support or, at the very least, feigned understanding. It was viewed as pure fabrication and dealt with harshly.

There was one older boy in particular, the typical bully who found great delight in tormenting me in whatever way he could.

Finally one day, I'd had enough! In an effort to bring about what I thought would be an end to his constant abuse, I boldly confronted him, punched him in his stomach – as that was the only area I could reach, given my small stature – and then ran like hell! When this bully recovered from the shock of my retribution, he immediately began his sincere pursuit of me and, as a result of this mad chase, I ended up injuring my arm and required immediate medical attention.

Ultimately, all this did was delay my adoption and immigration to the United States. No clear winner here! My convalescence lasted two whole months.

When I returned to the orphanage with my arm still in a cast, the first chance I got, I hit this bully over the head with it. Of course, this meant my arm needed to be reset, due to the reinjury caused by my revenge thus delaying, yet again, my journey to the United States and my adopted family. Was it worth it you ask? ... (smiling).

(Flashback)

Morning comes and Stephan awakes feeling groggy yet determined to secretly follow Lupo's unspoken directives. He rubs his sleepy eyes as he tries to clear the cobwebs in an effort to bring his young mind back into focus. Stephan leans up onto one elbow and then cocks his head as he attempts to make out the conversation that is coming from the nearby kitchen. He determines the voices are those of MaMa and Papa, but there's another one, an unfamiliar man's voice he doesn't recognize.

As Stephan slowly climbs out of bed, his little legs and feet ache from his nighttime trek. Cautiously, he opens the bedroom door in an effort to peek into the kitchen and tries to identify the source of this new voice. He notices that the farmer's children have already gotten up and are most likely off doing chores and wonders if they let him sleep because of what happened the night before. Not being able to see beyond the small crack of his bedroom door, Stephan opens it wide. Again rubbing his eyes as he pads his way into the kitchen, MaMa speaks his name softly as she approaches, taking his hand in hers and then leads him to join PaPa and the stranger sitting at the kitchen table.

"Stephan," PaPa begins in a gentle voice, "this is Mr. Mastriano. He runs an orphanage in a city not far from here called Milan. He's here to take you to Milan to another home where there will be other children like you waiting to find a permanent family to live with. Until then, the orphanage will be your new home ..."PaPa's voice trails off, holding back his rising emotions as he finds the words difficult to form.

New home? I don't want a new home! I like it here! PaPa, MaMa, and the others are here! Lupo is here! Stephan shouts inside himself.

When Stephan finds his voice, he begins to plead "I won't be bad anymore! I won't walk out at night again! I won't run away again!" In one swift motion, Stephan leaps into the safety of PaPa's lap, all the while pleading for another chance.

"This is not a punishment, Stephan. MaMa and I are allowed to care for children who are not our own for only a short time, or until Mr. Mastriano finds a permanent home for them. Mr. Mastriano is here because he has found you a new home in America. Isn't that exciting" PaPa explains unconvincingly.

America! Stephan has never heard of *America*. "Where is America? Is it nearby? Can I see you and MaMa and the other children?" Stephan's quivering voice pleads. PaPa's reply is of little comfort for a young boy who only knows the limited surroundings of his hillside home, with the exception of his nightly excursions with his "friends".

Struggling to contain his own emotions, PaPa slowly rises with Stephan still in his arms and then places him solidly onto his own stool and deliberately turns his head away to hide his deepening sorrow. Nervously pacing back and forth, PaPa begins his explanation telling Stephan how America is far away across a great sea and that they will not, most likely, see each other again. With these words, the room becomes eerily silent.

It is MaMa who breaks the palpable tension by rising from her chair and then begins to clear the table of the breakfast dishes in a futile effort to hide her own free flowing tears, for she has become deeply attached to this little boy and her heart aches at the thought of never seeing him again. *What will become of him?*, she tortures.

Stephan hesitates but a moment and then, to everyone's amazement, wipes away his own tears as he softly and calmly asks, "When do I have to go?"

PaPa's reply is barely audible, "Right away, my boy … right away."

Packing up what few belongings he has acquired in his short life and brief stay with his hillside family, Stephan walks over to MaMa who hands him a basket of food she has lovingly prepared for their long journey to Milan.

By now the other children, curious about whose car is on their land and what the stranger is doing here, begin to filter into the kitchen one behind the other. Antonio is the first to notice Stephan carrying his belongings under his small arms, while his mother kneels before the young boy, helping him put on the hand-me-down woolen coat, all the while speaking words of encouragement about his departure.

At the quiet urgings of the other children, Antonio finds the courage to ask PaPa what's going on. As PaPa awkwardly recounts the situation at hand, his children gasp at the reality of Stephan's immediate departure.

While it's true, they've taken delight at taunting Stephan when it came to his imaginary friends and his outrageous talk of flying off somewhere in a space ship, if the truth be known, the boys have grown quite fond of their smallest roommate. Though they're no strangers to the comings and goings of other foster children left in their parents' temporary care, somehow Stephan, despite his abnormalities, has become one of them, and they know his departure will leave a void that won't be readily filled.

One by one, the farmer's children approach Stephan with half embraces and childlike mumblings about how he will be missed and how exciting it will be that he'll soon be in a new home. The farmer has taught his children well in the ways of handling foster children's eventual departure.

With nothing more to be said, they all solemnly descend the catwalk stairs. After Stephan is helped into the back seat of

Mr. Mastriano's car, he locks his gaze with PaPa's as he settles into his fate. While the car slowly drives away, Stephan's takes one final look at his family waving in silent resignation as he journeys away from their lives and away from his beloved Lupo.

The trip to Milan is long and arduous, with little conversation between them. They only stop to partake of the delicious fixin's of chicken drumsticks, sweet bread, homemade grape juice from the farmer's vineyard, and — Stephan's personal favorite — fig squares that MaMa would bake at his insistence.

Night is falling and Stephan finds it nearly impossible to keep his eyes open. But open they stay as he has never traveled this road before, and his curiosity about the city betrays his body's urgent need for rest. Then he sees it! The lights of the city twinkle before him, announcing their impending arrival to his new life.

In typical kid fashion, Stephan excitedly asks Mr. Mastriano, "Are we there yet?" Mr. Mastriano's reply is gentle and engaging: "Soon," he informs Stephan, "very soon."

So many buildings, Stephan thinks, *and they're all right next to each other! Where do they keep their goats and chickens and cows?*, he ponders.

The car comes to a halt, signaling Stephan has, at last, reached his next destination. Mr. Mastriano helps him out of the car and then leads him up a long set of stairs that mark the entrance to an old, dark, towering building and then through a huge doorway, leading, yet again, to another long and winding staircase. Once at the top of the stairs, Mr. Mastriano is greeted by Sister Marguerite, an unfriendly soul who immediately commandeers Stephan and his belongings, then forcefully drags him to his new dormitory filled with dozens of sleeping children.

Never having been treated this abruptly, Stephan is understandably frightened. He's led to a small unoccupied cot amid countless others filled with sleeping children, Sister Marguerite tells him in a low, firm voice that he is to go right to sleep and to not stir until the morning bell is rung. Stephan, now terrified of this gruff woman, nods his head in acknowledgment and climbs thankfully into his bed, where he quickly falls asleep, no doubt emotionally exhausted from the day's stressful journey.

The next morning Stephan is awakened, not by the bell Sister Marguerite warned him about but by the dozens of sets of strange eyes peering, closely watching his every move as he awakes.

Then it happens…"GONG! GONG! GONG!" Over and over the earsplitting bell sounds.

"G-O-N-G! G-O-N-G! G-O-N-G!"

The other children scramble about in chaos to dress and then militantly fall in line by the dormitory door in specific order, smallest boys in the front with the bigger boys in the back, where they stand and wait. But wait for what? Stephan is dumbfounded and with no instruction, simply sits in confusion as to what he's supposed to do next.

As if to answer his unspoken question, enter Sister Marguerite accompanied by another lady dressed in the same odd attire; heads covered in cloth hoods with long, flowing, layered skirts. *But where are their hands?* Stephan ponders, as all he can see are their arms.

Never having seen a nun before, Stephan is not savvy to their demeanor or their conditioned posture, standing and walking with their hands hidden beneath their habits. *How strange!* He thinks quietly to himself. Now, while it's true Stephan has been witness to a lot of strange beings and behaviors in his young life, he decides to chalk this up to being just one more.

Without warning, Stephan is suddenly launched onto the floor by a slightly older boy, he guesses to be around eight years old. Having slept in his clothes, Stephan immediately falls in line behind another boy, similar in height and age. So, there he stands, barely awake, book ended by two strangers. Obediently Stephan falls in step with the others as they are marched down the same long winding staircase he climbed upon his arrival the night before. The procession continues in silence down yet another long, cold hallway where the only sounds are those emitted from the barrage of shuffling feet that echo off the cold, stone walls.

The parade comes to a halt before two oversized wooden doors that provide no hint of what lies beyond, at least to Stephan. Several more ladies dressed in identical clothing have joined the group and are now leading additional groups of children through the doorway; only these children are girls of all different ages, just like the boys.

With great effort, two nuns swing the cumbersome doors open wide to reveal an expansive dining hall where the children uniformly file in and are then instructed to take their seats and be quiet about it. The children obey with only a few rebellious exceptions, which are met with swift retribution for their disobedience.

Stephan inhales deeply – "Something smells good, really good!" Stephan shouts, "I'm hungry! Are we going to eat now?" In unison, a sea of heads turn in scorn upon his small presence, which instantly translate that it best he remain quiet.

As the children take their respective seats, an instantaneous bustle of activity surrounds the room. Platters of biscuits and hot cereals seem to appear from everywhere, delivered courtesy of the ladies in the hooded dresses.

As Stephan and one or two others begin to grab for their share, Sister Marguerite shouts a warning that no food is to be touched until the morning prayer of blessings has been said. Prayers? The only prayers Stephan has ever heard were those of the farmer when he unintentionally hit his hand with a hammer while mending a fence. He thinks it went something like "For God sakes … " then he simply can't remember the rest.

Oh well, Stephan resigns and then summons his last bit of patience and decides he can wait another minute until he thanks God for bringing him such great-smelling food. With the blessing said, let the games begin!

Stephan and the others hungrily grab at the plates of biscuits with one hand while holding their glasses up to be filled with delicious, fresh goat's milk brought around by a nice lady in yet another funny-looking garb. Only she is much younger than the others and seems to enjoy serving the children and even laughs along with them as they sputter out words of gleeful appreciation.

After the morning meal, Sister Marguerite introduces a painfully shy Stephan as a new arrival, however, goes on to explain that his presence will be short lived, as he's expected to be placed in to the charge of a local foster family as he awaits his adoption. What is she talking about? Stephan questions.

With swollen cheeks full of biscuit morsels, one of the older boys informs him of how lucky he is to leave this place so quickly and how he's been waiting for years to have a family outside of these walls to care for him.

Down deep Stephan does feel lucky; lucky to have lived with PaPa, MaMa, and the other children in their Castle in the Clouds. Now, he can only hope that his new family will care for him as well, and that he'll be happy once again in a wonderful new home until he goes to America.

With breakfast over, Stephan is singled out and instructed to follow one of the nuns to Sister Marguerite's office. Once there, he's placed on a very hard wooden bench, where he sits and sits for what seems like an eternity, in wait for his foster family to pick him up.

Finally, a large man with a big belly and a small woman —with a belly to match his—bound through the door to Sister Marguerite's office.

They eye Stephan briefly and ask if this is the boy they are to care for. When Sister Marguerite answers in the affirmative, they couple hastily signs the appropriate paperwork, abruptly grab Stephan by the hand and tell him to come with them.

"Stephan! My name is Stephan," he manages to utter as they hurriedly whisk him into the hallway, out the front door, and then gruffly plop him into the back seat of their tattered, smelly car.

Never casting a glance his way or a single kind word as they drive, this unlikely pair chatter away about things that have no meaning to Stephan. Soon they arrive at their destination and "... Stephan, is it? ..." is told he can get out the car.

His belongings in hand, he timidly follows their lead into an ugly house that is void of any embellishments; no pretty flowers, nor shrubs, not even a friendly climbing tree can be found nearby. An intuitive uneasy feeling begins to rise up in Stephan's stomach— *This doesn't seem like a very nice place* he worries.

As the trio approaches the front door, they're greeted by the squeals of four unruly children of varying ages, who boisterously welcome their parents home. They barely acknowledge Stephan as they jump in anticipation of what treats their parents have brought home for them. The parents, who apparently received an advance payment for Stephan's care, produce edible goodies for their children but deliberately neglect to share with Stephan.

As feared, this was the beginning of an unhappy experience with this foster family, who cleverly found way to take advantage of the welfare system so as to provide their own family with food and clothing, leaving the foster children to fend for themselves.

The first night went without incident...then, without his consent, it happens. Stephan's sleepwalking resumes and instantly becomes a source of major irritation for this new foster family, who are in dire fear of losing their meal ticket. So they decide the best course of action is to tie Stephan up in a closet each night with just a flimsy blanket for warmth, while they slumber comfortably in their own soft beds in their well-heated rooms.

For Stephan, the only relief he gets is during his nightly excursions with his *friends*, who take him to such amazing places and show him such incredible sights. At least, he believes he's visiting these places, for the truth of the matter is Stephan isn't sure himself anymore if these visits are real or not. But one thing he is sure of: real or not, they are a welcome respite to his otherwise hostile state of being.

His waking hours are torturous and so he purposely avoids

any contact or verbal exchange with any family members, for he's sure to be beaten or punished for something that is either imagined or misunderstood. Even at the age of four and a half, he is smart enough to know it's best to be ignored by these people, for fear of their abusive retribution.

Much to the dismay of the foster family, Stephan's adoption is close to completion and so he's taken out of their greedy charge and returned, temporarily at least, to the orphanage in Milan while the appropriate paperwork is put in order, then it's off to America!

For Stephan, it's become a matter of the lesser of two evils to either remain in an cruel foster home where he's neglected and forced to sleep in a closet, or to resume the chastising and beatings from the older boys' at the orphanage that is sure to follow his nightly disappearing acts.

With such horrific choices, Stephan decides to focus on his new family in America and all the possibilities that lay before him in a new land. *It has to be better...* he prays to himself.

As is the case unfortunate case with so many children, Stephan has a nemesis in the orphanage — an older boy named Michael, who is resentful of Stephan's cute appearance and, more now than ever, his opportunity to move out of this horrible place to begin a new life with a family in America.

One morning after breakfast, Michael takes it upon himself to instigate yet another day of torture for young Stephan. He continues his taunting by calling Stephan unspeakable names and then, in an effort to insult him even more Michael encourages some of the other boys to make an arsenal of disgusting spitballs and take every opportunity to assault him, awake or asleep. Only this time, Stephan's had enough!

Stephan picks his moment to confront Michael, all the while planning his escape to the girls' section of the play area, which is usually off limits to the boys.

Stephan masterfully releases a low blow to Michael's midsection then runs as fast as his little legs can carry him to the safety of the girls' life size playhouse. Because he is still so small, Stephan easily scales the doll house exterior wall to the temporary safe haven up on its pitched roof.

All too soon, Michael, now in hot pursuit, reaches Stephan on the playhouse roof and forcefully pushes him, causing Stephan to lose his balance and fall hard upon the concrete flooring, thus breaking his fragile little arm in two places.

The other children witnessing the fracas hysterically call for help, and one by one the nuns appear to clear the area to lend assistance to this fallen child. Stephan is taken to a nearby hospital for treatment, all the while being chastised by Sister Marguerite for his actions and how his injury will set back the timeline for his adoption by several months; not to mention her concern about having the authorities instigate an unwanted investigation that might put the orphanage in a less than desirable light, perhaps even jeopardize their funding.

After a detailed medical examination it is determined that Stephan's injury is more severe than first thought, and so he is confined to bed-rest and a hospital stay of two months. As it turns out, Stephan is not totally unhappy at this new prospect, as this provides him with guaranteed a breather from the beatings and the bullying, and instead will be well fed and cared for by the pretty nurses. *Having a broken arm isn't so bad….* Now that Stephan finally has a break in the action, strangely enough, his visitations cease as well, if only for the short time he is in the hospital.

After his two-month recuperation, it is time to return to the orphanage. How Stephan has dreaded this day. However, this time he decides to take matters into his own hands by taking the offensive. Immediately upon his arrival, Stephan begins his own reign of terror by launching an unprovoked attack upon Michael's head with his cast, only to re-break his arm, thus setting back his adoption for the second time. America will have to wait … again!

Coming to America

I arrived in America wearing blue short pants with a red-and-white horizontal-striped shirt. I guess whoever dressed me thought these were very appropriate patriotic colors for my new country. I, on the other hand, had no opinion on the matter.

Upon my arrival at Angel Guardian Adoption Home in New York, I was greeted by, yep, some more nuns, only they were very kind to me. Now in their care, they thought it best to remove my patriotic attire, washed me down, combed my hair, then put on some different colored clothes on me. No more red, white and blue. Now, I was ready to meet my new parents!

When I was finally introduced to them, I'll be honest, I felt no connection at first. But once I met my adopted mother's mother, who was a native Sicilian, the connection formed instantly, and a sense of well-being and acceptance began to work its way into my heart.

There were no other children in the home, and I remember not feeling particularly good about that. Being painfully shy and guarded, I spent my first few days imbedded in a corner of the living room, neither speaking nor listening to anyone.

Then one day, a neighbor from across the street came over to get a glimpse of the new arrival. He was a shoe salesman by trade who spoke not a word of Italian and, quite frankly, didn't even try, but for some unknown reason I felt a total affinity for him.

He would playfully tease with me, and before long I was allowing myself to settle into the security of an environment that was, until that gifted moment, totally foreign to me. I give him total credit for those early moments of comfort and ease. His name was Shelby and he made me laugh — something I hadn't done in quite some time. It felt good. It felt very good.

A key factor to my instant bonding with Shelby may have been his bald-headed resemblance to my nighttime visitors. At any rate, he made sure I had the best shoes for my feet. I'd never owned a pair of sneakers before. Never having been married and having kids of his own, Shelby made it his business — no, more his mission — to be sure I fit in with the other kids in the neighborhood. What a great guy!

My life was again beginning to change, but this time it was a welcome, comfortable change. It didn't take me very long to become a part of the neighborhood scene. There were children everywhere in my neighborhood. The houses surrounding my home were literally bursting at the seams with children.

The O'Malley family on one side of my house had eight children; the Cochran family on the other side had seven, while the Geracci family directly across the street had four.

My life was showing signs of normalcy, whatever that was, and partly because I had learned the English language in literally two short weeks; I did not feel like the outsider any longer.

By now the neighborhood kids had started to call me Steffe, a nickname I grew to like and feel comfortable with as it denoted their acceptance of me into their fold. It was proof positive that I was one of them, had roots, and was part of the landscape. I liked that a lot!

I was considered exceptionally bright for my age, so much so that my parents decided to no longer hold back the speed of my induction into American culture. I was ready!

So here I was at age five about to experience my first Halloween. My mother, who was a big Joe DiMaggio fan, dressed me up to look like him. Talk about waving the American flag and Mom's apple pie! This was truly the Americanization of Stephan, and my official initiation into Yankeedom.

Halloween was not a custom I had ever seen or heard of before, and yet it appealed to me greatly. While the other young children were frightened by the more gruesome costumes, I found the whole experience exciting – plus, don't forget all the candy I could carry at one time.

Of course, my mother would do the parent thing. You know, the part where you think you've got just about the most candy any kid could possibly conceive of in their possession at one time, then Mother says, "You can't eat this all now. You have to wait until after dinner."

I remember thinking, this is a dumb holiday. You go around for hours begging for candy just to have your mother say you can't eat it? I could only hope this American custom had some hidden meaning justifying the confiscation of my booty.

Tommy, a kid who lived two houses down from me, became my best friend. He had two older brothers – Matthew and Brian, who talked my mother into letting me go out after dinner for one more round of Trick or Treat. Well, of course as soon as we hit the street, Tommy's brothers took off with their friends, which left me, Tommy, and another neighborhood boy named Daniel to explore the dank and dark recesses of the Halloween streets by ourselves.

This was a pretty special moment for any five-year-old...one we were not going to squander. We didn't particularly see ourselves as courageous kids, let alone old enough to roam the dark neighborhood unsupervised. And yet, the thought of the endless possibilities that crept into our young imaginations sparked a few nervous giggles, if not a sense of false courage.

As we were walking along the darkened streets, we looked up at the clear night sky and began talking about stars and stuff. I told them, "Look up there. See that bright star? That's where I'm from." I was pointing to Sirius, which shone the most brilliant blue in the night sky.

For those who are unfamiliar with this star system, Sirius is located in the eye of the greater dog Canis Major and is only visible in the northern hemisphere from early fall until early spring ... but I could always find it. Sirius can easily be located by finding the three bright stars that form constellation Orion's belt. Just follow an imaginary line through these stars to Sirius, which was now just above the horizon.

Tommy and Daniel didn't show any particular reaction to my comment, other than saying something like "Are you kidding?" to which I replied, "No, I'm Sirius." I don't think they got my advanced humor. All they knew was that I was a foreigner; I was not born where they were born, and that I kind of popped up out of nowhere – so the rest was pretty much accepted.

I told them I came here in a big silver flying machine – to them that meant a traditional airplane. Five-year-olds don't have much of a concept of countries, never mind solar systems and galaxies. My friends were more intent on finding out what it was like where I came from.

My answer was always the same. With a finger pointed toward the heavens, I would always track the exact same star. It didn't matter that I couldn't explain anything else about Sirius. It was enough for me, and apparently for them.

(Flashback)

Stephan stands quietly beside the stewardess as she scans the mass of strange faces whizzing by. She anticipates the handing off of her young charge to the next relayer on Stephan's journey to his new home in America.

At last, a young woman dressed in the same funny clothing that the nuns wore in Italy approaches the stewardess and identifies herself as the emissary sent to escort young Stephan to his next stop—the Angel Guardian Adoption Home in Long Island, New York. With the word "Angel" in the adoption home's name, he's counting on it being a good place to stay while he waits for his new family to pick him up—or so Stephan hopes, anyway.

Once Stephan arrives at Angel Guardian, he is pleasantly surprised by the warmth and kindness extended to him — a vast improvement from his last experiences with the nuns at the orphanages in Italy.

Two nuns, one on each side, take him by the hand and lead him to what appears to be a sort of medical office, where he is given a quick once-over and presented with all new clothing.

His face is gently washed and his hair carefully groomed to perfection. Catching a glimpse of himself in the reflection of a metal cabinet next to the sink, Stephan likes what he sees and, for once, feels a sense of importance with all the fuss being made over him.

Mother Superior, who seems to be totally in charge of the entire production, has Stephan spin around in front of her for her final approval. Clapping in excitement she shouts, "Bravo, Stephan, Bravo!"

Within minutes, his new family finally arrives. "Stephan," begins Mother Superior, "these are your new parents, William and Francesca Wolf." Stephan is coaxed by one of the nuns to extend his little hand in introduction, which he declines as he bows his head, not wishing to make eye contact with these strangers. He's conflicted, as he wants to run into their arms but his recent history cautions him to do the opposite.

Deciding not to force the issue, the Wolfs mumble an excuse about needing to begin their journey back home so as to avoid rush-hour traffic. Mother Superior and the others bid Stephan good luck as they watch a timid five-year old walk independently between his new parents.

Once again, with his worldly belongings in hand, Stephan is escorted out of the adoption home to an awaiting car to travel to yet another destination — a lot of confusion and exhausting travel for this young boy.

Surprisingly, once situated in the car, Stephan falls into a deep, peaceful sleep and awakens only when their destination is reached. Still groggy from his cat nap, Stephan awkwardly trips out of the car onto his new driveway. His new parents chuckle as they help him up and brush off his dirty knees. Stephan quickly scans the area and stands wide eyed as he takes in the sight of his new home, which is most pleasing to the eye, as are all the surrounding homes in his new neighborhood.

With no words spoken, William and Francesca gently coax Stephen to follow them up the front walkway lined on either side with fragrant flowers that form a colorful pathway to a large porch that lovingly wraps around their modest home.

Inside the front door, the trio is greeted by several adult family members who have been patiently awaiting their arrival, one of whom is Stephan's new grandmother, Nonna Rosa. Slight of frame, she gives Stephan a playful wink and welcomes him in his native tongue – *Benvenuto, Stephano! Benvento!*. Stephan allows a hint of a smile to form on his face as he exchanges a few pleasantries with Nona Rosa, and begins to take comfort that at least *someone* can converse with him and understand his response.

Still painfully shy, Stephan chooses to distance himself from any English conversation, which he doesn't understand, anyway — at least not yet.

When bedtime finally arrives, Stephan is grateful to be out of the spotlight and putting on some fresh, clean, new cozy PJ's. In Italy, all he was given were filthy, ragged night shirts, so this was a wonderful first impression of his new home. Ready to bring an end to an emotionally exhausting day, young Stephan happily climbs into his very own bed in his very own room. As there are no other children, Stephan must admit to himself that this new family just might be okay, and he promises himself to be more friendly tomorrow. But for now, sleep is the order of the day.

When morning comes, it takes Stephan a few moments to orient himself to his new surroundings and remember the happenings of the past few days. His new mother waits patiently for him to adjust and studies him intently as he slowly begins to move about his new room, exploring what treasures are here for his use and enjoyment.

The irony that his new mother doesn't speak Italian well, even though her own mother, Nonna Rosa, speaks mostly all

Italian with very few English utterances, causes Stephan to wonder how these people ever understand one another. Then he gets his first lesson on their method of communication as his mother gestures for him to follow her downstairs, which he does with a slight bit of trepidation.

Upon entering the kitchen, Stephan's new mom leads his gently to sit at the kitchen table while she prepares his first American breakfast consisting of some freshly squeezed orange juice, bacon and eggs, with whole-wheat toast. Different foods for him to try, but they smell so delicious, his tummy begins to growl.

All of a sudden there's an unexpected enthusiastic knocking at the door which sends Stephan flying off his chair to the sanctity and shelter of the underside of the kitchen table. Chuckling softly to herself at such a sight, Francesca crosses the kitchen floor to answer the urgent knocking.

"Where is he? Where's the new arrival hiding at?" says a loud male voice resounding through the kitchen.

"Stephan, this is a friend of ours. His name is Shelby, and he is very excited to meet you. Come on out from under the table. It's okay. Honest", his mother reassures.

Not intending to wait a moment longer, Shelby boldly takes matters into his own hands crouches down under the table and smiles as he extends a friendly hand to assist Stephan out of his temporary sanctuary, and then lifts him high to the ceiling, laughing and carrying on. Francesca reminds Shelby that Stephan doesn't yet speak or understand any English, but Shelby assures her that won't be a problem between he and the boy. And you know what? ... Shelby is right.

Stephan finds himself giggling and smiling in no time at all as he exchanges hand gestures with Shelby in their nonverbal communication, which Stephan finds so familiar, recalling his nighttime visitors on the hillside farm. Or perhaps it's due in part to Shelby's physical resemblance to his galactic visitors, for he doesn't have any hair on his head either!

In the days that follow, Stephan begins to warm up to his new family and is introduced to more people and new customs every day. In record time, Stephan picks up the English language and can fluently articulate his every need, while still retaining a slight Italian accent that everyone finds quite charming.

However, much to his parents' dismay, Stephan not only excels in learning English but all its unsavory slang, as well. To Stephan's delight, the neighborhood children waste no time taking him into their private world of "No Adults Allowed!" *Cool! Very cool!*

Since Stephan is about to attend his first day of school in a few weeks, his mother takes great delight in dragging him from store to store, looking for just the right outfits for her new pride and joy.

After an exhausting day of shopping, Stephan collapses on the living room couch only to be literally uprooted by his new pal Shelby, who bounds into the house with a surprise package in hand. Eagerly, Stephan rips open the box and finds a new pair of sneakers for school. *Sneakers!* He had never seen sneakers before coming to America. He was so envious of the other children as they ran, jumped, and rode their bikes in comfort. Now he, too, can be just like the other kids!

Stephan's best friend and confidant is a neighbor named Tommy O'Malley. *How Irish can you get?* Tommy, a year older than Stephan, has two older brothers — Matthew, age ten, and Brian, age twelve — who take great pleasure in tormenting the younger boys. But Stephan and Tommy, while feigning injustice, participate eagerly in these exchanges and even instigate the majority of the interplay.

Adjusting to school is easy for Stephan. He is exceptionally bright, eager to learn, and gets along quite well with the other students. Surprisingly enough, his previous experiences with the less than desirable foster-home children and the abusive treatment at the orphanage didn't leave Stephan with any permanent emotional scars. His new friends fondly nickname him Steffe, and he likes that.

His parents, while not wishing to change his first name, decide to further Americanize him by changing his name's pronunciation from Ste-phan to Stee-phan, with the spelling remaining the same.

In an ironic twist of fate, Stephan learns how his adopted family's original name was Lupiano and was changed to Wolf when Stephan's adopted father's grandfather came to this America from Italy. Interesting indeed. Stephan can't help but feel Lupo is alive and well and still in his life, even in this far-away land called America.

With fall in full swing, Stephan is introduced to yet another new custom. Halloween is fast approaching and so his mother, who has been preparing for this moment for years, it seems, goes all out for Stephan's first Halloween costume.

No amount of protesting can change her intended course, so he decides it best to ride the wave. What's more American (besides apple pie) than baseball and its heroes? So there he stands, a pintsize, five-year-old replica of the man himself — Joe DiMaggio!

As his mother puts the finishing touches on his costume, Tommy comes crashing through the front door in full pirate regalia, with his exasperated mother in tow and yells, "Trick or treat! Trick or treat!"

"Why is he saying that, Mom?" asks Stephan. Realizing she's neglected to mention this part of the Halloween tradition, Francesca describes the entire process on how to politely partake of the goodies the neighbors have waiting for all the ghosts and goblins that roam the streets on this special night.

"Wow! Let's go then!" shouts Stephan. The boys race to the door while their mothers call after them to wait up. But it is wasted breath and energy as the two five-year-olds burst out onto the cold October streets of their transformed suburban neighborhood abundantly decorated with jack-o-lanterns and scary Halloween sights and sounds.

Being an American has so many advantages, Stephan muses to himself... Not only do you get to stay out late, but you can ring doorbells and get candy for just saying "Trick or treat!" *I love America!*

After an hour or so, the mothers agree it's time to return home, much to the disappointment of Joe DiMaggio and his pirate accomplice. Once in the house, Stephan's mom begins the daunting task of weeding through the candy, which by now he's opened and begun to eat all at once.

"Why are you going through the candy?" he asks. His mother explains how there are people, regrettably, who don't have the right spirit and attitude about children and Halloween that they might place harmful things inside the candy, so that's why the moms and dads check it all out before the children can eat it. Dumb rule, Stephan thinks, but acquiesces nonetheless.

All of a sudden, there's a knock on the door, and so Stephan races to answer, prepared to distribute more candy to "Trick-or-treaters." To his surprise, there stands Tommy and his brothers, Matthew and Brian who are costumed as a football player and a ghost, respectively, pleading with Stephan's mother for him to join them for one more go around the neighborhood.

Not wishing to be a considered stick in the mud by her son... *her son*, what a nice ring that has to it, Francesca agrees, but only under the condition that no candy be eaten until she has done her thorough inspection of his treasures. *Agreed!* Off the four boys go, with the promise to return in an hour.

They no sooner get around the first corner when Matthew and Brian announce they're going to meet up with some of their friends, and that Tommy and Stephan can continue on their own, but they have to promise not to talk to any strangers... and for heaven's sake don't go home without them, or they'll all be in trouble!

All agree to meet at a particular spot in a hour, not that Stephan or Tommy have any idea of the passage of time, but they do understand they have to go home eventually and will figure it out somehow.

A short way into their walk, Tommy and Stephan hook up with another neighborhood boy, Daniel, who's wrapped in ace bandaging from head to toe, with a fake bloodstain on his head and explains that he's an accident-prone mummy. *Halloween – what will they think of next?* Stephan wonders.

As the evening goes on, the air turns colder and soon the streets become less and less populated by Trick-or-treaters. The boys begin to wonder if enough time has passed and if they should head back to meet up with Tommy's older brothers. No one takes into consideration that most five-year olds can't tell time, and even if these three could, none are wearing a watch anyway.

Tommy guesstimates that they have a little more time and so collectively agree to travel down one last street in search of the last bit of candy that awaits their confiscation.

Growing weary and disappointed that the street they chose has no porch lights lit, they plop themselves down upon the curbstone for to take inventory of their treasure.

While Daniel and Tommy enthusiastically rummage through their containers filled to the brim with confectionary treats, Stephan gazes longingly skyward. Such a clear, crisp, crystal night sky, with stars twinkling endlessly above.

Tommy stops in mid-rummage to ask Stephan "What are you lookin' at?"

"Home," Stephan dreamily replies.

"I thought you said you were from Italy?" Daniel interjects, while continuing to count his confiscated treats.

"Well, I guess you could say I came from Italy to here... but I came from *there* first." He points to a bright blue and white, twinkling star near the horizon.

"How did you get from there to here, then?" Daniel continues casually while his mouth brims with chocolate delights.

"I don't really know...I just know it's where I'm from," Stephan replies in earnest.

Tommy quietly joins Stephan in his gaze at this amazingly bright star that seems to shout to be noticed with its ceaseless blue-and-white strobing.

In a brotherly gesture, Tommy drapes his arm around Stephan's shoulders and says, "Well, I'm glad you're here with us now, Steffe. Okay guys, I think it's time we find Matthew and Brian, and go home. I'm cold."

The Shrink

I guess the mastery of my disappearing act in the middle of the night — or perhaps it was my unabashed explanation of where I'd been all night — was the final straw that unnerved my parents enough to think I was compensating on some primal level for being abandoned by my real parents or, at the very least, that I had an unnerving overactive imagination.

I had become quite astute at hiding my true intelligence at school for fear of being ridiculed and cast out from the other kids. I would deliberately flunk tests just so I would be considered to be a normal child struggling with the same academic challenges as everyone else.

At any rate, the end result was that I began having "talks" with a shrink. He was no ordinary shrink, I was to later discover. His name was Dr. Umberto Francisco Ortega, and he specialized in "children like me," whatever that meant.

I still didn't understand what all the fuss was about relative to my artwork, which often detailed the inside of a spaceship or my aerial interpretations of the Earth below. These schematics were very clear to me from the nightly visits with my friends, so it was only natural that I would replicate on paper what I had seen first hand. After all, it was no big deal when I would make renderings of our home or the family pet or some scenic view while amusing myself in the back seat of the family car while on a road trip. So why this reaction?

Don't get me wrong, my family loved me very much. I was adored by all my relatives, even though I was categorized as a bit bizarre by some of them or how I often brought my parents to the point of being frantic with some of my stories and wild behavior. They truly struggled and couldn't decide if I should be labeled a genius or just plain weird. The latter ended up being the label of choice.

As a result of my nighttime meanderings, my family was the first in our neighborhood to install an alarm system to monitor my nocturnal whereabouts. Despite this expensive investment and the numerous safety locks placed strategically throughout the house, I still got out. I was often found in my PJ's in the early morning hours in a dazed condition, stating most emphatically that I was visiting and traveling around with my "friends" — thus the sessions with the shrink.

I even disappeared for a whole day while vacationing with one of my uncles in Lake George, New York. To this day, I have no recollection of where I was. I just knew that when those kinds of things occurred, I would always return safe and sound.

As if all this weren't enough, I was raised Catholic and constantly challenged the church doctrine, much to the horror of my devotedly religious mother and grandmother.

My natural psychic abilities, telepathic communications and telekinesis skills were all viewed as a deliberate blasphemy toward the church which ultimately translated to my family to be nothing short of witchcraft. As a matter of fact, Monsignor Monticello was finally called upon to perform a good old-fashioned exorcism to shut me up, but my beliefs never faltered.

To appease my parents and to be more accepted, I agreed to become an altar boy, a position I held for two full years, which ended on my fourteenth birthday.

During all this, I found time to embark on an entrepreneurial career by creating my own Space Club, which consisted of some neighborhood friends and those I connected with who also attended sessions with Dr. Ortega. No girls allowed though! I say this because there was one chubby little girl whose appointment followed mine who tried her best to join the club, but I wasn't about to break the code of our all-male bond. No way!

As strange as it may sound, I did enjoy my visits with Dr. Ortega, for he truly believed what I told him and showed great interest in the mechanics of it all.

One particular afternoon, when I arrived at his office for my standing appointment, two men in dark suits met me at the door and rudely asked who I was and why I was there. When I told them I saw Dr. Ortega all the time, they began to ask me all kinds of questions, one right after the other. The whole time this interrogation was going on some other men were emptying out the file cabinets of their contents and placing these materials into boxes, and then hurriedly whisked them out of the building.

When there was a break in the rapid-fire grilling, I found the courage to ask a question myself: "Where's Dr. Ortega?"

The answer not only shocked me, but the manner in which it was delivered went beyond definition. "Oh, he's dead! You can go now."

"He's dead? What do you mean, he's dead?" Those words hung in the air and echoed in my ears for weeks to come. Surprisingly, my parents were of no help, as they nervously declined to discuss the incident any further. What did they know and why wouldn't anyone tell me?

So my sessions with Dr. Ortega ended as abruptly as they had begun, with no talk about finding another doctor.

One last thing I was told – no I was ordered – not to discuss this with anyone! I also had to stop talking to the other children who had met with Dr. Ortega. End of discussion!

It wasn't until I got to college and reconnected with one of the boys who also saw Dr. Ortega that I found out what really happened to him and the possible implications it had on us all – but I digress.

(Flashback)

"Hey there, Steffe! Como esta?" greets Dr. Ortega. Stephan, who is comfortable by now with his weekly sessions with the doctor, responds with a grin as he bursts through the office door to the inner sanctum of the therapy room and then plops himself down onto one of the overstuffed chairs - the "hot seat," as Dr. Ortega affectionately calls it.

Stephan has missed a couple sessions with Dr. Ortega because he had been away on spring break from school.

"So, gone anyplace interesting lately?" Dr. Ortega prods in his familiar cavalier style, then reaches to turn on his tape recorder, which is mounted in an inconspicuous location somewhere beneath his desk. Stephan is at ease with this routine and knows it's all part of Dr. Ortega's job but, more importantly, it lends a certain amount of credibility on the good doctor's behalf that he takes Stephan's statements and stories so seriously.

"And they're off!" Stephan answers in a somewhat arrogant manner. They both let out a mild chuckle, then Stephan begins, "Actually ..."

Intrigued by his lead-in, Dr. Ortega presses Stephan further. Without much encouragement, Stephan recounts his latest episode.

"Over spring break, I spent a week with my Uncle Bill at his cabin on Lake George. Did I ever tell you about him? He's my mom's youngest brother. We get along really great, so he invited me fishing while I was on my vacation. I was psyched! The first couple days were kind of cold and rainy, but the rest of the week the weather got really nice."

Dr. Ortega interrupts Stephan: with "Sounds pretty normal to me so far. Continue." Stephan holds up his hand to gesture *wait, it gets better*, causing Dr. Ortega to lean forward in his chair, all ears.

"Wednesday — no, I think it was Thursday — morning I woke up early - I mean really early. Even Uncle Bill hadn't gotten up yet and he's up with the birds. I got dressed, grabbed a couple donuts and a carton of milk, then walked down to the dock that's not far from the front porch of the cabin.

"The lake was amazingly still and clear. I could actually

see fish swimming below the surface. Without much thought I decided to take advantage of the situation and take the boat out, maybe catch a few fish and surprise my uncle. We always kept the boat ready for fishing, with poles and bait, so I hopped aboard and began rowing."

Stephan stops his narrative and stares off, oblivious to his surroundings and obviously lost in his own thoughts. Dr. Ortega cocks his head and then clears his throat in an effort to nudge Stephan out of his self-imposed hypnosis, so he can continue his tale. Stephan, coming back to the reality of the room, adjusts his position in the chair and returns his gaze to Dr. Ortega, then quietly whispers "And that's all I remember…"

"What do you mean … that's all you remember? Did you fall asleep? Did you fall and hit your head and pass out? What do you mean?"

Stephan looks longingly at the doctor as if pleading to understand it himself, but all he can answer is: "I don't know. All I remember is being back in the boat beached on the shore by the dock—not tied up to it, just near it, and it's dark out. My Uncle Bill is shaking me by the shoulders, yelling at me to tell him where I've been all day and why I left without telling him. He was really upset, worried that something bad had happened. Like I might have drowned or something. But I really can't remember…anything."

Stephan is obviously shaken by recalling this event, yet Dr. Ortega doesn't want this moment to slip away, so asks Stephan if they can try hypnotic regression. Stephan has done this many times before with Dr. Ortega and is a willing subject to try it again, for he, too, wants to get to the bottom of what's happening to him and, most importantly, why.

"Okay, Stephan, let's go over to the recliner and get comfortable. You know the drill." Stephan readies himself as he has done so many times before, then hesitates. "This time I'm a little scared. I don't know exactly why, but I am. I just want you to know that."

49

Dr. Ortega reaches over to pat Stephan's shoulder. "I will always protect you," he says, "and if you get uncomfortable at any time as we try to figure out what happened that day, I promise to bring you back quickly."

This is exactly why Stephan trusts Dr. Ortega so much. While it's important to get to the bottom of all of this weirdness, Stephan knows Dr. Ortega is his friend and will do anything to keep him safe and minimize any trauma that may result from their findings.

"Ready? ... Let's begin." Dr. Ortega gently begins the process of regressing Stephan by having him close his eyes and breathe deeply. He is to listen only to the sound of the doctor's voice.

Stephan's breathing is slow and steady as he begins to relax and obediently shuts out all other sounds. "Relax, relax ... deeper and deeper." He goes into that place where unconscious memory resides. Where the soul keeps it secrets and holds them tightly until demanded to rise to the surface.

Confident that Stephan has reached that place, Dr. Ortega begins the dialogue: "Stephan, I want you to go back a few weeks to your vacation with your Uncle Bill at Lake George. I want you to put yourself right there. See it, smell it, hear the sounds. Are you there, Stephan?"

"Yes," Stephan answers calmly — then:

Dr. O.: *Good, very good. Now I want you to tell me what you see and hear.*

Stephan: *It's really pretty here. It's kind of cold and it's raining really hard, but I'm happy. I like being here.*

Dr. O.: *What are you doing?*

Stephan: *Uncle Bill and I are unpacking our gear and putting groceries away. We're talking about hiking in the woods, even though it's raining. I'm thinking, How cool is this? Nobody to tell me I can't go out in the rain because I might get my feet wet and get sick.*

Dr. O.: *Yep, that's very cool, Stephan. Now, I want you to go ahead a bit in time to the day when the rain stopped and you woke up early before your uncle did. Can you do that for me?*

Stephan: *Okay.*

Dr. O.: *You're lying in bed, just opening your eyes. ... Tell me what happens next.*

Stephan: *I'm looking around the room then out the window by my bed and see the sun is up, but it's barely up, so I know it's really early in the morning. I push back the covers and get up and throw on my jeans and a warm flannel shirt I left on the floor last night. I probably should put on a clean shirt, but I don't care.*

Dr. Ortega smiles and stifles a snicker as he thinks how Stephan can seem so normal at times. Just a typical preteen boy. But he quickly pulls himself back to the task at hand and asks Stephan to keep going and tell him what happens next.

Stephan: *I'm out in the living room, and I see that Uncle Bill's bedroom door is closed. Guess he's still sleeping. Boy, this is a first. Me waking up before him! I'm hungry. I see a box of donuts on the counter and grab two of the white, sugar-coated ones. I like those best. I'm opening the refrigerator and taking out a small carton of milk to wash it all down with. I'm looking out the front picture window at the lake and thinking, I want to go outside. So I do.*

Dr. Ortega decides to move the process along a bit faster and asks:

Stephan place yourself down by the dock and describe how you are feeling and what you're thinking.

Stephan: *I feel great. I'm not hungry anymore. I'm looking at how clear the water is. I can see fish! Lot's of fish. Big ones! Boy, I want to go out and catch some and bring them back before Uncle Bill even knows I'm gone. It's warming up. The sun feels good. I don't think I need a jacket. The boat is tied to the dock, with fishing poles and a can of live worms. Perfect! I'm going out to fish.*

Dr. O.: *Tell me what you're thinking now. Are you afraid to go out by yourself?*

Stephan: *No. It's not a big lake. I can row out a little ways and cast my line and still see the cabin. It's not far. I'm okay.*

Dr O.: All right. Stephan, where are you now and what are you doing?

Stephan: *I'm about a hundred yards out. I can still see the cabin, and there's no wind, so I'm not drifting or anything. I'm looking through the can of worms to pick out a couple lively ones. Found one! Great! I'm putting it on the hook and casting it over the side. This is cool. This is very cool … wait! Wait a minute … it's all black! It's all black! I can't see! I can't see! What's that noise?*

Dr. O.: *Okay, Stephan. I want you to relax and breathe slowly and deeply for me. You're all right. I'm here with you. Just relax … relax.*

Stephan obediently begins taking slow breaths in and out as he is told. Dr. Ortega reaches for Stephan's wrist and confirms his pulse is at a normal rhythm.

Dr. O.: *Good, Stephan. Just relax. You all right to continue?*

Stephan: *Yeah … sure.*

Dr. O.: *Okay then. Have you ever experienced this before?*

Stephan: *Actually, yeah. But never this dark and never for this long. Guess it kind of freaked me out.*

Dr. O.: *What does the blackness and the noise mean?*

Stephan: *It means they're coming. Whenever they come, it gets dark like this. But first, there's always a humming sound.*

Dr. O.: *Who's coming, Stephan?*

Stephan: *They're coming ... my friends are coming ... Lupo is coming!*

Dr. Ortega has regressed Stephan many times before, but this time he notices a different pattern in the boy's reaction to the regressive memory event. He is keenly aware that even Stephan, with his high level of paranormal experience, is having difficulty wrapping sense around this particular event, so Dr. Ortega must proceed ever so carefully, so as not to upset Stephan or, even worse, lose him in a post-traumatic episode.

Dr. O.: *Before we continue, I want you know I'm right here with you and that I'll stay right with you. You have nothing to fear. I want you to tell me exactly, in as much detail as possible, all that is happening – who you are with and what you are witnessing. I won't ask any questions for now. You just talk. But I do want you to tell me if you begin to feel uncomfortable. I promise I'll bring you out any time you ask. Quickly. Okay, Stephan? Go ahead. Tell me what's happening.*

Stephan: *It's getting lighter now. I feel better. I see lots of light. Really bright...white, white, white, no...now there are lots of colors. Like a rainbow, only it's swirling around me like I'm in some kind of tunnel. Colors everywhere!*

Wait! I see something. Looks like ... oh, I see ... it's them! Guess they found a new way to visit me. There are three of them. We're talking, but there's no sound. I hear them, but their lips aren't moving. We walk without using our feet ... kind of floating. They're taking me through a series of tunnels ... hallways ... I can't really describe – blurry, traveling really fast through them.

Two of them are no longer here. Don't know where they went. It's is just me and the third one. He feels more familiar to me. Somehow, I feel we've done this many times before, just not in this way.

He leads me to a door I float through. I mean — I don't open it — I just go through it. On the other side are many others. Five, six, no ... seven beings surrounded by more bright light. I mean it's REALLY bright, but my eyes don't hurt. They look like the others, only bigger.

The size of their heads and the dark coverings over their eyes freak me out. Sort of like sunglasses, but without the earpieces. I don't see any ears anyway.

They welcome me and speak of how long it's been since I've been with them. Then one moves closer and begins to ask me questions. I think this one's in charge.

I'm giving them a lot of information, but for some reason I can't remember exactly what I'm telling them. It's like I'm observing all this and not really part of it.

Now they're showing me some TV-like screens with charts with longitudes and latitudes. It looks like maps of the Earth.

I'm feeling a sudden intense surge of energy in my head. At first it's just like a humming, a buzzing that's getting louder and louder. Wait a minute ... it's starting to hurt ... I'm putting my hands over my ears to muffle the sound, but it doesn't help. I'm looking at them, pleading for them to stop this noise in my head, but they just continue to watch me.

Stop! Stop it! It hurts! Why aren't they helping? I feel like my head's going to explode. Help! Stop it! God ... help me!"

Stephan is thrashing about, screaming for the pain to stop.

Dr. O.: *Stephan, Stephan, it's all right. I'll bring you back now. You don't have to stay there. Just listen to my voice. You will only hear my voice. Stephan, can you hear me?*

Struggling to contain his pain, Stephan, eyes still closed, grips both ears as he writhes in agony, pleading over and over to stop the session.

Dr. O.: *Stephan, I'm right here with you. Together we're*

going to get you out of there. I want you to hear only my voice. Stephan, all is well. You are safe; you are in control of your body and mind. You can come back right now! You only have to focus on my voice and follow it back into my office. Breathe, Stephan, BREATHE!

Dr. Ortega is desperate to bring Stephan back unharmed, yet he knows he must do this slowly and deliberately. He continues his instructions and is relieved when he finally sees the telltale signs of Stephan's return.

Stephan's breathing grows less labored, and he regains a more normal rhythmic pattern. His face begins to relax and he no longer winces in pain.

Once confident that Stephan has fully returned to this reality, Dr. Ortega takes a moment to catch his own breath before instructing Stephan to open his eyes.

Stephan, exhausted from the mental journey, wipes his moist eyes with both hands as he slowly sits up from his reclined position and quips solemnly, "Wow! How was that, Doc?"

Dr. Ortega can only respond with wonderment of how surreal and unabashedly frightening this kind of experience must be for a young person. As an adult professional who thought he had seen and heard it all, he discovers that he was scared out of his own wits at what must have really gone on for Stephan, at least in his mind.

Above all, Dr. Ortega knows he must continue working with Stephan to uncover why he has been chosen and what he has been chosen to do.

Pouring Stephan a glass of water, Dr. Ortega comforts him as best he can and cautions him to not discuss this session with anyone. "We've just begun getting into some important new territory with this one, Stephan. Let's keep this between us until we can make some sense of it all. Agreed?"

With little more than a few exchanged words, Stephan and Dr. Ortega part company, with mumblings of ...See you next week.

After escorting Stephan out of his office, Dr. Ortega locks the door behind him as he has no other scheduled appointments for the day. He plops himself heavily upon the recliner reserved for his clients' sessions and tries to regain some semblance of professional objectivity to what he's just witnessed. Working with these extraordinary children has proven to be an experience that even he couldn't have possibly prepared for.

All of Dr. Ortega's young patients have unusual stories to share, but he has become acutely aware that Stephan along with two other children go far beyond the others in their intense experiences and aptitudes.

Dr. Ortega rises from the recliner and moves to his file cabinet, where he shuffles through its contents until he reaches the files of the two other children, Elizabeth and Nathan, who exhibit the same type of paranormal episodes as Stephan.

Moving slowly back to his desk, he opens the files and rereads excerpts from the other two children's sessions, searching for a common denominator that might link these three patients together.

Elizabeth is about the same age as Stephan, and Dr. Ortega smiles a bit as he pores over his side notes about how she compensates emotionally with her ordeals through overeating. Not an uncommon tool for children who are stressed and need to find comfort in whatever way they can.

Dr. Ortega then turns his attention to the other file. Nathan is a little older than Stephan and Elizabeth. Beyond the age difference, the doctor makes mental note of Nathan's odd physical appearance compared to the other two.

Nathan is quite tall and slender for his age, and exhibits a strange detachment from his environment. He displays almost robotic movements, along with eyes that don't show a lot of connection to Dr. Ortega or the world around him. He speaks in a monotone with little to no inflection to his voice, with the exception of when Dr. Ortega implements a regression therapy session. Then, and only then, does Nathan break out of his protective cocoon and show any type of real emotion.

Puzzling, indeed, to see three different children whose reactions to their extraordinary experiences are as remote from one another as they could possibly be, and yet there is a connection among them. Dr. Ortega is almost sure of it now.

He determines he must place the majority of his professional focus on these three specific children if he is to ever get to the bottom of this amazing mystery.

In his solitude, Dr. Ortega ponders the depth of what this all means in terms of reality. Reality. Is there such a thing? Sure, but there is never just one true reality. There are many, and these three children are displaying their abilities to cross over from one reality to another as willing guinea pigs on behalf of whom? And for what purpose?

When Dr. Ortega was first approached by a branch of the C.I.A. and wooed to leave his comfortable general practice of child psychology to specialize in working with children exhibiting paranormal prowess, he thought, Sure, why not? Could be an intriguing experience with groundbreaking results — not to mention a welcome professional challenge.

Little did he realize the enormity of the task at hand and, more importantly, the impact these children would have on him, not only as a professional but as a human being on this planet, in this galaxy, in this universe!

Now, as he sits dumbfounded by his latest session with Stephan and tries to connect the dots between Nathan and Elizabeth, he begins to grasp the enormity of the situation and begins to wonder if these children could possibly be in any danger — and not just from the aliens they purport to be in contact with.

He has no sooner finished that thought when he hears a noise that seems to be coming from his outer office. As he slowly rises from his desk to investigate, he searches his memory ... didn't I already lock the front door?

He opens the door from his private office to the waiting room and is shocked to see two tall, dark figures standing side by side before him, approaching without hesitation or saying a word.

Dr. Ortega demands: "Who are you?" but the figures keep coming, forcing him to instinctively back all the way into his private office, stopping only because he is met with the front of his desk and can go no farther.

His heart races wildly as he senses what is to come. The only sound besides the pounding of his heart is a trembling whispered prayer emitting from his lips as he utters his final plea.

Back on the Farm

Okay, so what kid wouldn't love to visit his aunt and uncle and favorite cousin, Paul, on their farm in Idaho for two weeks during summer vacation?

It was my thirteenth birthday. My coming of age. Knowing how much I missed hanging out with my cousin Paul, my parents thought they'd surprise me with this special gift. You know that old expression, "You can take the boy out of the country ..."

Oh, I adapted to living in the suburbs just fine and learned how to be an all-American boy in record time. But my heart always returned to those early recollections and happiest memories of my days with my first foster family on their farm high atop the hillside in Italy.

Farm life to me always represented a special connection to the earth and to nature and, most especially, those visits with my "special" friends — and Lupo.

What a blast I had with Paul and his rowdy band of friends. Farm life for teenage boys with raging hormones can be duller than watching paint dry. But Paul and his buddies always seemed to make the best of it and pushed the edge of the envelope just enough to stay out of any serious trouble.

Emerging into teenagehood held the promise of exciting changes and endless possibilities. Little did I know exactly how much my life was about to change, once again, in a way that even I couldn't have seen coming.

It was a typical sultry August day with the threat of impending summer thunderstorms off in the distance. Larry, one of the band of merry men, had liberated a pack of Winston cigarettes from his older brother's shirt pocket, along with several back issues of Playboy he hoped his father wouldn't miss for very long.

Sitting atop the ranch rail fence that bordered Paul's property with his neighbor's there we all sat, smoking, sipping Cokes, and talking about, – what else? – girls and how can we get their attention. Just five guys goofing off on a lazy Thursday in August in a wheatfield in Idaho.

To spice things up a bit, we challenged each other to a race through the cornfields and wheat fields to see who could run the fastest and sustain running the longest, in spite of our newly developed cigarette coughs. Nasty habit!

Whooping and hollering as we ran unencumbered through the fields was exhilarating, and we felt like fearless Masters of the Universe. That is, until we stumbled onto something that changed our lives forever – or at least mine.

I can't remember who exactly made the discovery first, but suddenly we all came to a screeching halt and surveyed the surrounding terrain in awe of what appeared to be one of those crop circles. Now we had heard of them, of course, and thought they were a bunch of hooey.

Now, here we were right smack dab in the middle of that hooey, frozen solid to the spots where we stood.

A couple of the guys stuttered some type of reasonable explanation for what or who could have done this, but their reasoning quickly fell apart as they crouched to inspect the crushed plants under our feet.

It didn't take long before one by one, or maybe two by two, the guys began to peel off in haste, shouting such nonsense as "Well, g-g-gotta go … my p-p-arents will be looking for me…D-d-dinner's about ready … see ya later! …" And off they all ran, with the exception of Paul and me.

For some unknown reason, Paul hesitated along with me. Maybe he wanted to see what I would do first, before he surrendered to the fight or flight syndrome.

Right from my first days in America, Paul was the one I confided in the most when others wouldn't listen or allow me to talk about my "other life" – how I knew things and how I believed I came from another place, a place called Sirius.

Even as a young boy, Paul humored my ramblings and let me speak about it all, never judging, just listening. Oh, once in a while he would say something like "Wow, that's really far out there, Steffe" and occasionally he'd ask a question or two. But for the most part, Paul accepted this part of who I was or, at least, who I thought I was. I was always grateful for his unconditional acceptance of me.

Both of us now silent, I began to walk even deeper into the center of the circle. Paul became increasingly uneasy and suggested maybe we, too, should head back home, as the other boys had done.

Without answering, I walked even deeper into the circle.

Paul couldn't contain his anxiety any longer and finally declared that he was leaving and that I could stay if I wanted to. Like a dog with its tail between its legs, Paul hurried off, all the while mumbling some inaudible warnings to me. So there I stood all by myself. Waiting. Listening.

(Flashback)

Standing inside the massive circle of wheat detailed with artistic swirls and intricate weaves, Stephan, now totally transfixed upon this discovery, begins to feel a low vibration, a pulsing barely felt or heard, but nonetheless there.

As he strains his ears to identify the source of this sound, the vibration becomes more pronounced and begins to take on a harmonic resonance that can only be likened to a symphony tuning up before a performance. "Hum-m-m-m, hum-m-m-m."

Slowly he begins to turn, first in one direction, then in the other, trying to identify the etiology of the sound as its volume increases.

"Oh-m-m-m-m, OH-M-m-m, OH-M-M-m, OH-M-M-M!"

There's a strange familiarity to this humming. Stephan cocks his head all the while turning, listening, and then turning again. "OH-M-M-M, OH-M-M-M, OH-M-M-M!"

It seems to be coming from everywhere now! Above him, below him, from the right, from the left, even from inside of him! Louder and louder.

"OH-M-M-M … OH-M-M-M-M … OH-M-M-M-M!"

His concentration is momentarily broken by a large flock of geese honking in flight formation above him. When the geese reach the epicenter of the crop circle, they chaotically disburse in every direction, squawking and screeching as they pass overhead as if some invisible force field has disrupted their flight path.

Then he feels it! An amazing, powerful, vibrating energy so strong that every fiber of his being pulsates in rapture with this enormous harmonic sound.

"OH-M-M-M-M … OH-M-M-M-M … OH-M-M-M-M!"

No longer in control of his body, he feels his arms rise from his sides, palms up, face tilted to the sky, eyes gently closed so he may relish each sound, each vibration.

"OH-M-M-M-M … OH-M-M-M-M … OH-M-M-M-M!"

Totally mesmerized, he begins a slow spin around and around like a dancer performing choreographic movements to the harmonies that now completely envelop him.

"OH-M-M-M-M-M…OH-M-M-M-M-M…OH-M-M-M-M-M!"

Totally lost in his reverie, he ignores the rustling sounds emulating from the undisturbed wheat that surrounds the circle. So absorbed in ecstasy, he will not be distracted from this moment.

"OH-M-M-M-M-M…OH-M-M-M-M-M…OH-M-M-M-M-M!"

As if on cue, they emerge from the thick magical blades of the wheat field's perimeter. First one, then two, then a half-dozen stealthful wolves surround Stephan. Licking at his legs, bumping their heads to his body in a low posture denoting their submissive greeting reserved for only the highest creature in the animal kingdom — the alpha male — Lupo!

"OH-M-M-M-M-M-M … OH-M-M-M-M-M … OH-M-M-M," blackness, then silence.

Stephan awakens bewildered, his body outstretched as he lies face up in the center of the crop circle floor. He is all alone in complete, deafening silence. Had he somehow fallen asleep? Was it all a dream? Is he still dreaming? *NO!* He knows better.

Even though it's been some time since he has allowed himself to be receptive to visits from his *friends*, due to peer pressure and that of his parents, Stephan smiles with the assuredness that this was anything *but* a dream.

Lupo has once again reactivated the wisdom of the Elders to this now-thirteen-year-old receiver, whose mission is clearer than ever before, a mission he will obey without question.

Stephan will not talk of this day to anyone, not even to his closest confidant, Paul. For he knows this is way beyond Paul's benevolent understanding. He also knows he cannot divulge, at least not yet, the honorary task assigned to him.

Recalling his recent studies in school of the Hopi Indian tribe, now — more than ever — he understands their prophecy: *"We are the ones we've been waiting for."*

Soon, he tells himself, soon they'll all know of this. For now, Stephan will hold tight to his mission.

The Other E.T.

*A*fter *graduating from high school, I set my sights on a career in the legal field. I had applied to several excellent law schools and was pleased to have been accepted to George Washington University. Although it wasn't my first choice, it certainly held its own reputation for graduates being placed in solid, well-established law firms. That was good enough for me.*

So at the end of a crazy summer of partying and saying goodbye to my family and my closest friends, I once again packed up most of my earthly belongings, at least those I could fit into my 1972 Chevy Camaro that my Uncle Bill gifted to me, and drove to Washington, D.C., and my new life at George Washington University.

While I purposely wasn't the best student in the world, I at least held my grade average and earned enough extra credits to obtain a partial scholarship. Between my parents' remortgaging the house and the generous contributions from my aunt and uncle on my father's side who had no children of their own, I was able to afford to attend such a prestigious school.

I was the "great white hope" in my family, as they were mostly working-class people who earned an honest living at a variety of crafts. My parents were literally betting all their money on me and my future as an attorney.

I'll never forget my father's tearful speech as he cornered me at my going-away party. Admittedly, he had imbibed in one too many Rum and Cokes while my mother played the perfect hostess in our small but well-appointed patio, ideal for just such a gathering. But the words he spoke stopped me dead in my tracks as he looked me straight in the eye and told me of how at first he wasn't so sure about adopting a child, but wanted to make my mother happy.

Before I could get my feathers ruffled, he continued to recount my early struggles as a "different kind of kid" who wasn't always understood, but was always loved and cherished beyond words.

He acknowledged my academic acumen in certain subject matters — such as math, science, and languages — and how he never dreamed I would someday choose to focus on becoming an attorney, which by his family's standards was right up there with becoming President of the United States. A proud father, indeed.

Seeing that his emotions were on the verge of running amuck, I quickly took control of the conversation by reminding him of some ridiculous stunt I had pulled one day at high school that resulted in my getting an inside suspension, which basically meant I could go to school but not to class. Go figure.

Now, while this type of behavior would bring most parents to their knees asking God what they had done wrong to have raised such a child, my father found great humor in my shenanigans, at least at this level. My sleepwalking, psychic premonitions, and disappearing acts were another matter entirely. Those he never understood, and I guess what ultimately happened was that he chose to ignore them altogether, which translated to him as their never having happened in the first place. Problem solved.

I was deeply touched by his words and that he took the initiative to send me out into the world knowing I am deeply loved. It meant a lot to me, as I usually felt so different from most of my adopted family. For that matter, from the rest of humanity!

My first week at George Washington University was just as you would expect a first week at a new school away from home to be. Chaotic, to say the least, but totally exhilarating, to say the most.

Here you have young men and women, most of whom are experiencing true freedom for the first time in their young lives, allowed to come and go as they please. Very empowering and confusing all at the same time. I, on the other hand, enjoyed the lack of structure and found great comfort in winging it.

Once I located my dormitory building and my room, I began the unmitigated chore of unloading my car, which, by the way, was parked in a lot so far from my room that I seriously considered paying one of the other students to drive me back and forth. Of course, I later learned there was a parking lot much closer to my new living quarters, but the upperclassmen weren't about to share that valuable piece of information with a lowly freshman. NO WAY!

Continuing with my lucky streak, my roommate was a quiet and unassuming guy from the Midwest, whose only focus was on his studies and sleeping. Actually, in hindsight, Jeffrey was probably the only roommate who would have worked for me at that stage in my life, as I was struggling to keep my "other" talents hidden, at least for now.

I had become quite adept at explaining how I would be found in my underwear or, on certain occasions, al naturale, standing outside my room or, better yet, outside the dorm building on my return trip from one of my visitations. The one good thing about college life is that anything and everything is expected, and usually there are no questions asked. Just a rolling of the eyes or a shaking of the head, accompanied by muffled snickering. Thank you, God!

My classes were mainstream pre-law with an occasional elective that was like a breath of fresh air. One such class was The Study of Psychological Phenomenon, which was right up my alley. Here the discussions and research focused on the paranormal, such as poltergeists, ghosts, possession, UFOs and, of course, E.T.'s.

As you can imagine, this was a no-brainer for me, and my professor found me fascinating as I went on with my postulations on space travel and life on other planets. I'd be willing to bet he thought I was either a genius or some egghead whose imagination was enhanced by one of many available mind-altering substances that could be readily found on campus. At any rate, he enjoyed my banter and the thought-provoking elements I brought to class. If he only knew ...

But it wasn't all business, as I was soon to discover. A late registrant to the class, Elizabeth Tanner joined our motley crew and, I must say, added greatly to the climate of the surroundings.

Appearing somewhat aloof at first, she had a terrific sense of humor and challenged Professor Nordstar daily with her unprecedented line of questioning that had us all waiting with bated breath to see how she would unravel his demeanor, yet once again.

It seemed like she knew something nobody else did, and she exhibited great joy in keeping her secret. I know this sounds corny, but there was something familiar about her.

She was an attractive, petite brunette with piercing crystal blue eyes — a most unusual color combination as her eyes were the most brilliant blue I had ever seen. The kind of blue one would associate with a towheaded blonde, not someone with her dark coloring.

As time went on, Liz, as she liked to be called, and I became very close and enjoyed sharing some pretty way-out theories on what is unseen by most. But there was one particular event that happened between us that became a defining moment in both our lives.

Liz and I wanted to take advantage of a day off from our studies, so we decided to make a day of it and head off campus to enjoy the sights. Our first stop was the Washington National Zoo.

As we walked about, taking in all the animal exhibits, we found ourselves stopped directly in front of the wolf enclosure. We both became silent as we observed these beautiful animals, each in our own thoughts.

I remember clearly that I was in one of my "exchange" modes with an alpha male wolf that sat directly in front of me, with the safety of the glass partition between us.

This was a familiar scenario for me, as I have been communicating with Lupo since I was a young boy. Unbeknownst to me, Liz was doing exactly the same thing.

She was the one who finally broke the silence by making a comment about how distressed this alpha male was in his captivity.
I, on the other hand, was shocked to hear her confirm the exact same information this Lupo had just shared with me!

Now, I'm not talking about a general assumption one would make that an animal held in captivity is unhappy. I'm talking about a verbatim recounting of what this alpha male shared with me just moments before!

This marked the beginning of an amazing discovery that would forever alter the course of Liz's and my individual journeys.

(Flashback)

"What? You think you're the only one who can hear them? It's about time you figured out who you're dealing with, Preppy," Liz teases.

Stephan stands in silent amazement as she arrogantly turns on her heels and heads toward another exhibit. When he finally regains his composure, he calls after her, "Whoa, wait a minute! Hold on a second!"

When he catches up to her, he reaches for her arm and spins her around, all the while searching her eyes for more explanation. Liz giggles and pulls her arm away stating, "I was wondering how long it would take you to figure it out."

Still confused, Stephan asks if they can sit a minute while he puts it all into focus. Liz complies, and as they sit on a nearby bench, Stephan wipes off the beads of sweat that have formed on his forehead. Seeing that he's having difficulty formulating the words he wants to speak, Liz decides to help him out. She takes a deep breath and begins her explanation.

"I guess I should start by apologizing for having some fun at your expense. Guess it's something I enjoy doing. I've had to create some jokes along the way, so I won't go mad myself."

Liz can tell her opening statement has not helped Stephan's confusion, so she continues in earnest, "Do you remember the feeling you had when we first met? That *I've met you before* thing that's hard to explain? Well, we did meet before, but it was many years ago, when we were both pretty young." She continues, "Like you, I have always been *different*. I, *too*, know things, see things.

"I was a patient of Dr. Ortega's, just like you, and for the exact same reasons you talked with him. I, also, was taken by aliens, E.T.'s—whatever you want to call them—and shown things I couldn't explain to anyone. They all thought I was nuts!"

By now Stephan's confusion has turned to complete focus on the words Liz is speaking. The roaring in his ears has stopped, and he is once again able to fully concentrate on and begin to comprehend what she is telling him.

"You were there, too?" he whispers when he finally finds his voice.

"Yes, and I remember you sitting in the waiting room. You always were before my appointments, Friday afternoons at four."

He rapidly blinks his eyes as he tries to remember those days, and finally raises his eyebrows as clarity sweeps over him. "Yes!" Stephan shouts, "Yes, I remember a chubby little girl sitting in the waiting room who was always eating a large bag of potato chips when I would come out of Dr. Ortega's office."

"Hey, wait a minute," she chimes in, "I was a chubby little girl because I found my only solace in food. Kind of a nervous eating thing. Anyway, I'm over that now", Liz says with pride as she runs her hands demurely down her curvaceous yet athletic form.

Stephan, with a million questions racing through his mind, blurts out some sort of feeble acknowledgement of her current more desirable appearance. But his real thoughts are still formulating.

"Answer me this," he continues. "With all our conversations, how is it I never knew you were from the same town I grew up in? Dr. Ortega was supposed to be one of only a few doctors specializing in 'kids like us.' But, more importantly, I'm blown away by what are the odds that you and I would attend the same college, let alone become friends. Help me out here!" he pleads.

In an effort to calm Stephan, Liz gently places her hand over his before she speaks. "Well, I wasn't exactly from your town. Actually, I lived in a town kind of far away. Over fifty miles away, to be exact. My parents, who are quite comfortable financially and still hold a high profile in our community, couldn't risk the scandal of a child of theirs seeing a shrink, let alone that their child believes she's the recipient of frequent alien abductions by them.

"Besides, as you said, Dr. Ortega was the only one in his field close enough to see me on a regular basis. Believe me, if he hadn't been so close, my parents would have shipped me off in a New York minute to some boarding school or somewhere else less obvious."

Beginning to accept Liz's story, Stephan still has difficulty trying to figure out the synchronicity of their scholastic endeavors.

For the first time, Liz hesitates before she speaks. Shifting her body to the edge of the bench, she leans into him, closer than a piece of paper or a coat of wax would be, as the saying goes.

Her eyes completely fix upon Stephan's, she places both her hands on his, and starts slowly, "When I was younger, I mean *really* younger, I ran away. At least, that's what they told me I did. There's a small patch of woods behind the house where I grew up, and for the most part I never wanted to go in there because my older brother and sister would terrorize me with stories of monsters and other creepy things in the woods.

"But one night, for whatever reason, I found myself smack dab in the middle of the woods, in my pajamas no less! I couldn't have been any older than three! I sat looking around in the dark waiting ... for what? I didn't know. Then this wolf appeared and walked right up beside me and sat down.

"The funny thing is I don't remember feeling scared at all. I didn't touch the wolf; at least, I don't think I did. I just stared into his big yellow eyes. I must have fallen asleep at some point because the next thing I remember was waking up still in the woods, but it was daylight, and I was by myself, with no sign of the wolf. I wondered if I'd been sleepwalking or dreaming, but I truly believed it all happened."

Without regard to Stephan's reaction, she continues: "From that moment on, I just knew I had something I must do."

"As I got older, my studies and research became almost obsessive when it came to UFOs, alien abductions, and other similar phenomena. But in answer to your question as to why I chose this particular school—I don't have an answer, Stef. … I really don't."

Stephan, still locked silently in full attention to Liz, finally looks down before he speaks. "I do, at least I *think* I do."

He clears his throat. "It's no coincidence we came together at this time in our lives. I had a similar experience at a very young age, an encounter with a wolf. Only I call him Lupo— Italian for 'wolf.'

"When I was three, I lived with a foster family on a farm in the hills of Italy, and I ran off into the night to find Lupo. As amazing as it sounds, I wasn't afraid either; in fact, I recall purposely going out to look for him.

"I, also knew some things I couldn't possibly have known or shared with anyone, for that matter, because I would have most certainly been sent away."

Now, it's Liz who sits speechless as Stephan recounts his parallel experience.

Trembling, Stephan adds, "I'm going to step way out on this very shaky limb and tell you what I think — no, what I *believe* to be so. You and I, and God knows how many others, have been 'chosen' to do something extraordinary. Alone, who knows how far we'd get? Together, I think we're unstoppable. Remember what the bible says: "Whenever two or more of you are gathered in his name …"

I suppose under ordinary circumstances Stephan's revelations would be met with some measure of resistance pressing him for further explanation as to what the heck he means. But these are anything but ordinary circumstances. In fact, there is nothing ordinary about either Liz or Stephan.

Liz finally breaks the long silent pause, nodding her head in complete affirmation as she utters, "… and so it is!"

With that, Stephan and Liz rise up off the bench in unison, still clutching each other's hand as Stephan gestures the universal "After you."

As they walk together, trancelike, toward the zoo exit, they find it's no longer necessary to speak. For they are now bonded in thought and purpose.

In their hearts they know they are gearing up for another kind of rocket ride. The rocket ride of their lives!

ॐ
Nathan

While I was attending sessions with Dr. Ortega, there was another boy that I would occasionally run into. His name was Nathan and he was really strange. By that, I mean he seemed almost disconnected from what was going on around him.

Whenever I would try to start up some small talk with him, he would vacantly stare back at me as if he were translating what I was saying into his own language, whatever that was.

After a while I stopped trying to have conversations with him, and we would just ignore each other whenever we found ourselves in the same room.

At any rate, imagine my surprise to find Nathan in one of my elective classes — The Study of Psychological Phenomenon — at George Washington University. Nathan was a bit older than I, but as far as elective classes go, any student may attend. Funny how some things never change, and Nathan proved that theory to be an exact science. He was just as distant, uncommunicative, and even more strange, if that was possible.

The dichotomy about it all was his uncanny coincidental run-ins with either me or Elizabeth (Liz) Tanner. Liz and I would often comment: "Okay, isn't it about time for that weirdo to show up?" — and sure enough there he'd be, sitting in some corner either reading or observing. Observing what? you ask. Who knew!

It was like he was taking notes or something on human behavior as he clearly lacked any semblance of that himself. And yet, I must admit that I found him fascinating in an Alfred Hitchcock sort of way. You know what I mean? The guy totally creeped me out, and yet I found myself riveted to his odd physicality and the way he would cock his head from one side to the other as if trying to assimilate what he was observing.

Liz told me that she had a very in-depth conversation with Nathan one day after class and that she found him brilliant, albeit strange. She commented on the blankness in his eyes and how even though she knew he was looking at her, she almost felt like there was nothing and no one behind those dark ebony eyes.

She admitted a strange attraction to him and found that while she consciously would try to avoid him at all costs, unconsciously she felt compelled to engage in rather intense dialogue with him postulating the possibilities of life on other planets and alien beings among us. Pretty much the kind of stuff she and I would discuss at great length, but somehow with Nathan it took on a more deliberate serious tone.

Liz and I would often chuckle to ourselves about how Nathan reminded us of an alien himself, with his lack of emotion and robotic movements seeming not of this earth. In hindsight, one might compare him to the emotionless Mr. Spock of the hit TV series Star Trek. Great analogy.

So you can imagine my shock when one day Nathan sought me out, wanting to know if I'd meet him for a bite to eat.

I searched desperately for a clever reason to decline but came up dry, so I agreed to meet him at a local pub just off campus at seven that night.

In an effort to ease my discomfort and since he and Liz already knew each other, I asked Nathan if he'd have a problem with Liz joining us. To my surprise, he responded with a resounding "Yes!" He would prefer we meet alone. No other excuses or explanations.

Okay! So I guess it would be just Nathan and me. What could he possibly want to talk about? The answer would soon be made clear. Very clear.

(Flashback)

As Stephan finishes preparing a mock brief for tomorrow's midterm exam in criminal law, he finds himself getting a bit anxious about his scheduled meeting with Nathan. He can't quite put his finger on why he's uncomfortable, just that he would feel a lot better if Liz were permitted to join them.

But it is not to be. So Stephan gulps down the last of his now-warm Coke and quickly checks his reflection in the silver metal lamp on his desk. He flies out of his dorm room, grabbing his light jacket that hangs disheveled on the doorknob. Once in his car, Stephan reaches for the radio to drown out the myriad of anxious questions he has about this impending encounter.

Arriving a few minutes earlier than scheduled, Stephan shuts off his car and sits in silence, contemplating the posture he will present to Nathan, so his true feelings will not be evident.

Taking one last calming deep breath, he boldly steps out of his car and walks to the entrance of the pub, only to find Nathan walking in at exactly the same moment. Coincidence? Perhaps.

With little verbal acknowledgement, Nathan indicates to Stephan to move forward, as the unlikely duo mutually agree to sit in a booth that is located in a far corner of the pub. It is at this moment that Stephan feels like a pawn in some kind of spy movie or some illegal covert operation. He muffles a slight giggle, no doubt brought about by his ever-growing nervousness.

Nathan breaks the uncomfortable silence by asking Stephan if he would like to order some food first. Stephan nods in agreement and summons the waitress over to take their orders. Once that's out of the way, Stephan decides to takes charge and asks, "Okay, Nathan … what's this all about?"

Nathan begins, "I had a discussion with your friend Elizabeth — I believe you like to call her Liz — a few discussions, actually, that I found quite intriguing. She's a very bright young woman, don't you agree?" he states in a flat monotone voice.

Stephan studies Nathan's body language, which reveals nothing more than a cool, detached body sitting in front of him while his mouth formulates understandable language. Weird, very weird.

Nathan continues despite Stephan's lack of response to his statement about Liz. "Liz and I spoke of many things. In particular, we conversed at length about the possibility — no, let me correct that — the probability of life on other planets, both in and outside our galaxy."

"I, for one, feel no need to explore this perplexity any further; nonetheless, I find the contrasting theories and objections by the human race on this subject to be so ... absolutely fascinating." Nathan concludes with no hint of excitement or emotion.

He goes on, "How do you respond to this ongoing investigation of other life forms?"

Stephan, still unsure what Nathan is leading to, answers briefly, "Well, I too, am intrigued by the subject matter and like to consider all things possible. Forgive me for pursuing the issue Nathan, but again, what's this got to do with me? I'm sure you didn't ask me here to meet you in some dark corner of a restaurant just to formulate or expand upon our personal theories on the status of possible galactic inhabitants, did you?", Stephan snips back.

Never losing his cool demeanor, Nathan replies, "Well, you're not totally wrong there. As a matter of fact, I suppose I do wish to expand this 'intrigue,' as you call it, but not in the way you may be anticipating. Let me clarify."

Stephan quips back a flat "Please do."

"I find our paths have crossed more than once. Were you aware that I, too, was a patient of Dr. Ortega's when I was a young boy, such as you?"

By this time Stephan is mesmerized and feeling a bit dizzy at this revelation. "Go on ..."

"Well, my reasons for seeing Dr. Ortega were similar to yours, I would assume however, there were some differences. I also believe Elizabeth's 'talents,' if you will, were a bit of a different nature as well."

Now Stephan is totally confused. What does Nathan know of Liz's connection to Dr. Ortega and himself?

Nathan coolly continues, "Oh, I remembered seeing Liz there. I have this ability to recognize familiar traits in people that they take with them into adulthood, so it was not difficult for me to recall the essence of her personality."

"Unfortunate about her need to excessively nourish her body so she might emotionally cope with all that was happening; however, I note that she has corrected that error. ..." He trails off with indifferent concern. "I shall continue."

"Actually, Liz and I spoke about our mutual encounters with Dr. Ortega and, interestingly enough, she divulged even more about her particular experiences, expanding on what she feels it all means."

Stephan is growing increasingly irritated by Nathan's arrogant knowledge of certain highly personal information about Liz and now himself. Nathan, sensing Stephan's mood, cuts to the chase.

"Dr. Ortega's death was not an accident. He was murdered by those who wished to silence him as he was about to uncover information the government wished to keep secret from the public. More importantly, Dr. Ortega was connecting the dots, I believe the saying goes, about the three of us—Elizabeth, you, and me.

"By human standards, we have unusual abilities and were individually chosen to be part of a greater endeavor. It is no mistake that we are, once again, in proximity of one another."

Stephan's anger has now turned into silent focus as he leans in to encourage Nathan to continue.

"It is my understanding that you totally know of what I speak, and that the time has now come for the three of us to begin to formulate that which we are intended to accomplish for the good of all."

Stephan, now sitting erect in his seat, nods in agreement and finds his voice again to ask Nathan... "What is it that we do now?"

"We all still have pertinent information to gather before we can implement our assignments. It is my suggestion to you that your next step is to travel to a place high in the Arizona desert, where there are many resources from which you may draw the information you seek in an effort to fulfill your destiny and complete your mission."

Stephan interrupts Nathan's monologue, "What about Liz ... and you? What are you to do? Will we be working together?"

As Nathan slowly rises from his seat, he informs Stephan that for this part of the journey he must continue on alone. It will be made clear to Stephan when the appropriate time is right and the three will be, once again, standing side by side, so to speak, in unison for the common good of man.

For now, Stephan is to talk to no one of this. Familiar advice for Stephan.Ever since he was a boy, he was constantly cautioned not to speak to anyone of his "visitors," Lupo, his sleepwalking, his special trips, his drawing, and now this!

Deep in his very being, Stephan realizes the importance of his part in all of this. There is a knowing that, despite his outward normal human life, there awaits a monumental purpose he was gifted to execute, and he intends to do just that.

As Stephan's awareness drifts back to the pub, he realizes that Nathan has left without a goodbye. A hint of a smile forms on Stephan's face as he rises to go.

Once outside, as Stephan approaches his car in the darkened parking lot, he takes a moment to glance skyward and instantly locates Sirius twinkling back at him. All is well, Stephan reassures himself. All *is* well!

ॐ Sedona

*A*s a result of my dramatic meeting with Nathan that fateful night at the Pub, I diligently embarked on some research of my own about the high desert country in Arizona that he so emphatically suggested I explore.

I stumbled upon an area in northern Arizona that was fast becoming a hotbed of UFO activity and paranormal events. The area was called Sedona, and it was purported to be experiencing an unusually large amount of unexplained sightings and paranormal events.

Sedona was well known for attracting New Agers and freethinkers, so I felt this community would welcome my casual investigatory presence without fear of skepticism or criticism. And I was right.

I booked a flight from Washington to Colorado and then continued on to Phoenix, Arizona, which is approximately one hundred twenty miles or so south of Sedona. What little reading I did about the area hadn't prepared me fully for the magnificent beauty I encountered as I drove up "the hill," as they say, from the desert valley floor of the metro-Phoenix area in my rented car.

At an altitude of four thousand five hundred feet, this was no ordinary high-desert environment – quite the opposite. After exiting off the highway, I found myself surrounded by towering red rock monoliths carved, no doubt, through centuries of wind, water, and natural earth shifts. It was almost impossible to fathom that this arid desert environment was once under water, with its primary inhabitants *being dolphins and whales.*

Just as amazing was the red clay ground cover that was meticulously dottedwith deep lush greenery of desertcacti, Ponderosa pine trees, and low brush. I remember thinking to myself, God is the Master Landscaper here, indeed.

The numerous mesas and buttes had very distinct shapes; in fact, many of these incredible formations were assigned names that perfectly fit their appearances, such as Cathedral Rock, Bell Rock, Courthouse Butte, and Coffee Pot Rock. One very popular formation totally resembled Snoopy lying on his doghouse as drawn by Charles Schultz. Amazing! But this was just the beginning of amazing.

I set aside my first few days for driving around Sedona, just to take in the magnificence of the rock formations and the clear, crisp cobalt blue skies prevalent there all year-round...and to get a feel for the area and its inhabitants.

Well, nobody warned me about the "feeling" part of being in Sedona, but I soon found out — sometimes the hard way — that I wasn't in Kansas anymore, Toto!

I purchased the usual tourist information guidebooks and noted the emphasis on hiking to the many vortexes found in the area, and their varied effects on the environment and on all living things. I was getting more and more intrigued by this magical place.

On my third day in Sedona, as I sipped my morning brew at a local coffee shop, I questioned my waiter about the purported UFO activities in the area. Without missing a beat, he pointed out a man sitting in a corner all by himself. The waiter then urged me to just casually wander on over and ask him my questions.

Before I could even mutter some inane excuse about not wanting to bother the man, the waiter had already moved back behind the counter and was busying himself with another customer.

So there I sat, trying to muster up enough gumption to get up out of my seat and meander over to this perfect stranger and pose some outlandish questions to him.

I cleared my throat as I slowly rose from my chair, and said to myself, Okay, here goes!

When I reached the man's table, I managed to mumble some meager introduction and asked if I could have a moment of his time as I had just arrived in town and was here to do some research – "Have a seat," he interrupted without even looking up at me as he sipped from a coffee mug cupped in both hands.

"Thanks," I said, and sat down.

I quickly began to formulate some kind of officious, highly intellectual dialogue in an effort to let him know I was here to research paranormal sightings in Sedona, and needed to gather some data on the mysterious events that I've heard so much about.

But before I even got my next full sentence out, he began telling me that he already knew why I was here and that he'd be happy to share whatever information I could fathom. He went on to state that I needed to keep an open mind about what he was about to reveal; otherwise, he didn't want to waste my time or his. Then he lifted his head and looked me straight in the eye, awaiting my response. I rapidly nodded my head in agreement.

As he began his monologue – I say monologue, as he made it quite clear his time was limited this particular morning, and that in order for him to give me a hint of what I came to uncover, it would be best if I kept silent and didn't ask any questions, at least for now. Wide-eyed, I nodded again in compliance and gestured with my hand for him to continue.

He said his name was Brad Phillips, and he was known around this area as the local UFO expert. He went on to tell me that over the past several years, he and a few of his close friends had unwontedly stumbled onto a bunch of unusual, unconnected sightings and encounters. What struck him most was the frequency with which these events were happening.

As a result, he had now become totally obsessed with getting to the bottom of it all. He went on to mention that he was diligent about keeping a journal of these experiences, and with a little prompting wrote several books about them, and was now sought out by other well-known international investigators seeking to pick his brain about these unusual phenomena.

Others who have had similar experiences have come to trust him and know he takes great care in recounting their paranormal events without revealing their true identities for fear of — just for fear.

One of the things I got right away was that Brad seemed to be a man of his word and that he preferred to keep a low profile, thus maintaining his integrity by not seeking publicity and, more importantly, preserving his own sanity.

He told me that what he was about to reveal would be enough for anyone to question if he was a victim of altitude sickness or just plain over the edge and totally lost his mind.

I took a chance and interrupted him just quickly enough to ask if it would be all right for me to take notes. He waived me off, saying "Not this time ... perhaps the next time we meet." Next time? This was encouraging.

Brad continued with some preliminary background of the area and how through history it has been touted as a sacred land of our Native American forefathers.

While I was paying close attention to his words, I couldn't help but be amused by the thought of his reaction when he discovers who I am, where I'm really from, and who began to visit me when I was only three.

Before I knew it, two and a half hours had passed with Brad doing all the talking. I was totally enthralled by his "tip of the iceberg" stories and hungered for more.

We agreed to meet at the coffee shop again in a couple of days. I attempted to provide him with information about where I was staying in town and how he could reach me, but he said that wouldn't be necessary — we'd find each other eventually. I knew he was right.

(Flashback)

Talk about a man on a mission, Stephan can't get enough reading materials on Sedona. Thank God the books he purchased at the local bookstores aren't very heavy reading, so he's able to pore through them in record time.

He takes advantage of what time he guesstimates he has before his next encounter with Brad to visit some of the more popular hiking areas and tourist attractions, such as The Chapel, a lovely ultramodern-designed structure built into a rock formation high upon a hill where he can see for miles and take in the panoramic view of so many other formations that simply take his breath away.

Stephan can't help but notice how peaceful he feels here, and that everyone he encounters seems to be walking around in an altered state of bliss. He takes advantage of the quietness and the plethora of opportunities to find isolated areas in which to be alone with nature and with his thoughts. Even though he has been in Sedona only a few days, he already recognizes a shift in his awareness and is very attuned to the hum of the Earth.

He feels the presence of many who have gone before him, and welcomes their kind spirits. He sits for hours deep inside one of his favorite locations called Boynton Canyon, absorbing the wisdom of the Elders who surely still inhabit this sacred space.

So deep in his own thoughts, Stephan is unaware that nightfall has begun. Even though it's midsummer, the desert temperatures drop drastically with the setting sun. Stephan reemerges back to reality and feels it best to begin his trek back to his car that's parked a few miles away.

Never planning to stay until dark, he now wishes he had thought to bring at least a jacket and a flashlight. He did have enough presence of mind to pack plenty of water, as dehydration in the desert can happen quickly.

Reaching into his backpack for a fresh bottled water, he takes in the majestic beauty of the day's fading light that spot lights the towering formations around him.

He suddenly startles at the loud snap of a twig in the brush behind him, but then concludes the sounds are most likely made by dessert critters that are awakening for their nocturnal outings, now that the heat of the day has subsided. Smiling to himself, he feels a closeness with the earth he hasn't felt since his early days on the hillside farm in Italy. How he loved his life then.

Even though the trails are well marked by cairns which are rocks contained in chicken wire mesh, he must strain his vision to follow what he believes to be the way out of the canyon to the parking lot by the trailhead.

Then he hears it again. Only louder and closer this time.

Stephan, no longer feels safe, so he picks up his pace, all the while hoping that he's headed in the right direction toward the trailhead and the refuge of his car.

The one thing Stephan has been able to determine from the sounds behind him is that whatever is making them is on his trail — directly behind him. Tracking him?

Stephan doesn't know exactly when he became afraid, but he is now just short of a full state of panic. Propelling himself forward even faster now, he is well aware that the only other sound he hears is that of his own heavy breathing as he struggles through the brush and craggy rock.

He has totally lost the marked trail now, but the constant snapping of twigs and rustling of brush continue just over his shoulder, closing in on him swiftly.

Now in a full run, he stumbles over large rocks and red rock gravel that lie loosely underfoot. His heart pounds furiously as he hears the muffled treading of what sounds like a large animal. He knows this area is full of mountain lions, javelina, coyotes, and whatever other beasts inhabit this canyon.

Suddenly, a voice deep inside him warns to step no further. He unwittingly obeys just in time to catch himself before he is about to step off a high ridge, preventing a fall that certainly would have caused him major harm if not his death.

With his heart racing so fast that he finds it almost impossible to breathe, Stephan contemplates his next move. Does he even have one?

Before he can evaluate his options for escape, he realizes that whatever has been chasing him has stopped as well. What does that mean? Is the pursuer gone — or is it lying in wait, knowing that Stephan is trapped with no way out.

Stephan's straining eyes dart first in one direction then another. Desperate to flee yet needing a plan, he chooses the only option open to him.

Slowly he bends over to pick up a heavy rock, in preparation to fight for his life. Before he can bring his body back up to a full stand, he hears a low guttural growl coming from more than one direction and from more than one source.

Oh God! More than one! Stephan holds his breath in an effort to concentrate on the sounds that surround him. What are they? How many are there?

His question is immediately answered. Two pairs of large, yellow eyes emerge from the brush as Stephan readies himself for battle. He doesn't even have enough time to think about his fate before a third pair of eyes appear from a rock ledge just above him. Oh, my God! This is it! There's no way out!

Just then, the newest arrival looking down on Stephan let's out a growl so deep it sends chills down his spine. But the growling is not directed at Stephan. It's aimed at the other two beasts standing before him.

Without warning, the large shadow of the animal above launches into midair and lands with a muted thud on the terrain between Stephan and the others. To Stephan's amazement, the larger animal attacks the two animals that stalked him to this perilous point.

Wishing he could block his ears from the frightening cries of battle and hideous rips of tearing flesh and flying fur, Stephan dares not drop the boulder he still holds tightly in his grasp for fear the largest of the three may decide to turn on him next.

Within minutes the other two predator's retreat, howling and yelping with obvious injury. Stephan quickly takes a deep breath as he widens his stance, gripping the boulder even tighter in his straining fingers, prepared to defend his life against the animal that remains.

As the larger animal approaches, Stephan — in a slow, deliberate motion — raises the boulder high above his head … then suddenly stops.

He becomes transfixed upon the gaze of the yellow eyes before him, and finds it difficult to bring his body to full command to heave the boulder at this threat to his very existence.

Beyond reason, Stephan is compelled to release the boulder, but not on his target. His arms aching, he drops his rudimentary weapon on the ground between himself and the approaching beast. His eyes strain to see the form about to take his life. With one last gasp for air, he exclaims: "Lupo!"

Lupo now at Stephan's feet, lowers his head, and bumps it in submission against Stephan's body while he circles. Stephan, half laughing, half crying, reaches down to pat Lupo's head and notices a warm wetness upon his fingers. He instantly concludes that Lupo is injured. Stephan joins him on the ground, hugging and caressing the wolf's body in an effort to determine the severity of his injury, and if there are others inflicted.

Lupo winces slightly as Stephan checks one of his forelegs, indicating he has, indeed, additional wounds. Despite his injuries, Lupo nips Stephan's shirt sleeve and tugs it hard, as indication for Stephan to get up. Lupo begins a retreat, imploring Stephan to follow — which he does obediently. Together, silently, the two friends walk in the darkness, only this time Stephan is confident that he will finally be led to safety.

They're Here

The day after my hiking experience in Boynton Canyon and my reconnection with Lupo, I got a phone message from Brad Phillips that basically said: "Anything unusual happen lately? How about we meet at 9:30 a.m. at the coffee shop?" That was it! I couldn't help but wonder if this guy was a mind reader, a psychic, or just a good guesser.

At any rate, I welcomed the opportunity to meet with him again and talk in more depth about what the heck goes on in this area. While I'm not one to point fingers — after all, look at my past history — I was a bit unsure about Brad's own motives for granting me this second audience. One way or the other I was going to get that question answered before I wasted any more of my time or his.

I drove the short distance on Highway 89A from my hotel in West Sedona to meet with Brad at the now-infamous coffee café at the exact appointed hour. When I got there, Brad was already seated in his usual spot, the table in the corner. He shared with me later on that he prefers to sit at that particular table as it's sort of out of the way and he can observe all that is before him, never needing to watch his back, which he keeps to the wall. Insecure? Nope, he tells me, he just prefers it that way.

After we exchanged the mundane "How're ya doing?" and before Brad proceeded with his monologue, I decided to start the conversation by asking him, point-blank, why he agreed to meet with me and what's in it for him. He lifted his head, which was bowed over his cup of coffee, and chuckled out loud as he commented on how he admired my directness. Then he got right to the point.

And the point for him was just this: he's been around this area for a long time and has experienced a ton of unusual happenings — not to mention the stories told to him in confidence by so many others.

As a result, he has become astute at recognizing a serious UFOer whenever he meets one, and apparently I fell into that category. If he only knew!

Satisfied with his response, I proceeded to ask my first question, with my pen poised to record his answer — which he graciously had agreed to allow this time around. He put his hand up to indicate "wait a minute" and posed a question of his own first.

"So tell me ... what happened with you yesterday?"

I was slowly becoming accustomed to his directness and not altogether shocked by his ability to "know" things in advance, so I took a deep breath and recounted my hiking experience in the canyon, with particular emphasis on Lupo.

His response was an affirmative nodding of his head and a smirk. I felt I was providing him with a confirmation of something he already knew, more than sharing my hair-raising experience.

He picked up his coffee cup, took a long, slow sip, and said, "Okay! NOW we can begin in earnest."

(Flashback)

As Stephan takes Brad through his harrowing adventure hiking through Boynton Canyon, he can't help but notice the sincere interest of his audience. Brad never interrupts Stephan's story until almost the very end.

At the point where Stephan describes Lupo's intervention — defending him from harm by the other beasts — Brad finally breaks his silence, lifts his baseball cap higher off his forehead, fully revealing his gaze, and asks how Stephan came to call the wolf Lupo.

"I didn't," Stephan replies. "At least, I don't remember coming up with that name. I just knew that was what he wanted to be called. While growing up in Italy, it was commonplace to call the wolves in the area Lupo. I discovered later while in college that L-U-P-O also means E.T. (extraterrestrial)." Of course, Brad thinks to himself. Of course.

Stephan continues by recounting some pertinent information about himself — telling Brad where he was born, when he first encountered the E.T.'s, and what "special talents" he has of his own.

Before he realizes it, three hours have passed, and he has not yet asked one question of Brad. Instead, this meeting ends up with Brad figuring out more of who Stephan really is. Brad seems to intuitively know that in time they'll draw their own conclusions about how they can join forces to find answers about UFO and E.T. activity in Sedona, or anywhere else for that matter.

Stephan ends their talk by detailing what he believes will be his participation in bringing a more concrete understanding of the role these extraterrestrials or inter-dimensional beings have with mankind, and whether their interaction and intention is that of friend or foe.

Duly impressed and more confident than ever that he is in the presence of perhaps a genuine offshoot of an E.T., Brad asks if Stephan would like to join him for lunch at his place, which is about four and a half miles off Highway 89A.

Stephan, pumped by the invitation, is more than willing. The unlikely twosome rise from the table and exit the café to their awaiting vehicles in the parking lot, their dialogue now bursting with enthusiasm. Brad halts the information frenzy by suggesting Stephan follow him to his home, where they can continue in complete privacy.

The short drive to Brad's provides just enough time for Stephan to get hold of his excitement and formulate pertinent questions to pose to Brad before their time together comes to a close. Stephan has final exams to prepare for as graduation is just around the corner. There's yet so much to ask and so much to see. Where to begin?

Brad turns off Highway 89A onto a remote dusty road with Stephan following closely behind. With dust swirling wildly around the two vehicles, Stephan finds it difficult to keep Brad in view. Brad is driving a four- wheel-drive Jeep Cherokee, while Stephan bumps along in his compact rental car.

As the road dust settles, Stephan notices Brad has parked and is emerging from his car. He signals Stephan to park alongside his modest house. The remote area seems to suit Brad and his need for privacy, not to mention the awesome view of the red rock formations and an open vista with its prime vantage point for stargazing.

Once inside, Stephan casually walks around the sparsely furnished room decorated in vintage Southwestern style, noting the oversized telescope standing in front of a huge picture window.

As he continues to gaze about the room, his focus turns to several different models of cameras, along with a vast array of recording equipment obviously used for Brad's investigations.

"You have quite an assortment of equipment. Pretty expensive stuff, isn't it?" Stephan quips.

"Believe it or not, a lot of it is either secondhand or donated. I've only purchased a few cameras and recording devices myself. I've been really lucky to have so many generous people provide me with this kind of stuff, so I can keep digging deeper into the phenomena that interest us all."

Stephan scans the bookcase spanning the entire wall opposite the picture window and comments to Brad on the abundance of UFO and E.T. reading material that dominates the shelves.

Brad chuckles from the kitchen immediately off the great room, where he prepares lunch for them both. "If you look close, you might find one or two of my literary works in there."

Stephan counts seven books in all that bear Brad's name as

author. Hanging on a paneled wall of the great room are a few plaques and framed newspaper clippings that profess Brad as one of the world's leading authorities on UFOs. "Wow! Now I really am impressed!" Stephan says.

Obviously embarrassed by all the attention, Brad announces lunch is ready, such as it is. "Come into the kitchen and pull up a chair."

Pouring them each a large class of ice-cold lemonade, he begins to provide Stephan with some additional UFO history of Sedona and the immediate surrounding towns.

Cottonwood, for example, is a small residential community approximately fifteen miles west of Sedona. Jerome is another town slightly farther west that is best known as an old mining ghost town. They both brag of some pretty strange occurrences and unusual sightings.

Stephan pulls out a mini recorder and indicates an unspoken "Can I?" to Brad as they both devour their turkey club sandwiches and pickles. Brad nods in agreement, as he knows that to take notes at this point would take too long, and besides Stephan can't eat AND write at the same time. His talents probably don't include multi-tasking at least not at that level.

Brad begins by introducing some not-so-nice experiences that both he and others have had in an area called Sycamore Canyon, which is about thirty-three miles long, runs north and south, and is approximately one mile wide. It's a long dusty ride on a gravel road from Clarkdale — another desert community just west of Sedona.

"During the 1800s it was a major cattle-drive route, but history states that the Basque sheepherders avoided this area because of strange, giant, hair-covered creatures that were reported to roam the terrain.

"Now, here is some of the good stuff. You might want to pay particular attention to this part. There is a purported tunnel system that is located on public property between the Coconino National Forest and the Prescott National Forest. There have been reports of people hearing loud underground and aboveground drilling sounds somewhere between Clarkdale and Jerome.

"But here's the real scary stuff — hikers have been known to stumble onto military-type soldiers, some carrying what look like M-16s or some other semiautomatic pistols. The hikers have been told in no uncertain terms that they'll be shot dead on the spot if they don't turn around and leave the area."

He goes on to tell Stephan that "An Arizona State employee was hiking one day and encountered a nine-foot alien creature. There was no exchange between them, but the hiker ran nearly five miles back to his car, never to go there again. Even though he reported it to local officials and the state police, and actually demanded an investigation of this incredible sighting, he was met with strong advice to keep his mouth shut!"

Stephan shakes his head in disbelief but understands better than most the denial that others are in when it comes to paranormal experiences. Fear is a powerful emotion that tries its darndest to refute these events because they don't fit into a familiar format or context.

Stephan interrupts Brad to inquire about the reliability of his sources. Brad emphatically states that all of his stories come from extremely credible sources, such as municipal employees, retired military personnel up to and including major generals, as well as U.S. Air Force intelligence officers who have been honorably discharged.

People from all walks of life have sought Brad out to share their stories. He's talked with prominent doctors; presidents of major banks; police officers; firefighters; and clergymen who, despite their religious background, knew what they saw and had to share it with someone.

One of Brad's most memorable accounts was from the son of a military man who recounted that back in 1955, when he was about ten years of age, he saw firsthand numerous space ships and pictures of dead aliens — some looking amazingly like human children.

His father had apparently smuggled him into the base, and somehow he eluded detection as he uncovered these artifacts. His father demanded that he never speak of what he saw for fear of retribution from the military or worse.

The son obeyed this request until his father passed away several years ago. He had carried this incredible information with him in silence all these years until he felt he could share it with someone. That someone was Brad Phillips.

Stephan could totally relate to the boy's vow of silence because he, too, was often told to never speak to anyone of his strange encounters.

"Do you have a pair of hiking shoes with you?" Brad asks Stephan.

"No, but I have a pair of sneakers in the car — why?"

"Well, change into them then. I want to take you on a hike just over the ridge behind the house. Got something to show you."

It is only around two o'clock, and the Arizona desert sun is still ablaze in the afternoon sky, so they have plenty of daylight left to explore.

Brad, while quite a bit taller than Stephan, offers him one of his cotton T-shirts to wear instead of his heavy polo shirt. The temperature this time of year can reach well into the low one hundreds, so it's wise to dress lightly and be prepared to hydrate often.

Once Stephan is garbed in his hiking clothes and armed with ample bottles of water, they proceed out the front door and head up the road on foot.

After walking a short distance, Brad turns right and leads them up a steep incline that turns into a challenging vertical rock climb some two hundred feet in.

Huffing and puffing from behind, Stephan asks where the heck Brad's taking him. Brad laughs as he reaches for another foothold in the jagged rock face and tells Stephan they are almost there. "You'll soon see how it is well worth the effort."

Brad reaches the summit first and lends a hand as Stephan struggles up.

Once atop their destination, the two stand in reverence of the panoramic magnificence laid out before them. "This view is rivaled only by the Grand Canyon," Stephan says.

As far as the eye can see are majestic white and red rock formations back-dropped by a cobalt blue sky and puffy white clouds. It is most surreal to Stephan as he watches a hawk circle high above with only the sound of the wind whistling past their ears.

"Unbelievable!" Stephan sighs.

Brad responds, "Yep, as many times as I've climbed up here, I still can't get over how small and insignificant I feel in comparison to this. It's God's best work, that's for sure!"

Pulling out a pair of high-caliber binoculars, he directs Stephan to look at a point off to the southwest. "See that formation over there? The double peak? Well, one night around dusk I was up here meditating and waiting to catch the sunset when my focus was drawn to a dark object in the sky. It wasn't silver like a plane; it was black and large. It was moving at what I estimated to be a high rate of speed and was fast approaching.

"As I watched it in flight, I remember thinking, *but I don't hear any engine noise*. At first I thought it was because the air currents were blowing in the opposite direction, and once it passed over I'd hear the roar of the engines. But I never did.

"In fact, when it did pass directly overhead, it was quite low — maybe only two or three hundred feet above me — with no noise. Just this big looming vehicle passing overhead. I instinctively ducked, you know, like you do when you think something is lower than it actually is.

"It seemed to hover over me for a minute or two, and it had a huge wing span and no propeller blades. I've never known of a traditional aircraft to be able to hover almost completely still like that and not make any sound!

"And then the most unbelievable thing happened. ... As I

lowered my binoculars to get a better look, a bright orange beam shot out of the undercarriage of the craft and encased me in a tube of light, you know?" Brad's emotions begin to rise with each word.

"Then, before I could figure out what part of the ship it was coming from or even if I should run, I guess I blacked out or something because the next thing I knew I was lying on the ground by my car in my front yard, and it was dark out. At first I thought maybe I'd fallen off the ridge, but that couldn't be right because, as you now know, the ridge is more than a mile away.

"Somehow I'd lost about six hours and ended up a mile and a half from where I stood on the ridge…"

While Brad's voice trails off Stephan gently places his hand on his shoulder. "Do you think they took you someplace?" Stephan asks.

It takes Brad a moment to realize Stephan is speaking. "What did you just say?"

Stephan rephrases, "Do you feel you may have been abducted?"

"Yes!" Brad looks surprised by his own answer. "Up until now I've never really been able to remember what happened."

Stephan thinks this is as good a time as any to tell Brad the full truth about his own "travels," so they can both better understand the nature of the "visits" Stephan has experienced.

He begins, "As a very young boy, I was visited by what I thought were other small children, like me. Only they didn't talk, at least not out loud. We spoke to each other without saying words, and I never felt threatened or frightened when they appeared.

"I unhesitantly followed them numerous times onboard their special ships and was taken for rides high above the Earth. The funny thing was I couldn't remember what I did when I was with them, but I could draw the inside of the ships right down to the minutest detail.

"My visitations, as I would call them, continued until I was a senior in high school. It was hard enough to 'know' things that others didn't know. I would shock some and freak out others with my ability to tell them about their grandmother who was about to die or their aunt who had a tumor in her head or their dead father wanting me to pass on some message that was exactly what they needed to hear.

"But my encounters with Lupo were the most amazing. As a young child I had no fear of being in the presence of a wolf — a wild animal that for all intents and purposes could have harmed me greatly. But Lupo wasn't really what he appeared to be."

Up until now, Stephan had been extremely careful not to divulge too much information about his "specialties," but he felt safe with what he was about to share with Brad. The only other person Stephan had discussed this with in detail was Liz, and then there was Nathan, who seemed to know everything anyway.

Stephan takes in a slow breath and continues: "Remember how I told you that L-U-P-O is Italian for 'wolf,' and that I discovered it also meant E.T.? Well, in my last encounter with Lupo a few days ago, when he saved my life, what I didn't tell you was what happened just before he left me safely by my car."

Stephan tries to calculate the best way to explain and decides to just tell it the way it happened. "Once Lupo led me down to the trailhead, he stopped in his tracks. He had sustained a serious injury while protecting me from the eminent attack of the other wolves.

"As he sat on the ground, barely visible due to the darkness, all of a sudden a beam of orange light illuminated him from a source high above us both. I couldn't make out the source, but like you described when you saw that dark craft, whatever was there made no sound."

Stephan takes a sip of water to relieve his dry mouth and continues his saga, "Right before my eyes Lupo, or the image I had interpreted as Lupo, morphed into what I can only describe as the familiar shape of the childlike visitors I traveled with on those ships. The beast Lupo had turned into one of my 'friends' from my early days on the hillside farm in Italy!

"This 'being' had an unusually large head and black slanted eyes, but no ears. He was dressed in some type of shiny metallic cloth that was silvery blue in color. Almost iridescent."

"Go on," Brad excitedly urges, who has been quietly listening up to this point.

"Without looking at me again, Lupo, or I guess I should say this being levitated up toward the source of the light, again without a sound. I stood there frozen as I watched this whole unbelievable event unfold.

"Then without warning, the light went out, the sky again darkened, and there I stood all alone in the parking lot next to my car. There was no sound, no sign of Lupo nor the light that beamed him up into the night sky.

"When I was finally able to move my legs, I opened the car door and just sat there. I don't honestly know how long I sat there, but believe me it was a while. When I felt I could drive, I fumbled my keys into the ignition and drove ever so slowly back to the main road and to my hotel room, where I collapsed onto my bed and fell instantly into a deep, deep sleep."

Brad sits there, speechless. Then he says, "I've heard many a strange tale, but this one is most unusual — and yet totally believable to me."

The two men continue to stare at each other, without speaking, then Brad lifts off his baseball cap, scratches his head, and wipes away the sweat dripping down his forehead. Then he lets out a raucous laugh. "Okay son, you got me on that one! Here's what I think. … I think you and I need to keep talking to each other. Even after you return home. I'll tell you what else … I think you and your 'friends' just may be the ones who can blow all this stuff right out in the open. I mean, push the edge of the envelope and get folks to understand
— it's not a matter of IF they are here, it's a matter of WHY they are here!" Stephan knows what Brad is suggesting rings true to him at his core. Now the biggest question is: –HOW?

The Arizona sun is setting, and both men are weary from the day's excitement. After the two return to Brad's homestead, Stephan bids his new compadre a good evening, with the promise of more meetings and discussions to follow.

This is not over between the two men…not for a minute. The time has come for stepping up their individual investigations and pooling as much information as they can gather, so Stephan will be well armed for his next paramount task — convincing the government it's time to let the public know who walks among them, and why.

The Lobbyist

*W*hen I returned to school after my life-changing visit to Sedona, I didn't immediately know what to do with all this information. Nathan had been incredibly astute in recommending I go there to search for additional information valuable to my mission. However, I couldn't help but wonder how he thought I could effectively merge my impending law degree with the ever-present UFO activity, in light of the government's blatant cover-up. There were hundreds upon thousands of documented accounts of alien abductions and UFO sightings, with just as many denouncements by the government stating they could all be easily explained, so what was I supposed to do with that?

While in Sedona I was in constant contact with Liz and shared with her every discovery, every event, every meeting with Brad. Liz had become more than an ally in this quest for truth. I had fallen in love with her. We both knew she would be by my side for a long time to come.

Liz had done some soul-searching of her own while I was away, and had an epiphany that changed the course of her life's direction. She told me that after graduation she was going to take some post-grad courses in psychology and that she intended to pick up where Dr. Ortega left off.

She knew her mission was to continue to guide "kids like us" and help these children find acceptance of their special abilities, so they, too, could be of value and utilize the knowledge and purpose gifted them. I thought, who better to understand these children than Liz?

As soon as I unpacked my bags, I called her to ask if we could meet as soon as possible, so we could figure out the next step in this crazy journey of ours. And, of course, I needed to talk again with Nathan to fill him in on my unbelievable trip.

To my surprise, Liz informed me no one had seen or heard from Nathan for over two weeks, and that the campus authorities had brought in local detectives to investigate his disappearance.

Deciding to put Nathan's MIA (missing in action) aside for the time being, Liz and I reviewed what we knew so far, and thought it best to sleep on it to let the dust settle (Arizona desert notwithstanding).

I did know this: I was on a fast track I couldn't get off of even if I'd wanted to.

My encounters with my "friends" and Lupo were big enough events unto themselves, but this new twist of my experience in Sedona along with my meetings with Brad Phillips left little doubt I needed to continue my research — thus arming myself with as much ammunition available for what I needed to do next.

So for the next several weeks, I isolated myself after classes, going to either the library or the confines of my dorm to read everything ever written about encounters with UFOs, abductions, and the government's continued denial of these types of phenomena.

Even though Brad expounded on the government's unmovable posture concerning UFOs, I was hoping against hope that his bias was unfounded and that, in the greater scheme of things, the government was finally at a point of acknowledgement of their existence — actually encouraging people to step forward with their stories. How naive I was.

(Flashback)

His eyes beyond weary from endlessly reading accounts of UFO sightings, alien encounters and abductions, Stephan succumbs to fatigue and reluctantly loosens his grip on the report in his hand and lets it drop to the carpet of his dormitory floor.

He drifts into a fitful slumber, as his mind refuses to stop its incessant analyzing and postulation. When Stephan awakes but a few hours later, he bolts upright in half consciousness and proclaims out loud, "Oh, my God … that's it! Of course!"

Ignoring the lateness of the hour, or more correctly the earliness of the day, he dials Liz's phone number as he struggles to clear away any cobwebs that remain in his head.

While Liz is just as committed as he in their purposeful journey, he reminds himself just how much she enjoys her beauty sleep and that disturbing her in the wee hours of the morning holds the strong probability of her not being in the same frame of excitement; however, he continues to dial.

"Hello? …" Liz's raspy voice responds to the telephone's urgent summoning.

"Liz! Liz! I've got it! I can't explain right now how I got it … but I've got it!" His voice explodes with enthusiasm.

"Wha—Who … Stephan, is that you? This better be good, Preppy, or—" She interrupts herself with a yawn as she attempts to become more awake.

"I'm on my way over. Put on some coffee, some very strong coffee. We're going to need it. I'll be there in ten minutes!" He slams the phone down and before Liz can reply, "Sure, Okay", Stephan is gone.

Liz rubs here eyes in the hopes the numbers on her digital clock can't be right as she struggles to raise her uncooperative body from its restful pose. "Coffee, coffee, coffee …" she mumbles, shuffling her way to the small kitchen located next to her bedroom. She flips on the kitchen switch and cries, "Good Lord!" at the intensity of the light that floods over her.

Coffee started, she stares blankly out the window over the sink, watching for Stephan's car. Believing she has a few moments before his arrival, she hurries to the bathroom to wash her face and brush her teeth. She doesn't care how much she loves this man, she can't greet him with morning breath and half-asleep eyes. She laughs to herself.

The loud banging on her front door announces his arrival, and she hurries to open it, not so much in anticipation of Stephan but to quiet him before he wakes up the whole building.

He hurries past her, blowing an indifferent air kiss her way as he reaches for a coffee mug hanging under the cupboard. Cocking her head to one side as she walks toward him, she asks, "Okay, what the heck is this all about?" He risks her growing impatience by taking one more big gulp of coffee, then he begins.

"Last night I could barely keep my eyes open while I was reading through some dull, redundant materials the government had written pretty much denouncing anything and everything that's been reported on UFO sightings to a small investigative task force they created called Blue Book.

"It goes on to explain that after all the hoopla coming out of the purported episodes in the now-infamous Area 51 in Nevada and the accounts of captured aliens in Roswell, New Mexico, they have concluded beyond a reasonable doubt that there's a manmade explanation for everything. Big surprise, right?

"They go on to denounce all of it and how the public's manic need to engage their fantasies by bringing Buck Rogers and the Star Trek adventures into reality has caused a gosh darn UFO epidemic! As I drifted off to sleep, I laughed to myself and thought, Man! You have no idea!" Stephan laughs.

Liz knows that to ask Stephan any questions at this juncture will be futile, so she nods and gestures for him to continue.

"So I fall asleep and begin to have these really vivid dreams. Nothing like when I'm about to have a visitation — quite the opposite.

"I recognize on some level that I am, in fact, dreaming, but I am also observing the dream from outside myself. Does that make any sense?"

"Go … go on, Stef," she urges.

"All of a sudden I'm standing in this huge room filled with people. I mean a huge room, like a rotunda or some other auditorium with a circular dais and sectioned seating. There are flags representing every country known to man flying all around the circumference of the room.

"I watch a man as he approaches the podium and slams down a gavel, which brings a hush to the crowd. Then I begin to hear his words. He is introducing a very important speaker seated just behind him, who then rises and takes his place before this assembly.

"In my dream I'm straining to make out the figure as he moves closer to the podium, and then I see — the speaker is me! I am speaking before the World Council of the Humanities!" Stephan concludes with excitement.

Liz stares for a moment then responds, "Of course! Exactly!" They both chime in together as they think aloud: "Is there anyone who has done this before on such a controversial subject as UFOs?"

They begin a frantic chatter, sometimes speaking over each other, about needing to figure out how to obtain an audience before the World Council of the Humanities, when the "Eureka" moment occurs to them simultaneously... Stephan needs to become a lobbyist, with his agenda being complete disclosure by the government of the existence of UFO activity — thus bringing a halt to the cover-up! But this is just a fraction of their mission; the more urgent part is to bring awareness as to WHY the aliens are here.

They both stop mid-sentence and look into each other's eyes and calmly declare, "This is it! This is what we are to do!"

With that, Stephan pours himself another cup of coffee while Liz hurriedly boots up her computer, all the while fumbling through her desk drawers for pen and paper so they can begin the ardent process of submitting his application to become a lobbyist.

As the hours go by, instead of appearing fatigued, Stephan seems exhilarated, not to mention wired from all that caffeine he has consumed.

Ultimately, Liz announces she has to get dressed for class, and Stephan reluctantly acknowledges that he has a pre-exam study group to meet up with. He informs her that he'll go to the campus library later to continue his fact-finding on how to proceed in becoming a lobbyist. He knows it won't happen over night, so there's no time to lose.

It never crosses Liz's mind that Stephan might not be truly ready for this. She just knows it's the next logical step in what they came here to do.

Before departing, Stephan gently brings Liz to his chest in a close embrace. He looks deep into her piercing blue eyes and tells her how much he loves her and how they are about to embark on one of the most exciting parts of their journey together. Liz smiles from ear to ear and says, "I go where you go. Bring it on, Preppy!"

ॐ Lions and Tigers and Bears, Oh My!

The baby-boomer era produced not only changes in consciousness but gave rise to intense focus and concentrated awareness to the possibilities of other life forms. Non-human — not us — life forms.

Nothing made that so clear as the master creation of television. A decidedly technological phenomenon for its day that brought families together to gaze endlessly hour after hour at a small box that produced black-and-white images for our amusement and occasionally our intellect.

While most people viewed this wonderful invention as a major advancement in modern technology, I on the other hand, found it an amusing, almost primal building blocks — like Legos, if you will. Don't get me wrong; for lack of something better to do, I, too, was glued to the "boob tube" as visions of game shows, comedy hours, and live dramas flashed before my very eyes.

But what drew my sincere interest were the initial feeble portrayals of space travel and the introduction of "aliens" right into our living rooms. As corny as it was presented, the accuracy of its delivery was somewhat comical, at least to me.

While programs like Flash Gordon *and, in later years,* Lost in Space *lacked credibility — with their humorous attempts to lure their audience with the portent of life on other planets, space travel, and alien beings — they ended up being a driving force that ultimately, if not deliberately, bred fear and hostility toward whatever else lay outside our galactic box.*

The mere thought of other beings that looked horrific and threatened our peaceful existence couldn't be any further from the truth, in my opinion. That's not to say there aren't negative beings, whether here in our dimension or in nonphysical, whose intent for a peaceful coexistence differs from ours. However, that old expression "one bad apple ..." certainly applies here.

Around the time Star Trek *was introduced to TV Land, at least those writers proved to display some level of intelligence and took responsibility to incorporate plausible scenarios of a less threatening nature. They also introduced the idea of a Galactic Federation of sorts that governed the unruly aliens and stood fast in mediation and arbitration for the purpose of joining together beings of difference in an effort to promote peace and harmony amongst the shared space of our galaxies.*

But the real heroes, the ones who thought up this whole idea of life on other planets besides our own and introduced the plausibility of technologies beyond our limited thinking, were sheer geniuses.

By the time Star Wars, Close Encounters of the Third Kind, *and* E.T. *were made, the mass consciousness was ready, willing, and able to acknowledge the seriousness of the subject matter, and began recognizing that the governments around the planet were in some sort of conspiring agreement to continue to let the public believe that interaction with these beings was detrimental to their very existence.*

Star Wars *kept the "good guy/bad guy" conflict alive and well, leaving fantasy as its genre and fear in its wake.*

Close Encounters of the Third Kind *was the breakthrough movie that not only took on the monumental task of acknowledging the government's cover-up policies but introduced recreations of actual nonviolent encounters through special effects and drama that had audiences everywhere unable to deny this fictional story was possible and most assuredly plausible.*

E.T., however, was the closet depiction to the reality of what some galactic neighbors are about and that they mean us no harm. It is the E.T. beings that I, personally, interacted with in my younger years while living on the farm in Italy.

Louise Rose Aveni

I had a special fondness for the movie E.T. and a profound appreciation of Steven Spielberg for having the courage to take such a giant step in the movie-making industry by venturing out of the proverbial box and portraying our alien neighbors as the gentle, benevolent beings that some of them are.

More amazingly, the physicality of the E.T. character was so brilliantly – dare I say, accurately – depicted that it caused me to ponder if Mr. Spielberg had, himself, been the participant in a close encounter of any kind.

Unfortunately, Mr. Spielberg took a one-hundred-eighty-degree turn from those types of films when he recently directed the updated version of War of the Worlds, undoing all the positive imaging he had brought to the masses over two decades before.

Just as we have many cultures and races here on Earth, so it is in this expansive galaxy of ours. We are not made up of only whites, blacks, Indians, and Asians – just to name a few. There are innumerous cross-cultures and hybrids walking around in human form.

The majority of alien beings come from Pleiades, Orion, Lyra, Vega, Sirius, Arcturus, Andromeda, and Cassiopeia (home of the praying mantis race of tall Greys).

The star beings that receive the most notoriety are the Greys (Zeta Reticuli Type A – who are more aggressive – and Type B – who are less hostile and display miraculous feats with their higher technologies).

Next come the Pleidians, also known as the Nordics/Swedes, who are here to observe and not interfere, at least not yet. It is purported that Pleidians appear most like humans and, because of this, can walk among us without detection. They are prophesized to be the ones who will ultimately bring humans into the light. They communicate telepathically; travel from place to place through a tube system; and are primarily vegetarians, although they do occasionally eat meat. They are in control of their own health, so no medicines or technological interventions are utilized. Their skin is whiter and smoother than human skin, and they have a seven-hundred-year life span.

Finally, there are the Reptoids, which are bird-like reptilian entities. They are anywhere from six- to eight-foot bipedal reptilians with large, yellow, vertical pupils. These entities have been part of the Earth since its beginnings and were best described in history as being prevalent in the now-famous dinosaur era. But, like I said, that's only three of uncountable others.

The most "popular" abduction tales are those of the Greys. I have firsthand knowledge of the Greys (Type B), and, unfortunately, some of the more negative beings of their species (Type A) have been instrumental in keeping the fear factor in the hearts of mankind.

The irony of the Zeta Reticuli is that their planet is located in the same Orion constellation as Sirius, my star home. Some theorize that the Greys are the observers and perhaps the creators of this third dimensional holographic program called the human experience on planet Earth.

It is speculated that this is only one of many in the grid of realities and that we humans are encoded and are guided by them through our evolution. Because the Zeta Reticuli are a dying species due to over-cloning that has weakened them, it is their intention to crossbreed with humans in an effort to create a better species. So ask yourself: Why, then, would they destroy the program?

My encounters have always been ones of cooperation. While I initially interacted with the smaller Greys, I continued my "education," as it were, with the taller Greys, whose height ranges anywhere from seven to nine feet. They also have the distinction of a large nose, which the smaller Greys do not possess.

I was never forced to go anywhere I didn't want to go. Once I adjusted to the process of interaction and how I came and went from one reality to another, I eagerly participated in their schooling and welcomed our encounters.

Very early on, it was made crystal clear to me that my participation in this part of the evolutionary journey was but a next step in what would be for the greater good of all — mankind and non-mankind.

ॐ
LUPO Speaks

When I look back on this incredible journey and all that has happened thus far, the most amazing thing to me is that it's really just begun.

Becoming a respected, credible lobbyist was no small feat. It took years of internship and research coupled with a ton of rejection and heartache causing me to wonder if this endeavor was ever going to be brought out into the light, let alone successful.

Blazing a new trail in this untried arena of UFO and E.T. awareness, I was fortunate, indeed, to have amassed people of like mind who saw the value of taking the huge risk and stepping out of the proverbial box for the sake of humanity and its future.

The people and the star beings I've encountered along this journey are but a few in an unknown number who hold a common vantage point, a positive perspective of a beautiful, harmonious coexistence in this brief episode we call life.

As much as I think I've learned, the knowledge and the immense insight I have gleaned through those interactions are but a minute particle of ALL THAT IS!

What I held as my perception proved to be an ever-changing metamorphosis of realities. As I crossed back and forth from dimension to dimension, confused for a while as to which one was real, I came away with my own truth that they are ALL real! It just depends on where you hold your focus at that moment, I guess.

I don't know how or why I, like so many others, were chosen to

*assist this planet and its inhabitants to expand their thinking by
becoming leading-edge creators of a new way of being, but I am beyond
grateful for my participation in this evolutionary process in the hope of
manifesting a world, a galaxy, an infinitum of expansive joy and peace.*

(Flashback)

As Stephan prepares for his trip to New York to speak before
the World Council of the Humanities, he has a moment of panic.
How can I possibly articulate all that needs to be said in such a
way that it is truly heard, he torments to himself.

He decides to clear his head by taking a walk along the
riverbank that borders his home. It is always so peaceful and
uninterrupted there, and that's exactly what he needs right now.

He reaches for his trusty handheld recorder, pops in a new
mini cassette, and pockets two more so he can immediately
record his thoughts and strategies for the most important lobby
of his life — no, mankind's existence.

With summer over, the early morning chill announcing fall's
impending arrival prompts Stephan to take along a lightweight
jacket. Walking along aimlessly in search of the right spot to
settle and focus, his thoughts turn to Liz — how blessed he feels
to have her love and how vital her role has been through all of
this incredible journey.

He flashes back to his earliest memories of her sitting in Dr.
Ortega's office, munching on a large bag of potato chips. He
marvels at the first adult impression she made on him when
she boldly bounded into his class on The Study of Psychological
Phenomenon that first year in college.

He recalls first being drawn to her outlandish sense of
humor, her defiant — dare he say, "cocky arrogance" — with
the professor as she constantly challenged and baited him into
one of her nobody-can-win debates on the probability of life on

other planets. If only Professor Nordstar were still alive today and could talk with her now!

Stephan's reverie is broken by a morning jogger passing by with his leashed dog panting in tow. Stephan stops walking to look around and spies a welcoming cluster of maple trees whose leaves are just beginning to turn their seasonal hue.

He chooses to sit beneath the largest in the group of trees that face the river's great expanse. The sun has now risen sufficiently in the morning sky, so its warming rays are beginning to be felt. Stephan sighs deeply, not knowing where to begin.

He momentarily changes his focus to observe a bright yellow kayak maneuvering gently down this placid section of the river. He sighs once again as he gently closes his eyes for but a moment. Then … he feels it!

At first the vibration is barely noticeable. His conscious mind rapidly concludes it's an airplane passing overhead at a low altitude. No need to open his eyes and interrupt his blissful moment.

"Hm-m-m-m, Hm-m-m-m-m, H-m-m-m-m."

Now the sound becomes ever louder:

"H-m-m-m, H-M-M-M, H-M-M-M-M, H-M-M-M-M!" Stephan can actually feel the ground vibrating in harmony beneath him as he sits beneath the tree.

Suddenly, Stephan is engulfed in "OH-M-M-M-M-M-M, OHM-M-M-M-M, OH-M-M-M-M, OHM-M-M-M!" and finds it impossible to ignore.

This sound has become innately familiar to Stephan, so he remains seated, eyes still shut as he relaxes even more into the deafening sound. "OOOH-MMMMM, OOOH-MMMMM, OOOH-MMMM, OOOH-M-M-M-M-M!"

Louder and louder the vibration tones take Stephan deeper and deeper into himself. With a whoosh, he senses himself speeding through a weightless tunnel. Not falling or plummeting, just moving forward at warp speed.

All of a sudden the forward momentum ceases, and Stephan's

body begins to float downward, where it finally lands softly on a solid surface.

Stephan slowly opens his eyes and looks around to orient himself to his new surroundings. To his amazement, what he sees is a similar scene to the one where he just sat but a few moments ago, only this environment's appearance is definitely altered from the other.

The colors are florescent in spectrum. Stephan observes the same yellow kayak passing before him as it had done before, only this time the water pushed out by the oars of the boatman glows iridescent blue, green, and yellow.

As Stephan attempts to adjust his vision to take in this new look, he glances around toward the cluster of trees that surround him and observes some leaves as they silently fall. They, too, are encompassed by an iridescent aura, this time of red, orange, and green. They seem to emit a muted musical chime as they lightly touch the ground: "Bing ... bing ... bing."

This has to be one of the most beautiful places he's ever seen. But wait a minute ... there is another sound emanating from the low-lying shrubs to his right.

He moves his gaze slowly to the direction of the sound. His squinted eyes attempt to focus in on the moving object as it emerges from the greenery in slow motion.

It doesn't take long for Stephan to recognize this familiar figure and shout, "LUPO!"

Stephan stands to greet his old friend, whom he hasn't seen in a long while — not since his rescue in Boynton Canyon. Stephan abruptly stops in mid-stance. As Lupo's canine form approaches, it immediately begins to morph right before Stephan's eyes into ... Nathan?

While Stephan's brain struggles to accept what his eyes are interpreting, Lupo's morphing continues. What briefly stood walking toward him first as Lupo, then as Nathan, now stands directly before Stephan as ... the "Visitor" — with oversized head and black sunglass-like eyes.

The ever-so-tall, lean figure, with no ears and pencil-thin lips, bows his head in greeting to Stephan, who is frantically blinking in disbelief.

Before Stephan can truly grasp any of this, a gentle voice commands him to sit down. Feeling weak in the knees, he has no problem complying.

Stephan's next thoughts are: *Am I dead? ... Am I even breathing? ... I don't think I'm breathing!*

"Of course you're still breathing, and NO you are NOT dead!" replies the being standing erect before him. "There is no death, anyway, but that discussion will come at another time," the voice replies to his thoughts.

Stephan's gaze is now fully upon this being who apparently is the source of the voice. He begins to ease into it all and silently declares to himself that he's having one of his "visits." *Isn't that right?* he thinks.

"Yes, you are correct. Welcome, Stephan. It has been some time since our last encounter. We have much to discuss, so listen carefully. The time has come for revelation."

As Stephan holds his seated position, the alien being remains standing before him. Floating before him, actually, as Stephan notices the being's lower extremities never quite touch the ground.

Stephan speaks: "You are familiar to me, yes? We've met many times before, haven't we? What name do I call you?"

The voice answers: "'Lupo' is fine. Our dialogue this time will be entirely on the task at hand. It is crucial that your thoughts remain focused, so you may relay this information accurately to the others. Do you understand?"

Stephan's reply is a strong and steady "Yes!"

LUPO: *When you came to this Earth School as a very young child, you were carefully and deliberately positioned in a place of easy access for us to watch and meet with you unnoticed. Your Earth family were simple, unsophisticated humans who were unknowing of beings such as we and others like us. They were riddled with foolish superstitions and myths about that which they could not explain, yet perfect for our purpose.*

Stephan: *Why was it, then, that I had to leave and go to that awful orphanage and suffer such abuse with that foster family before coming to live with my adopted family in America?*

LUPO: *We didn't have much control over that, Stephan. The time you ran into the night to find me, to find the entity you refer to as Lupo, so frightened your caregivers that they feared for your safety, living with them on the hillside.*

While they wanted you to remain with them, their concern for what was best for you left them no alternative but to contact the orphanage in the hope of providing you with a permanent family as a safe haven.

We were not allowed to intercede for fear of being discovered or, worse, eliminated from the project. Your stay at the orphanage and with the other unkind Earth family was unfortunate, but we needed a little more time to secure better arrangements.

Stephan: *You mean you were responsible for getting my adopted family and me together?*

LUPO: *Exactly. We even added in a bit of your Earth humor by finding a family whose original name was Lupiano but Americanized it to Wolf. Did it not catch your notice? My species is not generally known for exhibiting emotions of any kind, let alone humor; however, we found it intriguing to leave you clues such as this one, so as to follow your observations and discoveries.*

Stephan: *Actually, that one didn't escape my notice. But I've got a question for you. If you were in control of bringing me back and forth for our visits, how was it then that when it was time to return me, you weren't a bit more exact in your coordinates?*

I got into a lot of trouble for my "sleepwalking" and was constantly tied up or locked up, only to be found in the early morning hours outside of buildings or on the lawn of wherever I was staying. I was beaten many times for my disappearing act.

LUPO: *Admittedly your Earth density still holds some mystery for us. We continue to experiment with our calibrations, vectors, and coordinates for proper replacements; we are not yet perfect, as you say.*

But let us discuss your outrage at our minor errors another time and resume our discussion of more urgent matters.

Stephan: *Minor errors? Those minor errors nearly got me locked up in a loony bin! If it hadn't been for Dr. Ortega, I might have been placed in a hospital somewhere with the key thrown away! Speaking of Dr. Ortega, was he part of all this?*

LUPO: *Not exactly. He was allowed to have access to you and the others. …*

Stephan: *Like Liz?*

LUPO: *Like Elizabeth, but Dr. Ortega needed to go so much deeper with his studies of your kind that it became necessary to introduce Nathan so as to heighten the intensity of the investigation of children such as you.*

Unfortunately, there are those in your government who felt uneasy with Dr. Ortega's unanticipated diligent detective work, so once he got too close to uncovering some of their secrets, he needed to be eliminated.

You see, it was never their intention to let Dr. Ortega do anything more with you children than pacify your families, teachers, and anyone else who questioned your claims of abductions or your extraordinarily high level of psychic ability.

So we allowed Dr. Ortega a way to uncover just enough evidence to substantiate the necessity for the therapy sessions, thus providing a vehicle to cloak the increasing interest the government was demonstrating regarding you children.

It provided a failsafe for all of you to be pushed under the carpet, so to speak, so as not to encourage further examination of the growing phenomenon by the public at large.

So many children were being brought to Earth with their special abilities, and their detection was becoming obvious. Someone deemed it necessary to label them according to their unique abilities. They have been called Crystal Children or Indigo Children. Semantics ... just semantics.

Dr. Ortega was closely monitored, not only by government officials but by us as well. The information he gathered was only "smoke and mirrors" designed for the ultimate purpose of providing a distraction for the government. More accurately, the destruction of information.

We had no need to study you and the others, simply to instruct and guide you toward your ultimate humanitarian and galactic purpose.

Stephan: *Why didn't you stop them?*

LUPO: *It wasn't time yet. We thought it best to protect you children by allowing the events to unfold in the manner in which they did, so that you and they might be perceived as "less special" and resume a semi-normal childhood, with the exception of our visits. It was always our intention to reduce the number of visits for a bit until you got older so as to allow the human part of your experience to flourish and complement a balance between your duality.*

Stephan: *There would never be anything even close to normal for us. I remember the visits became more serious and not at all so playful.*

LUPO: *Indeed. Just as human growth experiences expand on Earth, we too have a propensity for more serious matters to be dominant.*

Stephan: *So, WE children/adults have been groomed right from the start? You've orchestrated pretty much most of our lives right up to this moment?*

LUPO: *Accurately stated. We knew even before you emerged into physical form who you were to become and what role each one of you would play in the execution of this mission born of the Galactic Federation.*

You were chosen, all of you, for your special abilities, individual personalities, and unique talents to be positioned throughout the galaxy to live, learn, and grow amongst the species until this moment of revelation.

I must add that all of you always had the free will to not participate. We gave you that option after each and every time of visit. It was not our intention to utilize your abilities against your will.

Upon the conclusion of each visit, each encounter, you were always asked if you wished to cease your involvement, to have your memories of any of this erased forever, and to resume a life of your choosing. For it is your birthright. You and the others made it clear that you wished to continue. And so it is!

Stephan: *Just how many of us are there? Enough to make a difference?*

LUPO: *The numbers are vast. There are many who have walked amongst the Earthlings for centuries.*

In the greater galaxy, where the measurement of time is not linear such as it is on Earth, it is almost impossible to describe in a format that you can understand. For clarity, let it be enough to use the Earth analogy of the theory of Critical Mass or the Hundredth Monkey. Does that help you?

Stephan: *Yes, that's clear. Now it comes down to the most important question of all: How do I convey the importance of what is about to happen when I go before the World Council of the Humanities?*

LUPO: *I will speak, you will listen. When I am through speaking, it will then be appropriate for you to request any further clarification. Let us begin.*

We and others like us have been part of Earth's beginnings. First as observers, still as observers. The interaction, while seemingly new to Earthlings, has gone on before. For as I mentioned, there is no linear time throughout space. Only here.

There were those from other galaxies of a more aggressive nature who attempted to dominate; however, the Federation intervened with swift and cataclysmic results. For example, I believe you refer to one such era as the Ice Age.

Earth is a living entity unto itself. It is source energy at its best. It breathes, thrives, and purges. Natural disasters are nothing more than Mother Earth eliminating that which no longer serves her wellbeing. The humans caught in that elimination are not unfortunate in their placement but destined, if you will, to fulfill their mission in non-third dimension. They ascend when they do, as they do, when all is in order.

There are many species that walk the earth, as do you. On Earth it is you, the human, who dominates and exhibits the higher intellect. For all others, their role is strictly lower vibration.

In the greater expanse known to you as the Universe, it is quite different. For example, the entities you refer to as insects and reptiles, while small and insignificant and most annoying on planet Earth, are a superior intelligent species with higher technologies that man has never seen the likes of. They chose to be part of this experiment as a subspecies rather than a dominant one.

That is not to say there aren't those in the infinite who would like to dominate; they are simply rebuffed from completing their intent by the powerful rule of the Federation. It is by their grant that other star beings are able to partake in this experiment.

For most, domination is not the intent, although your

governments would like to portray quite the opposite for their own suspect reasons.

While there are many who govern human societies with the aid of beings less focused on Earth's continuation, there are just as many in power who are willing to listen and have already set the wheels in motion for the upheaval of dysfunctional dominance.

Right now, there are groups merging into a powerful network for positive change. Humans resist change as it is an unknown with no discernible texture. Its success is not assured, so those in power keep the populous in fear as it is an effective means of holding them in denial and thus cloaking the truth.

Humanity needs to regulate its activity to better harmonize with the ecosystem. The people of Earth are ready for the elimination of harmful environmental toxins that help line the pockets of the greedy. They are ready for one government chosen by the masses, with currency no longer being regulated by those in power, but empowering those in need to generate their own form of exchange.

In Pleiades, for example, there is no need for currency. They share resources with all, based on contribution to society as a whole. So the responsibility rests solely on the being to either prosper or be accountable for their lack. Simple.

The human formation of religions, social structures, governments, and the like, are but negotiated agreements by those who hunger to dominate the masses. While it is not unreasonable to prefer order over chaos, it is the manner in which the order is established that dictates the outcome for the general good of all.

The Galactic Federation has allowed intervention when and only when there is threat of annihilation of the planet or a populous at large. In more recent times, intervention has been allowed in an effort to keep nuclear weapons with capabilities of mass destruction in their silos, never to be launched nor reach their intended targets.

Earth was created as an experimental oasis, a stopping-off point for the continuum of leading-edge thinkers. Nowhere else in the galaxy is there a place such as Earth that provides harmonious beauty and a soothing environment for beings who experience sensually; that is, with senses of auditory, vision, smell, taste, and touch.

Perhaps one of the most significant Earth experiences that is devoid in most other planetary environments is that of emotion. It is considered a point of weakness by other star societies, yet warrants closer investigation and evaluation for its usefulness.

And so it was that the Galactic Federation deployed emissaries from numerous dimensions, by invitation only, to take part in this experiment.

In response, planets such as your star family on Sirius evaluated young candidates, some in vitro; encoded the transmitter, your human brain; positioned these new lives around the planet at different stages of its evolution; then observed the results. A sort of holographic experimentation program.

Essential knowledge has not been erased from each candidate, but has been implanted deep, so you may use this Earth School to find ways to discover it. You and others like you were key elements in assisting the transformation of life to new levels of the Earth's healing.

This transformation process is one of healing your separateness. The Federation formed a partnership with other star beings to assist the enlightening of humanity, so it may move more completely into a course of wise action.

It goes without saying that there are numerous uninvited entities that feign observation while their intention is interference and, to use a human vernacular, upset the apple cart.

You and others like you chose this Earth School journey because you accepted the challenges of participation in this lifetime in the hopes of redirecting the current evolutionary shifts on your planet. With guiding influence of the Federation, your accepted larger role is to stabilize Earth's living environment.

This is a time of rejuvenation. You are to use your abilities and talents to heal the Earth. There is no one single truth.

I will say this, the program is not in jeopardy of termination. Far from it. We all have much to learn from this and so it is then … the program will continue.

There is much that has been assimilated, reviewed, and concluded.

While the experiment began with individual assignments, the conclusion is that separateness is useless and of no benefit. Joining together as one has proven to be of infinite value for the common good of all. And so it is that our message to those on Earth is to no longer separate from one another as your true power lays within the larger YOU.

This evolutionary period of renewal and stabilization is designed to expand awareness of sources less familiar, with the ultimate result being one of harmony of purpose.

So, I am complete. Go now, Stephan. The world awaits your contribution."

Imagine

*P*reparing for my speech before the World Council of the Humanities was the ultimate culmination of my journey, this far. But only the beginning of what was to be.

Knowing how unique I was and finding others "like me" gave credence to my existence. What I wasn't sure of was how I would become one of many voices that could ultimately change the world as we know it. How could I live up to such a responsibility? It was overwhelming, yet I knew I would give it my best shot.

The human side of me had doubts, fears, and a million questions. That "other" part of me was confident and all knowing. This duality made being Me a real challenge.

As I looked back on my journey from my first recollections of living with my foster family on the hillside farm in Italy, I couldn't help but wish I could regain the innocence and simplicity life offered back then. Being ... just being! Living each moment – in the moment.

Coming to terms with my abilities and my connection with others like me was a monumental task, to say the least. But convincing my family and friends that what was happening to me was nothing to be feared was nearly impossible.

The jury is still out with most of my immediate family on all of this, but I will say, the one person who shocked me by staying somewhat open to the possibilities was my dad. I thought he'd be the last one to accept any of it, but he genuinely keeps a crack in the door open because of his powerful love for his son. My mom just keeps walking around the *house blessing herself and muttering some prayerful verbiage that will keep me and those around me safe from harm. So be it!*

Most of my childhood chums have moved on, and we don't talk much anymore. To tell you the truth, I think they feel it best to give me a wide berth these days. My stories and talents were cool when we were kids, but unexplainable and just plain weird as adults. My only wish is that they will remember the wonderment of the experiences I shared with them while growing up together, and be receptive to their own children's "special talents" because it is this new generation that holds the key to positive global change.

I'm still in touch with some of my college buddies, but mostly the ones who were involved in my lobbying efforts. A seasoned lobbyist is capable of grabbing the attention of not only financial backers but a significant entourage of powerful supporters along the way. I was blessed with obtaining both.

With the subject matter of UFOs, extraterrestrials, and the granddaddy of all — the Great Government Cover-up, I was blazing a new trail in this industry and for the history books. Luckily, I had gained the confidence and respect of a small handful of "believers" who volunteered their time and talents to the cause. I am forever grateful for their generosity, compassion, and insight of what can be.

It goes without saying that Brad Phillips was an integral part of this process, so I invited him to join me and be prepared to answer some pretty tough questions. I was amused to see when I picked him up at the airport that he was laden with boxes upon boxes of written testimonials and recordings … just in case. I could always count on Brad to rise to the occasion.

With such a monumental task put before me, Liz and I couldn't have possibly accumulated the research materials all by ourselves. No way!

These volunteers were instrumental in compiling the hundreds upon thousands of written testimonials from key witnesses ranging from retired military personnel, government officials, prominent physicians, bankers, corporate bigwigs, celebrities, commercial pilots, all the way through to the working-class men and women who had firsthand accounts of UFO and extraterrestrial events since 1947, which earmarked the official beginning of the investigation.

As long as the government keeps the public busy focusing on the debate of the existence of UFOs and extraterrestrials, then the real issues of why they are here and what the government's sinister role is in their cover-up remain enigmas. More importantly, politicians can continue with their global environmental challenge for power, coercion, greed, and corruption in earnest. ("Watch the right hand, so you don't see what the left hand is doing" is their mantra.)

I had the undaunted task of ripping off the government's mask of illusion, and presenting a new way of perceiving our galactic neighbors as not only the high technological gurus they are but as benevolent emissaries capable of elevating our evolution into the fifth world. A challenging concept at best.

Just imagine a world united in purpose – a co-mingling of idealisms for the common good of man. Recalling the powerful lyrics from John Lennon's song "Imagine": "You may say I'm a dreamer, but I'm not the only one. I hope someday you'll join us.... And the world will live as one."

When the moment of truth arrives and the impact of my speech before the World Council of the Humanities is felt around the world, then and only then will I pass the gauntlet.

(Flashback)

His speech before the World Council of the Humanities was more than Stephan could have ever envisioned. Not only did he have the full attention of the entire assembly for over four hours but what was born of this amazing moment in time held the portent of a new life, a birthing of a new era for not only the people on Earth but throughout the galaxy.

As Liz and Stephan settle into their hotel room, Liz is clearly exhausted and draws herself a soothing bubble bath before retiring to bed. Stephan is beyond exhilarated and sits in a chair by the window overlooking this amazing city of millions, in awe of the day's unfolding. Pinch me!

As the flow from the bathtub faucet fills a well-deserved respite for Liz, Stephan relives the highlights of the day. He smiles to himself remembering being poised and ready for his announcement by the Majority Leader of the Dias and how this depicted exactly what he had seen in his prophetic dream the night he decided to become a lobbyist. It all seems so long ago … so long ago.

Standing before the mass assembly of the Council, not to mention the hordes of international media, Stephan recalls feeling but a fleeting moment of panic — would he say enough? Would he be able to share his experiences in a manner that would be taken seriously by the Council? Could he open the minds of this small representation of humanity to embrace the opportunity to be the ones to change the course of history for mankind and beyond?

Reliving that moment makes Stephan shiver. Then he recalls the calm that washed over him as he cleared his throat and began thanking the assembly for this opportunity.

Somehow the words flowed as he spoke evenly, confidently, and articulately. He felt altered in his state of consciousness — a puppet, if you will, to words that came from another place. His voice box was the instrument from which the transmission freely flowed.

Stephan chuckles to himself as he recalls a poignant moment when he pulled out all the stops by using a dramatic courtroom tactic he once saw in a movie.

He had over fifty of his volunteers in ready in the hallway outside the assembly room, loaded down with thousands of the written testimonials of UFO and extraterrestrial encounters generated by the masses of people from all walks of life.

On cue these deliverers of knowledge entered en masse, pushing and pulling wheeled metal pallets overflowing with undeniable evidence.

It was Stephan's intent to belay the question "Are they here?" The focus could now be directed on the "Why".

At the conclusion of his speech, he wasn't prepared for the deafening roar of applause that followed as the assembly rose to their feet in unison with undeniable approval. The applause was but a small token of the genuine acceptance that was to follow.

After what seemed to be an hour of congratulatory backslapping, with an abundance of kudos and accolades, Stephan remembers gathering his notes in preparation to find Liz and head back to their hotel for celebration and a much deserved rest.

Before he could leave the podium, two very high-profiled political figures approached him and offered their congratulations, which by itself filled him with pride. But what followed next was more than Stephan could have ever imagined. They proposed an immediate meeting with Stephan to discuss and formulate a plan of action to develop a unified coalition group that would be governed by the people, a cross-section humanitarian committee of his choosing, with the intent of being ready to interact with the Galactic Federation when they were sure of the people's commitment of cooperation for the good of all.

For what happens here on Earth is far-reaching into the galaxy and perhaps beyond. There are many species from distant star regions who have been watching and waiting to see how humanity utilizes the tools of higher consciousness, which is ever expanding in an effort to change and ultimately eliminate its course of environmental self-destruction, as its impact is infinite.

With this last thought, Stephan, still sitting in the chair by the window, drifts off into a deep, peaceful slumber. He is complete. Job well done!

Completing his speech before the World Council of the Humanities was exhausting enough for Stephan, but he has chosen this moment in time to introduce Liz to his family, as she has become more than a colleague in this endeavor — this mission — to change the world as we know it.

Stephan is beginning to think that what he thought was his biggest challenge pales at the prospect of articulating the past thirty-odd years' experience to his parents. After all, they were never aware of his continued "sleepwalking" visitations or especially Lupo. For all they knew, all this nonsense ceased years ago after Dr. Ortega's death. From their standpoint, that was the end of an extremely imaginative phase of Stephan's life, most likely brought on by his traumatic beginnings as a young child in Italy.

And yet Stephan finds that his dad, of all people, is questioning him more and more about the direction he has chosen to take as — in his Dad's words — "a lobbyist for UFOs is it?" Not quite. But his genuine curiosity is encouraging. Enough so that Stephan has offered to have his dad join him for a few days in Washington to visit his office and watch him go through his paces. Perhaps then his father will understand a little more… Perhaps.

The short drive from the hotel in New York to Stephan's parents' home in the upper portion of the state provides Stephan and Liz the ultimate luxury of a private audience with each other to formulate their next step. Liz seems somewhat apprehensive about meeting Stephan's family. She's worried they may perceive her as another weirdo who enables Stephan to continue his unusual quest for truth. Perhaps they're right after all.

Exactly how much should Stephan reveal about his relationship with Liz, in terms of their special talents? Running the risk of Stephan's mom fainting dead on the floor and his dad reaching for whatever his hands land on in the liquor cabinet gives them pause regarding their course of action.

It's not long before they arrive at their destination. Liz appears impressed with the loveliness of the neighborhood and the pristine landscape of Stephan's childhood home, obviously produced by the caring hands of his dad, who — according to

Stephan — loves to get his hands dirty and is always planting and pruning his small estate.

As they exit the car and open the trunk to retrieve their bags, Stephan's mom comes running out the front door, apron flapping in the breeze as she speeds forward in typical elderly shuffle to greet them.

"She looks wonderful," Stephan says more to himself than to Liz.

"Hey there, young man!" a voice booms from the open garage door. Stephan's dad emerges with a gardening tool in one hand and nothing but the promise of a hug in the other.

After embraces and introductions, the two couples excitedly enter the foyer of Stephan's first real home. How he's missed this place. Even with the passage of time and all the renovations over the years, the house retains its essence of home — His home.

The visit is a good one. Meeting Liz is a dream come true for Stephan's parents, who want nothing more than for their son to settle down with a nice girl and raise a family. While they may be, indeed, headed in that direction, for now Stephan and Liz have a full plate before them that takes precedence over all other personal future plans.

Stephan earnestly vows to his parents and to himself to visit more often, and Liz assures them all she'll make it her mission to see that he keeps that promise.

All too soon it's time to head back to Washington and to what lies in wait. Coming home was the best thing Stephan could have done for himself, for he knows that his mission is really just beginning. The past three and a half decades are but the preamble for what is to come.

Riding back in the car Liz finds it impossible to keep her eyes open, so she slips off to sleep. Stephan lovingly looks over at her in her peaceful slumber, the ever confident passenger trusting there's a competent driver at the wheel. Metaphor? You bet!

IMAGINE

Imagine there's no heaven
It's easy if you try
No hell below us
Above us only sky
Imagine all the people
Living for today...

Imagine there's no countries
It isn't hard to do
Nothing to kill or die for
And no religion too
Imagine all the people
Living life in peace...

You may say I'm a dreamer
But I'm not the only one
I hope someday you'll join us
And the world will be as one

Imagine no possessions
I wonder if you can
No need for greed or hunger
A brotherhood of man
Imagine all the people
Sharing all the world...

You may say I'm a dreamer
But I'm not the only one
I hope someday you'll join us
And the world will live as one

Wolf Wisdom

One evening, an old Cherokee told his grandson about a battle that goes on inside people. He said, "My son, the battle is between two 'wolves' inside us all.

"One is *Evil*. It is anger, jealousy, sorrow, regret, greed, arrogance, self-pity, guilt, resentment, inferiority, lies, false pride, superiority, and ego.

"The other is *Good*. It is joy, peace, love, hope, serenity, humility, kindness, benevolence, empathy, generosity, truth, compassion, and faith."

The grandson thought about it for a minute and then asked his grandfather – "Which wolf wins?"

The old Cherokee simply replied – "The one you feed."

Author Unknown

Book II

HYBRID

THE CONVERSATION CONTINUES

THE WORDS OF A HOPI ELDER:

"I have been in the hearts of many and there is, indeed, something happening that is distinct.

There are those clinging to the shore of familiarity, hiding from their true selves both in themselves and from the world around them and there are those who have left the shore and are seeking who and what will support their celebration, as they swim for home.

There is a river flowing now, very fast.

It is so great and swift, that there are those who will be afraid.

They will try to hold on to the shore, they will feel they are being torn apart and will suffer greatly.

Know that the river has its destination.

The elders say we must let go of the shore, push off into the middle of the river, keep our eyes open and our heads above the water.

And I say, see who is there with you and celebrate.

At this time in history, we are to take nothing personally, least of all ourselves, for the moment that we do, our spiritual growth and journey come to a halt.

The time of the lone wolf is over. Gather yourselves.

Banish the word struggle from your attitude and vocabulary. All that we do now, must be done in a sacred manner and in celebration.

We are the ones we have been waiting for."

For my grandsons, Scott and Cody
Believe in the possibilities…and watch what happens!

The only truth that truly matters is the one you seek deep inside. The trick is recognizing when it surfaces.

Louise Rose Aveni

Prologue
Stephan Remembers

*T*he arrival of the new millennium brought about many global
changes- some welcome, others not so welcome. It took me a long
time to prepare for what is now being touted as one of the most identifiable
galactic missions ever experienced in the history of mankind.

I've been a tenacious UFO lobbyist for over two decades and now,
here I stand locked and loaded as I prepare to take on yet another
congressional committee debate regarding the government's blatant
disregard concerning the existence of "Chemtrails".

What exactly are "Chemtrails" you ask? Just look up into the sky
and check out all the streaks of white plumed chemicals that defile
the very air that we breathe. However, definitively speaking: they are
highly visible streaks of chemicals, created in the air by spray systems
onboard airplanes that fly at varying altitudes with no known purpose.

Of course, the United States Government denies any knowledge or
responsibility regarding these Chemtrails, but consider this…if their
presence was not of our government's approval or acceptance, they
would have fighter jets ready to intercept and destroy the intrusion
into our air space. No questions asked - that's a known fact!

As I sit in wait for the anticipated rebuttal, my mind involuntarily
drifts away from the confines of the room and I find myself reflecting
on just how much my life has changed. Even now, I can vividly recall
my early days as a young orphan living with the foster family on the
hillside farm in Verese, Italy and how I befriended a lone wolf I call
LUPO, not to mention all my other "special visitors" who began their

143

unique tutorage in preparation for moments like these – or, as I like to refer to them as - my Galactic/Humanitarian missions.

As a kid, I had to get pretty creative at hiding my extraordinary psychic abilities and was never allowed to speak of my nightly excursions with E.T.s (extraterrestrials) for fear of being locked up or beaten by those who saw this activity as dysfunctional and just plain weird.

Once I was adopted by my American family, I was able to experience these special encounters more fully, albeit still secretively, for fear that I might sustain the same type of retribution from those who couldn't grasp what was happening. Of course that never happened but, once bitten…

It wasn't until I attended law school at George Washington University in Washington, D.C. that I discovered my true destined purpose. Before that, it was more than enough for me to acclimate to my "talents", all the while keeping my true identity hidden, even from those I loved most dearly.

College is also where I met and fell in love with Elizabeth "Liz" Tanner, my true soul mate, who not only shared some similar psychic attributes, but also lived a parallel history, to boot! Actually, it was Liz who quickly connected the dots and remembered our prior introduction as young patients of Dr. Umberto Franco Ortega, a wonderful child psychologist who specialized in "kids like us".

So, together we set our determined course and forged ahead full tilt as truth seekers with the intention of answering the questions raised after the 1947 UFO incident in Roswell, New Mexico of "Are they here?" and uncovered "Why they are here!"

I had my work cut out for myself because believe me, becoming the only UFO lobbyist in history, thus far, was no small feat. It took me years to cultivate serious financial and political supporters, never mind dodging all the brutal criticism from family and friends. But, with the help of dedicated colleagues and, more importantly, my friend, Brad Phillips, a highly credible, well respected ufologist from Sedona, Arizona, I not only obtained an audience before the renowned World Council of the Humanities but caught the attention of some high profile supporters in the private sector who offered substantial financial funding to further my study and research in this most controversial arena.

Okay, back to the present. I guess they're ready for me now. Have to refocus my thoughts on the task at hand. While I gather my thoughts, I'll use my tried and true stall tactic of first, straightening my tie, then -AHEM- clear my throat as I adjust my jacket, and NOW–let the games begin!

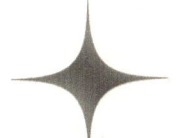

The Invitation

"Congressman Mansfield, am I to understand that your official posture as Chairman of this Committee on Global Affairs and spokesperson for the government of the United States is to unequivocally deny any knowledge and/or government involvement relative to the activity known as "Chemtrails?" Stephan blasts. "Is it also your intention to dismiss this investigation, born of the public's demand for answers, acceptable or not, to the anomalies that plague and obstruct our otherwise clean air and clear skies?" he continues.

"Mr. Wolf, just what evidence do you have in support of your accusations? I, for one, would be most pleased to address your concerns, providing they can be substantiated and validated." Congressman Mansfield arrogantly quips in response.

"If you and the Committee will kindly refer to the most recent report prepared that is now in front of you, you will find that it provides thousands of credible testimony from concerned citizens of science, medicine, education, clergy, laymen, and, yes, Congressman, even military personnel, I believe would be a good place to start - wouldn't you agree?" Stephan sarcastically replies.

As the individual members of the Committee quickly thumb through the over 800 pages of sworn testimony, mumbling to one another as they make note of its volume, Congressman Hobart asks permission of the Chairman to pose a question to Stephan.

"Mr. Wolf, while this lengthy report is impressive, if only by its size, I'm afraid I am at a loss relative to the nature of these so-called "Chemtrails". If you would be so kind as to provide this Committee with the *Reader's Digest* version and summarize the report, I can assure you that this Committee would be most grateful, as there are other pressing matters before us and the day is growing short."

This is such an old tactic by this particular Committee, one that Stephan has dealt with so many times before that he is more than prepared to give them exactly what they are requesting, all the while remaining poised and confident as he speaks.

In keeping with Congressional Committee protocol, Stephan turns to the chairman and begins; "Mr. Chairman, with your permission?" The Congressman nods in agreement for Stephan to proceed.

"Chemtrails- what are Chemtrails? One official definition of a Chemtrails is -"… highly visible streaks of chemicals created in the air by spray systems onboard airplanes that fly at varying altitudes with no known purpose.

He continues, "Years ago we attributed these streaks in the sky as either contrails from aircraft or simply "sky writers" and were quite cavalier about their presence. However, today people are reporting unusual activity in the sky with jets at low altitudes leaving trails and spray lines creating X's, S's and parallel lines - lines that slowly spread to create a "canopy of haze" and there have been numerous reports of unusual smells, tastes and even illness related to these trails.

"I also have in my possession the results of reports conducted by an independent lab of mutual choosing that details the contents and effects of a reddish-brown gel that's being dropped from low-flying aircraft. When samples of this substance were fully analyzed, they were found to be teaming with biological organisms!

It's a well known fact that the U.S military is extremely interested in weather control and so it is that I demand your confirmation that the Chemtrail phenomena is a part of that covert operation."

As the members of the Committee shoot nervous glances at one another, Stephan continues, "With all due respect gentlemen, if the etiology of these Chemtrails were of a humanitarian nature, such as assisting in reversing global warming or protecting our atmosphere from some form of radiation that puts the very existence of life on our planet in peril, it would be an understatement to assume that the government would rally to their fiduciary and moral obligation to advise the public of their intention and purpose. Do you agree?

"That being in question, the very fact that the government flatly denies their existence and touts them to be contrails, which are natural vapors emitted from the engines of aircraft, flies... pardon the pun, in the face of logic and, quite frankly, angers those intelligent folks who just plain know better.

"It is also a well-known fact that a contrail from an aircraft is brief in its length and dissipates leaving no discernable trail behind it. Chemtrails, on the other hand, can be seen from one end of the horizon to the other, fanning out into the atmosphere almost immediately, intersecting and merging with others in proximity forming the so-called "canopy of haze". In fact, after several hours of this activity, the once clear blue skies are now awash with filmed white clouds, obscuring the day's sunlight. Normal? I think not!"

Congressman Mansfield interjects, "Mr. Wolf, the Committee is aware of your concerns and those of the public but wishes to remind you that the United States Government is completely willing to cooperate in answering any and all questions posed relative to this matter. The United States Government has already assigned the Air Force Office of Special Investigation, headquartered at Andrews Air Force Base in Maryland to perform a thorough investigation into these allegations. As a matter of fact, as far back as August 1948, a specific felony-level investigative service was created in an effort to address the concerns of citizens of these United States regarding our changing world."

Stephan knew that this was Congressman Mansfield's pre-programmed response and that he was stealthfully laying the foundation for winding up this particular session and putting this whole matter on the Congressional back burner- again!

Before Stephan can respond, Congressman Mansfield glances at his watch then offers an insincere apology to Stephan and the rest of the dais about how time constraints prohibit the continuance of this session and so, it is ended. Stephan's frustrated posture is evident, although ignored, as the assembly quickly dismantles and exits the meeting room, post haste.

Gathering up his materials, Stephan turns to his associate, John Wells, and instructs him to immediately request a follow up hearing as soon as possible. He isn't about to let the Committee sweep this one under the proverbial carpet – not this time! John gives Stephan a *consider it done* wink and moves swiftly to take care of this urgent request.

Out in the hallway, Stephan is greeted by several fellow lobbyists who are there conducting their own committee meetings but were curious as to how he faired before one of the toughest committees in the entire Congress.

Always humble, yet direct, Stephan quips "Well boys, you know how it can be – *especially* when you've got Mansfield at the helm. But you also know me- I'm not about to let go of this one!" The small group laughs in unison, mumbling their well wishes for a successful outcome, as they disburse and go their separate ways.

Once outside the building, Stephan takes in a long, deep breath and lets out an audible sigh as he begins to descend the multi-sets of marbled steps and head back to his office, some ten blocks away.

It is a bright, sunny day in Washington, D.C. with an early spring temperature hovering around 68°. The apple blossoms are in full bloom and the clear, crisp air helps put a bounce back in

Stephan's step, after his grueling morning with the Committee on Global Affairs.

Taking a moment to absorb the beauty, Stephan's reverie is broken all too soon by someone calling out his name. "Mr. Wolf?... Mr. Wolf!" the voice cries out as it nears its target.

When Stephan spins around to answer, he is greeted by a petite young woman, dressed in a tan business suit, laden with several books of various sizes and a large briefcase. She awkwardly extends her hand in introduction - "Mr. Wolf, my name is Amanda Charles and I am the personal assistant to Byron Huxley of the Huxley Foundation. Do you know who he is?"

Stephan begins to answer in the affirmative, however, this young woman is on a mission and wastes no time in pleasantries as she continues, "Mr. Wolf, Mr. Huxley is having a private party this weekend at his seaside estate on Martha's Vineyard and requests your presence, along with your wife's, of course." While Stephan attempts to formulate a politically correct response, Amanda fumbles into her briefcase then, eventually, hands him a formal written invitation, complete with map and directions.

Stephan smiles to himself, for he is well aware of whom Byron Huxley is. A bit of an eccentric, Byron Huxley is well known for his deep pocket, philanthropic endeavors not to be overshadowed by his entrepreneurial prowess, earning him the well-deserved financial reputation, only rivaling that of Donald Trump. For years, Stephan has attempted to get his foot in the door of the Huxley organization in the hopes of gaining some political, if not financial, support for his various lobbies. Now he is being summoned by the man himself to attend a private party! Sweet, indeed.

Stephan graciously accepts and asks Amanda to thank Mr. Huxley for the invitation. Wasting no time or words, Amanda hurries off, then stops but a few feet away as she looks back over her shoulder and shouts, "By the way, Mr. Wolf, I admire what you are doing about exposing the UFO cover ups. Maybe I can tell you about my own unique encounter, sometime..." then she's lost in the maze of bodies bustling through the complex's courtyard.

Staring at the invitation in his hand, Stephan can't help but wonder what has prompted Byron Huxley to invite he and Liz to this particular gathering? While grateful for the opportunity, his intuitive gut wells with healthy skepticism. *Wait until Liz hears this one!* Stephan laughs to himself.

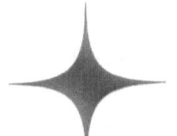

Bethany

*S*tephan and I met in college, re-met, actually, as we had already met in a psychiatrist's office when we were children. Okay, I can hear your "what?" but it's not what you think. As a matter of fact, no part of that whole experience is what you would think.

Stephan and I are what some people label as "special" or "gifted". As children we were challenged with experiences and knowledge beyond human comprehension, let alone understanding. To put it bluntly, we were abducted by beings – NOT from here! Stephan likes to refer to them as "visitations by other beings for the purpose of education and monitoring, as part of a greater galactic mission". Pretty heady explanation, huh?

As young children, we candidly talked about our times with our alien friends, only to be categorized as weird and majorly dysfunctional. Our parents dealt with us the only way they knew how, which was to take us to a psychiatrist. But he was no ordinary shrink. Dr. Umberto Franco Ortega – "Dr. O", as I liked to call him, specialized in "kids like us".

In those days, I coped as best I could and found solace in over eating. Classic Psyche 101, better known as "oral gratification complex". So, in addition to dealing with alien abductions, I had an eating disorder to boot! Lucky me.

Not far into my treatment, Dr. Ortega was found dead by a cleaning lady early one morning. The circumstances surrounding his death were never discussed by anyone and the ordeal was totally swept *under the carpet, like it never happened.*

I liked Dr. Ortega, I liked him a lot. Here was this man charged with exploring and defining the unearthly experiences of children, who not only verbally related their encounters, but also could artistically recreate the images of the beings and spacecrafts down to the minutest detail. While the kids ranged in ages from 5 – 15, their renderings were amazingly similar in content and form, only the little kid's drawings lacked sophistication.

I would often sit in the waiting room munching on a large bag of potato chips or pretzels in nervous anticipation of "my turn." I remember one particular afternoon, I kept staring at several of Dr. Ortega's medical certificates that hung on the wall and repeated his name over and over again, just slightly under my breath...Umberto Franco Ortega...Umberto Franco Ortega...Umberto Fran...U.F.O.! The initials of his name were UFO! What were the odds...?

I never mentioned that discovery to anyone before. I wondered if anyone else picked up on it? Anyway, years later while attending George Washington University, I bumped into Stephan, an extremely bright, articulate (did I mention handsome?) law student. We met in an elective class The Study of Psychological Phenomena, yes, I know – kismet!

We were drawn to each other right away. Stephan didn't have a clue that we had already met years before as patients of Dr. O's... but I did. I think I had a crush on him way back then. I was not as shocked as he when we reconnected in college - but more about that later.

Once we caught up to the present, post walk down "alien memory lane", we knew that together we had a calling, a mission that would forever bond our souls.

Through a series of amazing events, Stephan decided to change his scholastic focus and became a lobbyist, committed to uncovering critical documentation and credible testimony from others who knew that the UFO and E.T. experiences were genuine. Both Stephan and I had personal knowledge this was so, but he felt he needed to get the United States Government to finally acknowledge their existence and their role in the big cover up. A monumental task - but he was determined to do it.

I, on the other hand, switched majors and began focusing on earning my degree in psychology – child psychology, to be exact, as I wanted to carry on where Dr. Ortega left off and work with "kids like us" – who better to relate to these kids, but one of their own?

So here I am today, happily married to my soul mate, Stephan. While my practice is small, right now I'm working with an amazing five year old named Bethany. Her psychic aptitude goes far beyond any of the other kids I've encountered, thus far. At times, I question who's helping whom, here. I was soon to find out.

(Flashback)

Five-year-old Bethany sits fidgeting in her chair, feet swinging back and forth as they barely reach the carpet of the waiting room floor. Loudly smacking the wad of bubble gum that takes up the majority of her tiny mouth, she manages to ask her mother "Will it be much longer?" Looking down lovingly from the seat next to Bethany her mother, Rachel, gently pats the back of her daughter's hand as she impatiently drums her fingers in nervous, annoying rhythm and answers "Soon, baby...soon."

Within moments, Liz's office door swings wide open as eight-year-old Michael bounds out of his session, his Attention Deficit Disorder diagnosis evident to all that bear witness.

"See you next week, Michael", calls Liz as he races down the hallway, leaving his bewildered father behind, shaking his head and rolling his eyes as he prepares to sprint after his son who, most likely, has already reached the elevator by now.

"Hi Liz!" shouts an excited Bethany. "Well, hello there, Ms. Bethany!. And how are *you* today?" Liz responds with a warm and engaging smile. Liz knows she's not supposed to have favorites, but she allows herself to openly show her pleasure at seeing Bethany at each and every visit.

"Ready?" asks Liz.

"Ready!" answers Bethany.

"Let's go! See you in a little bit, Mom." Liz reassures Rachel.

Liz takes Bethany's small hand in hers and leads her into the private office. Once inside, Bethany immediately hops onto a soft, over stuffed chair that's designed especially low to the ground for smaller patients.

The office is well appointed with soothing colors of sea foam green and earth tone beige. The walls are featured with special images of clear blue skies dotted with puffy white clouds, fields of colorful flowers that seem to go on forever, and a star filled night sky that seems to beckon the observer far and away into the galaxies beyond.

Liz also thought it would be fun, as well as practical, to have all kinds of drawing and coloring materials with wads of blank paper for those moments of inspiration, when words just aren't enough to describe...

When the older kids are in session with Liz, she utilizes soft, relaxing music or recorded whale and ocean sounds on her CD player. It has been her experience that the mature kids are inclined to open up and focus more fully with these particular background sounds.

But not so with the little ones. Unfortunately, it has the total opposite effect on the younger set. They become too aware of and focused on the music and begin to dance or interpret the animal sounds by performing a kind of charades... "Look at me...I'm a whale!"

Because sessions with the children don't always remain on track, Liz agrees with the method of tape recording them, a trick she learned from her days with Dr. Ortega. This way she can re-listen, evaluate and then later transcribe their conversations.

Liz silently turns on the recorder undetected by Bethany who, most assuredly, would ask a million questions about it and begin performing instead of focusing on today's visit.

Liz begins: *Okay, sweetie, so tell me...what's been happening lately? Gone on any trips with your friends?*

Bethany: *Oh sure. Just last night I went to the playhouse with the others and we had lots of fun!*

Liz: *Tell me about the playhouse, again?*

Bethany: *Well, it's where we go to show the others how to play nicely with the toys. They're so funny...sometimes they hold them wrong...upside down like this.(She demonstrates with her hands to indicate flipping something over – upside down.)*

Liz: *Oh, that is funny. Tell me, Bethany, have they learned to talk to you with words, yet?*

Bethany: *Uh, uh - not yet. But I hear them anyway...in my head. Saves having to use the words. When they do make sounds, they sound funny and I laugh. (Bethany giggles.)*

Liz: *Do they laugh, too? Bethany: No, but I know they like what we're doing.*

All the while this dialog is going on, Bethany is roaming around the room, picking up books and examining stuffed animals that lay about. As long as she continues to remain focused on the questions, Liz allows her to *do her thing*.

Liz asks Bethany if she would like to draw a picture of her friends and what it looks like at the playhouse.

"No, not right now. Besides, I already did that before... remember?" Bethany reminds Liz.

"Yes, I certainly do and you did such a great job." Liz assures. "I just wondered if this time, it looked any different to you or, if there was anything or anyone new to the playhouse."

Bethany suddenly stops her roaming about and stares skyward, as if trying to remember something and says, "We-e-l-l, yes, there were some new playmates that I didn't know. They were kinda bigger...like this much." (Again, Bethany demonstrates with her hands held high above her head.)

Liz: *Did you play with any of them?*

Bethany: *Not really, they just sorta watched.*

Bethany resumes her stroll about the office. Liz decides this new revelation deserves more focus from Bethany, so she gently urges her to pick up whatever drawing implement she chooses and asks her to draw, as best she can, what the new playmates look like.

As Bethany picks up a box of crayons and spills its contents onto the carpet, Liz grabs a piece of blank paper from the supply shelf and plops herself down next to her, sitting Indian style, keeping quiet while Bethany intensely sketches her encounter with her new *friends*.

It is Bethany who finally breaks the silence by commenting on how she doesn't feel very good about one the larger playmates, who seems "kinda mean."

Liz finds an appropriate moment to resume their conversation:

Why do you say that? Don't you like him?

Bethany: *I dunno…he just makes me feel…he looks mad or something. I stop playing with the others when he's around and he gets mad, I think.*

Liz: *Why do you stop playing?*

Bethany: *Well, first of all, I got knocked down… (Liz waits.) He comes in and just looks at me… (She trails off engrossed in her sketching.)*

Liz: *Who knocked you down, sweetie?*

Bethany: *One of the others, one of my play friends.*

Liz: *Why do you suppose he did that?*

Bethany: *It's a she…and she got mad because I was playing with a toy she wanted.*

Liz: *Oh. (Liz can't help but draw the conclusion that "kids will be kids" no matter the species.) How did she knock you down?*

Bethany: *(Before Liz can give Bethany any options of method she blurts out), With her mind! She pushed me down with her mind! They don't like to touch very much so they do it in their heads, just like how we talk…in our heads.*

(Liz concludes it's telepathy and kinetics.)

Liz: *Bethany, what did you do when you got knocked down like that? Bethany: Oh, I cried and when I got up I went over to her and yelled in her face with my outside voice to STOP IT! (She demonstrates with a yell.)*

Liz: *(Stifling a snicker) What did she do then? Bethany: She ran over to one of the big friends who was watching and hid behind her. Maybe the big one is her mommy?*

Liz: *Perhaps. So tell me…what happened next?*

Just then Bethany hollers "FINISHED!" and holds up her drawing. "Wow! That's very good, Bethany." Liz praises, "Good job! Let's see…hm-m-m…tell me about this." "I just did." Bethany states with impatience. Then indignantly elaborates anyway: "Here I am playing with my friends and here's the big ones watching." Liz, no stranger to encounters with other beings, recognizes the larger ones as the "Grays" that she, too, interacted with as a small child. She suspected they were the ones responsible for Bethany's abductions, as indicated by her previous drawings of the other hybrid children. While more human in appearance, they still had the undeniable big, black, slanted eyes associated with the Zeta Reticuli. Now, it was confirmed.

"Are we done, yet?" Bethany breaks Liz's concentration on the picture and brings her back into the moment.

"Ah, yep. Actually, we are done." Liz declares as she spies the clock on her desk. How did she know that? Did she know it or was it just her way of saying she's had enough for today?

Anyway, this is one of the parts she loves the best working with these kids…their total candor and ability to switch gears instantly. But then, she remembers her own experiences and how it became paramount to be able to do just that, or else go mad. Kids roll with all kinds of stuff, but adults tend to over analyze and dissect… like Liz is doing right now.

Knowing the drill, Bethany puts all the crayons away without being asked to, humming as she continues to chew on the large wad of gum still in her mouth.

All the kids hum now and then but the melody Bethany is humming is not notes of a traditional song. They're more tonal in structure.

As Liz rises from her seated position on the carpet, she asks Bethany one last question: "Hey, that's a nice song. Did you learn that at school?"

Bethany: *Nope. It's what I hear at the playhouse with my friends. We all hum it, except they do it in their heads… always in their heads! Gosh, when are they gonna talk like me?*

Liz: *Do they try?*

Bethany: *Sometimes, but (she's now in full laugh and hard to understand) all that comes out is…ekgt, gloaub, naretty, gleebik… (inaudible sounds.).*

Liz joins Bethany in full laughter as the two embrace and then leads her young charge back to the waiting room and her mother, Rachel.

As Bethany takes her mother's hand in hers, Rachel looks questioningly back over her shoulder at Liz, who reassures her with a wink and a smile then softly says to them both "See you next week."

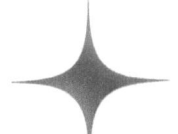

Vineyard Proposal

*W*hen I told Liz about our invitation to Byron Huxley's estate
on Martha's Vineyard for an entire weekend, she had mixed
feelings about it all. While she was enthusiastic about me finally
connecting with such an influential, high profiled individual, who
could certainly open doors for my lobbying efforts, she candidly told
me that there was something stirring below the surface in her "gut"
that didn't quite feel right.

Admittedly, she'd been working way too hard of late, especially
with one of her favorite patients, Bethany, who was displaying some
amazing abilities that Liz couldn't stop thinking about. She told me
that she wasn't sleeping very well and was constantly thinking about
how to work more effectively with Bethany, as she felt that she was
truly on the verge of a major breakthrough with her.

I told her, all the more reason to get away and relax on Martha's
Vineyard, while I conduct some business. In light of where we were
going, I even alluded to her thinking of herself in a quasi Jackie Kennedy
role, luxuriating to her up and coming husband's future endeavors,
sort of thing. She just rolled her eyes, laughed in my face and began
dragging out our duffle bags for packing. That's my girl!

I never let on to Liz that I, too, was a bit apprehensive about
this "audience" with Mr. Huxley, but in this political climate you
sometimes have to make nice and rub elbows with those individuals of
influence, if you want any chance of success as a lobbyist, especially
one who specializes in UFO activity. I trusted my instincts implicitly,

yet couldn't help wish that I could somehow connect with LUPO on this one. How's that saying go…Be careful what you wish for…?

(Flashback)

Stephen and Liz are picked up and transported to the airport for their travel to Martha's Vineyard via an elegant, dark gray, stretch limousine, courtesy of Byron Huxley. They are pleasantly surprised to find their transportation destination is not JFK Airport but a small private executive airport tucked away in a semi-remote area, just off the main highway.

As they are driven directly onto the tarmac, the limousine pulls up alongside a Beech Craft Super King Air 200 whose idling engines indicate an immediate departure.

The casually dressed chauffeur pops open the trunk before getting out from behind the wheel and officiously swings open the back door of the limousine so that Stephan and Liz may exit. Liz lets out an uncontrollable giggle and a "holy cow!" as they run their eyes from nose to tail of the sparkling, silver plane that waits to jet them off to their ultimate destination.

"I think this is one of those new Super Kings" Stephan whispers to Liz as they approach the short stairway at the plane's entrance.

Once aboard, they are welcomed to sit in any seat of their choosing, all the while the chauffeur hands off their bags to the flight attendant who is impeccably dressed in a light gray skirt and jacket, complete with blinding white starched shirt embossed with the initials "BHF" for Byron Huxley Foundation, no doubt. No ego here, Stephan chuckles to himself.

Just prior to closing the hatch for takeoff, the captain peeks his head around to the cabin to introduce himself and his co-pilot to his passengers. Then without hesitation, places his earphones on his head as the co-pilot gives them a wink before closing off the cockpit in final preparation for takeoff.

As the Super King begins its taxi towards the appropriate runway, the attendant offers two flute glasses filled with orange juice and champagne, commonly known as Mimosas. "Now, this is the only way to fly!" Stephan laughs, taking the glasses from the attendant and offers one to Liz, who graciously accepts, smiling from ear to ear.

After a smooth takeoff, the captain comes over the intercom and announces the typical welcoming speech, advising his passengers of their level of flight, estimated time of arrival and the all important current weather conditions for Cape Cod and the Islands. All appears to be routine, so Stephan and Liz sit back to relax and enjoy their short flight.

"Have either one of you ever been to the Cape or Martha's Vineyard before?" asks the attendant. "I have." Liz answers, "But it was a long time ago and all I remember about that visit was how quickly the weather can go from blue skies to gray and foggy in less than a heartbeat." The attendant smiles and acknowledges an old New England cliché, 'If you get tired of the weather…just wait a minute…' then trails off as they nod and laugh in unison.

Liz can't decide if it's the gentle motion of the plane, the Mimosa or a combination of the two, but decides to take advantage of her calm sense of well being and closes her eyes for a bit. Stephan, on the other hand, can't seem to shut his mind off as he anticipates what Mr. Huxley might offer in the way of support for his latest lobbying efforts.

As expected, the flight is short and so the plane begins its final approach to Martha's Vineyard Airport. Stephan decides to let Liz rest until the final moment before landing as he, too, has noticed a paling in her complexion and a slight slowing in her usual hyperactive pace.

The landing is uneventful and as the plane shuts down at it's final destination, both crew and passengers exchange pleasantries before leaving each other's company.

When Stephan and a slightly groggy Liz begin to deplane yet another Huxley representative wearing much more casual attire, complete with lapelled Huxley emblem, escorts them to a bright yellow Hummer at the foot of the plane's stairway. Beginning to suspect that Mr. Huxley just might have a more fun side to him in spite of his corporate persona, Liz sparks awake to declare, "Now, you're talking!"

Martha's Vineyard, or Up Island as the locals call it, is located just seven miles off the Massachusetts coastline. It's a beautiful island a world apart, offering a vacation ambience unlike any other. It exudes diversity with its six island towns along pristine shores where you can take a step back in time and relax to a more leisurely pace, which is just what the doctor ordered for both Liz and Stephan.

As the Hummer winds its way up the unpaved, sandy driveway, Liz marvels at the well appointed gardens and low lying beach rose bushes on either side that are ablaze in hues of fuchsia, yellow and pink. The vehicle stops in the middle of a circular driveway in front of one of several house structures that appear to be connected by porches and weatherproof, glassed-in walkways.

"Welcome to the Huxley Estate" emotes a voice from behind them. Byron Huxley enthusiastically strides up to Stephen and Liz with unexpected outstretched arms to greet his guests.

"I hope your flight was pleasant and uneventful. Let me tell you a little bit about your accommodations here." Proudly, Byron Huxley begins the grand tour: "As you can see, my home consists of four separate structures; the main house and three guesthouses, which I had connected by enclosed walkways in the event of inclement weather." Then laughs, as he is sure everyone knows about the ever-changing New England climate.

As Byron walks arm and arm with Liz, Stephan trailing close behind, he continues to point out the amenities that his home away from home has to offer. "I chose this particular guesthouse for you as it provides one of the more spectacular views of the bay, besides my own, of course. I'm sure you'll be very comfortable here. Please...let's go inside where I'll acquaint you with your surroundings, while Frederick takes care of your bags. You have a least an hour or so to relax before the other guests arrive for our little cookout down by the waterfront."

Both Stephan and Liz are more than impressed by their luxurious accommodations, but not surprised. While the guesthouse appointments are grand, the theme is one of comfort and casualness. They thank their host for his welcome and agree to meet in an hour.

While unpacking their belongings, Liz mocks Stephen's criticism of her packing too many clothes for just a weekend getaway and cajoles, "See...aren't you glad, now, that I gave myself so many clothing options? I told you, we woman know what we're doing when we bring the 'just in case' stuff." Stephan holds up his hands in surrender as he acknowledges those little words that are seldom heard from a husband to his wife..."You were right, dear."

Before they knew it, an hour has passed and it is time for the afternoon festivities. The setting for the cookout turns out to be one of the most lavishly catered affairs that either one of them have ever attended and qualifies as such, not only because there is a twenty-five foot grill, but it is manned by no less than four Executive Chefs from some of the finest restaurants on the East Coast. Minus that little perk, this is just your ordinary epitome of grandeur and extravagance. In fact, Liz comments to Stephan in private, how the entire estate is an amazing architectural feat of design that boasts a living room so large that you could land a plane in it!

Keeping careful watch on all his guests to ensure all their creature comforts are met, Byron seizes the opportunity to steal Stephan from his guest mingling by feigning giving him the grand tour of one of his newest purchases, a sixty-three foot cabin cruiser named "Sea Wolf" that's tied up to his private, deep-water dock.

Stephan congratulates Byron on his latest new toy and

pretends to know something about yachting by asking some general nautical questions he picked up from some of his seaworthy lobbyists such as..."What's her draft and how wide is her beam?" Of course he has no idea of what he's talking about, but he's hoping Byron doesn't figure that one out.

Once they arrive at the end of the dock away from the others, Byron interrupts the small talk and cuts to the chase regarding his real interest in Stephan and says, "I've been following your career for some time now and I must say that you've caught the eye of many movers and shakers in Congress", then gives out a chuckle " and, unfortunately, NASA and the CIA. Now, I'm not above boasting about my accomplishments or how my financial prowess, let's say, provides a certain influence to my fellow business opponents, but I think my reputation speaks for itself." By now Stephen is truly confused as to where this is all leading to, but he's about to find out.

"Stephan, I'm known for my directness, so I'll get right to the point. I'm dying of a rare form of brain cancer, one that has no known treatment, recourse or cure. I know *who* you are and *where* you're from...and I don't mean Italy. Get my drift?" Stephan nods in acknowledgement. "Good, so let me get to the bottom line here. It is imperative, no – let me rephrase that, *urgent* that you locate and act as liaison on my behalf with other hybrids that can provide me with either their medical technology to cure my disease or get me to their planet or star system in an effort to retard my ultimate fate."

Before Stephan can begin to protest about why Byron believes he's the one for this mission, he continues... " I also believe that you have been interacting with the Galactic Federation though some source that you keep close to your vest. I respect your unique 'talents' and won't ask you to divulge your source but, like 'Big Brother', I've been watching for some time and know these events to be fact."

While Stephan is stunned by this declaration, he is also cautious not to reveal his discomfort at being under anyone's microscopic surveillance.

"I chose you specifically because of your deep personal

commitment to locate others like you. That's where I come in. I can help you, more than you know. I have both the financial and political wherewithal to speed up your research and exploration process. Let me reiterate, *time is of the essence for me* – we can help each other reach our intended goal if we partner up on this one."

So far, Stephan has been silent and respectful as Byron boldly lays out his intention and leaves himself vulnerable should Stephan refuse to assist, but it's a chance he's apparently willing to take. Byron Huxley's successes, thus far, have not been random ones, so he trusts his savvy intuition that Stephan, for whatever reason, will acquiesce to his offer.

Stephan takes but a moment before responding to this request, which by most standards would be considered outlandish, but given Stephan's life and choice of career, it's pretty much in line with it all.

The two men exchange a deep eye-to-eye moment before Stephan speaks, "Mr. Huxley, while part of my life and abilities are an open book, I am impressed that you've been able to identify my other 'talents' which, up until now, have been kept, how should I say this – unknown, for lack of a better definition. I am also flattered that you feel I am the right person for this highly sensitive mission, which I am sure is a well kept secret of your own. I am, however, in need of a bit more time to process and assimilate this task that you ask of me before I can provide you with my honest response. Would it be reasonable to ask for one week to get back to you with my answer?"

Without hesitation "A week it is." Byron replies. "Let's get back to our guests, shall we?"

As the festivities wind down, Stephan learns that there will be two other couples who'll stay for the remainder of the weekend; one comes from Washington, D.C. while the other couple lives in downtown Manhattan. Stephan is not clear if they have any role in the paramount mission he's been asked to perform, but his gut tells him they are just business acquaintances who have nothing to do with any of this.

With the gathering officially over and early evening approaching, Byron asks his remaining guests if they'd like to partake of an evening sunset stroll along his private stretch of the beach. Still feeling fatigued, Liz passes on the offer but Stephan and the male guest from Manhattan are eager to see more of this beautiful area.

Whereas it's only early spring in Massachusetts, the evenings still bring about a damp, down to the bone chill, especially seaside, so Liz and the other two women choose to cozy up before a warm fire and chat while the men folk, minus one, go exploring the rest of the island estate on foot.

The three men walk shoeless along the shore while Byron shares some of the colorful history and folklore of the area.

Stephan laments about his early childhood years in Italy on the hillside farm and purposely avoids any mention of his "special friends" not only to protect his true identity but not knowing this other guest's views on the existence of other worlds, doesn't wish to freak him out resulting in a hasty retreat. Leave it to Stephan – he's always thinking.

As is typical for Cape Cod and the islands, without warning a thick fog works its way onshore and so it is suggested that they head back to the main house to join the others.

For whatever reason, Stephan decides to hang back and assures his host that he won't get lost and will be along shortly. Byron doesn't protest but insists Stephan take and use a special flashlight that he removes from the pocket of his windbreaker. It's one that he invented to cut through the fog and has submitted its design for patent approval before releasing it for sale to the general public.

Everyone agrees it seems like it should be a big seller, especially in areas like this one. Byron quips, "As if I need any more success." But Stephan knows better. For there is one more thing that he *desperately* needs that would prove to be the biggest success of all …life itself!

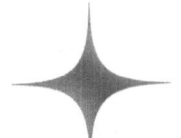

LUPO Returns

My trip to Martha's Vineyard turned out to be quite different from what I thought it would be. Concerns began to arise all around, not just about the mission Bryon Huxley proposed to me but I was becoming increasingly worried about Liz's physical condition.

Oh, at first I chalked it up to her long hours of work and inability to sleep due to the imminent breakthrough she was anticipating with one of her young patients, but more and more I observed her energy level depleting at the slightest exertion.

At any rate, as the island fog rolled in and shortened the sunset walk with my host and one of his other guests, I took the opportunity to isolate myself to digest and process everything.

I began to cautiously consider the repercussions of disclosing my identity more fully to Byron Huxley who, for selfish suspect reasons, might not honor my need for anonymity. Any premature disclosure could have catastrophic results on my mission. I truly had to get some answers and fast.

As always, I could turn to Liz for her input but given her yet unexplained waning energy, I didn't wish to be the cause of any concern for her, so decided to keep this one to myself to figure out. Oh, I know she'd be pretty ticked off if anything happened and I hadn't kept her in the loop about it, but that's a chance I chose to take.

Without much thought of my current whereabouts, I began to hike inland away from the shore, diminishing my point of reference of which way was which. I guess it became another one of "those moments" that *prodded me even deeper into the wooded area adjacent to the Huxley Estate.*

As I walked even deeper into a fog-laden forest with the day's last light ebbing, I felt a sudden pang of anxiety of what may lurk in there. I've been in this position before, like the time I foolishly hiked too late in the day into Boynton Canyon during my first visit to Sedona, Arizona then, as night fell, I was chased by some animals that meant me harm, only to be saved by LUPO.

The weird thing was, while I felt uneasy, I have to admit that there was an excitement that accompanied that feeling which kept me compelled to continue further into the woods, randomly walking into an area that was totally foreign to me. Was I nuts – or was there something I had to do right then and there?

(Flashback)

Deeper and deeper Stephan retreats into the thicketed forest. He decides to make good use of the flashlight that was given to him by Byron and chuckles to himself, *"not bad"*– as it truly seems to help him find the way through the dense fog.

At least he could make out the tall trees that stood in his path or the low lying brush that would, most assuredly, cause him to trip and fall at some point. Then, as he scans the ever-darkening terrain with this special light, he catches a quick glimpse out of the corner of his eye, off to his right, of something moving about forty - fifty feet away.

Stephan strains his eyes in an effort to make out what the flashlight beam is hitting. He suddenly gasps as he shares eye contact, only for a brief moment, with a large wolf before it darts off into the darkness. Now, most normal people would beat a hasty retreat in the opposite direction of any creature they might spot in the woods, especially at night, but not Stephan, who actually increases his pace in hot pursuit.

Ducking and darting his way through the wooded obstacle course, Stephen stops at a small clearing, all the while listening for the slightest hint of movement that will indicate his next choice in direction.

Before Stephan can formulate a plan, a low vibration begins to sound throughout the forest floor. A smile begins to form on Stephan's face as the rise in vibration emits a pleasant familiar, "oh-m-m-m, oh-m-m-m, OH-M-M-M, OH,M-M-M". As the tonal waves envelope all that surround him, lifting up through the low lying fog, beyond the canopy of branches that reveal the twinkling stars in a section of clear sky above, one by one the wolves enter the clearing.

Greeting Stephan in traditional submissive posture, heads down, bumping and licking at his legs, the largest wolf in the pack emerges from the darkness, his yellow eyes glowing in delight. "LUPO!" Stephan shouts and within seconds the beast morphs from the figure of the wolf into the Star Being who has guided and protected him since early childhood.

LUPO: *Greetings, Stephan. I anticipate you'll express your emotional response to my presence in one of your Earth terms relating to how long it has been since our last exchange. Is that accurate?*

Stephan: *That would be an understatement, but welcome at long last!*

LUPO: *It is my notice from reading your energy field that you are in need of an alignment. What may I offer in way of assistance in that adjustment?*

Stephan: *(chuckling) I love your metaphors, although awkward in language, however... here goes. It appears that my identity is not as -how should I say this...veiled as I would like. There is a man of power who wishes to utilize my abilities in an effort to locate and interact with other hybrids that might assist in prolonging his physical life, which is in jeopardy due to a serious illness. He offers this in exchange for his financial support and contacts so that my research and ultimate mission may continue with ease. I'm not sure that he is ...*

LUPO: *I know of this man and of his asking of you. His focus is born out of greed, a most undesirable human trait however, your species seems to make allowances for such beings whose only concern is that of self- preservation. You must look closely at his rationale and decide if this action serves the greater good of all, Stephan.*

Stephan: *Well, that's where I'm a bit stuck. I certainly could use his help and influence with those I must deal with in our government but to expose you, me and others like me that I seek...well, you get my drift?*

LUPO: *Get your drift? Does that equate that I understand? If so, why don't you just indicate that? If that is your meaning, then yes, you must show proper judgment in your disclosures that might not bode well for the tasks before you.*

We have spoken before of those who feign solidarity but in truth have another intent that is not for the good of all. They promise much but lack providing anything that is useful.

I wish to bring into your experience the knowledge that dis-ease is the result of consistent negative vibration -for well being is your natural state. It is only in those moments of disconnection from source that illness and imbalance prevail. This man has exercised his right of choice and focused on less positive action in exchange for power and currency. So, it is not unexpected that he has brought an illness into his experience that threatens his very existence.

We are not allowed to interfere with your judgment, but may bring factual information into your awareness for evaluation and clarity. And so it is I do this for you now. Are you complete?

Stephan: *Not entirely, but I'm closer than before. You're right - I must look to my own guidance to choose my next course of action on this matter. Thank you LUPO, for coming to my aide. How may I contact you if I need your help again?*

LUPO: *I am never beyond a thought - so it is that I may be summoned at will. Go now, Stephan, as Liz is in need of your presence.*

Before Stephan can inquire as to what LUPO meant by that, his friend was gone...literally into thin air.

He begins his journey back and somehow manages to follow the distant sounds of the ocean that help him navigate his way back to the estate compound. Realizing he's been gone for some time, he pretends that he got lost and thanks his host for the use of the flashlight, which provided a clear beam to safely guide his way back. .

Liz and the other women who have been visiting by the warmth of the fire, all declare that it has been a long day and bid their host and each other, good night. Liz notices that Stephan has that *I've got something to tell you* look and allows him to lead her back to their guest house in haste, bugging him all the way to tell her what happened while he was gone. However, Stephan ignores her pleas until they reach the privacy of their guesthouse.

Once inside the door Liz demands, "What's going on Stephan...? Where were you and why do you look like the preverbal cat that swallowed the canary?" Stephan gently pushes Liz up against the closed door and softly places his hand over her mouth, indicating she's probably going to freak out with what he's about to tell her and whispers... "*LUPO!*"
Mouth still covered by her husband's hand, Liz's eyes break out into an unspoken laugh.

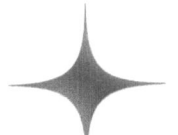

Breakthrough

*F*or what ever reason, Bethany had found her way into my heart *more than most. I delighted in that I possessed a genuine fondness and caring for all my special kids, but Bethany...well, I just couldn't explain it.*

It went far beyond my clinical intrigue regarding her intense psychic talents, her high level of telepathic communication abilities with the hybrids, not to mention her matter of fact acceptance to all that she had experienced, defied rationale. While chronologically only five years old, spiritually she was very wise and all knowing. I metaphorically compared her to the dolphins we think we're training when, in reality, it is they who patiently wait for us to catch up.

Stephan had commented to me, more than once, about my over the top focus on Bethany and pleaded with me to give it a rest, but I couldn't – at least not yet. I felt I was close to something... so close...

I'd been conferring with other child psychologists about Bethany, keeping her hybrid interactions to myself, only sharing with them that I had a high level, five-year old psychic in my charge. They all came to the same conclusion - that it would be quite beneficial if I were to perform a sleep study with Bethany, which may render invaluable data...I agreed.

After convincing Rachel, Bethany's mom, that I felt this type of experimental study would be of value and of no physical or physiological trauma to her daughter, I went ahead and began formulating exactly how I wished to perform this test on such a small child. I researched hundreds of previous studies of this nature on children and found I had issue with almost every method of procedure. Was I too close to all this? Was I loosing my clinical objectivity as a result of my emotional relationship with Bethany?

Then, from out of nowhere, came the answer!

(Flashback)

Stephan silently approaches Liz without notice as she sits at her desk in her home office, intently focused on the myriad of books that lay open before her. With pen in hand she begins sketch after sketch, only to utter sounds of frustration while crumbling up yet another ward of useless paper that joins the pile of discarded ideas on the floor below.

Sensing his presence, Liz let's out "Ugh! What's wrong with me? I can't seem to concentrate on anything at all these days." Stephan places his hand on her shoulders as he begins a soothing massage movement and feels her body's immediate grateful response.

"Listen Liz, you've got to take a break and get your mind off this bed or platform or whatever it is you're trying to design for Bethany's sleep study. Besides, it might not look so good if the head researcher passes out from sleep deprivation smack in the middle of the study, now would it?" Stephan chuckles.

"You're right." Liz sighs in compliance. "But I'm so close to coming up with a bed that's never been tried before, especially for a young child, that I don't want to stop…even for a moment." She defends.

While Stephan coyly removes the pen and paper from Liz's grasp, chattering all the while about how she needs her rest and how much clearer her head will be in the morning, he manages to extricate her from her office, albeit protesting all the way and leads her into their master bath where, to her delight, he's filled the Jacuzzi tub with glorious bubbles and scents of Lavender with an array of dimly lit candles that surround the entire enclosure, as the sounds of waves crash upon the shore from the Bose sound system that sits atop the vanity.

"Okay, okay...I give up." Liz giggles, flashing one of her *you always know what I need* smiles lovingly at Stephan, as he gingerly backs out of the inner sanctum of the newly created spa, softly closing the door behind him as he exits.

As Liz disrobes and slides her aching body into the warmth of the water that awaits, she finds it easy to release all thought and drifts into a complete state of relaxation. Deeper and deeper she slips into the blissful experience of weightlessness as her body responds to the water's buoyant support. Feeling like Scarlet O'Hara from "Gone with the Wind" she utters to herself.... "Tomorrow... I'll deal with it all tomorrow..."

The next morning, Stephan awakens to the delectable aroma of coffee brewing as a refreshed and exuberant Liz bounds into the bedroom, papers flapping in her hands while shouting, "Oh my God, Stephan – I've got it! Look!" With blurred excitement Stephan struggles to alert comprehensive mode to his wife's prattling description of the drawings that are whipped past his clouded morning eyes, then finally shouts, "Whoa, hold on, Liz. Let me at least open both eyes... Alright, now what's all this?"

Liz realizes that her zealous presentation might not be fully appreciated until Stephan has some coffee, so she rushes out of the bedroom only to return at warp speed with a large mug of black coffee and instructs him - no *orders* him to drink, drink, drink! Stephan laughs out loud and obeys, then clears his throat and declares, "I'm all yours."

Liz begins, "When I woke up this morning after an amazing good night's sleep... thanks to you, Stephan, it was like I was firing on all cylinders again. I headed into the kitchen to make coffee when I suddenly felt compelled to go to my office and began drawing... and this is what came out!" Liz proudly holds up a detailed rendering of what appears to be a round bed floating on top of a container filled with water that's covered with a clear dome. She explains to Stephan that this is a compilation of several separate designs used for previous sleep studies that resulted only in moderate success but by combining them, would make all the difference in the world.

Stephan asks Liz to further explain the concept, as he continues to sip his cobweb clearing coffee. "Stephan, while I was lying in complete relaxation in the Jacuzzi last night, I began thinking about how young children have the ability to retain the sensation of being in the womb surrounded by water, that's why they are soothed by rocking, etc. Then I thought, instead of utilizing the electrodes that are normally attached to the head to monitor the brain waves, we could replace that with a domed brain scanner... thus creating the perfect, non-invasive recording device!"

She excitedly continues with her presentation: "The problem with the old way of performing sleep studies, especially for children, is the propensity for the electrodes to interfere with the subject's sleeping comfort, not to mention trying to keep the wires attached as they fitfully toss and turn. With this device the subject feels weightless and so drifts off into a complete Delta sleep state but the real beauty is that the dome's sensors are able to record all brain activity no matter the subject's position on the bed, providing a complete, accurate recording of the data!"

Stephan is now just as excited as Liz and grabs her in full embrace as he yells, "Brilliant!" Liz chirps in "Now, it's just a matter of getting a prototype constructed and testing it out before I utilize it with Bethany. Okay, okay, I need to settle down and make some clear, concise notes before I call the team together and get them working on the bed. If this works, do you realize what a groundbreaking tool this will be for future studies with children?" Before Stephan can concur with his wife's declaration, she flies off the bed, bathrobe flying in the breeze as she races to her office to begin making copious notes for her colleagues.

Liz pauses for but a moment as she smiles to herself, knowing that this breakthrough will forever change researcher's abilities to delve even deeper into the phenomena of what really happens during the sleep state. More than that, she ponders her own core question of how this might assist her in defining just how many realities there are. She's about to find out.

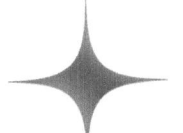

The Decision

*I*n the days following our visit to Martha's Vineyard and the proposal Bryon Huxley thrust upon me, I found myself in a bit of a quandary. On one hand, I wanted more than anything to secure the backing of a Byron Huxley, not just for his abundant financial contribution but for the political power punch he could bring to the table.

Let's face it; I could lobby for years (and I have) and only hope to get the attention and support of someone of Mr. Huxley's ilk, but it came with a hefty price. I had to weigh the pros and cons of a joint venture with such a powerful man – a man who was willing to sell his soul to the devil if it ensured his survival.

One of my concerns were, how much control he would truly exercise in this covert project but more importantly, how he could easily expose some Star Beings identity, which would put their lives in danger and perhaps even destroy their peaceful agenda.

I thought long and hard about the words of caution LUPO expressed to me that night in the woods on the Cape. While I know that LUPO doesn't interfere in any way with my free will, I also recognize a warning when I hear it.

Time was of the essence as far as Byron Huxley was concerned and so I needed to get clear on my direction and make a decision. If I did what Byron asked of me, it might alter the course of my universal mission with the Galactic Federation. Suddenly, I knew what I had to do.

(Flashback)

Stephan sits staring at his cell phone for what seems an eternity. The bright sunlight cascades over his office desk spotlighting some urgent paperwork that needs his attention, however, it will have to wait. While he is at peace with the decision he's reached relative to the proposal Byron Huxley has made to him, he wonders what repercussions would be sure to follow as a result of that choice.

Taking in a long, deep breath, Stephan dials Bryon Huxley's direct line. "Byron Huxley, here." "Mr. Huxley, this is Stephan Wolf. As promised, I'm getting back to you in response to your *unique* proposal." Stephan begins with confidence.

But before he can go any further, Byron Huxley interrupts Stephan and suggests they continue this conversation in private. "Since it's such a beautiful spring day, how about we meet down at the Southside Marina in... let's say, an hour? I have another boat called HUXLEY'S FOLLY that's tied up at Pier 6. Meet me there in an hour and we'll go for a short cruise about the harbor and talk. " Before Stephan can respond, the line goes dead. I guess that answers at least one of Stephan's concerns about control.

Stephan can't help but wonder if it is in his best interest to be at sea with Bryon Huxley as he delivers the news that he's decided not to move forward with his proposal. Feeling a bit paranoid, he wonders if he'll get the chance to explain his reasons in full for denying the request of a dying man before becoming fish bait.

Even though Stephan had initially withheld sharing Byron Huxley's outrageous proposal with Liz, in the end he couldn't, in good conscience, keep something so important from his partner in life amid all this craziness. So as a failsafe, Stephan calls Liz to bring her up to speed with his plans to meet the formidable Mr. Huxley...just in case.

With so much at stake, Liz deliberately avoids putting in her two cents about what she thinks Stephan should do about all this. She does, however, indicate her confidence in his ability to make the right decision and that she will support whatever that ends up being.

With a plan in place to check in frequently with each other within the next couple of hours, Stephan grabs his sport coat that's draped across a pile of file folders atop the bookcase next to the door as he exists. Driving through cross-town traffic to the bay front, he fortifies himself with the importance of his own agenda and how imperative it is that he not waiver from his appointed mission.

He arrives dockside and immediately locates the Huxley yacht, which is just as impressive as the one on the Vineyard. Exiting his car, he decides to remove his sport coat and reaches in the back seat for his green windbreaker that lays somewhat disheveled on the backseat. No need to be formal at this point, he concludes to himself.

When Stephan reaches HUXLEY'S FOLLY he is greeted by a man dressed in a crisp navy blue uniform who tips his nautical cap, identifies himself as Captain Miller, commander of the vessel and cordially welcomes him aboard. While boarding the yacht from mid-ship, Stephan is led to meet his host who is seated in the aft deck. Working his way toward the stern he can't resist stealing a quick glance at the magnificent interior and all the opulent appointments this particular boat has to offer.

As Byron Huxley rises to extend a warm welcome, the boat's engines roar in preparation for cast off. "Stephan, so good of you to come on such short notice. May I offer you a beverage – some wine, perhaps?" Stephan waves off his host's offer as they shake hands and then takes a seat in one of the canvas deck chairs next to the fully stocked bar that's shaded by the upper deck's overhang.

"If you don't mind, I think I'll just sit here in the shade." Stephan states as he pulls a pair of sunglasses out of his jacket pocket and places them over his squinting eyes. *Best not to give away my uneasiness quite so soon,* he thinks to himself.

While getting underway, Bryon shares how he came to name his yacht HUXLEY'S FOLLY. "While I was on a quick jaunt to Costa Rica, I spotted her moored out several hundred yards off a beach and asked who owned her. I then made arrangements to meet the owner and made him a most generous offer to purchase her right then and there. I guess, as they saying goes … an offer he couldn't refuse." he states with a laugh.

Once clear of the harbor and into deeper waters away from shore, the small talk quickly turns to the matter at hand. Stephan can't decide if he likes Byron's "get to the point" persona or if it is a strategic tactic that has the deliberate guile of keeping others off balance. At any rate, Stephan is prepared to answer in like manner.

Stephan: *Mr. Huxley…*

Byron: *Bryon…please call me Byron.*

Stephan: *All right, Byron…I want to take this opportunity to thank you for your sincere interest in the lobbying work I do… especially given the area with which it concerns.*

Byron: *If I may interrupt, Stephan…it is exactly because of the area it concerns that I have even given you an audience. Ask around, you'll find that up until now I've been… unapproachable. With very few exceptions, I only give my attention and/or money to matters that I find pertinent to technological advancement or that provide a substantial personal gain.*

Given the information I've shared with you about my current medical condition, I think the latter qualifies, don't you?

Stephan: *Indeed it does. While I truly appreciate your urgent set of circumstances, with all due respect Byron, regrettably I must decline your offer of financial and political support in exchange for the opportunity to locate the beings you seek in an effort to fulfill your own agenda.*

Stephan holds his breath as Byron Huxley slowly rises out of his deck chair, walks over to the bar, pours himself a straight shot of liquor and tips his head fully back to partake of every last drop. Dabbing his lips with a cocktail napkin, he clears his throat and in a calm, low, controlled voice states; "That's disappointing news, Stephan, very disappointing news."

With that, Byron Huxley reaches for a portable phone that sits atop the bar and calls to the captain to turn the yacht around and head for shore as, "Mr. Wolf will be leaving us, now. Thank you, Captain Miller."

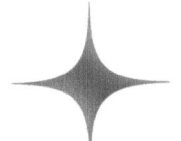

Dreams Come Through

What if you slept,
And what if in your sleep, you dreamed?
And what if in your dream,
you went to heaven and there you plucked
a strange and beautiful flower?
And what if, when you awoke,
you had the flower in your hand?
- Samuel Taylor Coleridge (1772-1834)

To say I was excited about inventing a cutting edge modality relative to sleep study research in children was the granddaddy of understatements, but realizing I was about to unlock some of the mysteries surrounding Bethany's interactions with her hybrid friends...well, there are no words!

I have to admit that while my team joined in my enthusiasm about this project, they let me know, just short of a full mutiny, of their frustration as I caustically rejected prototype after prototype until that miracle moment when I finally approved one of their last efforts.

Oh, I apologized of course, for my manic behavior and blamed it on the long hours and obsessive desire to make it work and work well, especially on behalf of my precious Bethany. But, if I couldn't guarantee her complete safety and ensure that this process would render some plausible results, I would most assuredly re-evaluate my accepted mission, no matter what the Galactic Federation asked of me.

187

Stephan's consistent support and encouragement provided me with the courage I needed to remain focused and confident in my ability, as I was about to take a great big giant step off the proverbial cliff and could only hope I'd catch air.

After weeks of my team and I acting as guinea pigs testing and adjusting the equipment, the moment of truth arrived and it was time to schedule the sleep study with Bethany and her Mom. I could only hope that Dr. Ortega was somewhere close by or, at the very least, watching in approval as I readied for this historic medical moment. Time, as they say, would tell.

(Flashback)

As Liz and her team fuss with the final preparations for Bethany's sleep study that will begin later that evening, she calmly asks for everyone's attention and then clears her throat to deliver her words of gratitude and praise for a job well done, although under less than desirable conditions, namely her unusual short fuse of late. Even Liz's team is becoming concerned about her lackluster and impatience but chalks it up to her need to get this one perfect.

"I want to thank all of you, most sincerely, for your tireless efforts and long hours away from your own families so that we could stand here today about to make medical research history. I cannot think of any clinicians more talented or individuals more dedicated who could have brought about these amazing results in such a short period of time...again, I thank you."

Liz takes in a long, deep breath and squeezes her own two hands behind her back hoping no one notices how nervous she is as she continues: "That being said, given the nature and sensitivity of this specific subject study with Bethany, I hope you'll understand that I've decided that *I'll* be the only other person present."

The team's expected moans and gasps were of no surprise and the anticipated evidence of their disapproval is duly noted, but Liz goes on, "Bethany, while a remarkable child, is still just that...a child. I have cultivated and earned her unconditional trust these past several months and cannot jeopardize loosing that trust, should she become unsettled with strangers around. So, I will ask that everyone please finish what you were doing and then, you are free to leave."

Liz can feel the heaviness in the room as, one by one ,the members of the team silently complete their assigned tasks. She takes one last opportunity to remind them that this study will be recorded and the findings will be reviewed with the entire team upon its completion. Being the professionals that they are, all wish her good luck as they exit the sleep lab.

Liz checks the clock and notes that she has two hours before Bethany and her mother arrive and decides to lock up the lab so that she may retreat to her office for some left over lasagna she brought from home. She wonders if she'll be able to take a quick power nap in the hope of rejuvenating her understandable fatigue and promises herself to visit with a doctor should she find her energy level does not recuperate once this study is completed.

Liz takes but a few bites of her microwaved dinner and finds it impossible to stay awake. She puts her uneaten meal in the mini-fridge next to her desk then heads over to a small couch by the office door that beckons her to rest. She reaches for the clock that sits adjacent to her temporary bed and thinks it best to set the alarm for one hour from now to ensure she has enough time to fully awake and clear any grogginess that will surely follow.

Liz is amazed at how quickly she relaxes and releases an audible sigh as she drifts off into immediate slumber. Her breathing is deep and steady as her mind slips off into an unconscious state devoid of any time, space reality.

Before long, she is suddenly jolted back to consciousness as loud music emits from the preset alarm clock radio. The hour passed in the blink of an eye and Liz is somewhat disappointed that she doesn't feel more refreshed. In fact, she finds it quite difficult to walk steadily towards the coffee maker, which she hopes will hold the key to reviving her to a better state of alertness. Unfortunately, the stale tasting coffee offers no assistance and, quite frankly, is making her nauseous, so she wobbles to the small bathroom adjacent to her copy machine and splashes cold water on her sleepy eyes.

Liz laughs to herself as she struggles to full consciousness and thinks how she should be the one they're doing the sleep study on, as she hasn't had very much of it lately.

Sitting at her desk, staring at the mish-mash of paperwork that is strewed across the surface in every direction she proclaims, "I really do need to get my act together and get this place more organized." The song from "Annie" rings through her head as she hums the melody "Tomorrow, tomorrow..."

The ringing of her cell phone forces Liz to gather her thoughts as she fumbles to retrieve it, knowing it's buried somewhere beneath the pile of reports on her desk. Finally finding its location she answers, "Hello?" "Hey there, beautiful!" Stephan's voice responds. "Just checking in on you and wanting to wish you good luck with your study tonight. Everything okay?"

Liz forces a cheery "Great! Just doing last minute stuff before Bethany and her Mom arrive, which should be pretty soon, actually. I don't mean to cut you short, sweetie, but I need to get moving and get back to the lab. Don't forget, I'll have my cell phone off for the night, so we'll talk in the morning – okay?"

Before Stephan can answer and say goodbye, Liz lowers her tone and adds "Stephan, I'm a little nervous about this... is that being unprofessional?" "Are you kidding?" Stephan reassures. "No one has ever done this type of sleep study, especially with a five year old...of course you're nervous. But I'll tell you this...I have the utmost faith in you and your devotion to Bethany - so my money's on everything going just perfectly. I love you...call me in the morning. Goodnight."

With that, Liz smiles as she whispers back her words of love to her amazing husband. She takes one last look of herself in the bathroom mirror and gives a wink to the image reflected back and says "Okay, kiddo…it's show time!"

Bethany and her mother, Rachel, arrive right on time and shyly greet Liz, indicating a joint feeling of trepidation about what's going to happen. In an effort to lighten the mood, Liz scoops Bethany up into her arms and twirls her around again and again, bringing about that wonderful giggle of hers, which contagiously makes everyone feel better.

Both Bethany and her mother have been briefed many times about the procedure so it will, hopefully, eliminate some of the anxiety, not so much on Bethany's behalf but for her mother, who has undoubtedly, got tons of it.

Bethany's carrying a colorful backpack filled with personal artifacts, coloring books and crayons. But her most prized possession is a long-eared, stuffed bunny she calls Fred, that she holds tightly in her grip. As Bethany says goodnight to her mother, Liz reminds and reassures her that, "Mommy will be sleeping in a room nearby and will see you first thing in the morning."

After Rachel exits the lab, leaving Liz and Bethany alone, it is Bethany who breaks the moment of silence to ask "This won't be scary, will it?" Liz stoops down to her level and makes direct eye contact with her and says, "If you ever feel that you want to stop, for any reason, just tell me and we will. I promise that you'll be safe and that I'll be right here with you from the time you fall asleep, right up until the moment you wake up in the morning. Okay?" In typical kid fashion, Bethany begins wandering around the room, curiously checking everything out. Question answered…next?

Liz knows that with a child this young you can't just ask them to lie down and say *let's get this ball rolling*, so she assists Bethany in putting on her PJs and then they both sit quietly together in a rocking chair that Liz had brought in specifically for the purpose of relaxing Bethany before placing her in the special bed chamber.

Liz watches Bethany closely for the cues that the moment of truth has arrived and it's time to move her to the sleep study bed and begin monitoring her brain wave activity. A half asleep Bethany moans slightly as she is placed in the chamber but easily resumes her slumber.

As several hours pass without incident, Liz finds it challenging to remain awake herself and so drifts off into a light state of rest. Not knowing how long she has been dozing, Liz is brought back to full awareness by the sound of Bethany's voice, that is quite animated as she talks in her sleep.

Bethany is lying on her side with her back facing Liz as her monologue continues. Liz notices the monitors that are recording Bethany's brain activity are indicating that she is not asleep and actually, quite alert.

While Bethany continues her chatter, Liz keeps watching as the data readings intensify and indicate a high level of activity, compelling Liz to leave her chair and move towards the sleep chamber to try to figure out what this all means. If Bethany is awake, is she comforting herself by talking to her stuffed rabbit, Fred?

When Liz finally reaches the chamber she covers her mouth so as not to startle Bethany who is lying next to an alien hybrid about her size! Unable to speak, Liz continues to watch as Bethany and the hybrid exchange glances and pass the stuffed animal back and forth between them. While Bethany is using audible language, the hybrid is not.

Feeling a bit woozy, Liz grabs for whatever is near by to steady herself which, ironically, is the outer surface of the domed chamber. With that motion, the hybrid breaks its stare with Bethany and turns its attention to Liz who stands wide-eyed leaning against the outside of the dome surface.

Shock turns to melancholy as the hybrid now stares deeply into Liz's eyes. Liz is in complete awe, not just of the hybrid's presence but is hypnotized by the amazing light that emits from its crystal blue eyes that seem to connect to her very soul. No longer freaked out by what she is witnessing, Liz attempts to speak... "B-B-Bethany?" her voice shakes as she asks "Who-who's your friend?"

"She doesn't really have a name... but I call her Daphne. I think she likes being called that," Bethany answers matter of fact. "Bethany...c-c-can you tell me how your friend got here?" Liz is almost afraid to hear her answer. "I'm not sure, but I think when I was playing with her at the playhouse a little while ago she asked if she could come back and play at my house, so here we are!"

Liz chuckles a nervous laugh and says "Okay, that makes sense. But h-h-how did you both get back here?" Bethany seems a bit exasperated by the question but answers it anyway with "All she has to do is *think* about it and ...*phoof!* Here she is!"

Desperately trying to comprehend the simple explanation that Bethany provides, Liz's thinks this is anything BUT simple. Her mind is racing trying to figure out if Bethany transported herself to be with her little friend, then transported herself back with her friend in tow and, if so, how? Oh God, how she wishes she hadn't fallen asleep so she could have seen it for herself. She makes a quick mental note to review the tapes and recordings with a fine-toothed comb to see if any of this has registered or been recorded.

But back to the moment at hand. "Bethany, what is your friend telling you right now?" Liz inquires. "Well, she says she doesn't like this place very much and wants to go back, but doesn't know how." *Oh great*, Liz thinks to herself. *What do I do now?* Before she can come to any conclusions, a voice suggests she contact Stephan. *What? Who's saying that?*

The voice answers in a more demanding manner. *I am! Call Stephan!* As Liz searches the room, first in one direction, then in the next to determine the source of the voice, her eyes slowly rest upon the hybrid whose crystal blue eyes yield that it is the source. "Okay, okay. I'm dialing….I'm dialing" Liz obeys.

Thank God for speed dialing, as Liz's shaking hands are just barely able to hold onto her cell phone that she miraculously remembered to take from her office and put in her lab jacket pocket.

After what seems like a million rings, Stephan answers… "Hi, I thought you weren't going to call me until the morning…" Liz stutters, "S-S-Stephan? S-S-Stephan? Y-you're not going to believe this…"

Liz makes every attempt to recount the events exactly as they happened to her husband who is now totally silent on the other end of the phone. "Stephan, this being…" Bethany interrupts… "Daphne!" "Sorry", Liz interjects "*Daphne* told me to call you. Isn't that interesting?" she continues in a panicked high-toned voice.

" Stephan, I need you down here now! I've got this alien hybrid…excuse me, Daphne…with us and I don't know what to do!"

Stephan finally breaks his silence and tells Liz to hold on, that he's on his way. *Hold on? Hold on? Just what am I suppose to hold on to?* Liz humors to herself. Forgetting that the hybrid can read thought, it responds to Liz by assuring her that Stephan will have an answer to their dilemma. She hopes *Daphne* - is it?… is right.

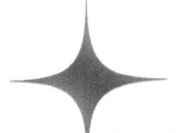

Plan "B"

I got Liz's frantic call to come to the lab because she had a "visitor" there who was asking for me... no, demanding that I come. Liz was breaking new ground with her study on hybrids and her star pupil, Bethany, was certainly earning her way into graduating Cum Laude.

Before driving the short distance to Liz's office where the lab study was taking place, for whatever reason I grabbed the digital camera that sat on the entry hall table... just in case.

Once in the car and on my way, I found my mind in overload attempting to formulate how this all might have happened. While LUPO had tutored me and shared a lot of information about dimensional travel, he also revealed that different species might not utilize the more familiar processes such as wormholes, portals and density manipulation.

When I finally arrived at the lab, I was careful not to bound into the room like one of the Super Heroes to save the day. I was hoping that Byron Huxley wouldn't get wind of this one, as I needed to protect these children as best I could from any negative entities from either side of the veil. I was fully aware that we had a delicate balance to maintain for Bethany and now, the hybrid.

(Flashback)

Just as Stephan parks his car by the rear entrance to Liz's office, he glances into his rearview mirror to see if the car that appeared to be following him since he left the house was anywhere in sight. It was not. He's beginning to wonder if he's becoming a bit paranoid since his unprecedented meeting with Bryon Huxley, who has a major vested interest in connecting with the hybrids. Dismissing the cloak and dagger scenario, Stephan still can't seem to shake the feeling that he is being followed. He vows to use more caution when talking on the phone or driving his car - just in case.

Stephan enters the lobby of the office building and takes the elevator up to the second floor suites that house Liz's office and the sleep lab. Once inside, he gingerly walks to the lab and opens the door quietly so as not to disturb the mood that awaits within.

The room is dark with the exception of a dim light that emits from within the dome structure. Liz had her team install a controllable lighting system so as to produce the desired reduction of light in an effort to assist the subject into a relaxed state.

Liz spies Stephan in her peripheral vision as he enters the room and silently says a *Thank you, God* under her breath. At that moment, the hybrid cocks its head in her direction and telepathically asks, *what is the origin of that word - God?*

Before Liz can worry about an answer, Stephan approaches her side and places a reassuring arm about her waist as he gazes inside the glass dome that encases Bethany and the hybrid, who are now in an upright-seated position. He, too, is taken aback not just by the hybrid's very presence, but its oversized, strikingly blue, crystal eyes that permeate his very being. He can't help but notice that even though they are all part of this unusual gathering, Bethany and the hybrid are each holding an arm of the stuffed rabbit just like most children would do under normal circumstances. But this is anything *but* normal.

Stephan stands in silence for a few moments and telepathically greets the hybrid. This exchange is a familiar one for him, since his early days with LUPO. Within moments Stephan lets out a loud laugh as he relays what the hybrid has shared with him, which is how funny our species looks and how archaic our method of travel is, referring to his need to drive a car to get over here. Funny, indeed.

As Liz, Stephan and especially Bethany share special *talents*, which include telepathic communication, there is no need for Stephan to translate the internal dialog that's going on between he and the hybrid any longer. Everyone gets it.

Bethany speaks aloud "She just wants to go home. Can you help her? I want my Mommy! Can I go home now, too?"

Liz is well aware of how this must be affecting Bethany but doesn't want to remove her from the dome until they figure out what to do with the hybrid, who obviously has an attachment with Bethany and might display some negative behavior should they be separated.

"Stephan, I have an idea." Liz quips "But we're going to have to work fast." Stephan is all ears and gives her the go ahead signal. "What if we have both Bethany and her little friend, here, lay back down and think about Daphne's returning home. Remember, they got here through thought… why wouldn't it work in reverse?" Stephan nods in agreement, but questions Liz on why the hybrid demanded his presence, if it's just that simple? Before Liz can answer his question the hybrid tells them *I needed to see you both, as together you will be instrumental in my evolution. I do not have clearance to speak further. Just know that all is as it should be. I'm ready to leave, now.*

With that, Liz instructs Bethany to lie down and as she does so, the hybrid follows her action. Both Liz and Stephan begin to move away from the dome but Stephan hesitates, as he pulls out the digital camera from his jacket pocket and quickly takes a random shot of the dome without aiming in the hopes he's captured this most unusual setting.

Once backed away from the apparatus, Liz reaches for the lab's console and slowly dims the lighting inside the dome to almost full blackout. She quietly instructs both Bethany and the hybrid to relax and dream. As Liz closely watches the monitors that record the brain waive activity, she is relieved to see that Bethany, at least, has reached Delta state.

In deafening silence Stephan and Liz peer into the darkness as they await for some indication that the hybrid has reached transition and is, once again, returned to its own state of being.

Within moments they get the confirmation they seek when Bethany shouts from out of the blackness "Goodbye! Thanks for coming! Can I go home *now*?"

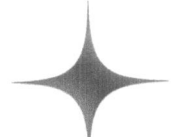

Back to Paradise

*T*o say that the Bethany's sleep study was a triumph was the understatement of the century. I couldn't help but notice how outside of the box our human lives had become, more than even we had thought possible.

So, I decided to take charge and booked Liz and I a well-deserved vacation to Sedona, Arizona. Okay, I admit that while I wanted Liz to relax and take a breather from her work, I also needed to step things up with my own research and to reconnect with Brad Phillips.

More importantly, I wanted to put some physical and mental distance between Byron Huxley and myself. I hadn't heard a word from him since that day on his yacht when I announced the bad news that I was unable to help him achieve his goal in connecting with other hybrids. I have to admit that his complete silence on our return boat trip back to the marina was pretty darned uncomfortable and, quite frankly, spooked the heck out of me, but I knew I had to put it out of my mind and refocus on my next task.

Brad had been emailing me about his recent visits with an Elder of the Navajo Nation, which is located just north of Sedona. It seemed that this particular Elder was willing to cooperate with Brad on a research project he was involved in about the role the Native American culture had in all the UFO and E.T. phenomena.

Apparently, he provided Brad with some fascinating Navajo folklore that is normally considered taboo to outsiders. While Brad chose not to go into detail about the specifics of this mysterious Navajo magic, he *did share with me that it was right up my alley. Enough said!*

To my surprise, Liz posed no objections to my taking some time off from our sightseeing schedule so that Brad and I could meet with the Elder. In fact, I think she was relieved to take a step back to absorb and process what had just unfolded with Bethany's sleep study.

She finally admitted to me that she was down right exhausted which, by itself, gave me the confirmation that a vacation was definitely in order and couldn't have come any too soon.

But her biggest concern was how the heck was she going to keep the results of all this from her team until she was sure it was safe to do so? We both knew she'd figure it out, but, in the meantime, it bore her no peace.

Since Liz had never been to Sedona before, I took great delight in prepping her for the unmatched sights and mysticism she was about to experience. I told her that a common Sedona phenomenon is the feeling that you've come "home".

Our bags were packed and our souls were ready for the next leg of our journey. Sedona…here we come!

(Flashback)

As the last call for boarding is announced, Stephan and Liz grab their carry on luggage and proceed to the jet walk. Just as Liz hands her boarding pass to the attendant she grabs for Stephan's arms, as the world begins to spin.

Both Stephan and the attendant ask if she's all right to which she responds, "Yeah, I'm fine. Guess I shouldn't have skipped breakfast, huh?"

As Stephan gives her a loving reprimand, she promises she'll eat something as soon as they are settled into their seats and airborn. Liz chalks it all up to her exhaustion and lack of proper diet of late. Keeping the long hours at her office coupled with her inability to shut her mind off when she's suppose to be sleeping, confirms her private diagnosis of being over worked. End of story.

As promised, once the plane has reached its cruising altitude, Liz reaches for her carry on and begins munching on a nutritional snack bar she packed and admits that she does, indeed, feel much better now.

Confident that all is well with Liz, Stephan reaches for his laptop and boots it up to check his emails. He finds a message from Brad marked "Can't arrive any too soon!!!"

Typing in his reply to Brad, knowing full well that Liz is reading over his shoulder, Stephan keeps his answer light so as not to alert Liz of any possible concern. He's decided for the first time in their entire relationship to edit how much he tells her about his research, as he feels she's got enough on her own plate these days.

Taking advantage of these quiet uninterrupted moments with his wife, Stephan closes the laptop and places it back into its carrier for the remainder of the flight. He then reaches for Liz's hand, kisses her lightly on the cheek and whispers "I'm all yours!" Liz returns his loving glance as she rests her head on his shoulder and switches the conversation to how excited she is to be finally visiting Sedona and seeing Brad again.

After an uneventful flight, their plane bumps onto the runway and heads to the gate as a refreshed Liz and Stephan gather up their belongings in preparation to deplane.

When they retrieve their luggage, which arrives on the baggage carrousel in record time, they give each other a wink and happily head over to the car rental counter.

While standing in line waiting their turn, Stephan casually scans the sea of traveler's faces as they come and go. His focus momentarily stops upon a man whose hair color is strikingly white and very well coiffed, not to mention that he's impeccably dressed in a gray three-piece suit, which seems an oddity given the temperature at the Phoenix Sky Harbor Airport is somewhere in the vicinity of the 110° mark.

Stephan's attention is diverted back for but a second to answer a question Liz has about the car rental. When he looks back in curiosity to see if the over dressed man has begun removing some of the extraneous clothing, he finds that the man is no longer in sight, so he simply dismisses it and proceeds to complete the car rental process.

As they begin their travel on Highway I-17 north heading towards Sedona, Liz begins to chuckle out loud as station after radio station plays one country song after the other. "I guess we must be out of range of hip hop and R & B, huh?" she quips. Stephan joins in her sarcasm and answers with a "Yep, purdy lady…out in these parts we purdy much frown on that *scare-the-cattle-'n-horses* kind of stuff you Easterners call music." Liz responds to his horrible attempt at a "cowboy" imitation with an "UGH!" then reaches for the "seek" button on the radio in the hope that they can pull in something more appealing.

Stephan and Liz find themselves relaxing and in no time at all they click off the 120 miles northward and soon spy the exit that reads "Sedona". Once off the exit they travel up Highway 179, where Liz gets her first glimpse of the red clay earth and comments on its beauty. Stephan chimes in with "Wait …you ain't seen nothin' yet!" and within seconds Liz gasps as the well known formation of Bell Rock looms large before her very eyes. "Oh my God, Stephan!" she shouts.

Stephan remembers how he reacted to the majesty of the area when he first came here and knows that it's futile to attempt to talk for the next several miles of this scenic road, so he lets Liz "Holy Cow!" and "Look at that!" until they reach their hotel destination. Not that those kinds of comments cease, as they exit their car and retrieve their bags from the trunk.

Knowing that Liz won't wish to stay one moment longer than is necessary inside the hotel, he recommends they dump their luggage in their suite, complete with panoramic views of the red rock and venture out for a bite to eat at any number of great restaurants in the area. He barely has time to finish his sentence when she's holding the hotel room door ajar exclaiming, "Let's go!"

Stephan chooses a fun authentic Mexican restaurant located atop a hilled plaza known for its pristine vantage point of the infamous red rock vista views.

Once the waitress takes their orders Stephan, who is seated across the table from Liz, gets up and moves to sit beside her, then wraps a loving arm about her waist and says "Welcome home, honey...Welcome home!"

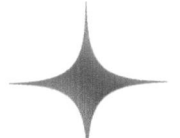

Reunion

I called *Brad the evening Liz and I arrived in Sedona to let him know where we were staying and to also let him know that I got his email that told me how anxious he was for us to hook up. The restlessness in his voice made it quite clear that something important had happened and while I understood his urgency, I had something just as important that I needed to do – spend some alone time with Liz for my own personal reasons. No further explanations needed.*

With Brad being a bachelor, I didn't really expect him to under-stand that it went beyond making the "little wife" happy. I think Brad knew me well enough to interpret that if I placed this above what he was indicating as a priority...then it was something that would just have to wait. He also knew how involved Liz was with all that we were doing, so I was grateful for his understanding. I also interpreted that while he understood and would be patient...he really hoped I'd hurry up!

It didn't matter what mundane things we did together, just seeing my love relax and regain some of the ol' Liz back was all that mattered to me. I have to be honest though, while I put my focus on her and enjoyed showing her some of the more popular spots in the area, I found my mind wandering now and then to what possibly could have Brad so fired up. After all he's seen and heard, it had to be something enormous. I was about to find out.

(Flashback)

After Stephan and Liz covered more sightseeing in a day than most people do in an entire week, Liz finally admitted that fatigue was setting in and decides she needs to get out of the hot desert sun and go back to the hotel for a much needed rest. Stephan takes this opportunity to suggest he will meet up with Brad while she recharges her batteries, to which she happily agrees.

Not wanting anyone else to hear what he needs to tell him, Brad asks Stephan if he remembers how to get to his house so they can talk in complete privacy. They go over the directions together and once assured Stephan has them right, they plan to meet in twenty minutes.

While driving the short distance to Brad's place, Stephan realizes he needs to switch gears and prepares himself for whatever he's about to hear. Just before he reaches the turn off to the dirt road that leads up to Brad's house, Stephan casually glances in his rearview mirror and notices a car following closely behind, whose driver seems oddly familiar to him. Why? he wonders.

He rationalizes how Sedona is a small area and how it's probably normal and almost expected to see the same people now and again while going about. But there's something else nagging him about all this. Then he spots it – the driver has the same strikingly white hair as the man wearing the three piece suit that caught his eye at the car rental section of the airport. Is he being followed and if so, by whom and why? Could it be that Byron Huxley is behind having him followed? If that's true, then it would explain a lot of things, especially why he appeared to accept Stephan's rejection so calmly. One way or the other,

Byron Huxley would not be denied what he wants – connecting with the hybrids.

For whatever reason, Stephan deliberately drives past the road to Brad's and erratically pulls into a nearby gas station, inconspicuously watching as the car and driver in question continues driving past. Once comfortable that it was either his over active imagination that he was being followed or just a coincidence, Stephan whips his car around and speeds quickly back to the road to Brad's.

When he finally arrives, Brad is standing outside waiting for him. By now, the dust kicked up as a result of his hasty driving catches up with him, causing Brad to cough and wave the blowing sand and dirt that engulfs him.

"Hey there, boy! I know I asked you to hurry up but you act as if someone's chasing you!" Brad says in jest. Not wishing to appear paranoid and not exactly sure of how to present his suspicions to Brad, Stephan chooses to laugh about it as well and perhaps, mention it to him later.

With the cordial greetings out of the way, Brad ushers Stephan inside. He offers Stephan a cool drink before they both sit at the small kitchen table and then he dives right in. "Stephan, you know how I've been doing some research on my own with some people from the Navajo Nation? Well, it took some time but I guess I've earned their trust, as one of the Elders requested my presence and began speaking about a phenomena that is taboo and mostly known only to the Navajos- its called Skin Walkers."

"In Navajo it is called Yea-Naa-Gloo-Shee, which means, *'with it he goes on all fours.'* It is an initiation for mostly the males into the Wichery Way using powers to travel in animal form. Apparently, only childless woman can become witches in this culture.

"The Navajo believe if you lock eyes with a Skin Walker they can absorb themselves into your body or, at the very least, read your thoughts. They avoid the light and it is said that their eyes glow like an animals when they reach human form."

Even though his mind is racing, Stephan listens with intense ears as Brad continues with his story. "While it's true other Native American cultures use the skins of animals in ceremonial rites, for the Navajo it is strictly taboo. Animal pelts from bears, coyotes, cougars and wolves are forbidden. It is only the sheepskin and buckskin that are used in ceremonies. But here's what I thought might be of real interest to you – a wounded Skin Walker, when morphed back into human form, will retain the same wound. Sound like anybody you know?" Brad asks with sarcasm. To which Stephan instantly replies, "LUPO!"

"Exactly! However, here's what I'm beginning to wonder... could the ancient Navajo folklore relative to Skin Walkers in actuality be Star Beings, such as Lupo, deliberately morphing themselves into the animals of the Earth as a more accepted form than they really are?"

Stephan adds "Some theologians propose that same question relative to sightings of angels. They propose that benevolent beings cloak themselves in a way that is nonthreatening and appealing so as to not produce fear to those that view their presence. This certainly falls in line with that theory. Go on..."

"Well, I also learned that the Navajos are extremely superstitious and obsessively cautious about this subject and to make sure the Skin Walker can't take over their bodies, they burn hair that has been cut and any of their nail clippings. And here's one for you...their spit! You'll never see a Navajo spit and they are paranoid to leave their shoes outside for fear the Skin Walker will take over and walk in their shoes."

Stephan thinks for a minute then tells Brad how he truly feels that while Lupo technically could be considered a Skin Walker by Navajo definition, he believes that he is more of what is categorized as a Wanderer, who are beings from other planets and incarnate here to help. He reminds Brad that Lupo first appeared to him when he was a young boy in the form of a wolf, then as a boy named Nathan, who also was a patient of Dr. Ortega and who exhibited extraordinary psychic prowess. But he must admit his confusion with all these labels, as Lupo has also come to him in the form of a Star Being.

He reiterates his focus is to find others like him, other hybrids that might provide him with the missing link to all this humanoid folklore.

At any rate, Brad tells Stephan that he has convinced this Elder to grant an audience with him, for which the Elder agreed as he feels that Stephan is a very wise Bila Gaana, Navajo for *white person*. Sensing Brad's sincere intention, the Elder agreed to this meeting on two small conditions, one; they come alone and two; it happen between the next full Ooljee (moon), which is in two days.

"Well, I guess that doesn't give us much time now, does it? How far away is this Navajo Nation?" Stephan ponders aloud. "About an hour and a half drive, so if we leave early enough in the morning, we can visit with the Elder then return all in the same day." Brad responds.

"Okay, let's make it happen. I need to talk to Liz about it, but I know she'll tell me to go ahead." Stephan concludes with some confidence.

"If there's nothing else, I'll head back to the hotel and spend some time with Liz and tell her about our little road trip and call you to confirm - we're a go."

With that, Brad walks Stephan to his car and jokes with him about not stirring up any more dust like he did when he arrived. Later, Stephan tells himself - later he'll share the truth with Brad about his suspicions about who might be following him and why. Just not yet.

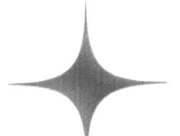

Revelation

*S*o here I was, less than twenty-four hours in this mystical and and I felt amazingly recharged and at peace. I was in awe of my surroundings, for sure, but the real surprise was how I was able to disconnect from all my work projects, at least for the time being.

Of course I still replayed the unbelievable event, when Bethany's surprise hybrid friend popped into this dimension. But for whatever reason, I was able to hold my obsession with it at bay until I returned home from our vacation. I truly needed this special time with Stephan in Sedona and hoped the bonus would be the return of my energy and the opportunity to regain my professional perspective on it all.

Stephan had been so attentive since the moment we arrived but I knew that Brad Phillips had an urgent need to speak to him about something very important. Oh, Stephan did his best to conceal his true curiosity about why Brad was so insistent to contact him, but I know him so well, did he really think it would escape my notice? Besides, we're both so highly telepathic I think he forgets I can read his thoughts…well, most of the time, anyway.

So being the good wife that I am, I told him that I had some souvenir shopping I wanted to do and didn't want to drag him along, as I know how he dislikes that sort of thing, so why didn't he plan on meeting up with Brad while I was gone.

He didn't even try to feign an "Oh honey, are you sure?" he simply said something lame like "Oh, okay…well, I'll call Brad to come pick me up so you can have the rental car to go exploring. I'll see you around dinner then? Bye." He blew me a kiss and off he went.

(Flashback)

As Liz flips through the Sedona Guidebook, she stops on the page titled Cathedral Rock, which is one of the most photographed areas in Sedona and is known for its peaceful Mother Earth vortex energy. While she reads up on this special formation, she's immediately drawn to the photograph that appears on the opposite page and just stares at it for a bit. Within seconds, she puts the guidebook in her backpack and heads out the door of the hotel to their rental car in the parking lot – destination – Cathedral Rock.

Cathedral Rock is a short drive from the hotel, about ten miles, and is located in an area called Red Rock Crossing. Driving down the spiral switchbacks just off Highway 89A to the crossing below puts Liz in awe as she takes in the long- range panoramic view of formations that burst up from the desert floor. She can't help but wonder if these towering monoliths might act as aerial markers for Star Beings who invisibly traverse across the Earth's terrain?

Liz comes back to the moment as she approaches the guardhouse that signals the entrance to Crescent Moon parking area. A pleasant park ranger welcomes her as he hands her a brochure that denotes the park rules and a parking pass that she's instructed to place on the windshield of her car.

Finding a parking space in the shade, Liz shuts off the car and begins reading the small brochure, all the while grabbing her backpack as she exits the vehicle. She decides to head in the direction of the smooth rocked area so famously photographed, which is located some five hundred yards from the parking lot.

She follows the paved sidewalk that leads to a man-made bridge built of wooden planks securely placed atop a line of rocks, some twenty feet in length that take visitors across the babbling waters to the other side.

Liz giggles to herself as she timidly walks across the boards balancing herself like a tightrope walker would, high above the crowd at a circus. Once across the bridge, she marvels at the smooth rock surface that lends itself to an easy walk, bringing her to one of the vantage spots featured in the brochure.

Even though there are other visitors milling about, Liz feels at peace and not distracted from the beauty. She's compelled to take off her sneakers and socks and dangles her feet in the cool, clear, crystal, rushing waters and spots trout and other fish as they amble by.

As the desert sun rises even higher in the cobalt blue skies, the once warm temperature is now, just plain hot. So, Liz decides it prudent to put her socks and sneakers back on and heads back to explore other parts of the park less exposed to the sun.

Referring once again to the brochure, complete with a detailed map, she follows a paved walkway to an area that takes her into the shade of the forest, stumbling upon an amazing spot where children are sliding off cascading slippery rocks that end in a deeper pool of water. Liz smiles and thinks to herself that no commercial themed water park could ever compare to what nature has constructed.

She continues further into the woods following a natural trail, most likely formed by frequent visitors enjoying the coolness the towering trees provide. Liz reaches for one of her bottled waters she placed in her backpack, as her thirst beckons.

Not far into the walk, she comes to a clearing that is covered with more of the smooth red rock that's so easy to walk upon. Greeting other visitors as they pass by one another, Liz stops dead in her tracks as she notices one of the most beautiful sights she has ever seen. There directly before her is a wide area of rushing water that bubbles over the rocks that form the creek bed below. This particular part of the creek bends from left to right, spilling its contents into another deep pool area.

Taking in the surrounding view, Cathedral Rock spires before her with trees of every size and thickness on either side of the sparkling water as it rushes to its unknown destination.

Again, Liz is compelled to remove her footwear and sits on the edge of a rock that provides an inviting seat, courtesy of Mother Nature. This spot seems to hold a sort of unspoken reverence as Liz instinctively whispers "Hello" to other visitors as they sit in silent meditation, a respected distance from one another.

It doesn't take much for Liz to follow suit and soon she finds herself drifting into that magical space of no thought and becomes one with the Earth. The relaxing sound of the water's rush, along with its cool temperature, takes Liz's spirit to places she's only read about. "I never want to leave this place," she silently says to herself.

Her reverie, however, is interrupted by the voices of some children who enthusiastically shout to their trailing parents to come look at the size of the fish that swim about in the depths of the pool.

Liz decides to pull herself and her gear together and travel even deeper into the wooded area, which is far less traveled, so that she may once again be in that consciousness of no space and time.

Before long, she finds herself upon an area that is overrun with rocks of every size and shape piled one on top of the other. They're symmetrically placed with the larger stones on the bottom all the way up to smaller pebbles at the very top. Some piles consist of only three or four rocks, while others are precariously balanced with many more. She laughs out loud trying to figure what this is all about.

Crouching low to inspect them more closely, Liz looks a short distance to her right and notices a man and a woman who are placing rocks one at a time on top of each other in the same exact fashion as all the others. Overwhelmed with curiosity, she finds her voice and asks, "Excuse me…but I'm trying to figure out what the piles of rocks symbolize. Is it a sacred Indian burial ground or something?"

The couple smile at one another, then the man explains, "No, not to our knowledge. We've been coming here for years and each time we come we find more and more rocks piled up like this. Actually, in the beginning there were only a few placed in this manner, so we decided to do our own thing. I guess it just became a way of people saying they were here. Kind of like signing nature's guest book."

With that, Liz gives out a great big grin and tells them that she doesn't want to break with tradition and begins searching the dried creek bed for her own signature rocks. When she's finished, Liz finds herself uttering a prayer of thanks for all that she has in her life.

Continuing on her hike, Liz goes even further into the woods to see what other little treasures this magical place has to offer and she's not disappointed, as she comes upon yet another clearing that beholds what can only be described as a sanded beach area with shade trees for protection from the sun.

"Good God!" Liz exclaims aloud. "It just keeps getting better and better. I wish Stephan were here to see this." She sighs. All of a sudden Liz feels a bit woozy and opts to rest beneath one of the shade trees that sits several feet from the water's edge. Thinking her dizziness might be from either the altitude, the hot temperature or perhaps something as simple as hunger, Liz reaches into her backpack and begins to eat one of the protein bars she'd packed, just in case…

She takes in her surroundings and makes note of the unprecedented beauty before her. She's never seen a place like this and didn't know the desert could even sustain this type of oasis. The creek is wide and winding at this spot with the water still and calm, unlike the rushing rapids found in the previous spots. On the opposite side of the creek are steep, treed, hills of red rock that form the bottom of Cathedral Rock. Liz has to tilt her head almost completely backward in an effort to see its peak.

Having finished her protein bar, Liz still finds herself feeling a bit weak and so gets up and walks to the water's edge to splash the cool water upon her face and neck.

After doing that a couple of times, she gasps in surprise as she notices a woman's reflection in the water, but not her own. Liz rises to her feet a bit too quickly as she turns around to see who is behind her and is thankful this person is there to steady her balance.

"Oh, you scared me. I didn't hear anyone coming up behind me. I guess I was too wrapped up in all this beauty." Liz explains. The woman smiles as she leads Liz up the small embankment to the shade of the tree and offers her some water. It is then that Liz becomes fully aware of the woman's appearance and is somewhat surprised to see that the woman is older than she first thought and that she is dressed in full Native American attire. Then she rationalizes that of course that's possible, seeing whereas they are in their own native environment, or perhaps this woman works for one of the reenactment tours.

Before Liz can come up with which answer would best fit her quandary, the woman speaks; "Are you well, now?" Liz assures the woman, whose gentleness is becoming more and more apparent by the moment, that she is, indeed, feeling much better. Liz finds herself rambling on and on to this perfect stranger about how she's not been feeling well lately and how she's been over working and didn't pay heed to the heat of the day and that she's probably just hungry.

The woman smiles and gently strokes Liz's hair and then moves, almost floats, down to the water's edge and takes a cloth from under her garment, wets it and wrings it out, bringing it back up to Liz, then places it on the back of her neck.

Liz sighs a heartfelt "thank you" for which the woman begins to speak again; "My child, the reasons believed to be cause for your condition are not so. What is happening to you is not uncommon for Wuti (*woman*)." Realizing that this woman is indeed an authentic Native American Indian and beginning to figure out that she is not *all* of who she appears to be, Liz questions, "Who are you? I feel as if I know you. Do I?"

My name is Chumana, which means *Snake Maiden* in my Hopi native tongue. I speak your English pretty good, but some words I express in Hopi. I will speak as best I can. Soon you will understand me without translation."

For whatever reason, Liz senses that it is best to listen and not ask a lot of questions and so nods for her companion to continue.

"I am mother of Lenmana (*Flute Girl*) and Kaya (*Older Sister*). We once walked Tuwa (*Earth*) when the Choovio (*antelope*), Moki (*deer*) and Istaqa (*coyote*) ran free. I now walk as Catori (*spirit*) and fly with Kwahu (*eagle*). There is much Nukpana (*evil*) now but you and others will once again restore Pavati (*clear water*) and Kuwanlelenta (*make beautiful surrounding*)."

Liz was beginning to understand that Chumana was here in spirit and came to her at this specific moment for a very special reason. She continues to listen...

"You carry Tiponi (*child of importance*) that will be born Soyala (*time of the Winter Solstice*). This Tiponi will be Qaletaqa (*guardian of the people*)."

Liz can no longer hold her silence and so stands slowly and asks "Are you telling me I am pregnant? That I'm going to have a baby around Christmas?" The old woman nods and smiles as she repeats... Soyala, (*time of the Winter Solstice*).

"Now it all makes sense!", Liz says aloud more to herself than Chumana. "Pregnant, huh?" She begins to laugh. "Oh, my God! Stephan! I must go and tell Stephan!" she shouts.

"Wait!" Chumana cautions. Liz's excitement is short lived as Chumana rises from her seated position, taking both hands in hers as she looks more seriously into Liz's eyes and begins to tell her – "there is more to come ...."

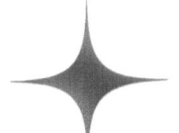

Up Canyon

*T*he day after our arrival in Sedona, Liz busied herself with some
hiking, while Brad and I headed Up Canyon to meet with a very
special Navajo Elder.

Brad had spent a lot of time researching the Navajo culture and
was extremely sensitive to their insistence of privacy relative to some
cultural dogma. The Navajos are a proud people, steeped in tremendous
spiritual connection to the Earth and the Great Spirit. They, along
with many Native American tribes, are all knowing of the Earth's
beginnings and the truth that has long evaded Western civilization.

As is always the case, the indigenous people of certain areas are
really the experts on life and living in harmony with nature, whereas
modern man, with all his arrogance, has chosen to ignore their wisdom
and disregard their warnings of catastrophic events, if man continues
to disrespect Mother Earth.

I had so much I wanted to know from this Navajo Elder and to ask
him about his take on our visitors from off planet.

What exactly does the Native American community know about
all this and are they in some way a major player in the mythology of
UFO and E.T. encounters? Somehow I knew this meeting would be yet
another "aha" moment for me and one that could reshape my mission.

Brad and I had a lot to talk about and this road trip provided us
with the unique opportunity of no interruption during our drive to
Pine Springs, which was some thirty miles northwest of Flagstaff, just

north from Sedona. Our conversation held our full attention, that is, until we noticed we had an uninvited guest following our every move.

(Flashback)

Stephan is full of anxious anticipation about meeting with the Elder, who holds a very prominent place in the Navajo Nation's Council. An extremely private man, this Elder granted an audience with Stephan as a result of his respect and trust for Brad, who has given his word that Stephan is a man of honor and "special talents" and would greatly benefit from his wisdom. He was also told of Stephan's mission to demand the government cease it's destructive assault upon Mother Earth and awaken humanity to the ways of those who have cherished the planet since the beginning.

While Brad expertly drives his jeep as they traverse the switchbacks of Highway 89A north towards Flagstaff, Stephan takes in the ever changing terrain that surrounds their climb. Then he sees something that begins to nag at his subconscious, but keeps it to himself, at least for the time being.

In no time at all, they arrive in Flagstaff, then continue west towards a small town called Pine Springs in the direction of the Grand Canyon where they will meet up with the Elder. Because of the nature of the conversation, Brad and the Elder agreed to meet in a secluded area there, so as not to alarm the other Navajo elders who still frown on the intrusion of strangers amid their sacred space.

Since they were making good time, Brad suggests they stop at a little eatery just off the main road to refill his coffee thermos and grab a quick bite, as the day could get away from them and neither one wanted to allow hunger to interfere with their intended mission.

After purchasing some sandwiches for the road, the two men head back to the jeep to resume their journey, when Stephan notices the same white haired man standing next to their vehicle smoking a cigarette. He's positive this is the same man he noticed at the Phoenix airport when he and Liz arrived and is sure, beyond a doubt, that this is the same man who has been following him all around Sedona. But why? Who is he?

Brad is aware that Stephan is wary of something and looks at him in puzzlement of what's wrong. As they get back into the jeep, Brad's astute intuition keeps him from voicing a question and instead leans in past Stephan and retrieves a piece of paper and pen from the glove compartment, hands it to him indicating...*write it down.*

Stephan jots down, *Being followed–seen him before–BE CARE-FUL!*

Brad turns the paper over and writes, *Just keep talking – small talk!*

Stephan nods in agreement, as Brad starts up the engine, puts the jeep in gear and then heads back onto the two-lane highway, once again. Within moments, without warning, Brad quickly pulls the jeep over to the soft, sandy shoulder at the side of the road, while Stephan tries to figure out what he is doing now, all the while keeping the stranger in his sites through the side rear-view mirror.

Brad leisurely jumps out of the jeep and lifts the hood, eyeing Stephan to *play along.*

Faking having car trouble, the pair wait to see what the stranger will do, when sure enough, he pulls over behind them, then steps out of his car and asks, "Hey there, do you need any help?"

"Nawh! Just a loose cable is all. Happens all the time. Guess I should listen to the little woman when she harps at me to get a new car. But thanks..." Brad says casually. Stephan laughs to himself at Brad's Academy Award performance as for a minute there, he almost believed it, himself.

When the white haired man gets back into his car and pulls away, he gives a friendly wave then continues up the highway at a slow speed.

Brad closes the hood of the jeep, gets in the car, then hands a small piece of metal to Stephan and indicates *sh-hh-h!* Reaching into the glove compartment once again, Brad removes what looks like a small scrambler device and plugs it into the socket where the lighter goes. Now, they can talk.

Stephan remains silent as Brad explains that the metal piece he found under the hood is a tracking device and that a microphone is, most likely, planted somewhere else in the vehicle, but by engaging the scrambler their conversation will be distorted, making it impossible to understand.

"Okay, Stephan…it's time to talk. Who is that guy and why is he following us?" Brad questions. Stephan brings Brad up to date on his meeting with Byron Huxley, recounting that Huxley is dying of a rare form of brain cancer with the clock running out and how he's asked him to connect with other hybrids in the hopes of curing his disease, or at least relocating to their planet in an effort to retard the inevitable.

Stephan then tells Brad of his suspicions about the guy with the white hair being some thug of Huxley's whose been following him ever since he refused to cooperate. A scary, but plausible scenario.

"Sorry for keeping you in the dark, my friend, but I thought the less you knew, the more likely you'd be out of jeopardy…" Stephan apologized.

"Okay, so now that I know we've got a '007' on our tail, let's see how creative I can get to loose 'em." Brad chuckles, "Hang on!"

With the skill of a professional racecar driver, Brad makes a sharp turn onto a dusty, unpaved road, or at least one that he's making as he drives over the bumpy terrain. Bouncing around like a ping-pong ball, Stephan lets out a "Whoo Hoo!"
as they kick up a rooster tail of flying pebbles and twigs.

Just when Stephan thinks his insides are going to disintegrate like strawberries in a Quinzinar, Brad places the jeep in a lower gear and heads towards a mountainous area surrounded by tall Ponderosa Pines.

"Need to not kick up so much of a trail, so it will be less likely that we could be followed by ol' whitey, there. Besides, that Ford Focus that dude rented would never make it fifty yards on the terrain we just came through. No siree!" He states with a tone of arrogance.

"Where did you learn to drive like that, you maniac? You could have at least warned me!" Stephan quips back. "I did! I told ya to *hang on*, didn't I?" Brad answers back with a wink.

As Brad maneuvers the jeep more gingerly through the bumps and rocks that now underlay the jeep's path, he tells Stephan that more than once in his twenty odd years of UFO research he's found himself in some pretty precarious situations that warranted becoming a master of the quick escape, for which they both laugh heartily out loud.

Slowing the vehicle to a crawl, Brad points to an area just ahead between two towering rock formations and says "There! That's where we're headed." Then adds, "Time to hang on again, my friend. Think you had a crazy ride just now? Wait 'til you see what you're in for next!"

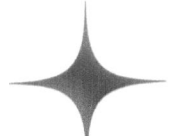

William

I have to tell you, Brad's Mario Andretti impersonation was enough to make my own hair turn white, not unlike the guy who had been following me for the past few weeks.

I guess I had foolishly underestimated Byron Huxley's apparent lack of retribution regarding his disappointment to my refusal to expose my hybrid connections. Lesson learned!

Keeping it real, I needed to focus on this meeting with the Navajo Elder, whose name I still didn't know, as yet. Every time I'd ask Brad, "Who are we meeting with?" he'd simply reply "You'll see."

I hate to admit it, but I was expecting some stereotypical, full Indian headressed, well tanned, Native American entity to lower himself down before me in some grandiose entrance from the heavens above. And why not? After all, look at all my experiences with LUPO's comings and goings, quasi-the Good Fairy from "The Wizard of Oz".

So, can you imagine my surprise as we reached our clandestine destination that there waiting for us, standing next to a white Ford Explorer covered in dust and dirt, stood a man dressed in faded blue jeans wearing a yellow and brown Tommy Bahama palmed tree shirt, topped off with a cowboy hat with a long black and gray feather in its brim and introduced himself as WILLIAM HUBBARD HODGE! Go figure!

(Flashback)

As Stephan and Brad step out of the jeep, Brad takes the lead and commences with the introductions, "Stephan, it is my honor to present..." "Okay, that's enough" William interrupts, "I'm William. It's so nice to finally meet you, Stephan."

As Stephan extends his hand in greeting, he laughs aloud, albeit a bit confused about such informality. After all, isn't this guy the big wig, Navajo Elder Brad's been bragging about, whose wisdom is sought out by so many?

"William, it's a pleasure to meet you, too." Stephan replies, then adds, "I hope you will forgive my directness and naiveté, but aren't you ..." William interrupts, "A Navajo Elder, a man of wisdom and prophecy? Actually, yes to both. When I am off the reservation, I chose to dress and conduct myself in a less conspicuous manner. Is that displeasing to you, Stephan?"

Stephan smiles as he assures William that in his experience, what appears before him, is not always what is. William nods in agreement. "So then, if you're ready to begin, please follow me inside." *Inside? Inside where?* Stephan wonders as he scans the immediate area and all he sees is a big hunk of mountain and a flat plain of dessert brush and tumbleweed.

The question is no sooner asked then answered, as Brad follows behind William signaling Stephan to fall into step. As they approach what looks like a solid wall of rock, William lifts both hands toward the sky and begins a low, melodious chant, barely audible, even though they are standing within three feet of one another.

Then, as William's chanting tone rises and his volume increases, a flow of white mist appears as it engulfs the three figures and before long, completely obliterates the scenery that once was before them.

Stephan is soon aware that he, along with Brad and William, have been transported into the interior of the mountainous rock and are now surrounded by ancient artifacts and petroglyphs depicting civilizations of long ago. An inviting fire lights the interior walls and illuminates a magical glow about the three visitors.

William gestures for Stephan and Brad to sit before the fire upon the handmade rugs that are evenly placed around the circumference. Once seated, Stephan observes William as he solemnly removes his hat and quietly mutters some final words of gratitude to the Great Spirit and asks for clarity of heart for those who are present. The mood has suddenly changed to a more somber one and Stephan sits in silence as he recognizes that the "lesson" is about to begin.

William begins to speak: "The Creator, Great Spirit, bids welcome to our new brother, Stephan, who seeks to keep pure his heart and learn the clarity of wisdom passed down through the elders. The Creator wishes me to provide you with some history of our great people, their ancestors and our purposes on the Earth.

"The people of the Navajo Nation have been placed between four sacred mountains that represent the four cardinal directions, Dibé Nitsaa (North), Tsisnaasjini (East), Tsoodzil (South) and Dokó Ooslid (West) teaching the ways to live in harmony with nature and The Creator.

"The Navajo people have long lived in harmony with nature and the beasts that roam the Great Plains. This great land was given to us by the Holy Ones, who came here through the sky. The Creator of the Universe entrusted us to honor this land. The Holy Ones taught us to take care of Mother Earth, to honor and delight in Her gifts; the mountains, the trees and the animals.

"There are many who hurt Mother Earth and dishonor and disavow Her as a living, conscious entity. A future day will fast arrive when the people of the Earth will seek out the ways of the Navajo to save and rejuvenate Her. We will be ready, when that day comes."

Stephan gives a quick glance over to Brad and wonders when it would be appropriate to speak. William answers his thoughts, "You may speak, Stephan. What is it that you seek?"

Stephan wonders where to begin and picks his question wisely, "William, I have many questions, but the ones that need immediate focus are these; I know that you have knowledge of who I am and why I am here..." William nods and gestures Stephan to continue.

"I represent all men, let me correct that, all of humanity, under the direction of the Galactic Federation. It is my task, my honor, to speak with your wise counsel so that I may gather the knowledge and tools to helps those who also wish to heal Mother Earth, for there are growing masses who realize the travesty that has taken place in destroying that which sustains us."

Stephan goes on, "William, what can you tell me about your people's interaction with those who come here from off Earth?" William takes a moment then answers, "Our people have long known of those you speak of, they are not foreign to us. Just look around at the depictions on these walls...these petroglyphs are representation and documentation of the ancient's cooperation in their schooling. The Navajo people understand the consequences of denying Mother Earth's protection. We view it as foolish to live otherwise. What more?"

Stephan wonders how William will receive his recounting of his own unusual history of abduction and interdimensional travel and decides to approach it in another way before speaking more fully about it. Brad has debriefed him on several of the Native American terms regarding E.T.s taking the shape and form of familiar living beings and hopes that is an appropriate place to start. Unfortunately, when Stephan mentions the terms, "Skin Walkers" and Walk Ins" he is taken aback by William's strong reaction.

"This is forbidden talk! But I will forgive your indiscretion, as I believe your heart truly does not know that this is taboo in our culture. I understand that Brad has explained about the Yea-Naa-Gloo-Shee. Our people fear this entity for it is unknown to us of who takes this form and what his intention is.

"However, it has been told that you walk alongside one who comes to you as Yea-Naa-Gloo-Shee and is not of the dark energy but of the light. I find this confusing as our ancient ones know only evil doing from one such as this.

"Your medicine must be very great, if you are able to harness the evil one and have him do your bidding. The other elders would bow to you and your powers, Stephan.

It would take too much explanation to recount the entire story of how he and LUPO met so, Stephan wisely chooses to ask another question of William, as he senses their time together is growing short. "William, what can you tell me about the "walk ins"?

William regains his comfort and ease and answers, "Ah, the 'walk ins'. They are highly evolved souls who, through agreement with another soul, exchange places so that the 'walk in' may incarnate at a more mature age, so that their intended mission may commence immediately. They do not have the time or desire to go through the many years of physical development, so the first soul agrees to move out of the way, usually because it is ready to leave, anyway.

"These 'walk ins' are of the light and are viewed as sacred beings who are here to save humanity from itself. Does that answer your question?" Stephan bows in acknowledgement then asks William, "What can you share with me that I may take back to impact those in our government that I am to speak before, so as to bring full awareness of the consequences of continuing to let Mother Earth struggle as She has been?"

William doesn't hesitate, "It is not a matter of choice, here Stephan. The prophecies of all nations have spoken of the impending disasters if man does not alter his ways.
The scientists and physicists are all in agreement, that the continued accumulation of burning fossil fuels along with the

polluted waters and air, will render this planet uninhabitable soon. Mother Earth is dying and her people are the ones who are poisoning her without conscience!

"All I can say to you is, the need to return to honoring the Earth is of paramount importance. The technologies that are of the future can be of benefit if those in power will only take the knowledge given to them over a half century ago, and utilize them in a humanitarian way, the way they were intended. Their misuse of these gifts have benefited but a few, for their reasons were born out of greed and personal power over the masses.

"Take this message to those who now hold the future of Mother Earth in their hands. By this I don't mean the leaders of each country, I mean take it to the ones who can make a difference...take it to the people, for it is *they*, who now hold the true power!"

And Baby Makes Three

*G*od bless my Liz! She's an amazing woman. Not only did she give me the green light to take the day and go with Brad to the Navajo Nation but she provided me with the peace of mind that she was feeling so much better and, in fact, had more tourist things and souvenir shopping to do. Quite honestly, she smiled like a Cheshire cat from ear to ear and acted like she couldn't wait to get rid of me. I swear I'll never be able to figure out woman.

Brad and I had left at the crack of dawn and spent the majority of the day Up Canyon. So when I finally arrived back at the hotel, it was dinnertime. Without even changing my clothes, I told Liz to grab her purse as we were going to dinner at a restaurant that had been highly recommended by the concierge of the hotel. I had a feeling that Liz was itching to tell me something, so this provided a nice atmosphere no matter what the reason was for her "I know something you don't know" demeanor.

I was truly interested in hearing about her day and where she went. I felt a little guilty not being able to share some Sedona "firsts" with her, but knew there would be many other opportunities to explore this magical place together, now that I'd gotten the trip with Brad out of the way. But what did I know…?

(Flashback)

Liz and Stephan are ushered to a private table that sits by floor to ceiling windows letting in the panoramic view whose rock formations are now spot lit by the sun's fading light. This has become Stephan's favorite part of the day and now he can share it with his beautiful wife, who for all intents and purposes, seems to have a glow all her own.

The waiter appears immediately and asks if they would like anything to drink. As Stephan begins to order a bottle of champagne, Liz tells him that she doesn't feel like drinking liquor tonight but tells him to go ahead and order whatever he wants for himself. Stephan takes her cue and asks the waiter if the restaurant has a non-alcoholic sparkling wine, which they do and so orders a bottle for their romantic dinner.

With the drink orders out of the way, Stephan reaches across the table for her hand and tells her how wonderful she looks. "Man! See what a little shopping and all this fresh air can do for you?" he teases. Liz agrees and can't stop smiling as he questions her more about what she did all day.

Not being able to contain herself any longer, she reaches into her bag and pulls out a small package that's wrapped in soft pink tissue paper. "What's this?" Stephan asks with curiosity. "Just open it – you'll see" Liz leans in with enthusiasm.

As Stephan unwraps the tissue paper, his expression turns to one of confusion as he holds up a tiny pair of beautifully beaded moccasins. "Okay" he starts. "These are cute, very cute, but aren't these for a baby?"

"Yep, they are." Liz answers with no other words to follow. "Alright then…but we don't know anybody with a baby." Stephan states emphatically. "We do now!" Liz sparkles at her husband.

It only takes but a moment before Stephan's eyes dart to meet those of his wife's and reaches the "AHA" moment and says in a voice barely audible, "Are you kidding me?" As Liz continues to shake her head in the negative, all Stephan can say in an ever-increasing volume is... *"Are you kidding me? We're gonna have baby? A BABY?"* With that Liz tries to shush her husband, whose enthusiasm is not far away from being out of control as his voice reaches a decibel that only dogs can hear.

Laughing and crying all at the same time, Liz and Stephan reach across the table for each other to embrace almost knocking over their water-filled glasses and sending silverware flying in all directions onto the floor.

As the waiter rushes over to retrieve the displaced utensils, Stephan shares with anyone within earshot that they're going to have a baby and receives a spontaneous applause from their fellow dinners.

"Boy, if ever there was a time when I wanted a drink...but, No...oh no, I get it...no more alcohol for you, young lady!" Stephan states in earnest.

"So, I guess this explains all my crazy symptoms like no energy, feeling queasy on the flight and not being able to concentrate for the past couple of months. I was blaming it on working too hard, but, that's doesn't seem to be the case." Liz states with a giggle.

Too excited to eat, both Stephan and Liz ask the waiter if they can hold off ordering dinner for a bit as they bask in the news and absorb what this all means for them. The waiter congratulates the couple and gives them a wink as he tells them to take their time and to let him know when they are ready to order.

Now a bit calmer, but not by much, Stephan moves his chair closer to Liz and begins "You know I've always wanted children. It's just that our lives were so busy, so consumed with our work and our mission that we never came to the decision about when would be a good time and all. I guess the Powers That Be said 'How about now?' I am beyond happy with this amazing news

Liz, and I promise that no matter what our mission asks of us, that this baby will always come first. We have been given a special gift and I can only imagine how amazing this child will be."

Liz jokes back "Yep, with your brains and my blue eyes…"

"It goes beyond that, Liz. I think you know what I mean." By now Stephan is whispering into his wife's ear so no one nearby can hear his words. "With you and I being hybrids, this child stands to have some pretty phenomenal abilities." Then he laughs "We may be in for it, you know?"

Liz wants to share the rest of the story with Stephan about meeting Chumana, the Hopi Indian spirit and all that she had to share with her, but she will wait until they are completely alone as she knows in her heart of hearts that she will not divulge everything to him that she was told …at least not yet.

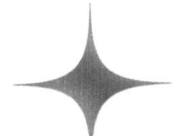

Disclosure

*W*hen Stephan and I returned from our amazing visit to Sedona, I had so much to process. We were so excited about the baby that would be entering into our experience before we knew it and that, alone, was a big enough event in our ever-changing lives. Add to that what happened during Bethany's sleep study…well, need I say more?

What I hadn't allowed myself to think about was exactly how I was going to relay this huge breakthrough to my team, who had been extraordinarily patient with me, what with all my mood swings and erratic behavior – God bless 'em!

Wow! And now I was about to hit them with a double whammy… my pregnancy and the unexpected appearance of Bethany's little friend, Daphne! Those eyes, those piercing blue eyes that seemed so innocent, yet wise beyond her estimated hybrid years. I had no way to properly gage Daphne's age, only that she appeared childlike, so I assigned her age to be similar to Bethany's.

As strange as it may sound – ha! trust me, everything was strange for me lately, I kept feeling that the little hybrid and my encounter with the Chumana, the Indian spirit at Cathedral Rock, was somehow connected.

I had enough on my plate for now, so I decided to hold that thought for another time.

(Flashback)

Even though Stephan and Liz had just returned home from their amazing trip to Sedona, Liz tells him that she must call her team together and, hopefully, find a way to recount the unprecedented events of the sleep study without completely freaking them out.

"Can't it wait just one more day?" Stephan asks his wife, who is zipping around their apartment gathering her notes and folders in preparation of her departure. "Nope, gotta do it today! I've kept them in the dark for too long as it is and now, with the baby coming…I need to bring them up to speed as fast as I can." Liz says with a smile, as she gently strokes the life that grows within her.

"I'd offer to come along for moral support, but I'm more than sure you've got it under control." Stephan says with a wink. Liz smiles back at her adoring husband, sighs and then says, "I have to admit though, I'm a bit nervous with all I have to tell them. Where do I begin?"

Stephan and Liz glance lovingly at each other; no words need to be spoken. They don't have to – it's all there; the love, the trust, the commitment and the belief in one another.

Liz breaks the spell by giving Stephan a big hug and passionately kisses his lips then whispers *"Wish me luck?"* He assures her, "You won't need it…"

As Liz drives over to the lab, a nagging thought about something Chumana said to her regarding *"that which is to come"* keeps her unsettled but she quickly dismisses it for the time being, as her focus must be in the now.

Driving into the parking lot Liz sees that her team has arrived before her, as one by one she identifies their cars.

"Oh boy!" Liz sighs as she puts the car in park and shuts off the engine. "Here I go!"

Deciding to take the stairs rather than the elevator to her second floor office, Liz stops to catch her breath on the landing. Her heart is beating so hard she's sure it will burst right through her chest at any moment now! She can't tell if it's because of the physical exertion, or just plain nerves. Doesn't really matter...

When she finally reaches her office, she's greeted with warm enthusiasm and "Welcome Back!" from her entire team. Although the group consists of only five people, they are considered to be the brightest and most forward thinking in their field.

Liz feels very blessed, indeed, to have these futuristic minds as part of her coalition, especially now.

"Okay everyone...if you wouldn't mind taking a seat *(you're gonna need one)*" Liz mutters under her breath, "We'll begin."

Before she realizes it, she has complete command of the room and commences her unplanned speech, as if she's on automatic pilot. She gets the mundane items out of the way and musters her courage to get to the meat and potatoes of it all.

"First, I have some exciting news, some very exciting news to share. Stephan and I are pregnant!" With that, the room fills with a roar of sincere congratulations and Liz is amused to see one of the team members turn to the other, hand extended palm up and states, "Told ya so! You owe me twenty bucks!"

"Whoa!" Liz blurts out in laughter, "You mean you already figured it out?" In chaotic unison, everyone speaks at once acknowledging his or her suspicions. Stacy, a clinical technician and one of Liz's closet friends, takes the lead and reminds Liz that she's dealing with scientific professionals who take in all the data, analyze it, then draw the most plausible conclusion, based on the facts. She goes on to say that in this case, they observed Liz's irrational mood swings, which draws a chuckle from the group, coupled with her general fatigue, not to mention the stash of junk food not hidden very well in her office, and voila... pregnancy!" With that, the room explodes in applause and laughter at Stacy's articulate summation of the facts.

Of course, they take great delight as they joke about what the alternative to this confirmed diagnosis would be. Meaning of course, that Liz had gone insane!

As the laughter dies down, Liz clears her thoughts, then her throat and begins anew, "Um, thank you for being so supportive and enthusiastic, as Stephan and I are about this, for it was a long time coming."

Okay Liz, now for the next revelation, "However, I have something else to share, something so amazing that I'm having trouble finding the right words…but here goes. First, I want to thank all of you for not giving me a hard time when I asked you to allow me complete privacy with Bethany during her sleep study a few weeks ago. I know it was disappointing to not be witness of what may or may not happen, for we were creating a new model for sleep studies for children and I apologize for that."

Liz knew she was dragging things out, as evident by the *get to the point* expressions on her teams' faces.

"Okay, okay…" she takes in one huge breath and continues, "All seemed normal for most of the early evening hours as I followed our predetermined protocol to the letter. Bethany was relaxed and comfortable and fell asleep in a reasonable amount of time. All the readings were in range and nothing unusual was evident…until…" At this point the team was in full attention to Liz's words.

"Apparently, due to my now known condition, I was unable to stay awake and so I drifted off to sleep for a bit. I guess I wasn't concerned about missing anything, as we had rigged a highly sensitive alarm system that would immediately indicate a change in the pre-programmed data ranges."

She pushes on, "I awoke suddenly, not due to any alarm going off but to the sound of Bethany talking out loud." Liz recounts, point by point the next steps as they unfolded, then drops the proverbial bomb; "As I approached the clear dome over her body, I saw a small hybrid lying next to Bethany playing with her stuffed animal!"

The gasps in the room couldn't out weigh the barrage of questions that began being fired at Liz. "People! People... please... please! I know you have a lot of questions, but if you wouldn't mind holding them until after I've finished? Thank you. I know how excited you all are, believe me...I know... but there's more!"

At this point, Liz darkens the room and begins running the film that documented the unfolding of events that best spoke to their curiosities.

As the close up image of the hybrid with her piercing, crystal blue eyes stares back at the observers, Liz quietly turns the lights back on, fully expecting a bombardment of questions, but they never come.

The team is in complete and utter shock after having witnessed what, for all intents and purposes, was a scientific breakthrough of gargantuan proportion, never mind from a humanitarian one! Even Ken, the newbie of the group, who usually drives the team to distraction with his incessant questions and postulations, is eerily quiet.

Without speaking, Liz passes out some materials she had prepared that contained all the clinical data read outs along with her personal notes of observation for them to study.

Finally breaking the silence, Liz thanks her team for coming and strongly advises them to maintain the utmost confidentiality about all this for the time being. All heads nod robotically in agreement as they thumb through the documentation and then, one by one, gather up their belongings and leave the lab in a trance like state.

It is Stacey who musters the energy to utter "Thank you... and congrats on the baby..."

When at last all alone in her lab, Liz takes a moment to reflect on what has just happened then is suddenly overwhelmed with emotion, as she buries her face in her hands and allows the tears to flow freely. For she knows, from this point forward, her life will never be the same again.

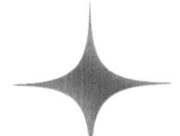

The Federation Speaks

*W*hen I first began my encounters with the Galactic Federation, I was on a whole different level of awareness. When I was a child, I interacted only with the "visitors" as I called them, whose main purpose was to tutor my human side while my hybrid side began to remember.

As I evolved into manhood, one of my rights of passage from the non-physical part of me, began connecting with a higher, more evolved entity. I immediately felt the difference in my vibration and intuitively knew that I'd graduated from "high school", if you know what I mean?

It wasn't until I spoke before the World Council for the Humanities during my fledgling days as a lobbyist that I began my dialogue with Adakor, overseer of The Federation Council. Adakor and The Council advised me of my mission and that the time had come to "step things up", as Earth was in jeopardy and both the surface dwellers and the light beings of the interior (Agartha) needed to make a choice on how to save the planet... or not.

According to Adakor, the time for the Elevated Spiritual Shift was at hand, so the mass consciousness of this fragile environment had charge of the outcome. Evolution...or degeneration. The Federation awaited the decision.

(Flashback)

As Stephan stands before Adakor, Magistrate for the Council of the Galactic Federation, he recalls how nervous he was as he prepared to address the International Press and the World Council for the Humanities, so many years ago. Now he realizes how that all pales in comparison, as he receives yet another directive from this powerful body for galactic order.

"Stephan," Adakor begins, "It is good to be in your presence, once again." Stephan bows in acknowledgement and awaits more. "This time, for the sake of ease, I will transmit data to you from The Council in your Earth words."

Normally, communicating telepathically, Stephan can't help but wonder why the change. Forgetting they can "hear" his thoughts, he is aware of laugher emitting from the others present as Adakor continues:

"We chose this method of communication with you for the reasons of complete clarity. While it is accurate to state we struggle with your Earth terms, we also view the value of ease in which you receive that which is of importance."

Once again, Stephan bows in silence, ready to receive.

"Long before your planet was inhabited, there were many who wish to lay claim to this unique environment, for it is rich in elements suitable for regeneration. While it is true that it holds a denser vibration, producing challenges of teleportation and interaction, it is of no surprise that others sought to control the planet as their own to mine and farm so as to match their own agenda.

"Prior to the formation of the Federation, there was much conflict and disharmony throughout the galaxy as to which species would provide ultimate rule. And so there began a competition, a race, if you will, to suppress dominance of others.

Each species who sought dominance needed Earth's inhabitants as seedlings to propagate and create a superior consciousness and intelligence.

"Your mythology inaccurately depicts certain civilizations as being the first to colonize Earth, the data then, is incomplete and flawed at its premise.

"It matters not who was first upon the Earth, nor should focus be upon the battles for dominance that ensued. What should be of concern is the NOW. Your planet, whose inhabitants originate from many, both inside and outside your galaxy, is in peril." Adakor looks around as the members of The Council nod in agreement, for this message is a powerful one.

"Never, in the history of the Galactic Federation has there been a mission of such importance, for what happens here on Gaia is far reaching into the cosmos. Hybrids exist on Earth in great numbers, whose etiology is just as vast. This is why your planet commands such attention and concern.

"The Federation is comprised of over two hundred and fifty members and continues to expand. Earth, however, has not earned such distinction, as yet. Thus the urgent need to determine its relevance and continuance.

"You stand before the Council as the invited guest of the entity you refer to as LUPO. In reality, his identity, while not pronounceable in Earth words, due to its tonal origin, is one of high relevance within our structure. You were chosen from your star seed family from Sirius to participate in this holistic experimentation as emissary to assist raising the mass consciousness in preparation of this great, imminent Spiritual Shift. LUPO was assigned as guardian, to protect and instruct, as your mission is far reaching.

"The time has come, Stephan to unite the hybrids, no matter their origin, so that all may continue and be elevated into the new Earth. Your task, along with many others, has not been an easy one, yet all indications are in harmony that the vibrational level on your planet has greatly lifted. I, along with the Council, am most encouraged – but the biggest challenge remains unmet.

"Mother Earth's ecosystem is dying, unless certain efforts are implemented and enforced immediately! Stephan, you have a voice of influence that has caught the attention of many government leaders. Do not underestimate your value or power. Use it to awaken the masses, now! While we are not able to interfere without request, we do possess certain latitude in orchestration of events providing a clearer path of intention.

"Your search for other hybrids, such as you, presented unexpected challenges, such as those brought forth by a human called Byron Huxley and those in his charge who maintained surveillance of your movement. We wish to advise that these humans shall no longer interrupt or interfere with your mission, for the one called Huxley is in a suspended state of mind now, I believe the Earth term is "stroke" and his follower has "forgotten" his assigned task.

"We wish to make clear that this Federation has full authority in these matters and will intercept negative actions in manners appropriate under all Universal Law. There will be no more talk of this man and others of his following.

"The living elements of the natural world do not struggle to live together, although there is struggle in the nature of their existence. Non-verbal communication is the language of the Universe. You must accept a willingness to observe and live without judgment or condemnation. Draw together for a common purpose of cooperation as part of your evolutionary continuance.

"Your poets and songwriters speak of the word LOVE. The LOVE that we offer you and all of humanity is encouraged to use in all ways throughout your time, space reality.

"Your planet has a purpose, as do you. It works within itself to provide well-being and involves bringing all levels of life together into a harmonious balance. The technologies that we have shared with your governments have not been utilized as intended. You have to demand that your leaders disclose their interactions of the past in an effort to seek corrections, if there is to be a future Earth.

"Soon there will become an era of 'no time', which means that the old ways will not be viewed or recorded as before. There are those who wish to continue to spread fear about our existence and agenda, so as to maintain their own continued control, right up to the end of their rule.

"Know this, Stephan, when the inhabitants of Earth realize the truth that has long been held behind the veil of the Cabal, and how they have the power within them to make a world of their choosing, then, and only then, will the ascension manifest into the glorious prophecy that has been foretold.

"One more thing, prepare to meet 'One of Five' hybrids who will disclose their true identity to you very soon. One, in particular, will be of great surprise.

"Go now, Stephan, there is much to do."

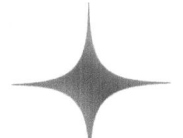

A Change of Heart

I *have to tell you, that when we got back from Sedona and all that*
happened there, I was physically and mentally spent. Not only did
I have the excitement of the baby that would be coming into our lives,
but chose to meet with my team the same day I got back to fill them in
on Bethany's remarkable sleep study events.

Yeah, I know, I asked for it. Stephan tried his darndest to, at least,
get me to relax for a day or two, but NO! I had to forge ahead full-
steam, as is my usual way. However, due to the physical changes my
body was going through with the pregnancy, like it or not, a slow down
was inevitable.

My body was obeying the request but my mind was saying "Okay
body, that's fine for you, be a wimp, but I've got more research..."

I'd already lost time going to Sedona with Stephan. While I loved
every minute of it, I knew I'd have to hit the ground running if I was to
pull all the data together, consult with my team and get my dissertation
ready to present before the scientific and medical communities and
hopefully published in the Journal of Psychiatry & Neuroscience and
the Journal of the American Medical Association.

Without sounding egotistical, what I was able to assimilate and
record with Bethany's study, would not only put my name on the
tongue of every researcher in the world, but the impact this would have
on the exploration of interdimentional interaction, especially through
children, was mind blowing!

I needed to formulate a post study evaluation with Bethany on how all this affected her and if this interaction with the hybrid could be controlled, would it mean that we could literally send out an invitation to them to pay us a "visit" or, are WE the ones who'd be granted an audience? Needed to find out…for sure!

The thing that concerned me the most, however, was Bethany. I'd kept in close touch with her mother while I was away, but I wasn't sure if I was being paranoid or not about her less than enthusiastic responses to my emails inquiring about Bethany's post sleep study demeanor.

I know this had to be a lot on them both, and, quite frankly, unless Bethany blurted out to her mother what had happened, I made the unilateral decision to wait until I could gather every bit of information and process what it all meant before I sat down and laid it all out for her.

Bethany's mom, Rachel, made it quite clear that the only reason she was doing any of this was for her daughter's well being, for as far as she was concerned, this was all a bit too far out there for her to comprehend. She just wanted me to "fix" whatever the problem was and make it go away. Sounded all too familiar.

That being said, my challenge was now going to be to spoon- feed her mother with this whole concept of actually manifesting a being from another dimension and was it going to freak her out? What do you think?

As I was about to call Rachel to schedule an appointment for another session with Bethany, my phone rang and she beat me to the punch. However, this punch blindsided me, as I was not prepared to hear what was about to happen next.

(Fashback)

The ringing of the phone startles Liz as she was just in the process of reaching for it to place a call to Rachel, Bethany's mom. "Hello?" Liz answers. There was a long silence with no response, so Liz repeats, "Hello? Anybody there?"

Again, met with silence. Liz was just about to hang up when she hears, "Dr. Wolf? Dr. Wolf...this is Rachel....Rachel Wilcox, Bethany's mom...um...sorry to bother you...but we need to talk."

Liz is immediately concerned and a bit alarmed, as any sentence that includes "...we need to talk..."can't be good. Liz jumps right in and gets to the point, "Hi Rachel, is Bethany alright? Is everything alright?"

For what seems like an eternity, Rachel finally answers with a more firm response, "Well, actually no, it's not! I've been quite upset since the evening of the sleep study with Bethany and I'm calling to tell you that she won't be coming to your office for any more of those damn sessions!"

Totally caught off guard, Liz's mind is racing in a million directions trying to comprehend what she is hearing and prepares to do damage control for...what? She hasn't a clue.

"Rachel, I'm so sorry that you're upset. But you need to tell me what this is all about so I can understand and perhaps do something to ease your anger. Please, tell me what's wrong" Liz pleads.

"I'm going to be brutally honest with you, Dr. Wolf, the only reason I brought Bethany to you in the first place is because all the other doctors wouldn't touch her...they thought she was suffering from some post traumatic event, even inferred that my husband and I might be guilty of some sort of inappropriate behavior with our own daughter...can you imagine that?"

"Well, I knew my Bethany just needed to get some of her crazy notions about playing with imaginary aliens out of her head and you came highly recommended, seeing whereas you worked with kids that talk about stuff like this. But never, never did I think that you'd actually make things worse!" by now Rachel is sobbing uncontrollably.

Liz quickly comes to the conclusion that Bethany must have told her mother about the hybrid, Daphne, appearing next to her the night of the sleep study then asks, "I gather that Bethany has shared the remarkable event that happened that evening..." Before Liz can utter another word, Rachel yells into the phone, "EVENT? That *event*, if it even happened at all, has my daughter crying all the time for someone named Daphne and how she can't see her anymore! What the hell went on that night, Dr. Wolf? I need to know..."

"Rachel, I want you to calm down. I'll be happy to tell you everything, but you need to take a deep breath and calm down." Liz's mind immediately races to Bethany's state of mind, so asks, "How is Bethany doing? I really must talk with her, Rachel. I need to know what she means that she can't see Daphne (she caught herself before slipping and using the word "hybrid", which surely would cause a catastrophic meltdown)...anymore? I can meet you at the office right away..."

Liz could hear Rachel still sniffing on the other end of the phone and continued to plead for a meeting at the office as soon as possible. Reluctantly, Rachel agrees, but on one condition, that she will be right there in the room when Bethany is questioned.

Oh God! Liz thinks to herself. She was hoping to have Bethany all to herself so that they could talk openly as before, but it was not to be. "Okay, Rachel, of course you can sit in. I'll meet you and Bethany at my office in twenty minutes?" With that Rachel confirms that they'll both be there, but warns, "If any of that *funny stuff* goes on, I'm taking my daughter out of there and reporting you to the authorities. Putting crazy ideas into an innocent child's head...I mean of all the..." then she hangs up.

Liz grabs her car keys and heads for the door, her mind whirling in all directions. "*Focus, Liz, focus!*" she shouts to herself. There is so much riding on how effectively she handles this crisis that her head feels like it will literally explode any minute.

The drive over to the office finds Liz riddled with nervous energy, which she knows she has to harness by the time she meets with Rachel and Bethany.

As Liz pulls into the parking lot, she is grateful that she is the first to arrive and quickly exits the car and heads up to her office. Once she enters the inner sanctum, she feels a sense of calm come over her while she turns on the lights and reaches for Bethany's file that, ironically is on top of a pile of records that she wanted to review.

Grateful that she has these few moments to go over Bethany's file, Liz stops only long enough to utter a private prayer that Rachel will allow Bethany's sessions to continue, as this is a crucial time in her therapy and one that Liz feels could result in less than desirable results, if interrupted so abruptly.

Liz hears the outer office door open and whispers to herself "Okay, here we go…"

"Hi Liz" Bethany acknowledges in a less than enthusiastic tone while her mother's stern expression tells it all. "Well, Hi there, yourself, Ms. Bethany! I've missed you while I was away. How are you doing?" Liz attempts to not let Bethany feel the tension that engulfs the room, but decides to keep it real, after all…this is Bethany, the wonder child who probably knows more than any room full of adults.

"Hey there, kiddo, what do you say…you, Mommy and I go into my office and visit for a bit? How does that sound?"

"Okay" Bethany says with a sigh. "Can I draw some pictures?" she perks up a bit when asking the question. "I don't see why not…Mom? Okay with you?"

Rachel nods her head in agreement as they all move into the session room to sit. Liz walks over to her desk and discretely reaches into a desk drawer to turn on the tape recorder, catching Rachel's eye indicating that she is doing so. Rachel nods again and let's Liz takes the lead.

"So, Bethany. What's been going on since the last time I saw you? Mommy tells me that you've been a bit upset. Want to tell me about it?" Normally, Bethany is a chatterbox at this juncture but with her mother sitting in, appears to hesitate slightly before she begins to recount for Liz, "Well, I'm mad at Daphne…"

Liz prods her on, "Why? Did she do something to upset

you?" Bethany's eyes dart in the direction of her mother then back at Liz, then looks down shyly before stating, "Yes. Yes, she upset me..."

Before Liz can ask why, Bethany gets emotional and begins to blurt out, "Because she won't play with me anymore! She told me she doesn't want to play with me anymore!" she cries.

Liz reaches for a tissue and hands it to Rachel to wipe Bethany's tears then urges her to go on, "Remember how Daphne and I would play at the playhouse...then she came to play here...that night? Well, she got real mad when she had to leave and got into a lot of trouble because she came to play with me, here...the night I slept over...remember?"

Softly Liz says, "Yes, I remember...go on". "Well" Bethany continues, "Mommy and Daddy didn't know that Daphne came to play and when I told them about it THEY got mad, too!" Now Bethany is in full hysterics, "I don't want Daphne to go away! I want to play with her...and the others...why can't I play with them anymore?"

Liz, now facing Rachel, asks her how she feels about all this, hoping that she'll remember to be careful with her choice of words while in Bethany's presence, "I...we...her father and I never asked Bethany what went on during your sessions with her. We were always advised to let that be between you and her...so, you can imagine our...surprise when Bethany shared her 'experience' with... Daphne, is it?"

Liz now has a full grasp on Rachel's outrage that's clearly born out of fear and lack of knowledge. She tries to use another tact, "Rachel, I want to apologize for keeping you out of the loop about my sessions with Bethany. I realize now that was unfair and it's no wonder that you were ...freaked
out by what you heard."

Liz knows that the next words out of mouth had better be good ones, or she'll loose Bethany as her special patient. But it goes far beyond that. Bethany has become so much more than that to Liz and she has always tried to let her know that and hoped that Rachel knew it, too.

"Rachel, I would like to suggest that you and your husband come to see me, alone, so that we can talk about all this and perhaps you'll feel more comfortable with Bethany continuing her sessions with me."

Liz has to get across to Rachel how imperative it is for Bethany to continue, especially now. It doesn't matter at this point what Rachel and her husband believe about all this, because, quite frankly, they may never understand the unique and special talents their daughter possess. However, Liz is determined to at least educate them slowly into the possibilities of their child's interaction with beings from… well…not here. *God help me!* She prays to herself.

Liz begins again, "Rachel, wouldn't you agree that since Bethany and I have been having our little "chats" that she has been happy and on target?" "Yes…" Rachel replies. *Good!*

Liz thinks and continues… "And wouldn't you agree that her mood swings and outburst have decreased, if not ceased all together in the months that we've been meeting?" "Yes," Rachel was weakening.

Bring it on home, Liz "And while this latest event was a bit of a shock to you, wouldn't you agree that Bethany's interaction with…Daphne is extremely important to her and to disallow it at this time could be detrimental?" "Yes, I agree." Rachel acquiesced.

Success! "Bethany, how would you like to continue coming to see me and together perhaps we can figure out how to talk with Daphne to see if you can play again? Okay?" Bethany brightens, looks at her mother and says "I want to Mommy, can I? Can I please…please?"

"Okay, Bethany, okay, sweetie." Rachel then turns to Liz with tears in her eyes as Bethany heads for the door and softly says to Liz, "I'm sorry I got so mad…I'm just so scared. don't understand any of this…but I'll try. I really will try.."

With that, Liz gives Rachel a reassuring hug and tells her

to speak with her husband and let her know when would be a convenient time for them to meet. She also reminds her of how special Bethany is to her, especially now, that she's about to become a mother, herself.

Rachel's mood turns from somber to joy as she shrieks "You are? Oh, Dr. Wolf, that's great!"

"Please, call me Liz" she says to Rachel. "Liz, it is."

Once Bethany and Rachel leave the office, Liz sits down behind her desk to shut off the tape recorder, then stares off into nowhere uttering her words of gratitude to whoever is listening, "Thank you…thank you…"

Christmas Hike

O	*kay, so here I am about to begin my ninth month of pregnancy and Stephan announces that he'd like us to spend Christmas in Sedona. Before I can raise any objections about traveling and all the "what if's", he tells me how he has worked it all out with my obstetrician who took the liberty of forwarding my medical records to a more than competent colleague in Cottonwood, which is only some fifteen miles away from where we'd be staying. And they say pregnant women are unpredictable and fickle?*

Don't get me wrong…I definitely wanted to go, for what better place to bring a new life into the world than in Sedona! So, in the end I agreed and chuckled to myself at the spontaneous whims that my darling husband continued to subject me to.

Despite all my joy, I have to admit there was still some foreboding that lurked deep inside that I'd not been able to shake off. Perhaps it was just nerves about being a first time mom or the foretelling of how special and unique this child was going to be – which to me, is no big stretch, seeing whereas this baby is the product of two hybrids, herself. Oh, did I forget to mention…we knew it was going to be a girl!

Besides, even though I was full term, I hadn't gained much weight (20 pounds, tops) and because I had kept myself physically active, I didn't have that debilitating pregnancy waddle that plagued so many woman by this stage. In fact, I planned on doing some easy hiking at one of my favorite spots – Cathedral Rock.

(Flashback)

After arriving at the Phoenix Sky Harbor Airport, Liz and Stephan pick up their rental car and head "up the hill" to the unprecedented beauty of Sedona.

Never having been in the high dessert during the winter months, both Stephan and Liz are pleasantly surprised to see not much of a difference to the terrain. While it's true, some of the deciduous tress have lost their fall yellows and oranges and are now bare, the greenery from the low brush and the towering Ponderosa Pine still dot the red rock splendor.

Stephan surprises Liz as they turn onto an unpaved road and travel but a short distance that brings them to their destination. Stephan has rented a beautiful 2,500 square foot hacienda for a month that boasts a panoramic view to die for!

The first couple of weeks are filled with relaxing spa treatments, romantic dinners and lots of Christmas purchases found in some quaint shops in the surrounding area. Not wanting to travel too far from the medical facility in Cottonwood, Liz confines her trips to no further than Flagstaff, which is some thirty miles to the north driving through some challenging switchback roads. Of late, she has been experiencing a lot of false labor cramping called Braxton Hicks contractions, which is quite normal around the final stages of pregnancy.

Stephan on the other hand, keeps himself busy meeting with Brad, preparing for his next presentation before the World Council of the Humanities, the assembly that first recognized Stephan's contribution and connection to the Galactic Federation.

Like it or not, even though it's three days before Christmas, Brad has gathered an impressive group, some of the most brilliant minds of modern times, whose credentials include a quantum physicist, a former NASA psychologist, a retired

U.S. Air force General and a former military neurosurgeon.

The plan is to brainstorm and share vital information in the hope that this presentation will be the granddaddy of them all, resulting in a final resolution to move forward with saving the planet before its too late.

With Liz's blessing Stephan agrees, under one condition, that the meeting be held at the house they've rented so he may remain close by, should Liz suddenly go into labor.

With all in agreement, the meeting is set. Liz deliberately makes herself scarce for the day to finish some last minute shopping and perhaps take a short walk though Cathedral Rock, for all too soon, she won't be able to do so, what with the baby's arrival due any day and they'll be returning home soon, thereafter.

Mother Hen, Stephan, makes sure Liz is properly clothed in warm layers and that she takes ample water with her, as even in the winter months, dehydration is always possible and the "must have"…her cell phone, which he made sure is fully charged.

As Liz swings open the front door to leave, she's met by Brad who has four other men in tow, whom Liz concludes must be the "science geeks", as she fondly refers to them, which is all in fun, as she considers herself one, as well.

After brief introductions are done, Stephan invites his guests in and tells them to make themselves comfortable, then walks Liz to the rental car where he holds her close for what seems an unusually long embrace, looking directly into her piercing blue eyes and mouths "I love you". She smiles and gives him a wink and tells him softly "Right back at ya, Preppy", a phrase of endearment from their college years together. Stephan asks "Had any more of those fun contractions, lately?" to which she responds "Nope, not a one. Stop worrying…"

With that, Stephan watches as Liz backs out of the driveway, then is suddenly overcome with a heavy feeling as he waves goodbye. Not understanding where that was coming from, Stephan shakes it off and heads back into the house to join his guests.

Liz enjoys driving around Sedona, now that the tourist traffic has eased from the seasonal chaos she experienced when she first visited, some six months ago. *Six months ago, look at how much things have changed in such a short time,* she thinks to herself.

Bored with shopping and recognizing that she'd bought way too much for Christmas and, as it is, will need to ship most of it home anyway, Liz decides to head towards Cathedral Rock to take one last hike, while she still can.

When she arrives, the parking lot is virtually empty, so she easily finds a spot by the restroom facilities, which she is sure to utilize frequently…baby resting on the bladder sort of thing.

Stepping out of the car, Liz glances up at the once clear blue sky and makes note of the dark gray clouds that are fast approaching. Zipping up her hooded winter jacket in an effort to keep out the biting chill that now fills the air, she hastens to the trailhead so that she can complete her hike before foul weather sets in

A shiver enshrouds her entire body, making her question the wisdom of this decision to hike, but feels compelled to do it anyway…for this could very well be her last hike for a while to come.

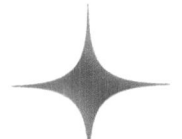

Meeting of the Minds

*V*acation? What a joke? Brad had me working almost as much as I did when I was at my office in Washington. You want to know the truth? I really didn't mind and, thankfully, neither did my darling Liz.

Seeing whereas she was in full bloom with her pregnancy, she slept a lot and with Christmas and the baby's arrival just around the corner, she was just as happy to do some last minute shopping and get in a hike or two on some of the easier trails around Sedona.

I know, I know, you're wondering...should she be hiking the remote trails in Sedona in her condition? Let me tell you, if I had my way, the answer would be a definitive NO! But my Liz defiantly had a mind of her own, always did, so she approached her safety and reasoning in her usual pragmatic way assuring ol' worry wart, me, that the exercise was actually beneficial in keeping her fit and preparing for the baby's birth - besides, she'd have her cell phone with her. Enough said!

So off she went for the day to do her thing, while Brad and I hosted a meeting at the house for the distinguished guests who'd be joining us; Quantum Physicist, Jack Wheller, General Donald Bailey, retired U.S. Air Force, Dr. William Wentzel, former NASA psychologist who specialized in working with abductees and our astronauts upon their return from space, and last but certainly not least, Dr. Paul Baker, former neurosurgeon for a military facility in Bethesda, Maryland, now a major UFO activist.

We made for quite an eclectic group, all right. Through his years of research involving UFO and E.T. encounters, Brad had either met or heard of these brilliant minds and their individual roles in the government cover up. Now, they not only wanted to talk about it, they were prepared and desperate to form a consortium in an effort to expose the lies and make humanity aware of the truth, as they knew it.

The truth...now there's an ever changing concept; for it was becoming more and more difficult to decipher the good guy from the bad guy, but one thing remained constant and true...our planet was in serious trouble and we needed to do everything within our power to save her, even if it meant getting the assistance from our galactic friends and neighbors, if it wasn't already too late...that is!

(Flashback)

Stephan watches as Liz drives away headed for last minute holiday shopping and perhaps a hike while his prominent guest pull up one by one, immediately following her departure.

As they each exit their vehicles, Brad gives out a laugh and shouts "What...did you all synchronize your watches or something to arrive at exactly the same time?"

It is Dr. Paul Baker who responds, "Well, you shouldn't be surprised...look at who you're dealing with...!" and leaves the interpretation of that statement up to Brad and Stephan. "Well, at least he has a sense of humor." Stephan mumbles to Brad who stands next to him by the driveway entrance, both cognizant of the somberness of the others as they retrieve their briefcases and other materials from their vehicles.

While Brad introduces the guests individually to Stephan and to each other, Stephan searches their eyes for any kind of clue or indication that might shed some light on if any of them might be the "One of Five' hybrids foretold he would be connecting with. But nothing is apparent to reveal his identity, at least not yet.

Stephan graciously escorts his guests inside the well-appointed rental home and offers coffee or beverages to each as the small talk quickly subsides and they sit down around the large oak dining room table that sits before an amazing panoramic view of the red rocked terrain.

Brad begins, "All right gentlemen, let's get down to business. First things first, Stephan and I want to assure you that we have made a thorough sweep of this house for electronic bugs and cameras and found none. I personally placed a half dozen scramblers around the interior and exterior of the premises to ensure our privacy, just in case we missed anything. So, that being said...Stephan, it's all yours."

"Welcome gentlemen. I want to thank you all for coming. I understand that some of you had some travel challenges but made it nonetheless...thank you. I also understand that Brad has informed and advised you as to my credentials and I anticipate that the information to be shared here today will not only be, pardon the pun, Earth shattering, but provide a solid foundation to finally move forward to getting the UFO phenomena out into the open and explained to the people of the world once and for all."

All heads nod in agreement. General Bailey takes the initiative, "Gentlemen, I'm going to drop my usual military protocol and speak to you as your fellow man, your fellow HUMAN, who has seen things that can only be described as downright frightening, surreal and just plain unbelievable! I don't have to remind you how military personnel are desensitized early on in their training to accept and not react in a negative way to whatever they may see, hear or be asked to do."

He continues, "As a "lifer" in the Air Force, I received special training and had extensive exposure and expertise involving specific, highly sensitive materials relative to national security. I was privy to things only seen in sci-fi movies. I assure you, that I have first hand knowledge that UFO vehicles and their crews are flying within our air space, some have been shot down and their crews have been captured and studied. But that's not all…I can tell you, unequivocally, that the U.S. Military and the government have indeed, been working with alien species for more than sixty years for their own suspect reasons." General Bailey states that he will elaborate more as the meeting evolves.

Before anyone has realized, two hours of non-stop discussion have passed when Stephan is suddenly overcome with a wave of discomfort, but why? He suggests they all take a five minute break to stretch their legs, then excuses himself while he steps out onto the large patio to check his cell phone to see if Liz has tried to call, for he has set it on "vibrate" so as not to disturb the meetings flow.

He notices a "missed call" and upon further investigation, finds that it is Liz's number that shows up but she hadn't left any message. Strange, very strange.

Not exactly sure if this is why he felt that pang of concern in the middle of this intense meeting, Stephan attempts to call Liz back but she doesn't answer. Poor cell phone reception is not unusual in Sedona as the mountain ranges often interfere with the signal, so he decides to change the phone setting to "ring", should she call again. Stephan doesn't care if it disturbs their meeting or not and knows that his guests would understand completely.

When the discussions resume, Stephan notices Brad looking out the window a lot, tipping his head first in one direction, then in another. When Stephan asks him if everything is all right, Brad hesitates then comes back more fully into the room and states "Oh, sorry, sure. Go on."

As the hours pass, there is much information that blows the non-scientific minds away. One thing is clear, the world of science, physics and that of the metaphysical philosophies are finally finding a unified agenda, a common thread that is forming our new mythology.

Metaphysics has long touted that we are all star seeds, hybrids if you will, whose amnesia has kept us from reaching our full potential to be highly evolved, fully conscious beings, whose mission is to assist Earth into the Golden Age at the turn of the millennium and now, here we are!

Scientists and physicists are discovering that our genetics are encoded with a "wake up call" and that humanity's memory is being restored at varying degrees. One of the most interesting and provable anomalies is that our DNA is morphing and we are adding a third helix to the existing two.

Children born today are emerging into life already "wired" with this third helix. Some children have the ability to fill up an empty container of water simply by thinking about it. Supernatural? Not at all, they are simply what we are evolving into. There are those who like to put labels on everything and call these children Indigos, or Crystals or Rainbow children. While they can't explain how or why they have these abilities, in an effort to keep the unexplainable in a format that won't upset their primal balance, they place tags on the unknown, which at least provides a definition to what is considered abnormal.

But the truth is, we are quickly moving into a new way of living. Scientists and astronomers alike are all in agreement that the entire Milky Way galaxy has been making a 26,000 year journey around the sun since time began, which is known as the Solar Precession. Within this precession is a 2,000 year period when the solar system passes through a band of extreme high energy known as the Menasic Radiation, or more commonly called the Photon Belt.

As a result of this march through space, this radiation brings all forms of life to a higher frequency or vibration. It is purported that humans will no longer be carbon based but as we move towards a higher dimension of being we will become more crystallized with over 1,200 functioning DNA strands!

New science has its own challenges with the discovery that Sir Isaac Newton's' Laws of Physics are no longer relevant in the ways understood in the past. Simply put, items with constant mass (size) such as planets that are close to a gravitational influence (sun) travel at different speeds than those further away.

What they've found out now, challenges the very premise of such a law. Scientist have discovered with "new eyes" that when matter gets super small there is a different interaction between mass objects, meaning that smaller particles don't have constant mass such as planets or the moon. Through computer controlled mirrors in telescopes, they are clearly showing that stars rotating around the center of the galaxy don't follow Newton's' Law!

This has surprised and amazed the astronomers who claim that this new information changes the way we look at our galaxy. While they don't know how, they do know that there is an unknown force that creates unseen energy that's affecting Newton's' Law.

So, after all these centuries of believing our Universe exists and functions in a certain way, is now in question. So why is it then, such a stretch to consider other life, dimensions, black holes and the like are a new reality?

Stephan and the group came to some obvious conclusion; Traditionally we've used labels such as UFO, E.T., EBE and Alien, to describe that which is unknown to man, at least on a conscious level. These identification names have a tremendous amount of fear attached to them and, deliberately so. For if we were to view them as benevolent or friendly, the general population or mass consciousness would then be in line for contact and interaction, thus arming the common man with knowledge and technologies that would level the playing field of those who wish to have dominance over the masses.

The inhabitants of Earth would not care to be referred to as "Mutated Primates" for it would demonstrate a stagnant mind. If we were to send a time capsule out into space, we wouldn't want our species to be represented by the likes of Hitler or Suddam Hussein, so why are we limiting our thoughts to assume that all beings are out there to destroy us?

If that were truly the case, with their advance technologies they could have conquered and destroyed us and our planet, long ago.

As the group's initial fact-finding comes to an end, Stephan notices Brad looking out the window again and can't help but ask, "What's so interesting out there?" "Snow!" Brad answers, "Just looking at the snow that's falling."

With that Stephan bends over holding his stomach in obvious pain. The men in the group ask if he is all right and he states that perhaps he's coming down with some sort of bug or something. But he knows better.

Everyone agrees that with the snow beginning to fall more rapidly and since they'd been at it for over eight hours, it was time to wrap it up and schedule their next meeting, only next time, in Washington.

As the men shake hands and say their goodbyes to Stephan and Brad, Stephan feels another wave of pain wash over him, but keeps it hidden from the group because he's beginning to understand what it all means.

Once the men depart, Stephan tries to reach Liz one more time on the cell phone but to no avail. He quickly turns to Brad and asks if he can borrow his jeep as he senses that Liz is in some sort of trouble and needs to go find her.

When Brad passes the keys to his friend, he grabs his arm to gain his attention and says "She's at Cathedral Rock, Stephan. You need to go to her now!"

In his haste, Stephan stops just long enough to question Brad, why he knows this – for which he answers, "I am the one Adakor told you about. I am the one you've been seeking all this time. During the meeting I 'saw' Liz at the area where the water is wide at the base of Cathedral Rock. The baby is on its way. Hurry, there is no time! We'll talk more when you return."

With that Stephan grabs the keys out of Brad's hands and jumps into the jeep, throwing his winter jacket into the back seat. Just then Brad shouts "Wait!" and as he hands Stephan a large warm blanket he utters "You're going to need this."

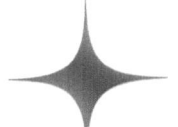

Ready or Not....!

L iz slows her pace a bit as another Braxton Hicks contraction cramps and hardens her distended abdomen. Knowing these are "dress rehearsals" for the impending labor, she slowly breathes through the mild discomfort, which is usually short-lived.

Resuming her trek along the well-marked trail through the lower regions of Cathedral Rock, Liz pauses at one of her favorite spots, an open expanse covered in smooth red rock that displays a fast running water feature at its far end.

During the warmer months, this is where Liz loves to take off her shoes to refresh her feet in its cool waters, but not today. Instead, she's brought along a healthy snack of dried fruits and nuts and plenty of bottled water to ensure staying hydrated, not just for herself, but for the life that waits within.

Noticing the dark clouds that now blanket the entire sky, Liz laughs to herself as she makes note of a few white flakes that lazily float past her. "Snow! Okay, better get moving if I want to finish my hike before it storms", she utters aloud, feeling that this is not exactly where she'd choose to be to watch the first snows of winter in Sedona.

Hiking further into the wooded area, she comes upon another delightful spot she visited where travelers stop to create small monuments of stone and pebbles in evidence of their passage through this sacred spot. Having done this herself during her last visit, Liz awkwardly bends down to retrieve pebbles of various sizes to erect her own tower of stone in homage of her rite of passage.

There it is again...another Braxton Hicks contraction, only this one seems a bit more intense than the others. She gently strokes her stomach as she mutters "Okay, baby...I hear you. Only do you think you could hold off just a bit longer, as we're not exactly close to any help, if you know what I mean?"

The discomfort passes so Liz continues to walk a short distance further until she reaches her final destination, a small clearing she calls – The Beach. Finding a large, flat rock to sit on, Liz slowly lowers herself upon it, releasing a sigh of relief and says "Whew! We made it!" While catching her breath, she takes in the magnificent view, which is why she came here in the first place, for there is none other like it.

The calm of this hidden gem reveals a sandy shore with a large pool of clear, crystal water that gently bends to form a babbling brook that flows swiftly to the awaiting creek below. During the summer months the water is normally muddied with dust from the red rock, keeping the treasures that lie just below the surface hidden in its veil.

Across the way, about 200-300 feet, hangs the remnants of a tire swing that someone erected to frolic a la Huck Finn style over the water on a hot summer's day. Liz smiles as she recalls this is the exact spot she met Chumana and first learned of her child's existence.

Then suddenly, Liz doubles over as another cramp envelopes her stomach only this time, this one means business!

Realizing she's about a mile or so from the parking lot and at least another twenty minutes from Stephan, she decides it's best to head back. She doesn't need a 2 X 4 to hit her over the head again to recognize that she's in the early stages of labor.

Just as Liz rises to start back, she's gripped with an excruciating pain so intense, that she has no other choice but to lower herself back down upon the cold, hard surface of the rock she'd been sitting on.

Not wearing a watch, she opens her cell phone in an attempt to begin timing her contractions. Her birthing classes assured the new mothers not to be alarmed as first babies usually take hours to be born. Once the contractions get closer to five minutes apart, then it was time to head to the nearest hospital.

Has it been five minutes, or longer? She wasn't really sure.

Once again, Liz attempts to stand, only to be overcome with pain, forcing her to resume her seated position. Just about the time she contemplates using her cell phone to call Stephan, she cries out "Oh great! NOW it's really starting to snow? Perfect!"

With that she flips open her cell phone to dial Stephan, but to her dismay she notices she's unable to get a signal here. She concludes it must be due to the interference of Cathedral Rock that looms large directly in front of her.

"Okay, okay...need to stay calm. I'm not that far away from the parking lot. If I can just work my way back a little closer and away from the interference..." she rationalizes aloud. But it's no use.

Each and every time she attempts to move away from the rock, she's gripped by overwhelming, debilitating, pain. There's is no question in her mind that she's now in active labor, as her contractions are clearly five minutes apart, if not closer.

As the snow begins to fall in earnest, Liz is forced to scout the area with her eyes for shelter. Of course, she's not exactly sure how she'll get herself to it, but she'll deal with that next.

Panic begins to set in as her contractions now come in rapid succession and with vigorous intent. Ready or not, this baby is on its way...and soon!

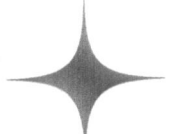

Emergence

Hee, hee, hee, hoo, hee, hee, hee, hoo -Liz breathes as she was taught in her Lemmas birthing class. She mutters aloud "Need to work with my body...this is a natural thing...mother nature has helped women since the beginning of time to birth babies in all kinds of situations...but here?"

She can't help but wonder if she's provided The Powers That Be with an exceptionally challenging task. "Leave it to me..."she says trying to maintain her sense of humor, as another contraction grips her hard.

As the cold, wet snow now completely blankets the terrain and frosts her outerwear, Liz has one vital question – can she get her body and baby to cooperate just long enough to allow her to move some fifteen yards to a thicketed area of trees that will protect her more from the heavy falling snow?

Knowing this is her only option, Liz prepares to make her move. Bracing her arms upon the surface of the rock, she gives out a huge grunt, all the while rising from her seated confinement. Success! "Okay, now," she thinks, "I only have to get myself over to those trees..."

Stepping slowly and cautiously, Liz aims in the direction of the haven of the trees. But she doesn't get very far before she's racked with a pain so intense that she's brought to her knees amid the snow, which by now is several inches deep.

"Damn! What do I do, now?" she shouts in desperation. No longer able to move in any way, Liz begins to fear for her very survival and that of her unborn baby.

Hoping against hope, she flips open her cell phone one more time in an attempt to call for help, but to no avail. Still no signal.

Just when Liz thinks that things can't possibly get any worse, she looks down upon the snow only to be horrified at what she sees. The snow between her crouched legs is bright red...blood red – she's hemorrhaging!

"Oh God!" she cries out, "Help Me!" Now sobbing almost uncontrollably, Liz is suddenly aware of her peril. "Why? Why would you allow this to happen?' she cries out in full anger. For but a moment she recalls her encounter with Chumana on this very spot some six months ago, who foretold of her mothering a child of special gifts and what a blessed event it will be for the entire world.

Liz, now blind with fear hadn't noticed the form that stood before her until a voice speaks, "Liz, my child...stand and walk with me," the voice urges. 'Wha...who...who's there?" Liz pleads, lifting her head while shielding her eyes from the pulverizing snow and sleet in an effort to view her rescuer.

"Come, Elizabeth" the voice continues, "It is time to go into the water, for the child awaits." By now Liz's ears are roaring as her mind attempts to decipher all that's going on and what is being asked of her, more immediately...what's about to happen!

Through her tears and falling snow, Liz is finally able to make out the shape that stands before her. It is Chumana!

"Help me, Chumana! I'm afraid! I don't want my baby to die!"

"There is nothing to fear, my child. Come, the water awaits." Chumana instructs with more urgency.

"Water? I can't go into the water...it's freezing! I'll surely die and so will my baby! No! I can't...I won't..." she declares with fervor. Just then, Liz becomes aware of the baby moving lower into the birth canal. So low, in fact, she could swear she felt the head about to emerge.

"Come Elizabeth. There is not time to waste." With that, Liz finds herself struggling to her feet and moving toward the frigid water with the help of Chumana.

Now beyond fear, Liz can only make whimpering sounds as she calls out Stephan's name, while Chumana guides her into the depths of the pool of water.

To her shock, Liz finds the water is not freezing at all, in fact, it feels warm and soothing. Confused but grateful, she doesn't care if her mind is playing tricks on her or not. All she can focus on is that this baby is coming...NOW!

Chumana begins to speak and chant in soothing tones explaining; "This child has lived in water since it's beginning, shielded from sound and light. Emerging into this world is made easier in the water, especially this water. It is not unfortunate to have your child born into these waters, Elizabeth...it is part of the enormous gift. For your child will be *Tiponi - Child of Importance*! One who leads."

" This moment has been destined exactly in this way. Allow the help of Mother Gaia...Surrender to All That Is, for this emergence will fulfill a miraculous prophecy brought forth by yours and Stephan's love and purpose."

"Now, Elizabeth...behold your miracle!"

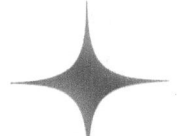

Stephan's Intuition

I drove like a maniac. On a good day, it was probably about a twenty-minute ride to Cathedral Rock, never mind having to maneuver through the slippery roads that were quickly being buried by the fast falling, wet snow. I estimated that there was already a good five to six inches on the ground. First, I had to contend with the narrow, winding, two lane Highway 179 and no safe way to pass the slow traffic in front of me.

My head was spinning. Liz was first and foremost in my mind, but somewhere back there was the unbelievable revelation that Brad had just hit me with. HE was a hybrid, himself! HE was the one Adakor had told me would reveal himself. Brad, my friend, an invaluable ally, who's been by my side all this time helping me to find others like me… The irony of it all would have to wait.

Once I reached the area known at the "Y", I was able to make up some time as I headed west on 89A, as the plows and sanders had already made one pass through. Thankfully, the traffic lights were in cooperation with my need to hurry, or perhaps it was the Powers That Be that paved the way, didn't matter. All I knew was that Liz was in trouble and with Brad's revelation of who HE is and that he, too, sensed the urgency to find Liz, just propelled me forward with even more determination.

When I arrived at the light where I needed to take a left onto Upper Loop Road, I threw the jeep into the lowest gear I could, as this steep switchback is a bit of a challenge on dry pavement, let alone with six plus inches of wet slippery snow and ice.

At every turn of the steep road, my stomach hurt more and more. I drove bent in half, holding my abdomen when I was able to let go of the wheel and with only one hand, I deftly maneuvered the sharp turns. I was feeling her pain!

Once reaching the bottom of the hill, I skidded past the road on the left that would lead me to the Crescent Moon parking lot. The jeep whined as it fought for traction as I attempted to back up as fast as I could. Realizing that was the worst thing I could do, I took in a deep breath and prayed aloud for help, which came swiftly in the form of solid traction.

When I was finally able to make the left turn, which was the last winding road that led to the park's entrance, I was somewhat relieved to see what appeared to be our rental car, covered in snow, parked by the restroom.

As I approached the guardhouse, a ranger told me to "Hold up a minute! You can't go in there! We're closed due to the storm!"

I lowered my window as I drove past and shouted "My pregnant wife is still in here. Call 911!"

I drove the jeep past our rental car and followed my intuition and my stomach pains that were now indicating which way to head, like a child's hide and seek game - "hot, hotter, hottest!"

I threw the jeep into park and shut off the engine, grabbing my jacket and the blanket Brad had given me back at the house.

Never having hiked in this direction before, I had to trust my intuition that I was indeed, headed in the right direction. I fell several times and in frustration, began yelling out loud at Liz for doing such a stupid thing.

I had no idea if I was following a trail or if I were blazing my own. All I knew was that I had to get to Liz and fast.

When I reached an open area, I saw a fast flowing stream ahead and remembered Liz talking about a spot just like this that was one of her favorite places to rest and soak her feet, Ha! I thought to myself, bet that water is beyond freezing now.

I began working my way through a wooded area just past the water but thought I might be headed in the wrong direction until I spotted some unusual mini-towered rock and pebble formations. Eureka! I remembered Liz telling me about this place too, and how she erected her own signature of her passing through this sacred spot. No time to figure out which one might be hers. Had to keep moving. Pains getting worse!

My hands were beginning to freeze up, as I had neglected to bring any gloves. I was grateful that I had a jacket, never mind being fully outfitted for an emergency hike through the snow.

I emerged out into an area that had a large pool of water before me. As I scanned the area, I began to shout "Liz! Liz! Where are you, Liz!" Within seconds I heard a faint, "Stephan…God! Stephan… over here!"

See You Soon

As Stephan rushes up to where Liz lain upon the snow under the protection of a group of trees, he is shocked to see the baby, whose piercing blue eyes look directly at him as they exchange greetings.

"Oh my God, Liz! The baby…the baby, she's beautiful! Liz, you're soaking wet!" Stephan reaches for the blanket, which he threw to the ground upon his discovery of Liz under the trees.

Gently he takes his new daughter from Liz's tight grasp, whispering to her "It's all right, sweetheart, I've got her now." Stephan wraps the baby in the clean, dry blanket then turns to attend to Liz. Carefully, yet gingerly, he removes Liz's wet clothing, then quickly unwraps the baby for but a moment, as he lovingly places her on Liz's chest, then rewraps them both in the blanket.

Realizing that the wet snow will eventually penetrate the blanket in no time at all, Stephan sweeps both mother and child up and places them on his lap as he sits for but a moment admiring his girls.

"Stephan" Liz begins barely audible, "Stephan you have to get help…" "Yes, I know. I already told the ranger at the guardhouse to call for help, but I don't know if they'll know which direction to go in. I'll try my cell." Before Liz can indicate don't bother, Stephan finds out for himself that he can't get a signal, either.

"Okay, Liz, here's what we're going to do...I'm going to carry you and the baby out. I've got Brad's jeep and if the rescue team isn't there by the time we are, then I'm driving you to the nearest emergency facility." Stephan has to think fast. Wasn't there a walk-in emergency clinic or something just up the top of the hill on 89A? Doesn't matter, first things first.

When Stephan attempts to lift Liz and the baby, he is shocked to see the large amount of blood staining the new fallen snow just beneath her. The look on his face tells Liz what she has feared all along, that she is still hemorrhaging and its getting worse.

"Liz", Stephan begins, "you're bleeding... a lot. I've got to get you some help."

What happens next is beyond Stephan's imagination, for there before him stands Chumana in full ceremonial headdress and garb. As Stephan looks at her quizzically, she softly tells him who she is and how she and Liz met in this very spot some six months ago. She goes on to tell him how she told Liz that she was to give birth to a *Tiponi* - child of importance.

"Yes, yes I remember Liz told me all this. But something is wrong, something is *very* wrong and we need help, right now! Can you help her?" Stephan begs as tears flow freely from his eyes.

"Stephan, my son, this child was prophesied by the Great Spirit to emerge at this time, in this place, in this way. It had also been foretold that the *Wuti* (woman) who would bear this child would leave this *Tuwa* (Earth) by the *Kuuyi* (water)." Chumana waits to see if Stephan understands what she is telling him, but sees that through his fear, is in denial of that which is to come.

Stephan looks down through tear stained eyes at Liz and the baby then softly asks her, "Did you know of this, Liz? Did you know that this was going to happen this way?"

Liz struggles for the strength to answer her beloved husband and whispers "Yes, Stephan. I knew. I always knew..."

"But why...why didn't you tell me? I don't understand!"

Stephan is hanging on to control his voice and his emotions as he finally realizes what Chumana is speaking of.

Turning to Chumana, Stephan asks "You are of the Source, you have ways that are known only to your people, surely you can do something to change all this. Surely you can make my Liz…"

"No, my son, I cannot interfere with that which is to be. For it has been decreed that this journey you have shared with one another has served it purpose and that the child will carry on for the mother."

Unable to control his emotions, Stephan bends over and brings Liz and the baby close to his chest as he softly cries, "No, Liz, not now…Please don't leave me…don't leave us now."

As Stephan pulls back to gaze upon her face, he notices that the light that shone so brightly in her amazing blue eyes all these years they've been together is all but gone, ebbing with the very life she once held in her being.

"Liz, oh God, Liz please don't leave me. I can't say goodbye…I won't say goodbye…"

As the life's light of his beloved Liz pulls away, she finds the strength to say, "All right, Stephan, we won't say goodbye, my love. Let's just say…see you soon…?" and with that, Liz's body relaxes into Stephan's arms signaling her departure.

Lost in his grief, Stephan embraces the physical body of his darling wife and partner. He gazes upon his new daughter still held in her mother's lifeless arms and wonders how she will ever know the amazing sacrifice her mother has made so that she may emerge and be an integral part of the evolution of man.

Time has all but stopped as Stephan continues to cradle his wife's body that once encased the life force that held him captive since the day they met. His eyes blurred with tears, Stephan lovingly looks upon his newborn daughter, whose piercing blue eyes stare back with empathetic wisdom of his loss…their loss.

Something unwittingly catches Stephan's attention and when he is finally able to look away from Liz and the baby, his focus is drawn to the pool of water adjacent to the shoreline where he now sits. Although numb within his grief, Stephan begins to feel a lifting from his broken soul as he views Chumana and his darling Liz in ghostly image standing side by side before him by the water's edge. Knowing that the time has come for her to truly go, Liz gives Stephan one last brilliant smile and a wink as she bids farewell … "See you soon, Preppy. See you soon."

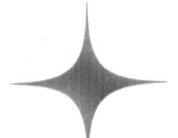

Epilogue

It's been three years since Liz departed and so now I journey every year at Christmas time with our daughter, Krystal, to Sedona where we bring flowers to Cathedral Rock and lay them upon the waters where she left us.

Taking Liz back home to Washington for a formal funeral for family and friends was difficult but more than that, I knew my Liz wouldn't want her final resting place to be there, so I took her cremated remains and climbed atop Cathedral Rock where I released her to the wind, so that she may soar among the eagles in a place she came to love as home.

Getting back to my routine was the most challenging of all. While my constituents were all sympathetic and more than supportive to my loss, no one knew...no one, of how much I hurt and how I truly missed my Liz.

I was, at least, successful in getting the government to declassify more documentation about UFOs and form an International Coalition for the Restoration and Recovery of Planet Earth, which took some of the sting away, but only some.

Liz and I continue to have our "visits" and "talks" with Krystal who, at age three, is demonstrating remarkable psychic abilities, as prophesized. More and more, everyday, I hear her exchange conversations with Liz and giggle, telling me how funny Mommy is. Yes, she did...does have a great sense of humor, that's one of the things I love about her the most.

One day, while taking Krystal to a restaurant that caters to children, I stood by as she frolicked upon the playground structures located at the back of the building. All of a sudden Krystal shouts out "Hi Bethany!" at an older child I guessed was somewhere between eight or nine years old.

The young girl approached Krystal, looking at her for a moment, somewhat confused then shouted "Daphne!"

I walked up to the little girl and said "Hi, honey. No, this is my daughter, Krystal. She's three years old. How old are you?"

"Hi, Mr. Wolf. Don't you remember me? It's Bethany…I use to visit with Liz. Boy, I sure miss her."

I was a bit unsteady for a moment, but when I recovered and looked more closely, I surely did recognize Bethany and gave her a hug. "Well, you've certainly grown a lot since I last saw you. Is your Mom here with you?"

Bethany pointed over to where her mother sat sipping on a Coke while watching her daughter play. When Bethany resumed her conversation with Krystal and I, she corrected me, "No, her name is Daphne…don't you remember…don't you remember the night I slept over at Liz's office and Daphne came to visit? Boy, were we surprised, huh?"

By now I was sizing up Krystal and Bethany as they appeared to be "exchanging" conversation without words. Bethany began to giggle and said, "Oh, Daphne, you're so funny. You still don't know how to say some things with words, do you?"

With that, Bethany's mom called for her as it was time for them to go. Before leaving, Bethany turned to me and asked. "Mr. Wolf, can Daphne come to play at my house some time? Now that she's here…"

I thought for a minute, looked into my daughter's beautiful, piercing, crystal blue eyes and answered, "On one condition…you call her Krystal." For which Bethany answered… "See you soon, Krystal."

The Farewell

There is something I know, that I want to say
When the sprit so moves and takes me away
To that special place where I come from
Where time and space are all but one
Where whispers beckon and thoughts come alive
Where all is still possible to nurture, survive
It is my home, I long to be there
Where stars shine above and my thoughts crystal clear
Please let me go home, feel the peace that I know
The wisdom of ages of times long ago
Where man doesn't hurt the surroundings he lives
Where peace and harmony abound
Where joy and love lives
I soar with the eagles, I float on the wind,
I play with all nature, for it is my friend
I am all that is, all that will ever be
I am the source of creativity
I blend with the earth and the heavens above
I come to this physical place
To bare witness of love
When my journey is over
And I'm at last home
Let my essence remain with those I have known.

Channeled from Tanee Estashae

Book III

KRYSTAL
2012
A NEW BEGINNING

"When the Blue Star Kacchina makes its appearance in the heavens,
the Fifth World will emerge.
This will be the Day of Purification."

~Ancient Hopi Indian prophecy

"I've had dreams in which I'm at a place
and a small group of people comes over a hill.
We all embrace and say, 'Brother, Sister, you survived'
- After the cleansing, we will see only people
who now how to reach out and learn.
People will know that their survival came about
because they had made good effort
to live in love and harmony."

~Sun Bear Tribe
Medicine Society and Native American visionary

"A great wind will come,
a wind that will make a hurricane seem like a whisper.
It will cleanse the Earth and return it to its original state.
That will be the punishment for what we've done to creation."

~Iroquois Quote (anonymous)

"You have been telling the people that this is the Eleventh Hour.
Now you must go back and tell the people that this is the Hour."

~Reading from Hopi Nation

"And the third angel sounded
and there fell a great star from heaven,
burning as it were a lamp
and it fell upon the third part of the rivers
and upon the foundations of waters:
And the name of the star is called **Wormwood."**

~Revelation Chapter 8, VRS 10 & 11

For Christine, Vicki and Peter
An open heart and mind creates a world
where everything is possible!

Prologue - Signs

In a small remote village just outside of La Paz, Boliva in a humble dwelling, deliberately obscured by thick green foliage so as to ensure its occupants complete privacy, a small group of self-appointed investigators pore over the voluminous materials strewn across the large, rustic wooden dining room table that include hundreds, if not thousands, of crop circles images photographed from around the world.

Dr. Ramón Fernandez, known for his ground breaking studies in astrophysics, famed geologist and amateur astronomist, Dr. Miguel Alvarez; Dr. Alberto Cruz, leading Peruvian archeologist; and Dr. Alicia Morales, PhD in Sociologic Science and Behavior, have been at it for hours, attempting to ascertain a common thread that would provide them with something, *anything* of value in their, thus far, futile attempts to decode the messages they're sure lie within these intricate circles.

Their concentrated focus is momentarily disrupted by an urgent plea from Dr. Fernandez's six-year old son, Joaquin, who has been quietly playing on the living room floor with Dr. Morales' five- year old daughter, Pilar and her older brother, seven-year old Marco. "PaPa, we are hungry" cries Joaquin, the other children nodding in pathetic agreement.

"Okay, my little one", Ramon answers his young son, as the grownups mumble in unison how they, too, could use a break and welcome having a bite to eat.

With all in agreement, the adults push back their chairs and move ensemble into the cozy kitchen to prepare some sustenance. Knowing it won't take long before the adults return, the children eye one another and then stealth fully approach the table that holds the amazing crop circle images upon its massive surface.

It is young Pilar who signals to the others to gather up the photos and follow her to an open area in the adjoining living room. As they carefully lay out the strange designs atop the partially carpeted floor, one by one, they unquestioningly choose specific images and then silently begin placing them in deliberate order, lining them up, as if assembling a storyboard.

Muffled giggles emerge as they deftly move about, carefully positioning each image into its assumed rightful place. When finished, the children sit back to admire their work, but their reverie is short lived - "Joaquin...what have you done!" shouts his father who, along with his colleagues stand frozen in bewilderment , all the while balancing plates of prepared delicacies in their hands.

Startled, the children jump instantly to their feet, heads bowed in trepidation of what is about to happen next. It is Marco who speaks first, "Dr. Fernandez, we meant no harm. For so long, we have only been able to sneak a peek at these beautiful images and simply wanted to look at them more closely...that's all"

"Silencio!" barks Dr. Alvarez. "What you children fail to recognize is that we've been working very hard for months trying to figure out what these photos mean. We've spent untold hours painstakingly putting them in order and now, you children, have messed everything up!"

Having a PhD in sociologic behavior, but more importantly, being the only mother in the group, Dr. Morales jumps in to defuse the adults' escalating anger and calmly reminds them how children have a normal curiosity about such things; then brilliantly touts how - "after all, they are the offspring of such great minds..." and goes on to point out that they should be proud that their children possess such avid curiosities that compel them to explore the unknown, just like their parents.

While Dr. Morales and Dr. Alvarez continue to *express* their different points of view about this occurrence, Dr. Cruz interrupts the grownup banter and speaks directly to the children... "Why did you place these pictures in *that* particular order?" It is young Pilar who provides the ingenuous answer, "Because this way, it tells a story...it's like a puzzle... and when the puzzle pieces are put together *just* right ...it tells a story."

The room takes on an eerie silence as these four brilliant adult minds, who have been eating, sleeping and breathing these images for the better part of a year, stand freeze-framed to their spots gazing at the photos, attempting to "read" them but still fail to see the significance of the order or what the children obviously deem as a translatable story.

"What do YOU children see? What are these pictures telling YOU?" Dr. Morales inquires.

The children excitedly begin babbling their explanation in unison. "Whoa, wait a minute! One at a time...one at a time..." instructs Dr. Fernandez.

Unexpectedly, it's six-year old Joaquin who boldly begins the explanation as he points to the first image - "This tells us how life began..." and then moves to the subsequent images that follow. As he continues to educate the adults, Joaquin secretly delights in being the center of attention and feels powerfully in command and so presses on - "Now these, tell about what happened a long, long, long, long time ago to the people and how *they* simply disappeared off the Earth. But *these*..." he points to the last five images that have, ironically, been of particular interest to the adults, "*these* tell us that something BIG is about to happen! Something not good..." Joaquin's voice trails off. Marco chimes in, "But don't worry, THEY'RE here now... to help us!"

The room is suddenly overcome with a deafening silence. Beginning to feel weak in the knees, one by one the adults find it impossible to remain standing and so begin lowering themselves, one at a time, onto the nearest chair, all the while trying to comprehend this innocuous translation coming from the children.

Justifiably, the grownups have many questions for the children but the one that seems most paramount is WHEN? *When is this all going to happen?*

Once again the children answer in unison, only this time - their answer is quite clear. "Now! It's happening NOW!"

As Dr. Morales slowly lowers herself onto the hardwood floor, perusing the crop circle images before her, she drags her hand across her face from forehead to chin and mumbles, to no one in particular, "It was all here, right in front of us. Here we are... with our brilliant education..." And then bursts out laughingly, "If you want to know the truth...ask a child."

Krystal

*M*y name is Krystal, spelled with a "K", but that's not the only unusual thing about me... you see – I'm a hybrid. What's that? The simple answer is I am, in part, biogenetically human and the other part...well...Alien. I prefer to call myself a Star Child however, until humanity stops groping with the whole concept of Beings such as me even existing... A-L-I-E-N it is. Thankfully, my dad, his friends and their kids, accept my uniqueness and actually embrace my somewhat unusual way of expressing things and then of course, there are my prophetic visions. I am a high functioning telepath, empath and psychic, among other things. I am what the Hopi's call "Tiponi" which means Child of Importance or Child of Destiny.

Oh, I guess don't mind. In fact, I think it's kind of cool being me! Do I sound convincing? I'm working on using more human colloquialisms so I blend in more easily, at least that's what my dad suggests I try.

Physically, I look like a normal, soon-to-be twelve year old girl, although I'm a bit tall for my age; I have long, curly dark auburn hair that I wear hanging down most of the time. For some reason I'm fascinated with clothing and take particular care in selecting what I wear and when. I'm drawn to the color blue, that seems to enhance my bright blue eyes, which my dad claims are just like my mom's. Like most dads, he tells me how special I am - a human trait I've come to accept and be at ease with. While all Beings are special and live, for the most part, in unintentional purpose, every so often, one emerges with *an overriding universal mission…that would be me.*

Where I come from, our species is not all that different from Earth children, with a few exceptions of course, and so it was decided that an experiment would be most useful to determine if we could be taught the ways of human children so that we may blend in more easily when the time of integration arrived.

By integration I mean, there are those throughout Earth's solar system, including my ancestors who have been watching Earth and its inhabitants for some time and were aware of a cyclical astronomical event…sorry- rephrase…a returning planet that was due to be dangerously close to Earth by the year 2012. So, the Galactic Federation, a group of diverse benevolent Star Beings concluded that if Earth's human civilization was to evolve and become part of the galactic neighborhood, due to their…how can I say this diplomatically?… insufficient knowledge of the workings of the Universe and lack of advanced technologies, an intervention was necessary. Whew! That was really difficult to put into Earth language, but I know you get what I'm trying to say.

Well, as it happened I was one of the off planet newbies who were selected, some of us en vitro, to assist in this experiment. Of course it was a choice, not a mandate that we participate and so it followed that we would choose our Earth parents. Just how I did that is hard to explain but let it be enough to know that I could "experience" energy and after "reviewing" the candidates, was inclined to choose two hybrids for my mother and father. I'll explain all this in a minute.

At any rate, I'm about to celebrate the 12th marking of my emergence into physical…I mean my birthday but let me tell you, everything surrounding this celebration is anything BUT normal!

I was born on December 21, 2000, the day of the Winter Solstice in the new Millennium. My birth was, how shall I say this…extremely out of the ordinary, for my mother gave birth during a snow storm, at the base of Cathedral Rock in Sedona, Arizona… in the water! Okay, so now you're beginning to get the picture.

A Hopi Indian spirit named Chumana, not only prophesized my birth but was present and aided in my emergence into physical form.

Sadly, she also assisted in my mother's transition – for she died right after I came forth. I miss her very much.

Okay, I can hear you ask "How can you miss someone you never knew?" but you're wrong; I not only knew my mother before my birth but actually specifically chose her and my father to be my Earth parents, for they too, are hybrids. Again, I'll explain how this all unfolded in a moment.

While here, my mom was a psychologist specializing in children who interacted with hybrids, who provided them with fundamental instruction on human characteristic behavior but were often mislabeled as abductees or contactees. As a hybrid herself, who better to understand these child emissaries whose parents and peers considered them majorly dysfunctional or just plain weird? She was brilliant at what she did.

Just prior to her passing, she developed a unique sleep study platform with electromagnetic sensors built into a clear plastic domed covering, thus eliminating the need for attached sensory wiring that inhibited complete relaxation. The platform floated on water, replicating the sensation of being inside the womb, the most primordial protected environment that rendered amazing data. Now, as a result of this ground breaking study, scientists, psychologists and physicians can delve so much deeper into the phenomena of what really happens during the sleep state and better understand dimentional travel.

As for my dad, he's a well-known and highly respected lobbyist in Washington, D.C. who advocates for full disclosure by the United States Government regarding UFOs and the presence of what Earthlings refer to as extraterrestrials (which, I guess again, would be me). He's also demanding the acknowledgement and reasons for their covert involvement for so many decades and to hold them accountable for the failed galactic treaties that have brought humanity and the planet to this now critical point in time...2012!

But that's not...um...how is it referred to... oh yeah,"the only game in town", for there are countless ancient prophecies that are in harmony with current day scientific theories postulating what's about to happen on Earth and to her inhabitants, both above and below her surface. Yep, you heard me correctly - I said below the surface, but that discussion is for another time.

Now, back to me - my hybrid side appears to be dominant, which encourages my peers at school to tease me repeatedly. When I emerged into this physical body, I just naturally assumed that everyone else came equipped with the same...um... abilities as me; meaning they communicated telepathically, used telekinesis to move objects (I know that one in particular freaked out my grandparents), could transport themselves into other dimensions at will, interact with Beings from other realities, and could foretell certain future events. Normal stuff, right?

Well, my dad was quick to point out that wasn't the way it was for most humans, and so began my education in recognizing when I needed to implement limited Accelerated Human Behavior or AHB, as the psychologists referred to it. I could no longer do what came natural for me and had to consider my audience before engaging in any "special" action or communication. That was hard for me – really hard! To me, it was the equivalent of asking a bird not to fly.

As I was highly advanced by most scholastic standards, I was home tutored. I begged my dad to let me attend school, so I could be around other children with similar attributes. After much debate, he finally gave in and enrolled me at a private school for exceptionally "gifted" children. Unfortunately, even they didn't always get me, and took every opportunity to taunt me about how different I was from them. It was challenging for me to understand the way they felt, because I thought it was so-o-o cool having these abilities; to know something was about to happen and then have it happen, exactly the way you saw it!...but I suppose that could be unsettling, if you weren't used to it. Being able to "hear" their thoughts really caused a lot of alienation; some called me a "witch" or "evil"...so, I didn't have any friends to speak of, except for Bethany...at least for a while, anyway.

Okay, now I'll tell you how I came to choosing my parents and how Bethany was the catalyst for our first introduction. Ready? Here goes: Bethany and I first...um... "met" before I came into human physical form. Let me explain: As an exceptionally elevated psychic who was also able to traverse between dimensions, Bethany was the perfect "playmate" for young future hybrids such as me. Bethany and I had already become inter-dimentional playmates, so when she was scheduled for a sleep study, that presented the perfect opportunity for me to see if I could transport myself back with her to "view" my soon-to-be parents, which were Elizabeth and Stephan.

The fact is, children from all dimensions share a common universal thread with one another – they have a natural curiosity and they love to play.

While it's true, what's considered "play" varies significantly throughout the Universe. For example: Zeta Reticuli offspring enjoy dissecting smaller species. Since they lack emotion, there is no malice either expressed or intended. Their mega-minds hold an unusually high level of inquisitiveness and so need to satiate the need to evaluate and conclude the data found in their...ah..."toys". I know this all sounds a bit macabre, but to them it's just...play.

For me, my mind was my toy; I was, and still am, able to move objects just by pure thought. Great fun, at least I thought it was until I came into this physical reality and began showing off to my human playmates or my grandparents; believing they, too would enjoy this feat of folly, but boy, was I wrong! Earth school was going to be tough, alright.

It was mostly the older kids that messed (is that the right colloquialism "messed"?) with me, constantly criticizing my behavior and comparing it to some old fictional TV character, Mr. Spock I believe was his name, due to my non-emotional, often verbose demeanor, but I'm working on that one, too. As a matter of fact, lately, I've been confronted with an onslaught of varying emotions which I can't, for the life of me, determine their purpose or value. My dad simply laughs and tells me I'll understand it all shortly...something about becoming a young woman...and how I will react biophysically to other humans. I am more than astute in understanding the biologic and physiologic composition of the human body, so I'm unclear as to the vagueness of his reference. (There I go again...need to rephrase...) So, guess I'll just have to wait and see for myself, as he suggested.

Anyway, even though Bethany was part of our little secret, in time she found that she couldn't handle the peer pressure any longer and so...well, she...she broke away from me, even shunned me. I still struggle with that...

Getting back to the timing of my birth and how it relates to the prophecies, well, it goes something like this...it has been prophesized that the end of the Mayan calendar ,which is December 21, 20012 (my birthday), translates into the "End Times" from the human 'Book of Revelations'. Some feel it is the end of the world and that catastrophes will envelop the Earth and mankind will cease to exist.

But I'm here to tell you, that will not happen....at least not the way and to the degree these people who are portraying it, will be. That's why this trip is so paramount. Part of my dad's mission is to locate other hybrids like him and mom, who volunteered to come to Earth from various interplanetary civilization (yes, there are many other cosmic hybrid species roaming the Earth) at this particular time, so as to assist humanity in finally reaching its next evolutionary stage.

When my dad and I journey to Sedona each year, it's a very private time for us; one that's shared only with nature. For this is where I was born. This is where my dad and I can unite with my mom and be a complete family once again.

Oh, I talk with my mother all the time, so does my dad... telepathically, that is. But when we're united in this magical portal of no space, all at the same time...well, you get the picture.

I'm all packed and ready to go, only this time, it means so much more. Why? Two reasons, actually, one; I'd recently been betrayed by my only friend, Bethany, and so I need to distance myself from that event and two: because shortly after we get there...it will be December 21, 2012 – the date of cataclysmic prophecy. Hold onto your hat!

The Hat

Having a daughter like Krystal with such extraordinary psychic abilities, presented certain challenges. Being a hybrid myself, I struggled through my own early years and was, unfortunately, on the receiving end of much ridicule, not to mention cruel and abusive treatment from those who just plain didn't understand.

I was determined to protect Krystal from all that and did everything in my power to surround her with others of like mind, or at least those who'd remain open to consider her unique abilities as a good thing.

Physically, Krystal looked like any other human child with the exception of her eyes...those amazing, piercing blue eyes with her dark auburn hair that she inherited from her mother. A most captivating combination. Her unique eye color is a biogenetic result of her high level psychic abilities.

Aside from that, what truly gave her uniqueness away was her dialogue, which went far beyond that of a normal human child, no matter the age. Krystal began full verbalization by her first birthday and by age two, could speak several languages fluently and compute college level mathematics, which would freak most people out. So I encouraged her to use her advanced telepathic skills to communicate with me whenever we were out in public, thus eliminating the double-takes. Well, most of them, anyway.

My parents were fantastic, stepping in during the early days to help a grieving father and his newborn baby. But as Krystal grew, her telekinetic abilities began developing more fully – and so you can only imagine how my folks, of all people, handled that one.

It was challenging enough for them to adjust and finally admit that their son experienced visitations with his E.T. friends but now, here's their brand new granddaughter who was openly displaying some of her own special talents...

That old expression "The apple doesn't fall far from the tree", would be a great statement by most grandparents, however, they wrestled with their own demons when I was growing up – as a "different kind of kid". So, in reality, I couldn't see them adjusting to yet another high-level hybrid's growing "special talents" - not just yet anyway.

I'll never forget the day I arrived home from work to find my poor, dear mother looking like the proverbial deer caught in the headlights as her little nine- month old granddaughter, Krystal, had apparently opened the refrigerator door and "summoned" her bottle, using her telekinetic ability a la Bewitched style, to where she lain in her Pack 'n Play! God help us all!

Not fully sure, myself of what to expect next from my galactic offspring, how could I risk my mother suffering a complete breakdown or worse! Needless to say, I decided it best for all concerned to make alternate day care arrangements after that. Enough is enough!

I was fortunate to have a great support system after Liz's passing, in particular, Stacy, who not only was a fellow colleague of Liz but, more importantly, her best friend. It was Stacy who took charge immediately after Liz left us all and kept her private practice and sleep studies going so that "kids like us" had someone to talk to about their special abilities and encounters with beings from other worlds and dimensions.

I have to admit however, in spite of Krystal's high functioning intelligence she remained emotionally deplete and needed a tremendous amount of attention and guidance when it came to expressing her feelings and understanding the simplest of actions or, should I say, reactions to normal everyday situations. So, I guided her with great care as her human side was perhaps a bit overshadowed by her hybrid biogenetics.

Even though I was a hybrid myself and understood, quite well, what Krystal was going through, I'm still her Dad and so I needed to find someone who could tutor her in female human behavior. That's where Stacy came in and I was and am most grateful to her for that.

To outsiders, Krystal carried the label of genius, but that's not who she is. She is so much more.

It would not be unusual to hear Krystal chattering away late at night when she's supposed to be sleeping. More than not, I'd go into her room only to find her sitting straight up in bed holding some conversation with Lord knows who. Sometimes, I was able to "see" and "hear" who she was conversing with, but not always.

The normal question and answer exchange would go something like this - "Krystal, who are you talking to tonight?" Her answer would be either "Mommy" or "My friends", which translated into other hybrids. The downside was that these nightly conversations were increasing both in frequency and duration, lasting well into the wee hours of the morning only to render a very cranky two- year old the following day.

Quite frankly, I didn't know what I could do to help her shut if off - that is until the night I heard her yelling "Go away! I don't want to talk anymore!" then it got eerily quiet.

Of course I immediately leapt out of my bed, ran full speed to her room, feet never touched the floor, only to find her sitting upright in bed, covers thrown over her head a la pitched tent style. "Krystal, are you okay, honey?" I asked, stifling the chuckle that so desperately fought to make its way out of my mouth. Just picture it.

Then in typical Krystal fashion she shot back "There Daddy...I did it! Now I can't hear them anymore!" She had figured out, perhaps by default, that if she covered her head, the chatter would stop. Brilliant!

Apparently, by covering her head as she did, she defused or blocked the energy waves that bombarded her normally uncluttered clear channel, especially at night when she was less distracted by other noises or incoming vibrations.

At any rate, the next day, after finally getting a decent night's sleep, I called my good friend, Brad Phillips in Sedona, Arizona to share the latest hilarious incident with my little genius. Funny, when I first met Brad in Sedona, some fifteen years ago during my early days of research, little did I know what a huge role he'd play in my mission to find other hybrids, let along how intimately involved he would become in my personal life.

"Uncle Brad", as he became known to Krystal, was instrumental in keeping it real for her, mostly due to the fact that he always emphasized the need to remain grounded and to keep full focus on this time-space-reality that we'd chosen to be part of - at least for now.

Brad's no nonsense persona left little to the imagination - that he's anything but a regular guy who cuts to the chase and bottoms lines everything! What you see is what you get...well, not quite for you see, he kept his true hybrid identity close to his vest, with the exception of a very few. We are so grateful, Krystal and I, to be two of those exceptions.

After Brad and I had a good laugh reliving the image of Krystal bolted upright with her cuddle blanket securely draped over her little body to shut out the late night conversations, he came up with a great idea.

"Hey, Krystal's birthday is comin' up, how about you buy her a cute little hat that she can place on her head anytime she wants to close off the connection she obviously has with other dimensions?" And so began the tradition of buying hats in all colors, shapes and sizes so Krystal could manage her ever increasing galactic abilities and allow the human part of her emotional and sociological development a chance to flourish.

While I bought the majority of Krystal's ever growing hat collection, it was Uncle Brad who always managed to find the coolest ones to send for each and every one of her birthdays. But I have to tell you, I'd pay good money to be a fly on the wall whenever this rough and tumble, "manly man" Brad would march into a department store or wherever he finds these things, sifting through every chapeau, looking for just the right one for his girly-girl back east. Cracks me up, every time!

Although I preferred to have Krystal tutored by those who knew her, she kept after me to attend a "real school" so she could meet other kids and make some friends. Who could argue with that?

Wearing her hats allowed her to partake in a more traditional educational setting, once I found a prestigious private school that catered to other kids with extremely high IQs, that is.

Krystal loved going to school and made friends easily and quickly. All was going quite well until the year a new teacher arrived and had zero tolerance for the quirky props these special children used to quell their various unique eccentricities, like Krystal wearing a hat.

For some unknown reason, this teacher zeroed in on Krystal and demanded that she remove her hat while in her class. Big mistake! I'm not exactly clear, even to this day the order in which the events unfolded but all I do remember is getting a frantic phone call from the principal at Krystal's school insisting I come to collect my unruly child immediately!

Apparently, Krystal's new teacher was most insistent that she remove her hat even in the school yard during recess. Krystal very politely advised the teacher that she really couldn't do that right then, knowing full well that if provoked enough her "friends" would come to the rescue and assist in responding to any outside hostile threats to her. A sort of galactic mafia, if you will. They take care of their own.

Well, as you can imagine, Krystal's courteous refusal to comply with the demand to remove the hat only enraged the teacher, who then took it upon herself to remove it from her head and tossed it randomly, where it landed in a puddle of muddy water from an early day rainstorm.

What happened next is probably still being talked about. Krystal began reciting events and recounting private conversations, word for word, the teacher had when she was upset at the School Board and the principal regarding her unbending methodology concerning the education of" these spoiled little brats".

Krystal went on to recite the teacher's words further, stating that she thought the parents were being manipulated by their "little darling geniuses" but who cares, because she's getting paid very well for the aggravation and that these maladjusted, weirdo-psychic kids would probably all grown up to be serial killers and, at the very least, a menace to society…

Well, needless to say, the shock of having her most private and unpopular perspective was overheard not only by the children in the playground, but their parents who were in the process of saying goodbye to their little prodigies' as they dropped them off for the school day.

So, that was the end of Krystal's traditional education and the beginning of private tutors.

Andrew

*A*s a lobbyist, I've met a lot of well-known people, from high profile political figures to eccentric philanthropists. Now, the challenge here was that everyone had their own agenda, including me. I learned early on that there are those who feigned support of my desire to end the Truth Embargo but were of suspect motivation regarding their true intention.

Such was the case with billionaire philanthropist Byron Huxley, who learned, through some intelligence source, who I really am and by that I mean my hybrid etiology and Galactic Federation connection. Mr. Huxley pledged his political and financial support alright - but with a major string attached to it. It seemed he was dying of a very rare, inoperable brain tumor and would only help in my lobbying efforts in exchange for a discrete introduction to my hybrid buddies or, at the very least, get him a one-way transport to another planet where his imminent demise would be retarded.

My ultimate decision was easy. I wasn't about to risk further detection, nor would I expose my "friends" and our galactic mission. So, I found myself boldly denying this powerful man his dying wish... literally.

At the risk of sounding like some dime store novel, as a result of that decision, it got a bit dicey for me. For weeks, some of Huxley's goons stayed close on my tail, even followed me to Sedona with my wife Liz in tow but my galactic overseers took care of those who sought to *interfere with our mission. As a matter of fact, not long after that trip, I heard that Byron Huxley had suffered a massive stroke and then died shortly thereafter. Checkmate!*

I must admit, that unfortunate episode didn't deter me, one bit. I was determined to continue my search to secure heavy hitters who'd back my UFO lobbying efforts for full governmental disclosure, more than ever. Especially now, that I knew what was about to happen on the planet... and soon - but more about that later.

There was one prominent person whose audience consistently escaped me. Andrew Bishop, world-renowned nuclear physicist, who not only boasted working alongside some of the greatest minds in nuclear fission rockets and power plants for space, but blazed new trails with his lifelong commitment to prove that we are not alone in the Universe and that UFOs and extraterrestrials were real and had been interacting with our government for decades. We needed to talk.

The 1947 UFO incident in Roswell, New Mexico amused the majority of people, frightened others and piqued the curiosity of a select few. Andrew Bishop was the latter.

With Andrew, it was like someone flipped a switch and so put all his focus on uncovering the long held secrecy behind the UFO cover up. But there was more.

Beyond his courage and wisdom to break with scientific tradition, Andrew was privy to some very unsettling information concerning credible imminent astronomical threats to Earth.

Can you see why getting an audience with this man was so important to me? As it was another necessary piece of the puzzle that I needed in order to fulfill the mission I came here to do. For whatever reason, it just never happened...until...

(Flashback)

Stephan slowly opens the heavy, oversized wooden door that leads into the Senate committee hearing room where renowned nuclear physicist, Andrew Bishop sits fidgeting with his microphone, as he awaits the commencement of the meeting before the Congressional Sub-Committee for Planetary Environmental Issues.

Taking the first available seat in the rear of the already packed room, Stephen is just in time as Andrew Bishop is about to begin his much anticipated dissertation on the yet undeclared intention of the United States Government regarding the forecasted dire astronomical events that hold the portent for global cataclysm.

Stephan can't help but wonder if his colleague has the chutzpa to include the unconfirmed, controversial theories that continue to swirl around the HAARP (High Frequency Active Aural Research) Program, whose well-crafted public relations persona simply identifies it as an investigatory project on the ionosphere, whose goal is to establish whether its properties can be utilized for communications or surveillance purposes. The fact that it's funded by the US Air Force, US Navy, along with the University of Alaska and DARPA (Defense Advanced Research Projects Agency), only increases the level of concern relative to their suspect agenda, which is believed to be a highly covert testing of weather control around the globe. "Control the weather and you control the world".

The repetitive piercing bang of a gavel brings a hush over the crowd, while the meeting is called to order. Stephan lowers his head and chuckles to himself as he spots his old nemesis, Congressman Mansfield, who will be presiding over these proceedings. Stephan mumbles under his breath, *"Fasten your seatbelt, Mansfield. You're in for a ride!"*

Andrew begins:

"I wish to thank Congressman Mansfield, Senate Sub-Committee Chairman Kuperman and the members of the Senate Sub-Committee for Planetary Environmental Issues for this audience.

"I'm going to get right to the point, here gentlemen; Earth is in trouble – and I'm not just talking about global warming. There's something out there, something big that's headed our way and we need to stop hushing this subject up and start formulating a real plan of action, if there is, indeed one to take.

"Let's start with what we *do* know. In 1982, NASA acknowledged by official statement, made by mistake or by purposeful design, of the plausibility of a Planet-X or some other immense mysterious object that's in our solar system and headed our way. What their statement does is confirm the ancient Sumerian pictographs of some 6,000 years ago that spoke of an entity sometimes referred to as 'Nibiru' – which means 'Planet of the Crossing' and how it is purported to come into dangerously close proximity to Earth by 2012.

"But this goes way beyond speculation, as the very next year, 1983, proved the existence of what is believed to be this dark planet with the launch of a satellite called IRAS (Infrared Astronomical Satellite) which determined and confirmed the ominous planet's trajectory was headed towards …Earth!

"It is still undetermined if Nibiru is, in fact, a planet, an asteroid, a comet or a constellation with a cluster of planets in tow. It is, however, believed to be a rogue, celestial object with a questionable orbit, albeit slightly elliptical, that appears to remain in deep space most of the time. It is purported to make its way into our galaxy every 3,600 years or so, thus causing scientists to postulate that it is to blame for certain geologic catastrophes to our planet. Some have dubbed it the 10th planet, with an unprecedented orbit that defies normal planetary predictability.

"If it is an asteroid or comet, it most assuredly will drag space debris in its wake that would have the capability of causing horrific catastrophes on Earth."

Despite Congressman Mansfield's obvious restlessness, most likely the result of the accusatory direction Andrew is headed in, the rest of the panel sits in attentive, silent respect as they allow him to continue, uninterrupted.

"Ancient civilizations such as the Maya, Egyptians and Incas, as well as numerous indigenous peoples such as the Hopi Indians, have kept this cosmic event alive and well in their folklore and mythology. But for the purpose of this meeting, I feel compelled to cite modern day scientists, astronomers and cosmologists, who deftly concur with the ancient prophecy and historical recordings. They also agree that something *big* is out there and headed our way...yet again! Ancient civilizations have documented this event for centuries and so it has been concluded that certain cataclysmic Earth events are directly tied into this phenomenon and can no longer be ignored!

"You know, one of the most disturbing concerns brought about from ancient recordings is that this mysterious planet does not provide much, if any, warning of its imminent arrival, due to its lack of luminescence – it simply becomes more pronounced in the sky – but by then it's too late!"

The committee members eye one another with raised brows and sit a bit taller in their seats in anticipation of Andrew's next outlandish statement. He's been known to be a bit of a grand-stander, engaging in some theatrical emoting, just to make a point, but regardless of the reputation, Andrew Bishop *does* know of what he speaks and has the documentation to back up his words. He's no longer viewed as just another advocacy do-gooder trying to get press coverage and perhaps sell some books. He continues:

"What you have before you, is a 550-page report, prepared by some the greatest minds in the world, who have studied this matter for decades. Some are, admittedly, very healthy skeptics, while others are more scientifically pragmatic and stick strictly with the data. However, all concur that by its very size alone, should it, indeed, even glaze by Earth, would provide an undeterminable gravitational effect, such as to cause the Earth's crust to slide, thus causing our planet to change its axis of rotation, otherwise known as a critical Pole Shift. Think about that for a moment, gentlemen. You need to let that one sink in." Andrew allows a dramatic pause, then adds:

"On December 21, 2012, the Earth will be in exact alignment with the sun and the center of the Milky Way, a galactic event that takes place only once every 25,800 years! This is in direct conjunction with other prophesized astrological events that could prove to be a major turning point for humanity, as we're most emphatically and assuredly moving into unchartered scientific waters.

"Back in 2006, NASA predicted that a massive solar storm, one of the most intense solar events in over fifty years will occur.

"As recent as 2008, NASA's five THEMIS spacecraft discovered that the sun had a decrease in pressure from solar wind, thus causing a huge magnetic bubble to form around our entire solar system, which basically translates into our planet having a dangerously high level of exposure to catastrophic radiation.

"Also in 2008, theoretical physicist, Dr. Michio Kaku, went on a major mainstream media news program and boldly issued an alert stating that "Scientist made a mistake by a factor of 20." In simple layman's terms, he was referring to the miscalculation of the sun's shield that normally flips every eleven years which predictably produces massive radiation that is received by Earth. But scientists erroneously anticipated that the next cycle was going to be quiet.

"Please bear with me as I put this statement into context for you; solar flares are rated in classes: B-Class, C-Class, M-Class and X-Class. Each class is 10-times more powerful than the previous category. X-Class solar flares can be harmful at the very least or lethal at the very worst. It has been dubbed the "Electrical Kill Zone" and with good reason.

"In 2003, Halloween to be more specific, Earth experienced an X-Class Solar storm which caused some major problems with the Earth's magnetic field. Now imagine, if you can, what a Y-Class solar storm could do, for it would be 10-times more destructive!

"Dr. Kaku poignantly emphasized the need to produce redundant systems as when this Y-Class solar storm hits Earth, it would produce volatile radiation that would, most assuredly reduce, or wipe out completely, our communication and weather satellite technologies. Why we'd be forced back to utilizing 20th century vacuum technologies. This event by itself, would, in fact, bring our industrialized global economy to a grinding halt, thrusting us all into third world societies!"

The large rotunda is under siege by Andrew Bishop and he's not about to let up or waste any precious moments with poetic pausing.

"Latest scientific and astrophysics calculations, continue to be alarmed by the discovery, some six years ago, of two major leaks, massive holes 4-times the size of Earth in our magnetosphere that shield us from these types of severe solar storms. These serious solar storms have the capability of disrupting, if not totally disabling satellites and all our major power grids on Earth, perhaps permanently!

"And as if that wasn't enough, geodynamic scientists have definitive proof that the Earth's rotation is slowing down – but why? This deceleration is actually affecting the atomic clock to the point where an 'extra' second was added to accommodate the Earth's slow down. Now, while that doesn't sound like a big deal to most, in fact, it truly is! This slow down directly interacts with Earth's magnetosphere, which controls the very motion of charged particles which ultimately translates into Earth's magnetic poles shifting.

"Clearly, this is alarming, as even minor fluctuations can produce some most unfavorable results. Now, add in the propensity of the approach of a dark mysterious object like this Planet-X – well, I think you're getting my point. The evidence is overwhelming! The potential… let me rephrase…the plausibility to lose 90% of ALL species exceeds being alarmed!"

Andrew pauses for a moment, staring off into nowhere and then, takes in a long, deep breath and begins again, only this time his voice is softer, almost pleading.

"So, here we are in 2012, the year of the prophetic 'End Times' and some thirty years after our own government acknowledged the presence of something *unknown* that could ultimately end life as we've known it and this knowledge STILL remains under 'gag order'.

"Even the average citizen is becoming aware of *'something looming out there'* with the random planetary physical effects evidenced by the unprecedented rash of severe weather patterns, the increase in volcanic eruptions, the numerous tsunamis, not to mention the mystery surrounding the need for Chemtrail aero spraying, but that's for another time. Suspected weather control is the least of our worries right now.

"Gentleman, non-disclosure is unacceptable, if not just plain arrogant! "How dare *any* government withhold such vital information from its people? I'll go one further, on page 232 of the report before you, not only recaps Executive Order # EO12938 instituted by then President William Clinton, but has, in fact, remained open even until this date, 2012.!

"Allowing our government to be able to declare martial law while relinquishing all of our constitutional forms of government, should bring pause to all Americans about why the government, of the people, for the people and supposedly by the people, will have NO SAY, whatsoever and be left in the dark about those specially known threats to our very existence!"

Feeling he's given the committee enough to chew on for now, Andrew brings it on home.

"I see Congressman Mansfield is checking his watch, so I'll wind this up. I'm *not* going away, gentleman and I want to assure you that I have hundreds, if not thousands of credible witnesses, and whistleblowers who are poised and ready to take this matter to its conclusion, which is full disclosure to the American people! We will settle for nothing less!

"It is THEY who have put you in office, trusting and believing that you're commitment to do what's in their best interest and for the highest good for humanity is steadfast and unwavering. You have all been charged with the stewardship to protect the American citizens from ALL types and forms of threat and possible destruction to these United States of America. Gentleman – do your job!"

As Andrew takes a crumpled handkerchief from his sport coat pocket to wipe his moist brow, a thunderous roar of applause explodes throughout the assembly room, while committee members nervously pack up their belongings in an attempt to escape the throng of questions that will surely plague their hasty retreat from the dais.

Stephan, too, decides to cut out of the room while he can and then heads for the parking lot to go home, for he has much to do in preparation for his trip to Sedona with Krystal the following day.

Once out of the building and into the cold fresh air, Stephan briskly walks towards the parking lot, when a voice calls out amid the sea of parked cars that all but obscure the snow covered asphalt of the congressional parking lot. "Stephan! Stephan Wolf!" the voice barks.

Stephan strains his eyes to locate the direction and source of the voice demanding his attention. Much to his shock, the lumbering figure closing in on him is none other than Andrew Bishop, who's awkwardly weaving his way towards his intended target, trench coat and woolen scarf flapping in the bitter cold Washington, D.C. winter wind.

Stephan hastily puts on his gloves to keep his hands from freezing, still looking around to see if perhaps Andrew Bishop is not the voice vying for his notice. How long has it been? Two, no three years since Stephan last ran into Andrew, who was a co-participant in a congressional sub-committee reporting their findings on the effects solar flares and sun storms have on the Earth's magnetic biosphere.

Stephan mentally recalls the brief casual exchange with Andrew: "Mr. Bishop" Stephan began. "Andrew. Please call me Andrew", he generously responded. "I've been following your career and I must say you've done one hell of a job keeping these clowns off balance." he continues letting out a robust laugh.

"It's not been easy, Andrew", Stephan replied with a humbled smile.

"Nonsense! These jackals have no idea who they're dealing with." Andrew quipped back, as he quickly walked past Stephan, headed into yet another important meeting.

Stephan waved in acknowledgement and appreciation as he watched Andrew Bishop disappear behind the oversized wooden doors to the meeting room and chuckled to himself - *and neither do you, Andrew. Neither do you.*

Stephan is quickly brought back to the present when he confirms to himself that Andrew Bishop is, indeed, seeking him out but can't imagine why.

Andrew comes to a complete stop once reaching Stephan's side and then, breathing heavily he leans one hand upon the parked car closest to him as he attempts to catch his breath. Without missing a beat, he wastes no time getting right to the point: "Stephan, if you can find some time this week, or next, I'd like to have a private meeting with you to discuss something of a most urgent and highly sensitive nature."

Stephan's mind is racing as he ponders what could possibly be so important that commands such urgency and secrecy? Whatever the case, Stephan can't believe that he's about to disappoint Andrew Bishop, the man whom he's been trying to meet for years because he's leaving for Sedona, Arizona the next day to celebrate Krystal's twelfth birthday and the Christmas holiday.

When Stephan informs Andrew of his previously arranged plans, Andrew pleads to meet with him that very afternoon. Stephan rolls his eyes and can't believe he's about to deliver yet the second blow, for he has a long awaited, pre-scheduled meeting with Congressman Mansfield and how Andrew, of all people, knows how tough it is to get this man's ear.

While Andrew fully understands, he is beyond impatient for this paramount meeting to take place. Stephen clearly sees his impatience and then jokes, "Unless you want to fly to Sedona and we can meet there?"

Visibly deflated, Andrew searches Stephan's eyes for an alternative and then, sensing there is none, arrogantly remarks, "I just may do that, young man."

The Gift

*B*y the time we reached Sedona, abnormal weather events were already popping up around the world and while Krystal and I knew a whole lot more was about to happen within a few days, if not hours, I needed to do something equally, if not vitally, important that couldn't wait. I had to give Krystal her birthday gift.

I know that sounds bizarre but more than ever Krystal and I needed to take the time to journey to Cathedral Rock to remember and honor her mother's passing and to celebrate her birthday, as we've done these past twelve years. But most imperative was the gift itself, for it was going to provide her with invaluable knowledge that would hopefully eliminate her struggle with her emotional human side, but of more importance, arm her with the critical balance between her genetic duality of hybrid-human.

I purposely waited to present her with this special gift on this particular birthday, as a symbol of another kind of emergence, one that would take her into womanhood and endow her with an important element that was missing from her experience...how she came to be!

Despite all her amazing psychic and prophetic abilities, her hybrid-human genetic makeup shortchanged her ability to connect the dots with certain emotional growth markers. For without them, she'd miss the whole point of her emergence into this physical time, space continuum.

(Flashback)

Not long after their arrival in Sedona, Stephan is surprised at Krystal's willingness to travel to Cathedral Rock, given that they are both highly aware of what is about to happen. He's keenly cognoscente that she possesses the highly intuitive insight to evaluate the dire cataclysms that are about to engulf Earth and all its inhabitants. The question was no longer about these events being the result of uncontrollable cosmic forces, or the diabolical co-creation of the Black OP, all that mattered was that they were here and needed to be dealt with. Krystal's surprisingly calm demeanor speaks volumes about this amazing young lady - his daughter - and how ready she is to begin her true mission as Tiponi, *Child of Importance*.

"Ready, Dad?" Krystal asks with enthusiasm, while reaching for her backpack that's crammed with bottled water and snacks, slipping it over her winter jacket. "I'm good to go, kiddo. Let's hit it!" Stephan replies, grabbing the rental car keys that rest upon the small entry hall table of their leased home.

Pretending he's just remembered something, Stephan slaps his forehead and then spins around to scoop up the festively wrapped present that has been conspicuously placed on the entry hall tile floor by the front door. Obvious that it contains her mysterious gift, Krystal chooses to forgo using her special abilities which would easily allow her to "view" its content. Instead, she plays along, rolling her eyes to the heavens while her father continues his pretense of almost forgetting to bring it along. She chuckles to herself as she ponders - *Who's the real child here?*

Not able to contain how humorous she finds her father's inept acting ability, Krystal lets out a giggle and then takes the lead out the front door, into the melting snowy driveway where their chariot awaits. Simultaneously reaching for their respective car doors, Stephan pauses for a moment to gaze lovingly at his daughter, knowing in his heart that this will be the last time his beautiful Krystal will ever view life in the same way. For her world is about to change in every way possible. But... first things first.

"Whew! It's warmer than I thought" Stephan remarks as he removes his winter parka and throws it onto the back seat. Krystal follows suit, then they're off!

Father and daughter make small talk as they travel the short distance on slushy Sedona roads and easily maneuver the switchback decent off of Highway 89A until they reach their destination, the entrance to Crescent Moon Park, located at the base of Cathedral Rock and adjacent to Red Rock Crossing.

The unusually warm temperature quickly melts what little snow remains on the parking lot asphalt, leaving random white dotted piles of snow having survived only by the grace of the tree-shade. As Stephan and Krystal exit the rental car, they hastily gather up their back packs and the mystery birthday gift. "Whew! It's so warm we should've brought our bathing suits" Stephan mocks as they simultaneously throw their winter jackets over their arms and begin their trek toward the area they affectionately call "the beach".

Without speaking, Krystal leads the way - for she has walked this path many times before with her father - every year, actually, to honor her mother's passing and to celebrate her emergence. A true emotional dichotomy for them both.

Working their way through the tree-lined pathways that wind and bend past familiar landmarks; the natural water slide where children frolic during summer months; the clearing where huge, smooth red rock boulders floor the walkway to a rushing brook that empties into a calm pool of magical liquid below; past the dry creek bed of towering stones of varying shape and size piled one atop the other, deliberately fashioned markers decreeing each visitors' passage through this mystical place - then finally – the beach.

No doubt that many an unsuspecting traveler who has stumbled across this magnificent oasis comprised of slate- grey river rock and red-beige grainy sand, bordered by towering green Ponderosa pine that edge the cool crystal clear waters, stands in reverence as they acknowledge *"We're not in Kansas anymore, Toto"*.

But for Stephan and Krystal, it goes far beyond the awe, for this is the exact spot where a beloved wife and mother left this motley coil called Earth so that her daughter could fulfill her galactic mission.

The reverence is palpable. There they stand, father and daughter in contemplative silence by the shore of the beach, gazing upon the still water, each in their own thought. Stephan, remembering the love of his life, his partner and mother of his amazing daughter, Krystal. *How I wish you were here, Liz, to enjoy this moment…*

Solemnly, Krystal removes the hat her Uncle Brad bought for her birthday - her all important, "coming of age" twelfth birthday, so that she can let in the voices that whisper her name and share their wisdom to this *Child of Importance*.

"Krystal" Stephan begins "I wanted to give you something very special this year to mark your twelfth birthday and didn't know, quite frankly, what I could give you. Then your Mom came to me in a dream and presented me with what she thought would be the perfect gift and I agree…" and with that he reaches into his backpack and pulls out the mystery gift wrapped in soft pink tissue paper, adorned with the same color satin ribbon and hands it to his daughter.

Smiling, Krystal takes the package and, ever so gently, removes the ribbon, then tears away the outer wrapping to reveal a royal blue parka, but not just any parka, for it's the one her mother wore the day of her birth - the day her mother left forever. Her head bows in silence as she inspects every inch of the garment.

Stephan clears his throat, fighting to control the overwhelming emotion that wells up inside, then continues, "Krystal, your Mom wants you to have this, she wants you to put it on so you can *see* and *feel* the events of that day...the day you were born, to fully understand the prophecy surrounding your emergence into physical. But more than that, honey, she wants you to *feel* the love she has for you and how happy she was to have had even those few physical moments alone with you before I arrived and how precious you were...*are*...to her."

Head still bowed, Krystal lets the wrapping and ribbon fall to the ground as she hands her jacket to her father and then places her mother's parka about her tiny frame, embracing the warmth that exudes from within. Walking slowly down to the water's edge, Krystal lowers herself onto a large, flat rock and then closes her eyes and takes in long, deep breath as she readies herself for what is to follow.

An invisible force commands Krystal to open her eyes where the landscape before her blurs as her head whirls into an indistinguishable sight. For a brief moment, a mass of swirling color distorts her vision until all is silent and still, once again. Slightly disoriented, Krystal strains her focus to identify the familiar view of the beach that leads to the water's edge some ten feet from where she sits, but the terrain is suddenly different and covered in snow, lots and lots of snow. *When did it snow? Am I dreaming?*

Krystal's ears begin to ring deafeningly loud, so much so that she's forced to cover them with her hands so as to block out the excruciating, painful noise. Thankfully, within seconds the ringing subsides, revealing what appears to be a conversation between two women. Krystal turns in several directions, in an effort to determine where the voices are coming from, then hears... "My name is Chumana, which means *Snake Maiden* in my Hopi native tongue." The voice continues but is not speaking directly to Krystal, "You carry Tiponi, *Child of Importance* that will be born Solaya, *time of the Winter Solstice*. This Tiponi will be Qaletaqa, *Guardian of the people.*"

Krystal realizes that she's listening to a conversation that happened between her mother and Chumana, some twelve years ago. The conversation continues: "Are you telling me I am pregnant? That I'm going to have a baby around Christmas?" Liz demands from Chumana. "Pregnant, huh? I've got to go and tell Stephan!" Chumana then replies, "Wait! There is more…"

Just as Krystal fully tunes in to the scene before her, it begins to change yet again. Now, Krystal sees a very pregnant Liz some six months later, and she's wearing the infamous blue parka. She observes her mother walking across the Crescent Moon parking lot and then on to a narrow path that leads through the woods, past the babbling brook, and beyond the towering rocks that empty on to the sandy beach…but something is wrong…there's pain – a lot of pain!

As an empath, Krystal feels everything and now bends over holding her own stomach , oblivious to her father who's kneeling by her side, helplessly watching his daughter *experience* her mother's active labor.

Krystal vacillates between being the observer and then, the experiencer. She's part of her mother's every movement, hears her conversations, and then *feels* her mother's pain and emotions – emotions she's never felt before – anxiety and fear!

The flashback continues: *With pains coming every five minutes or less, Liz attempts to stand, only to be overcome with racking pain, forcing her to resume her seated position on the rock by the water's edge. She attempts to use her cell phone to call Stephan for help, but there is no signal available here among the towering rocks.*

The snow is falling in earnest, and so Liz is forced to scout the area for shelter. Panic begins to set in as her contractions now come in rapid succession and with vigorous intent. She spies an area some fifteen yards away that is protected from the elements by thicketed trees. She attempts to head for the haven of the trees but is, yet again, racked with pain so intense that she's brought to her knees.

Krystal falls to her knees, doubled over in pain, completely unaware of her father's presence and how his tears flow freely, tortured as he watches her relive her mother's plight...things that even *he* never realized had happened. The remembering resumes:

The snow beneath Liz is bright red, blood red! – she's hemorrhaging! Liz is suddenly aware of her peril. For but a moment, Liz recalls her encounter with Chumana some six months ago on the this very spot, where she was foretold of mothering a child of special gifts and what a blessed event it will be for the entire world!

Now blind with fear, Liz hadn't noticed the form that stands before her and then, a voice speaks, "Liz, my child...stand and walk with me." It is Chumana "There is nothing to fear my child. Come, the water awaits. Come Elizabeth, there is no time to waste!"

Chumana guides Liz into the depths of the pool of water where, to her shock, it feels warm and soothing. Chumana begins to chant and then speaks, "This child has lived in water since its beginning, shielded from sound and light. Emerging into this world is made easier in the water, especially this water. It is not unfortunate to have your child born into these waters, Elizabeth...it is part of the enormous gift. For your child is Tiponi, One who Leads. This moment has been destined exactly in this way. Allow the help of Mother Gaia...Surrender to All That Is, for this emergence will fulfill a miraculous prophecy brought forth by yours and Stephan's love and Divine purpose. Now, Elisabeth, behold your miracle!"

Krystal lets out a primal yell - then falls eerily silent. Tears stream copiously down her face, she is now back into *this* reality with her devoted father by her side; his own eyes soaked with emotion, for he had no idea his beloved Liz had gone through such an ordeal prior to finding her and his new born child there in the snow covered woods.

With the help of her father, Krystal pulls herself upright and sits back atop the boulder from whence she first began this journey of remembrance. Taking in a deep breath, she wipes the remaining tears from her eyes, then asks "What happened next, Dad...?"

Stephan kneels before his daughter, grasping both hands in his and recounts "I, too, felt your mother's pain that day even though I was several miles away. She wanted to take one more hike by Cathedral Rock. Not sure where she was in the park, I followed my guidance and when I finally found her, you had already been born. Krystal, when I first laid eyes on you, I was so excited, then, as I looked upon your mother's face, I knew things were bad, but I had no idea *how* bad."

Stephan's voice cracks; his emotions almost too much for him to bear as he recalls that moment. Unsure if he can continue, he takes a moment to gather himself, knowing that he's come this far with Krystal's initiation into womanhood, he can't stop now. Drawing his hand from his brow all the way down to his lips, he stutters:

"W-w-when I realized that your M-m-om's physical body was in grave jeopardy, I told her that I would do *everything* possible to get medical help. She g-grabbed my arm and, in a barely audible voice, told me that she knew this was going to happen in this way and that I must be strong for our new baby." *Hold on Stephan…you can do this*, he commands himself.

"Then Chumana appeared and began to explain what your mother couldn't but I refused to listen at first. I even begged Chumana to help. I remember pleading with her that surely *she* could do something… but that was not to be."

Emotionally deplete, Stephan finishes his part of the story: "It wasn't until I looked into your mother's soul through her *amazing* blue eyes, that I saw the light that shone so brightly - was all but gone, ebbing with the very life she once held in her being."

Summoning up the last ounce of his emotional strength, Stephan continues, "As her life's light pulled away, she said, 'I can't say goodbye to you, my love. Let's say…see you soon?' and with that… your mother's body relaxed in my arms, signaling her departure."

Krystal gazed longingly into her father's eyes, wishing she

could speak the words that would ease his pain, but that was not to be, as she was struggling still with her own. Feeling somewhat stronger, Stephan draws up his trembling hand to gently wipe the single tear that remains on Krystal's flushed cheek and whispers:

"Time had all but stopped, as I continued to cradle Mom and you in my arms. When I could, I looked down at you, Krystal, and noticed that you had the same amazing crystal blue eyes that your mother has. Here you were, just minutes old and yet you looked back at me with such calm and peace and empathetic wisdom of my loss…our loss. Your mother and I never did get around to picking a name for you but at that very moment…I knew she would agree…those eyes…those amazing eyes that emitted such light…we would call you Krystal."

Krystal unwittingly reaches into the pocket of her mother's parka and finds a monogrammed hanky with the initials K.E.W. Time stands still as Stephan and Krystal gaze upon the hanky that her mother had made, serendipitously bearing her initials… *Krystal Elizabeth Wolf.*

Every young woman attains her rite of passage into womanhood, one way or another, but Krystal has been blessed with an experience that few others have or will ever know…of how she came to be and exactly how much she is loved.

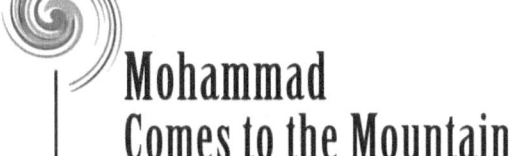

Mohammad
Comes to the Mountain

I *was beyond frustrated that I was unable to meet with Andrew Bishop,*
a man I not only revered but so respected his expansive knowledge
and dedication to uncover the truth relative to the E.T. presence, my
presence, actually – however, it would all have to wait. This was one
disappointment I didn't take lightly but I also realized how important
this trip with Krystal to Sedona was for us both...personally and as
part of our mission.

So, you can imagine my shock when I found a message on my cell
phone from, none other than, Andrew Bishop advising me that he was,
indeed, in Sedona and asked how soon we could meet!

"If the mountain won't come to Muhammad, Muhammad
must go to the mountain".

No, the "mountain" reference wasn't about me...it was about
coming to the magic of Sedona, with its towering, mystical monoliths
and working with cosmic energies that permeate the very air that you
breathe there.

While I knew my reasons were for wanting to hook up with
Andrew, in all honesty I was completely stumped as to HIS reason and
his urgent insistence to meeting with me A.S.AP.! Thank God, that
curiosity was about to be answered...and just in time!

(Flashback)

Within hours, all the major radio and TV stations were reporting the ever increasing outbreaks of unusual weather events and the unprecedented amplification of earthquake and volcanic activity across the globe. Even in Sedona, the small newspapers that normally focus on local news couldn't ignore these calamitous happenings. It appears to all that the dire prophecies have begun.

A misty rain begins to fall as Stephan and Krystal work their way back up the winding switchbacks from Red Rock Crossing in their rental car. Father and daughter ride in contemplated silence in the aftermath of what might have been their last trek to Cathedral Rock, at least for a while.

Krystal is cognizant that she has been given the most precious of gifts for her coming of age, the gift of witnessing the events surrounding her birth and actually experiencing her mother's transition, not just imagining it. But without a doubt, the biggest benefit was being able to *feel* her mother's love for her – a mother who now resides in the realm of the non-physical. For this virtual journey has allowed Krystal to fully bridge the gap between realities but even more overriding is her new comprehension and appreciation regarding the value emotions play while in this human experience. *Now* she gets it!

Stephan has one burning question that he's hesitant to ask of Krystal – *Did your mother suffer during her transition?* Forgetting for but a moment that Krystal wasn't wearing her hat and could clearly *hear* his thoughts, she replies "No Dad. It was very natural and peaceful for her. Just like walking from one room into another."

Stephan looks lovingly over towards his daughter, who

gazes passively out the car's passenger window and can't help but hope that this gift has done its job and that from this point forward they may take the next part of their journey together with renewed purpose and focus. He no longer worries that Krystal's emotional interpretation will be jeopardized by her overpowering hybrid side and is confident that balance has been attained in the biogenetic vehicle that houses her amazing spirit. His heart swells with pride

Realizing how they've been out of contact with the outside world for the better part of three hours, Stephan reaches for his cell phone which he'd deliberately turned off to ensure uninterrupted privacy. Not surprised to find several messages have been left, he listens intently to each one and then suddenly laughs aloud and shouts "No kidding?"

"What?" Krystal asks as she turns toward her father. "What's up?" Caught up in her father's exuberance, she begins to giggle and insists again, "What's going on, Dad?"

"It's Andrew – Andrew Bishop is here…in Sedona! Son of a gun, he did it! He took me up on my offer…"

Knowing Krystal's avid curiosity will prod him to tell her more, Stephan begins to recount the events surrounding his brief encounter with Andrew Bishop in the parking lot of the Congressional Building the day before they left for Sedona and how insistent he was that they meet and that Stephan joking offered that if Andrew really needed to talk to him, perhaps he should board a plane and fly out to Sedona, himself – apparently he did!

"Boy! Given all the chaos that's going on, Andrew must have a damn good reason for doing this now. Guess I'd better call him back to find out why, huh?"

Figuring he'll need all his focus on this chat with Andrew, Stephan pulls the rental car off onto a widened sandy shoulder off of Highway 179 and then places the call. "Hello?" the voice on the other end inquires. "Andrew, it's Stephan – Stephan Wolf. Sorry it's taken so long to get back to you but my daughter and

I ..." Andrew cuts Stephan off and asks where he is right now. When Stephan advises him of his location, Andrew asks if he could meet with him immediately at his hotel, as it's urgent.

Stephan attempts to interject some humor with a sarcastic, "Yeah, I kinda got that impression by the fact that you're here..." and is again cut off mid-sentence by Andrew who's detailing his exact location and asks how soon Stephan can get there.

"Of course", Stephan replies "I'll come right away, but I've got my daughter, Krystal, with me so I'll need to make arrangements ..." Andrew jumps in "Bring her with you!"

Stephan shoots Krystal a questioning glance, her return gaze answers a resounding *Sure!*

"OK, Andrew. We'll be there in ten to fifteen minutes." And with not so much as a goodbye, Andrew hangs up.

Just as Stephan turns the car around to head back towards Andrew's hotel, the rain begins in earnest. Not just a steady rain but torrents of water descend like the monsoons of summer, accompanied with blinding flashes of lightning and deafening thunder that explode like cannons echoing off the mountainous terrain. Krystal asks her father if he is going to divulge her *uniqueness* to Andrew, to which he replies, "No time like the present. In fact it's more a case of...no time for much else, it would seem."

Despite the foul weather, Stephan pulls into the hotel parking lot in record time, all the while straining to see through the pellets of rain his windshield wipers struggle to clear. Luck is on his side as he finds a parking space a quick sprint from the hotel's front door. Krystal and Stephan emerge from the car and dash through four inch puddles of water that have quickly accumulated onto the pitted asphalt and then bound into the hotel lobby, dripping wet. Squeaking wet sneakers announce their arrival to the front desk clerk who lifts his head, then smiles to himself as he watches the duo traverse the tiled floor that lead to the hotel elevators.

Once inside the elevator car, Stephan pushes the button that will take them to the third floor and Andrew's room #317. Once off the elevator, Stephan makes quick note of the wall plaque indicating the direction of Andrew's room. Krystal and Stephan briskly walk the long corridor eyeing each door number until they arrive at Andrew's room. Just as Stephan lifts his hand to knock on the door, it unexpectedly flies open and there stands an anxious Andrew, who graciously greets them with clean, dry hotel towels in hand. "I've been watching for you. Man, this rain is unbelievable! Here, take these to dry yourselves off", Andrew offers. As Krystal and Stephan take off their soaked jackets and sneakers, Andrew performs his own introduction. "You must be Krystal – Andrew Bishop. Nice to meet you... and I understand it's your birthday. Best wishes." Krystal shyly extends a dampened hand in greeting and thanks Andrew for the acknowledgement.

"Krystal, if you'd like, you can watch some TV while your Dad and I talk..." This time, it's Stephan who interrupts Andrew and boldly states, "Andrew, if you don't mind I'd like Krystal to be part of our meeting" and continues with slight trepidation "You see...Krystal...well, she's...she's a hybrid...a high functioning hybrid...the likes of which you've never seen, I'm sure."

To his surprise, Andrew projects a knowing smile and then states, "Stephan, you underestimate me. I've know of your own... how shall I say this...*talents*, for the lack of a better word and also of your late wife's...um... *expertise*. Now, I realize that as a man of science I'm expected to have a conventional skepticism about such things that might be construed as paranormal or unproven but to the contrary...I've had my own, let's say...encounters and know that there *are* Beings, such as yourselves that have walked the Earth for eons of time. It would only follow then, that two hybrid parents, such as you and your deceased wife, Elizabeth, would have a high predisposition of having a hybrid child of extraordinary characteristics. Have I got it right, so far?" Andrew chuckles.

Krystal smiles and demurely takes the cue, "That's correct, Mr. Bishop – in fact you have it exactly right." Stephan is beyond surprised at Krystal's candor and mature demeanor and proud that his daughter has begun to find her confident voice.

"May I offer either of you something to eat? Perhaps a hot drink to warm you? I'd be happy to call room service and then we can get started" however, Stephan and Krystal wave off his polite offering and indicate how they, too, would like to get down to business. Andrew begins:

"Stephan…Krystal…while I'm not 100% sure as to your… um…mission, it is my belief that you're part of some galactic group…shall we say, perhaps connected to the Galactic Federation, and will be instrumental in coordinating, if not orchestrating, some sort of survival plan in the aftermath of the predicted disasters. Am I right?" Stephan and Krystal nod in agreement, but wait for Andrew to finish his questioning before they set out to clarify their roles further. Andrew goes on:

"As you know, I've spent over forty years of my life devoted to not only getting the government to acknowledge the E.T. presence and the existence of UFOs but I've also done a tremendous amount of research and, if I may brag, some pretty diligent detective work regarding governmental interface with extraterrestrials and their joint clandestine scientific experimentation, at enormous risk to the people of this planet.

"It's no secret that I've been focusing my guns on HAARP and the Chemtrail issue. Krystal, are you privy to any of this information, or shall I explain?" Andrew politely inquires. Krystal answers, "Mr. Bishop, while my universal knowledge is quite extensive, some of what you refer to is foreign to me; even though my father has spoken of such things, I would be pleased to hear what you have to share."

"Thank you, and so I shall. Well, Krystal, as you know there are humans, here on Earth who have their own agenda on how this planet should be run and who's going to run it. For reasons of power, control and greed, not to mention biogenetic control of the species-at-large, these people have been creating new ways to alter the natural flow of life…if not its actual creation. Pretty scary stuff!

"Perfect example; Chemtrails have been implemented to disburse specific chemicals into our atmosphere with many intentions; for one, the control of weather. These aerosol sprayings lay down a chemical grid, of sorts, that can be utilized to bounce off Extremely Low Frequency Waves, also known as ELF Waves, into the ionosphere that can render several desired results.

"The fact is, there are natural occurring ELF waves present on Earth that resonate between the surface and the ionosphere and are sometimes initiated by simple lightning strikes. Without going into a lengthy diatribe, it's best that I cut to the chase and discuss what's presently being done today.

"Back in 1994, HAARP, touted simply as a scientific project funded by the US Navy and Air Force to explore the interface between Earth's surface and the ionosphere, officially went online as one of several such operations throughout the world; the United States ended up constructing three sites, with Russia having two such operative sites and the European Union having one known site.

"The United States site consists of forty-eight, of the one hundred eighty that are to be built, seventy-two foot tall antennas that are located approximately two-hundred and sixty miles northeast of Anchorage, Alaska. Simply stated, they have the capability to focus all the radio waves from these antennas into one single beam and bounce it off any part of the grid constructed by the Chemtrail sprayings, thus creating endless environmental applications such as causing floods or even droughts; giving birth to major hurricanes and then directing them at will, and most diabolical of all, causing massive earthquakes and the tsunamis that will most assuredly follow, just by artificially exciting the atmosphere.

"You can see the propensity to have these sites under your

control. *Control the weather and you control the world,* is the popular phrase. So, the problem we're facing at this very moment is we have legitimate transitory bits of nature coupled with the suspect agenda of HAARP, all converging around the same point in time...well, I think you get where I'm going.

"We in a real pickle here. We have extremely credible scientific evidence that something rather big is out there and headed towards Earth; that, all by itself, holds the plausibility of annihilation to all life on the planet, if not the planet itself. Now, as if that weren't bad enough, we have these mad men who are hell bent on ruling the world and in their effort to do so, are completely careless about what scientific missteps may occur, thus threatening mankind's continuation. Their blatant indifference regarding their actions may, in fact, directly cause the destruction of the Earth, without any assistance from whatever cosmic catastrophe that looms ahead, staggers the mind!

"So, what do we do now? Here's what I think...no, what I believe...there is, indeed, an entity such as the Galactic Federation and that Beings throughout this solar system and beyond... and you may be two of them... have joined forces to assist the people of Earth to reach their evolutionary step and be part of the Galactic neighborhood...if we don't kill ourselves first!

"Stephan...Krystal...I want to be part of that assemblage and offer up my scientific expertise ..."

Before Andrew finishes his thought, Krystal turns to her father and whispers *William...Let him come with us to meet with William.*

Stephan pivots back to face Andrew and shares how he, Krystal and Brad Phillips plan to head Up Canyon to Pine Springs to meet with Navajo Elder, William Hodges and together they are to set the true purpose of their mission in motion. Stephan hesitates to share the next bit of information, but then decides it is best to divulge all, if they are to be effective with their intended destiny. For he truly believes it is no coincidence that Andrew has found his way to this group and at this specific time.

"Andrew…there's one more thing that I need to share…or should I say prepare you for…a representative from the Galactic Federation will indeed be present at this meeting, as will an entity that has been my mentor, my guide, since childhood. I call him LUPO, which is Italian for wolf, but I chose that name as he first came to me when I was a small child as a wolf but has the ability to shape-shift into a benevolent Star Being.

"I was told that there would be a Council of Seven that would meet to formulate and then orchestrate a plan to assist humanity in the aftermath of the cataclysmic events that have been prophesized to commence now, in 2012. Well, here we are and now the time has come to take affirmative action and do what we came here to do. It would be an honor to have you as part of this process."

With little more to be said, Stephan shares some final instructions in preparation for their monumental journey Up Canyon the following day. The mood in the hotel room is solemn as each is lost in their own thoughts. The wheels are now in an unstoppable motion and they can only pray that their efforts will not be in vain.

Road Trip

*B*rad took his cue from the escalating catastrophes that were exploding around the globe and took the initiative to obtain an immediate audience with Navajo Elder, William for the very next morning. Time was of the essence and so we had to move… and move quickly!

It was beyond unnerving how many earthquakes, tsunamis and floods were happening simultaneously around the planet with an unending prediction and uncertainty of more to come. Luckily, so far, being in the high desert terrain of Sedona, nothing of note had reached us as yet, and the fact that William's property was on even higher ground was a definite perk to this emergency excursion.

Krystal had grown extremely quiet but knowing her as I did, I knew she was preparing herself, gearing up, as were we all. Andrew insisted upon coming along in Brad's Jeep and I wondered how he'd get back to Phoenix, knowing full well that he'd want to, or more to the point, need to head back to Washington as soon as possible. No time to waste…we'd deal with the logistics of that later.

Having to launch into action so quickly didn't leave much mental space to appreciate what was about to happen. Here we were, a nuclear physicist, a Navajo prophetic, sprinkled with three intergalactic hybrids, attempting to put our collective knowledge and intelligence together with the ultimate intent of choreographing the crucial steps necessary to execute our respective planetary missions. However, Krystal was the one who bore an undefined burden, and yet somehow *remained outwardly detached from the ever increasing insanity.*

During one of our special meetings, Adakor, Magistrate for the Galactic Federation, had revealed to me that I'd be one of a Council of Seven and how we'd be charged into action with our real mission. Always prepared to expect the unexpected, I couldn't for the life of me figure out who the seventh member would be, as I counted off, Krystal, Brad, Andrew, William, his grandson, Daniel, another high functioning psychic, and myself. I couldn't help but ponder…who was number seven?

Unsure of when, or if, we were going to return to Sedona right away, Brad suggested we pack whatever personal and key items that could fit into his jeep and leave the rest behind for…whenever…

It was the "whenever" that brought Krystal and I to look up from our respective packing efforts, lock eyes and telepathically reassure one another that ready or not, here's what we came here to do!

(Flashback)

"Not too much stuff, there young lady! Remember, Uncle Brad's jeep can't hold a lot of extra gear" Stephan reminds his daughter as they prepare for Brad's eminent arrival. While the car Stephan rented from the Phoenix Sky Harbor Airport was so much roomier, they thought it best to take the jeep with its 4-wheel drive, not knowing what type of terrain or weather anomaly they may encounter, which now seemed like a smart move, given the dark, ominous clouds that have already formed above, promising some form of precipitation. Since the jeep's 4-wheeled traction fares well in the snow and ice, as well as the summer monsoon rains that often has the dry creeks overflowing their beds, thus washing out even paved road passage, the jeep is the vehicle of choice.

Evidence of the planetary shift was never more prevalent than with the abnormally warm December temperatures experienced of late, especially here in the high desert country. Wearing only a long sleeved jersey and khaki pants, Krystal stands by the front door and shouts "He's here!" announcing her Uncle's arrival. With that, Stephan gives her a one arm hug as he gestures with the other for her to pick up her belongings and head out the door. "Vamonos, Chiquita!" Stephan calls to his daughter. "Si, Si, Papa!" Krystal quips in return, attempting to keep the mood light, at least for the moment.

Close on Brad's heels, Andrew pulls in directly behind in his rented vehicle, leans out his driver's side window as a warm light rain begins to fall and asks "Where should I park my car? And what's with this weather? Shouldn't this be snow?" Good question. As if what's going on around the planet wasn't bizarre enough, now here was this modern day physicist about to mind meld with a Navajo Elder and all he can ask about is the weather? Stephan and Brad lock eyes and relay an unspoken *God only knows what's going to happen next!*

Stephan starts to load his and Krystal's duffle bags into the jeep when Brad jumps in "Whoa! Hold up there buddy! Not enough room inside." Stephan gives Brad a shrug to indicate "So where, then?" But before Brad can answer, he spots a small trailer hitched to the back of the jeep that is laden with full camping gear. "Brilliant!" Stephan shouts to which Brad responds with a wink "Just in case…" Enough said.

Once Brad and Stephan tie down and secure the last of their belongings and prepare to leave, Stephan automatically heads for his usual shotgun position in the front seat but finds Andrew settled in his spot instead and isn't budging. It doesn't take long for everyone to realize that due to Andrew's large physique it would be far easier for Stephan to stuff his 6' 1" frame next to his daughter in the back seat.

Stephan shrugs his shoulders and then lopes around to the back of the jeep only to find a snickering Brad flipping the driver's seat forward with a thump so as to allow his entry. "Very funny…" Stephan whispers, as he deliberately bumps

Brad's shoulder, causing him to lose balance and fall against the driver's door, all the while displaying the crooked smirk that Stephan has grown to count on in times of question.

Once everyone is inside the jeep with seat belts fastened, this unlikely quartet heads out onto Route 89A north towards Flagstaff, and then continue on to the west to Pine Springs and William. A short way into their drive, Andrew breaks the silence to ask "I assume William knows why we're coming?" Surprisingly, it is Krystal's voice that chirps in first to confirm "He knows...he knows." Stephan reaches over to pat his daughter's knee in approval.

Brad is uncharacteristically quiet as he maneuvers the jeep up the winding switchbacks that lead them out of Sedona and on toward Flagstaff. Stephan can see Brad's eyes in the reflection of the rearview mirror and notices how he's scrutinizing the every changing sky, yet remains intently focused on the twisting the road before him. "Weather's comin' in. Hope it holds off just long enough for us to reach William's."

Silently, one by one, the other passengers' gaze goes skyward to observe the large billowing black clouds that are swiftly traversing across the high desert sky. "Don't usually see that type of cloud formation this time of year. More like the summer monsoon clouds. Whatever they are...can't be good..." Brad's voice trails off and then down shifts the jeep as it clears the final wind of the hilly climb, putting pedal to the metal, causing his riders to lurch back into their seats and states "Hang on!"

Krystal's intuitive mind responds silently... *In more ways than one!*

Daniel

*T*he majority of our drive to Pine Springs was traveled in silence with only an occasional comment from either Andrew or Brad. The small talk had all but ceased and the mood had become more somber. The weather was beyond bizarre with monsoon downpours one minute, only to turn into sleet and then a full blown snowy white out, causing the road to become slick and treacherous with zero visibility. Andrew postulated that due to the numerous earthquakes and volcanoes erupting, causing major chaos and disruption in the normal air currents, there had to be a smorgasbord of weather systems colliding, with the dominant system having precedence, if only for a few moments. As a matter of fact, a major hurricane was bearing down on southeast Florida – and it's the end of December – way past the end of the Atlantic Tropical storm season.

Brad did his best to anticipate the next driving challenge and was skillful at holding the jeep steady throughout the ever changing road conditions and keeping all of us safe. I'd experienced Brad's stealth driving skills once before when he deftly maneuvered us away from one of Byron Huxley's goons who'd been following me, after I'd refused to cooperate with Huxley's request to connect him with other hybrids as a self-preservation effort to stave off his imminent death. So I knew we were in expert hands.

Krystal remained pensive and so I'd reach for her hand every now and then and gave a fatherly squeeze of assurance. Seemed to work.

I know I've said this before, but more than ever I was fully aware of Krystal's accelerated transformation into womanhood...human womanhood. Her dominant hybrid side was finally giving way to her developing human emotions...she was evolving into a true blended being.

(Flashback)

After two hours of white knuckle driving, the weather has temporarily calmed, finally allowing Brad to relax his tight grip on the jeep's steering wheel. The sight of the small green and white sign that read "Welcome to Pine Springs" has everyone releasing a collective sigh of relief, as Brad announces "Well, with luck and the cooperation of the weather, we should be there in about ten minutes, or so. By the way, enjoy the comfort of this paved road because that's about to change", meaning that he'll soon be taking them off-road and over rough terrain to the seclusion of the Navajo village and William's home.

An anticipatory excitement brings the chatter back into the confines of the jeep. Stephan jokingly recounts his first visit to meet William. "Picture this..after ditching one of Huxley's goons who had been following me for a week, Brad drives the jeep off-road onto some the roughest terrain I'd ever seen. He heads us towards this big mountain that sits in the middle of nowhere and then brings the jeep to a sudden stop and who's standing before us, dressed in a short sleeved shirt with gosh darn palm trees all over it, wearing a huge black ten-gallon hat with a large eagle feather sticking out of it, leaning against a white Ford Explorer? William!"

Stephan is in full laughter as he continues "Here's this revered Navajo Elder, a man of ancient wisdom whom Brad had to go to great lengths to convince that we should meet...well, I guess I expected him to appear from out of the ethers in full Native American regalia or something... not decked out like some

Floridian tourist..." And before Stephan can finish his story, there before them stands William, himself, minus the infamous flamboyant shirt, sitting on a handmade rocker on the front porch of his humble home. Gesturing with both hands held upward, William shouts "You made it!" his amazing white teeth glisten against the backdrop of his beautiful dark complexion. "Wasn't easy, either!" Brad answers as he climbs out of the driver's seat and then throws it forward so that Stephan can at last free his six foot frame from the confines of the jeep's backseat.

One by one, they step out of the vehicle that has brought these travelers safely to their destination. While the ride wasn't a particularly long one, nonetheless, it had its share of white-knuckled drama. Before gathering their belongings, introductions are in order and so Brad takes the lead; "William, you remember Stephan? And this is his amazing daughter Krystal...whom I told you about." William's smile broadens even wider, if that's possible, as he steps down off the porch and then unexpectedly pulls Krystal into one of his bear-hug embraces and wishes her a Happy Birthday!

Stephan chuckles and jokingly warns Krystal to "Watch out for William... he can be quite the charmer." William's attention then turns toward Andrew who stands by the passenger side door waiting an introduction. Stephan apologizes for his oversight "Sorry...William, this is Andrew Bishop. I've asked him to join us, if that's alright. You'll know why very soon..."

"Ah, I love intrigue" William quips back with a wink, as he extends his huge hand in greeting. "Welcome Andrew! Krystal, why don't you come on inside and have something warm to drink to take the chill out of your bones. We'll just let the men unload all your gear before the rain starts again." he suggests, all the while his eyes scan the ever darkening sky.

Once inside, William tells Krystal to make herself at home while he puts a kettle to the heat of the stove for tea. Awkwardly, Krystal begins to walk around the small living space of the cabin's great room, taking in all the colorful artifacts and homemade treasures that reside within. In no time at all, she's drawn to the warmth of the fire that blazes in the hearth and plops herself before it, hands extended to receive its bounty. She has decided to leave her hat on for the time being, as she is quite tired and isn't in a receptive mood at the moment. They'll be plenty of time for that.

The front door swings wildly open as a huge gust of wind takes it out of Brad's control, signaling that another storm is fast approaching. Arms laden with gear, Brad asks "Where do you want us to put this stuff?" William shows the men where they'll be bunking in together and where Krystal will have her own private room, of course.

While the logged cabin home is small and only has two bedrooms, it exudes comfort and a safe haven for all who enter. Built by his father and his uncles, some eighty years ago, William takes great pride in maintaining his heritage, which is evidenced by the abundance of ancestral hand-me-downs that are found within its wall. Perched atop a graveled knoll, the oasis boasts the most magnificent panorama of this high desert community that is reserved for the tribal elders, such as William and his father before him .

Once settled in, William invites his guests to sit by the fire to relax, for the days that follow are sure to bring much turmoil. Just then, the front door bangs open and there stands a young man, around sixteen years old, who stumbles into the room, arms are laden with firewood. "Everyone, this young man is my grandson, Daniel. Daniel, go ahead and put the wood by the hearth for later. Thank you."

Once again, introductions are in order and it is only when Krystal's piercing blue eyes meet those of Daniel's do the real sparks fly into the room. Although Daniel is four years older than Krystal, there is a palpable energy exchanged between these young people. A moment of awkwardness is soon replaced with Daniel's query, "Hey! Is anyone else hungry?"

Usually shy, Krystal smiles and pipes up with "Yeah, I am!"

And with that William begins preparations for dinner. Daniel, apparently no stranger to the kitchen, jumps right in to assist his grandfather and then Krystal, yet again, surprises everyone by inquiring if she can help, too.

Stephan chuckles to himself as he watches his once somewhat inhibited daughter engage in and embrace the normal day-to-day activities, such as preparing a meal, that have, until this moment, been of little interest to her. He wonders; *could it be that this sixteen year old boy has awakened Krystal's biogenetic hormonal psyche? Was bound to happen sometime, I guess...*

Then he notices it...where is her hat and when did she take it off? She'd been wearing it more than not these past few days, so the reason for its absence was puzzling.

All during dinner, while the adults make small talk about the unusual weather events, Krystal and Daniel are having an exchange of their own but it has nothing to do with raging hormones or a young girl becoming enamored with an "older" man. It goes far beyond that. Without knowing much about Daniel, as yet, it would appear that he possesses some special abilities himself that seem to rival Krystal's. But she is careful not to divulge her suspicions, at least not yet.

The day has been a long one, and now that the rain and howling winds have subsided, Krystal is the first to retire and so bids everyone goodnight and heads to the privacy of her room. Once inside, Krystal finds herself feeling giddy – *What is this feeling? I can't stop smiling. It has something to do with Daniel... When I'm near him...I feel...funny!* Before she can ponder this new emotion any further, there's a gentle knock on her door. "Come in" she offers. As Stephan enters the room to say a private good night, he's taken aback by an immense glow that surrounds his daughter's form. For sure, something has changed within her. He assists Krystal as she climbs under the covers, bends down, kisses her gently on the forehead and then begins to leave the room. Krystal calls out to her father and begins to speak of her fears of how she's not worthy to take on such a powerful position that's about to be given her by the Federation. Stephan does his fatherly best to encourage her dialog, as he has many questions himself. But he's also keenly aware of how spent she is and decides that his own questions can wait until tomorrow.

Being so tuned into her father, Krystal knows that he has more to ask of her and she wants to answer but fatigue wins out, so she dons her hat and in no time drifts off into a deep slumber.

LUPO'S Reveal

*T*he cataclysmic events had begun with the promise of even more about to unfold, so I knew it was just a matter of time before Lupo and I were once again having one of our little chats.

I was also becoming somewhat concerned about Krystal's recent inability to control her psychic downloads, which were generally contained by simply putting on one of her hats. But now, with all the calamities simultaneously exploding around the planet, she was literally being bombarded by unparalleled energies from all directions. Poor kid!

From the moment we were chosen as galactic evolutionary emissaries, Krystal and I have known that something big was destined to occur here on Earth and so we shared an unwavering responsibility relative to our individual roles in helping humanity stave off, or more likely, recover from what was about to happen. But for Krystal, this was her destiny to be one of many who'd lead the way towards Earth's rejuvenation and humanity's final evolution. Big job for such a young girl, hybrid or not.

Even though we were preoccupied with our soon to occur historic get-together the Federation referred to as the "Council of Seven", we remained cognizant of the plague of earthquakes, floods, fires and volcanic events that continued to increase by the hour around the globe. And as if that wasn't enough, electronic communications had been severely compromised and all but ceased due to the dubious breakdown *of our satellite systems, causing world panic, as no one knew for sure, what was happening, when, how, or why.*

I couldn't help but wonder – would things reach the dire epic proportions as prophesized, or did WE have it within our power to alter the course of Earth's potential annihilation and the end of human civilization?

I was about to find out.

(Flashback)

Subsiding rains give way to clearing skies just in time to allow a glimpse of the winter sun as it quickly sets behind a mesa off in the distance. Krystal can no longer stifle the yawn that betrays her desire to remain awake; and so, she bids her father and the rest a good night as they sit entranced around the blazing fire that William has built in his rustic quarry- stoned fireplace.

As Krystal makes her way down the short hallway toward the comfort of the guestroom bed which William has lovingly prepared for her, Stephan excuses himself and follows closely behind, wishing to spend a moment alone with his daughter. Once inside the cozy bedroom, Stephan edges the door to close, leaving it slightly ajar and then gingerly makes his way to the twin bed which now holds his precious daughter. His towering body slowly bends down, allowing access to kiss her forehead, all the while adjusting the handmade quilt about her neck, keeping out the nightly chill that permeates the unheated room.

As Stephan begins his exit, Krystal unexpectedly bolts upright in bed to say the words she's compelled to utter, "Dad!" she almost shouts, stopping Stephan dead in his tracks. "What, Krystal? Are you okay..?"

"Yeah, I'm fine…it's just…I just…" Realizing that his daughter is untypically struggling for words, he tenderly moves his way back to her bedside, then lowers himself to sit next to her, taking her hand in his and begins, "I know, Krystal...I know. Our lives and our world as we have known it, are about to change..." But before Stephan can offer further comfort, Krystal takes both of her father's hands in hers, then states, "It's not what I know is about to occur that frightens me, Dad...it's what I *don't* know. There's something...something even *I* can't seem to access...and I'm scared!"

Seeing her eyes moist with the emotions of a child, Stephan is reminded how his special daughter, this Child of Importance is *still* just that, a child...and that part of her genetic makeup is struggling with the assignment placed upon her.

While Krystal and her father are well versed on their Universal call to service, the unknown wild card has exposed raw nerve, allowing uncertainty to creep into their otherwise unwavering commitment to carry out their mission to its conclusion. They've never even considered an alternate ending...or perhaps failure.

Stephan holds Krystal close to him, kissing the top of her wavy chestnut colored hair and then, ever so slowly, lowers his face so that his eyes make direct contact with hers and declares how proud his is to be her father; And how raising her, albeit as a single dad, in his mind, *is* the single most important role of his life!

"Krystal, I'd sell my human soul to have things easier for you, we both signed on for this gig and need to see it through. Your mother and I both knew that you would be such a big part of not only our lives, but to the whole world! We can't quit now. We *must* go on..."

A lump forms in Stephan's throat that threatens his composure and so decides to end the conversation where it is. He knows how Krystal feels and of her full awareness of his loving devotion and how he'd go to the ends of the Earth and beyond to protect her. With that, Krystal returns a long embrace and within moments, she falls into a deep and peaceful slumber, for it has all been said, for now.

Assured that his daughter has drifted off into some peaceful realm, hopefully disconnected from the tribulations of this reality, Stephan exits the bedroom, stopping one last time to look back upon his sleeping child, and then wipes away a single tear that betrays his otherwise stoic bravado.

With heavy heart, Stephan ambles his way back into the living room where Andrew, Brad, Daniel and William sit in silence, each lost in their own thoughts, as they gaze blankly into the ebbing fire that crackled and roared only moments before.

"Krystal asleep?" Brad asks with genuine concern. "Yep, she's finally asleep" Stephan sighs, as the weariness from the day's events have finally caught up with him, as well. And yet, while his body longs for rest, he unexpectedly announces that he's going to take a short walk around the property before retiring. "Want company?" Brad offers, all the while hoping the answer will be in the negative, for his own exhaustion has hit an all time high. He knows his friend is struggling, not just with the events that are about to unfold but more with his fatherly concerns. Tiponi or not, in their dominant human minds, Krystal is *still* only twelve years old.

"By the way", Brad continues, "I've noticed Krystal's been wearing her hat most of the time, lately, that is, with the exception of dinner. Just though you should know..." "Should I be concerned?" Stephan pleads to Brad who diplomatically responds with "Naaw, I just think she's shutting things out as long as she can. Can't say as I blame her, either" and with that, Brad is next to turn in. In the background Andrew, William and Daniel mutter something similar under their collective breath, then follow suit.

William offers a flashlight to Stephan for his walk, but he refuses, stating the light of the near full moon that has broken through the swift moving clouds will be enough to light his way. Grabbing his parka that's lying across a small birch wood chair, positioned like a sentry by the front door, Stephan steps out into the night.

Once outside, the surprising evening chill forces Stephan

to quickly don his jacket, pulling the zipper all the way up to where the neckline stands firm against his lower chin. Just as anticipated, the light from the moon illuminates the terrain, allowing an easy choice of paths to walk in either direction.

Not far from the house lies a cluster of rocks that form a mini-mesa and beckon Stephan's presence. As he walks toward his destination, he's keenly aware that the critters of the night are fully awake and within their divine natural right to roam this land without restraint. It is their time now, making Stephan the intruder in their domain.

Having made his way to the rocks without incident, Stephan is mindful of where he sits, taking respectful heed of those creatures that hibernate by day among the cracks and crevasses of this stone haven. Time becomes irrelevant as Stephan gazes skyward, following the faded outline of the Milky Way as it cuts its clear path across the desert sky.

Once again, the snapping twigs and rustling brush keep Stephan alert and present to his nightly position upon the desert floor.

Then it begins...ohhhmmm...ohhhmmm...OHHMMM... louder and louder, the welcoming, familiar vibrations rise as they herald only one thing...LUPO!

Then, just as has been in the past, ever since he was that small three-year old on the hillside farm in Italy, the lone wolf with his magnificent big yellow eyes emerges from out of the low lying brush, out of the darkness of night and into full view; illuminated from of a distant source millions of miles from Earth. And so, as has been the tradition, the large grey wolf bumps his head against Stephan's form in greeting, quickly shape-shifting into the hybrid form of the *Visitor*.

Being somewhat versed on human colloquialisms, Lupo makes an attempt at Earth humor "You ring?" Stephan laughs aloud, then answers mockingly, "The phrase is... 'You rang?' and yes, Lupo, I hoped to have an audience with you." Lupo reminds Stephan of his promise to him... "I'm only a thought away." Stephan chuckles, nodding his head in light agreement as he remembers that very vow professed to him so long ago.

Stephan begins to speak of his concerns, "Lupo, I'm unsure right now. I mean...um..." Lupo interrupts, saving Stephan's struggle and recounts how he can read his mind that presents itself as a complete energetic block of thought to him, which is then translated and evaluated.

Stephan, there is much to say, so I will talk and you will listen." Stephan chuckles again. "So, what's new with that process?" Ignoring the sarcasm, Lupo gets right to the point:

LUPO: *Stephan, the time of great change is upon Earth and its people, impacting your neighboring planets and even farther out into the entire galaxy. There is a saying I will paraphrase from one of Earth's ancient writings, the Emerald Tablet, which states, 'As above, so below'. More accurately translated it says:*

True, without falsehood, certain and most true, that which is above is the same as that which is below, and that which is below is the same as that which is above, for the performance of miracles of the One Thing."

Humans... let me rephrase... arrogant humans dispassionately ignore the existence, let alone the plausibility of other intelligent beings cohabitating in what is perceived as their time, space continuum and so falsely believe they, alone, are in control of all that surrounds them. They care not for others, or their right to personal sovereignty for their solitary agenda is self-preservation, greed and control.

You have many great minds of science, as well as the Native American descendants, whose ancestors are the true stewards of the Earth and are joined into a harmonic communal intention to save your planet, which is good...very good, indeed. However, the data they conclude as so, is incomplete and partially inaccurate and so the conclusions drawn remain flawed at their premise.

The lack of knowledge that dimensional laws impart upon one realm to another are a vital missing element to the Universal laws of creation and action. It is this omitted knowledge that keeps humanity in bondage and away from that which is sought. What is about to occur is not catastrophic cosmic punishment but rather the natural order of things. But take heed; there are human generated contaminants and catastrophic devices that are nonetheless threatening to Earth's continuance.

I will confirm, there is now, as has been so for many millenniums, secret, covert and deliberate interference from dark energies whose vile agenda and intentional debilitating mind control have produced severe negative reactions and consequences in response to those actions.

These destructive procedures have interfered greatly with the natural order and so it is that those who feared such negative response from more benevolent entities, have, in fact, been the direct cause of that which they fear most. Are you following me? Just nod.

Good, I shall continue. While they are, in comparison, few in their numbers, even so have gone ungoverned with their acts of war and disruption, much to the concern of the Galactic Federation and its members. And so it is that the Federation may now intervene and assist in the efforts to defuse and defend any further destruction brought about by these few. I must advise, however, that certain cosmic catastrophes are unavoidable and will be unfortunate in their occurrence. The Federation and other benevolent Star Beings are in chorus to prohibit and stop that which is stoppable. The rest will unfold, as interference is not possible.

Some Earth changes will be felt immediately by the quakes and floods that will result from unpredictable forces and uncharted cosmic events. Again, unfortunate. Once these have subsided, in linear time it will take three Earth days; the remaining alterations on your planet will unfold more slowly, as man's response to these matters will also be relevant and part of the equation.

There is no one source or type of Being that can accurately calculate the level of destruction, salvage or even renewal that will take place. Only the Creator has that knowledge and yet, may *choose to see how the species respond and participate in their own salvation.*

Many walk and have walked the Earth as Her steward, preserving Her gentle spirit and awakened consciousness. Just as many have been designated teachers, while others are warriors. A precarious balance, at best. You and others like you, Liz, Brad and now Krystal, have accepted your mission to be part of this evolutionary process that is unique unto this planet and at this time. Who you are and where you come from will be fully revealed soon. Your evolutionary history has been of major distortion and totally inaccurate, conceived by those who wish to control the masses for their own greed and power. That will all end!

Stephan, I have more to share with you that pertain only to you. You have performed well. The members of the Federation wish to commend your dedicated actions, as do the Galactic civilizations-at-large, which owe and express much gratitude. Your steadfast focus of service is unwavering and you've displayed immense courage and sound judgment as you carried out your specific part of the mission. Well done!

You are complete now, Stephan. What has been required of you is finished; And so it is time to stand aside so as to allow the next force to implement their assignment. Upon my specific request, The Federation granted me the high honor to act as your liaison, beginning as early as your third Earth year, and so allowed me access to that which I hold most dear. While it is not customary or within Universal or Galactic protocol to mentor one of my own, an exception was considered, evaluated, and then allowed.

Being your mentor, tutor, guide and advisor and being part of your mission was an honor that was bestowed upon me, upon us both, for nowhere else throughout the history of the Galactic Federation, have those of the same genetic code been granted such a specific request. I am proud to call you, son!"

Council of Seven

*O*ur impromptu meeting at William's had a major impact on us all, in more ways than one. It went beyond the melding of Andrew's scientific data with the ancient prophetic wisdom that William shared, and only re-enforced our collective determination to do whatever it took to get through the next few days, and hopefully beyond, but there was more to it. For unbeknownst to any of us, it became the moment of truth for Krystal...as it marked her emergence as a bona fide member of the Galactic Federation; and one of the most profound experiences of my journey with her, thus far.

As a fellow Earthling, with all the cataclysms happening simultaneously, I couldn't have been more concerned. And yet, as a father...I couldn't have been more proud!

(Flashback)

The dawning of the second day of planetary catastrophe found Stephan, Krystal, Brad and Andrew up and about early in anxious anticipation of their planned meeting. William and Daniel busied themselves by preparing a light breakfast for their guests, keeping in mind that appetites were going to be sparse, with nervous expectation being the order of the day.

As Daniel pours coffee, William butters slices of homemade cornbread, courtesy of a neighboring tribal member's wife. As the men sit in contemplative silence, Krystal is the last to emerge from her room, fully dressed, hat in place. Daniel's face illuminates, then speaks "Hey, mornin' Krystal. Would you like some juice…or…um …do you drink coffee?" Krystal fumbles her response "Um…sure…c-c-coffee is fine. Thanks."

Brad shoots Stephan a raised eyebrow which is returned with a knowing wink. For the moment, everything horrific is forgotten as all witness the awkward flirting of the young. Like a breath of fresh air, the room is instantly filled with hope and promise of tomorrow…tomorrow… Then, just like a popped balloon, the room deflates in collective wonder…will there even *be* a tomorrow?

The talk turns to the plan for the day. Glancing through his kitchen window, William cautiously observes the thickening clouds that threaten deluge within the hour. "I think it best that we take the horses today. Can't risk either Brad's Jeep or my SUV getting stuck in the mud." Krystal nervously adds "But I've never ridden a horse, so I'm not sure…" Daniel pipes in with a big dimpled grin "It's no big thing. Besides these horses know every inch of this land so all you have to do is hold on and enjoy the ride. I'll be right there if you get into any…um…" Before he can finish his thought, William, walks over to Daniel and then places a grandfatherly hand on his shoulder and interrupts "Krystal, Daniel is right. These horses, like most animals, enjoy being in cooperation with man, so all you have to do is let them know you honor and respect them and they will respond in kind." Krystal looks deep into William's eyes, sharing an unspoken exchange. Now fully comfortable with the decided mode of transportation, Krystal joins the others at the kitchen table.

Apparently, it hasn't crossed anyone's mind as to whether or not Andrew has ever mounted a horse, so they missed his *deer in the headlights* expression when it was suggested they ride instead of drive to their destination. Being a man of pride,

Andrew stoically excuses himself from the breakfast table, then walks out onto the front porch where he inhales deeply, silently mustering the courage to elevate himself some eleven feet off the ground and be at the mercy of some twelve hundred pound, four legged animal. *I'd rather face Congress in a heated debate than do this*, he thinks to himself.

With breakfast over, William and Daniel head out to the barn to tack the horses they'll use for their journey. The others gather up their warm jackets, hats and gloves, then head out to the barn as well. Once inside, the sights and smells of the stable are surprisingly calming as one by one the prepared horses are matched up with their intended rider. William provides some quick riding tips, but mostly reassures his friends how these horses are not some wild mustangs that will bolt off into the desert with them flailing helplessly on their backs. Andrew mumbles *God, I certainly hope not!*

Andrew's fears are somewhat diminished when he sees the horse that has been chosen for him; a black and white seven year old Gypsy Vanner named Lucy, who's normally used for hauling and working around the property. *Seems tame enough*, Andrew convinces himself, as several hands provide the necessary aid to place him securely atop his horse.

With everyone comfortably saddled up, the group begins their short trek, taking it slow and easy. William takes the lead, followed by Stephan, Andrew, Brad, and Krystal, with Daniel bringing up the rear. The way is fraught with displaced tree branches, tumbleweeds and rocks. The muddied terrain confirms William's assessment that the vehicles would surely get caught up in the sloppy landscape. It's a good call.

Rumbles of thunder are present in the distance, causing William to step up the group's pace. Daniel reminds Krystal to plant her feet toes up, heels down into the stirrups so as to provide a more controlled ride, especially during a trot. Krystal complies with a smile, actually enjoying this equestrian outing, forgetting for the moment, how they'll soon be discussing the planet's immediate peril in some remote hidden sanctum, with Stephan being the only one privy that they'll be a seventh member joining them, albeit that person's identity remains unknown, even to him.

Not long into the ride, there before them stands a mountain of solid rock, which is their ultimate destination and the exact spot where Stephan encountered William for the first time. Stephan smiles to himself as he recalls how they gained entry into this looming formation and is intrigued to see how the others will respond to the whole process, especially Andrew. After dismounting, the novice riders are shown the best way to secure their reins on nearby branches.

The moment of truth has arrived and just as before, William summons his group closer to the mountain's base and then asks "If you're all ready...please follow me inside." As everyone moves closer to William, Andrew nervously scans the area for an entrance, but all he sees is solid rock before him. And then William begins ...

With both hands outstretched skyward, William begins a soft melodious chant with Daniel echoing his song. Boisterous claps of thunder herald the arrival of the storm that has been brewing all morning. As William's chanting increases in volume the rain begins to fall, seeming to match his escalating tempo.

Hypnotically entranced in the mantra's rhythm, no one pays notice to the gentle white mist that now envelopes the group, completely obliterating the solid mass that once stood before them. When William's singing subsides, all become aware that they have been mystically transported into the mountain's interior and find themselves surrounded by images etched upon its walls, depicting life of a civilization long since gone.

In wonderment, Andrew's scientific mind considers their transference into the interior of the mountain. *Is it mass hypnosis? Or is this simply a holographic projection?* His questions are put aside for the time being as he, too, begins to explore the intriguing cavernous interior. With great interest, Andrew formulates his own interpretation of the petroglyphs and begins to render a seemingly plausible story that would suggest there was an undeniable interaction with off-planet entities and the indigenous people of that time.

Even though William, Daniel, Stephan and Brad have all been in this magical place before, they can't help but remain in awe of its meaning. Krystal's focus is drawn to several geometric designs and so perceptively voices "These are *exactly* the same type of formations and designs as some of the crop circles that have been discovered around the world! Remember the news report about the three Bolivian children who claim to have decoded the circles meaning? It appears they may be right...for these symbols, when put in proper order, seem to tell the story of how life began here on Earth. Separately, they are nothing more than beautiful geometric images, but when put into proper sequence, make known the secrets of the Universe." William and Stephan telepathically communicate their unified agreement.

"*Someone* knew we were coming..." Andrew remarks, while gesturing toward the blazing fire pit surrounded by Native American handmade blankets, which beckon to be sat upon. As the group makes their way over to sit by the fire, a low vibrating hum begins to fill the cavernous enclosure. The sound, while familiar to Stephan, is foreign to the others and so they look around in trepidation as they attempt to figure out what it all means.

Their question is quickly answered by Adakor's materialization before their very eyes. Once fully emerged, he joins the group by the fire. *Ah, so it is Adakor who completes the Council of Seven,* Stephan quietly concludes to himself and then speaks: "Welcome Adakor. I believe you know everyone here, with a few exceptions." Not waiting for Stephan's formal introductions, Adakor scans the group then offers "You are Andrew Bishop? I know of your...um...efforts on behalf of your Earth. It is good to be in your presence." Not being privy to the rules of proper galactic protocol, or even if there *is* one, Andrew bows in respect and mumbles a weak *Thank you*.

Adakor turns his attention toward Daniel "You are Daniel. Daniel, grandson of William...you have much yet to offer. For you too, are a *Destined One*. It is good to be in your presence, as well." Daniel nods sheepishly. Adakor adds: "Humility is a good trait. Hold on to it."

Without further hesitation, Adakor moves his gaze to meet that of Krystal, who sits tall, awaiting her turn. "Ah, Krystal" Adakor speaks, almost reverently. "Progeny of Stephan and Liz. The one referred to as *Tiponi*. It is, indeed, an honor to be in your presence."

Krystal is shocked to feel the heated blush that comes over her face. Other than her father and her Uncle Brad, no one has ever placed such emphasis on her importance, so she's surprised that her emotional human side has taken precedence in this particular moment.

With the introductions complete, Adakor begins:

"This gathering is historic, not just here on your Earth, but throughout our shared solar system; for it represents an unprecedented comingling of species whose focus and intent has common purpose – evolutionary survival. We are but a handful of the *chosen ones* – for some, their mission is that of warrior, seeking truth where none has been, while others champion Earth's evolutionary future. All present, are here to compare knowledge in our specific areas, with the unified intention to help change the course and destiny of this planet and its people and bring them fully into their rightful place in their evolutionary journey."

William interjects: "Adakor, with your permission...the Navajo, have a long lineage of communication with those we call the *sky gods* - modern man refers to them...*you*...as extraterrestrials or Star Beings. Contact has been occurring since the beginning of recorded time as is evidenced by these wall drawings. Communicating with those so distant from Mother Earth provided challenges and yet The Wise Ones intuitively knew that sound and light were too slow to reach such vast distances and so employed thought transmission to call upon those gods.

"It is our belief that each Native American tribe has its own extra-terrestrial race or ancestry. The oral traditions of the Navajo refer to them as Star Nations and prophetically warn of the End Times, also known as The Great Purification. It is now time for the old world to give way to the new; and for people of all walks of life to live in one spiritual harmony and abide by the natural laws of the Universe.

"While the Hopi and Navajo tribes to have long held differences between nations, one thing is agreed upon – there *will* be an astronomical event of such magnitude that will cause the waters to flow upstream instead of down and the sun to rise in the west and set in the east, forever changing Gaia and Her people.

"Navajo elders who could not write passed down this ancient wisdom in the form of chants so it would be remembered. Daniel and I intoned such a song so as to allow entrance to this dimensional space for our gathering.

"Prophecy states that there will be two signs announcing the New Spirit. The first sign will be a *Nine Pointed Star*, as the number nine symbolizes the highest unity, and that it *must come from the east*. The second sign talks about the coming of a great chief from the east, wearing a headdress with twelve feathers, symbolically representing the twelve great principles the Creator will bring to mankind, offering to bring all people together in understanding and love.

"Mother Gaia is dying and has many grave threats upon Her. As ancient stewards of the Earth the Navajo, along with all other Native American Nations, stand in ready to help usher in a new life, once the old one has been destroyed. It is not out of fright that we speak of such things, but in preparation of that which is to come and that which is to follow, that we offer our knowledge and wisdom.

"The natural ways of the land *must* be restored if we are to survive what our ancestors did not. We *must* change our ways and be prepared to embrace a new way of living. All the signs are there, the answers are clear…the time for action is now!"

Andrew nods in agreement as William completes his words and then speaks: "You know… science has long held a bad reputation for always disputing ancient prophecy when in fact, most prophecy can be scientifically validated and supported. Did you know that? Let me explain, if I may – while there just isn't enough time for me to share all that I know, let it be enough for me to interject some facts, as we currently know them to be. .."

Taking in a long breath, Andrew continues passionately, "We now know that there is a lot more going on in our solar system then officially acknowledged by world governments and their secret operations. While I question modern man's reluctance to share what the ancient cultures of the world have held in belief for eons of time, the fact remains…there IS something big out there, headed our way, there ARE governments preparing for an apocalyptic event and we DO need to take an active role in our destiny! Whether or not we're successful is another story, but to do nothing at all, is completely unacceptable and just plain suicidal!

"Astronomers and scientists agree that there is a cyclic timing of a so-called 'Planet of the Crossing' that has the potential to cause catastrophic damage to our planet. We're already experiencing massive floods, earthquakes, even volcanic eruptions, whose direct cause remains unknown, at least some of it. Again, I'll explain: It's no longer a secret that The United States, along with several other countries have been tampering with Mother Nature in their efforts to control the weather, predominantly for military reasons, but also in aid for specific corporate monopolization.

"Everyone is aware of the increased Chemtrail sprayings of late and how HAARP publicity gives the impression that it's mainly an academic project with the goal of changing the ionosphere to improve communications for our own good, but are actually in cahoots with an organization referred to as the Black Op with a more diabolical agenda.

"Simply stated, I'm just as concerned that they may choose to give the upper atmosphere a big zap with its steerable electromagnetic beam and wait to see what happens next, because, quite frankly even they don't know exactly what may occur. Should HAARP attempt one of its tests now, with an already compromised atmosphere…well, the dangers here are obvious. They're playing with fire AND our lives!"

Not missing a beat, Andrew adds, "Back in 2009, NASA issued a report quantifying the effects that extreme solar eruptions would have on our planet and was seeking ways to prevent communication and other technological damage from this extreme space weather. So you see, our problems are no longer solitary in focus.

"I plan to return to Washington, if I can get there, as soon as possible to evaluate the situation with my colleagues and can only hope that we'll find some solutions as to what can be controlled. While I'm a man of science, I am also a human being with a spirit. Yes, I admit it, I have a strong….let's say… curiosity about what cannot yet be proven scientifically. While I was raised within traditional religious parameters, I always liked to consider a wide range of possibilities, so it would naturally follow that I'd find quantum and nuclear physics so appealing.

"Now, here I am in the company of hybrids…um …sorry Star Beings, a revered Navajo Elder and his amazing grandson and you, Adakor, a member of the Galactic Federation…well, at the risk of appearing, pardon the pun, star struck, my whole world and the perception of what I thought was real has changed dramatically! "

Andrew pauses and then closes his final thoughts, almost in a whisper, "As a boy I dreamed of such things, and now… to know they *are* real…well, it breathes hope of better things to come, if we can make it through all this, that is…"

A contemplative lull washes over the group, as each one tries to process the parallel warnings of science and prophecy and how ironic it is that both have simultaneously reached this critical point at the same time.

Adakor speaks: "Brad, you have performed well in your clandestine mission as a human researcher and investigator, holding your hybrid identity in restriction for Earth decades. Convincing those who are cosmically asleep of our existence, your existence actually, with the intention of paving the way for optimal communication between the species has produced many challenges for you – they have not gone unnoticed."

He continues: "Stephan, your mission has been most complex. Your interface as a young human with those members of your Star family caused you much consternation from those who feared what they failed to understand. Even now, those who have great knowledge remain unsure of our existence and our role in their evolutionary process. It is only due to the planetary distress of these past few days that mass consciousness reaches for assistance from those they hope may alter their fate. *Such a peculiar species.*

"As your courageous participation in this mission is all but complete, I am most pleased that you now hold the knowledge of your true etiology and the revelation that the entity you refer to as 'Lupo' is in fact your sire." Everyone but Brad is astonished with this information. While the others sit dumbfounded, Stephan and Brad lock eyes in knowing affirmation.

Krystal breaks the mood with an unwitting attempt at humor "So, let me get this straight...I have a wolf for a grandfather?" The cavern fills with riotous laughter, which is a welcome relief from the somber discussions.

Adakor speaks again: "Krystal, it pleases us to see how you're progressing with your human elements. I would ask that you remove your hat so that you may clearly receive all that I am about to pronounce."

A more somber atmosphere permeates the fireside as Krystal

silently slips her hat from her head and waits for Adakor to continue: "Krystal, Child of Importance, your true mission has just begun. In your twelve short years here on Earth, you've struggled with your duality, dominant hybrid and submissive human. It was compulsory to reach a more blended state so that you could appropriately relate to the plight of humanity in an effort to efficiently evaluate how best to lead them into the next level of their progressive evolution. Not an easy task for one so inexperienced in the ways of human behavior.

"For those who came before you, your mother, Elizabeth, your father, Stephan, the one you call Uncle Brad, William and even grandson Daniel, here, the path to enlightenment has been fraught with hindrances of epic proportions. For never has a species placed so much resistance on that which is for their highest good. It has been extraordinarily disconcerting to watch a civilization pray so intently for a peaceful, harmonic planetary co-habitation and then demonstrate such horrific self-destructive action, thus denying their desire so completely. Puzzling indeed.

"For those who signed on as emissary, this behavior is considered most disturbing and quite illogical. So, your challenges will continue. However, we wish for you to understand and take comfort in the knowledge that these tribulations can be overridden by the symbiotic actions orchestrated by the members of the Galactic Federation.

"Krystal, what I wish to convey is that the time of full implementation has arrived and it is my honor to commence your initiation as a full member into the Galactic Federation of Star Nations, now, before this esteemed company. This privilege has rarely been bestowed upon one so young, if ever, in the 4.5 million year history of the Federation.

"There are many who will assist you in your capacity, so fear not. The abilities you currently hold, while impressive to humans, will be enhanced 1,000 fold at a ceremonial to be held in a secluded area of the place known to those on your planet as the Grand Canyon and shall commence in two Earth days.

"Now that your human side has satisfactorily developed, it will be of no consequence to advance your natural hybrid capabilities to their maximum. I wish you all safe journey as you put into operation your assigned missions. If there are no further inquiries, I shall return to the Federation. I am complete." And with that, Adakor dematerializes leaving this eclectic group preoccupied with thoughts of their next plan of action.

Daniel breaks the contemplative spell, "Grandfather, there is nothing more to be done here. Perhaps it best for us to take our leave and head back to the reservation, as there is much to plan." Daniel's eyes are locked specifically on Krystal who slowly places her hat back to its rightful place atop her head as she meets his gaze. It has been made clear that it is the young who will now take the lead.

Eye of the Huricane

*R*eady or not, everything Brad, Krystal and I, not to mention the hundreds of thousands of other hybrids, had been preparing for was upon us. No more lessons, no more training, no more postulating. What was happening around the planet was no longer theory or prophecy, it was real and it was bad!

But Brad and I shared an even more unique anxiety, for we'd been charged with getting Krystal to a specific designated area in the Grand Canyon the next day so that she could receive further instruction from the higher echelon of the Galactic Federation. It was now time to galvanize the hybrids and commence implementing their pre-assigned missions in earnest. We had to succeed. That old expression "failure is not an option" was never more real, than now!

Krystal, Brad and I were all locked and loaded and ready to spring into action and begin implementing our individual instructions.

Meanwhile, Andrew prepared to head back to Washington, if he could get there safely, that is, to work alongside some of the world's greatest minds in an effort to get a handle on the status of these catastrophes that were simultaneously erupting around the planet and what counter action, if any, was feasible before it was too late.

Andrew's concern wasn't about keeping the masses in conformed order; that was the insurmountable task for the military. As a matter of fact, he heard that troops overseas were being hastily flown back to the United States to assist in whatever capacity was needed. Weather had become one of the major deterrents and a dangerous one, at best.

Military, commercial and even private pilots were being commandeered to perform emergency evacuation of all high level government personnel and to bring them back to the United States as soon as possible. Sooner, than later was the order of the day.

(Flashback)

By the time Andrew makes his way back to Washington, the president has issued a full-state of emergency for the entire United States, placing everyone under complete and unbending martial law, which in effect is the equivalent to "battening down the hatches".

Andrew's flight from Phoenix is the last one allowed in or out of the Ronald Regan Airport, as airport officials prepare to completely shut down all operations, due to hurricane force winds that have hit the city within the last hour and the fact that the infrastructure is almost non-existent. As he and the other nervous passengers deplane, Andrew is met by a two-man military escort who whisk him away through a series of private corridors that lead to a secluded tarmac where a military helicopter with motor blades turning, sits in wait for his arrival.

Climbing aboard, Andrew is greeted by Doug Lafferty, a prominent figure in the United States Geological Service, a.k.a. the USGS. "Glad you made it back in one piece, Andrew" Lafferty yells above the roar of the helicopter blades, then gestures for Andrew to put on the headset that lies adjacent to his seat so they can at least hear one another.

"Doug, what's the status?" Andrew cuts to the chase. "Not good, Andrew… not good. The president has issued a full-state of emergency for the entire country and ordered all military and government personnel to active duty. I'm supposed to take you to an emergency meeting with the president along with Bill Hadley from NASA, Jonathan Coakley, the human aerospace computer from M.I.T. and of course you know Jason Beckwith, who's working furiously on the latest astrophysical data."

The short helicopter ride is riddled with extreme turbulence and forces Andrew and his companion to hold on for dear life until safely landing on the White House lawn helipad. Silently, Andrew acknowledges the honor bestowed upon his arrival, but more than that he's keenly aware of the urgency of the situation, so his ego's *fifteen minutes of fame* is short lived.

Just as Andrew and Doug are about to deplane, the heavens open up yet again. Within seconds, two White House aides appear with oversized umbrellas which provide little protection as they contortedly bend in the opposite direction due to the violent winds which accompany their exit.

Feverously running across the slippery soaked lawn, Andrew grabs onto Doug's arm for dear life, in an attempt to remain upright on his waterlogged feet. Once inside, they are met with yet another human convoy of escorts that lead them through the winding twists and turns from corridor to corridor until they reach their final destination... the infamous Oval Office.

Once cleared to enter, Andrew and Doug step inside this inner sanctum reserved for but a selected few and spot the president, who stands back to the door talking in low tones to an unknown party. Becoming aware of their arrival, the president spins around and cuts her conversation short.

Being the first woman president of the United States holds a plethora of historical significance however, Jocelyn Summers never anticipated experiencing this type of terrorist threat from an unknown galactic foe during her presidency.

Dispensing with the formalities, all in attendance nod their greetings and then President Summers gestures for them to take a seat and begins, "Gentlemen, I'm glad you're here. Someone... please get Mr. Bishop and Mr. Lafferty some dry towels. I'm going to skip the rhetoric and let Jason bring you all up to speed with the latest data. Jason..."

"Thank you, Madame President. Gentlemen, what we're

dealing with is unprecedented, even in our study models, so I won't mince words…we're flying blind here. Let me tell you what we DO know and what we've gleaned from what few systems are still left in operation.

"A giant mass, which we believe to be solid, at least ten times the size of Earth with an incredibly strong gravitational signature, has passed in close proximity to our planet, thus disrupting all of our electromagnetic fields and systems. We believe this could be the arrival or at least a glancing fly by what has been referred to as Planet-X."

At this point, Bill Hadley from NASA slams both hands down onto the arms of his overstuffed leather chair in protest and objects, "Oh, come on, Jason! You're not going to start that ridiculous Planet-X bullshit again, are you? I suppose next you're going to blame this all on HAARP, as well!"

In unison, the room erupts into chaotic chatter as the five men begin talking all at once, unsuccessfully attempting to dispute one another's statements and theories; some touting that Bill Hadley and NASA are maintaining their steadfast covert posture about withholding critical data not only from the public, but the office of the presidency, as well.

President Summers, who has been listening intently, arms folded across her chest, leaning against the front portion of her oversized desk, quickly rises to full upright deportment and demands silence.

"Gentlemen, this is not the time, nor do we HAVE the time to debate this matter. What we Do need and what the American people demand are answers and a plan of action… so do I! If you cannot, or are unwilling to fully cooperate in accomplishing this same goal, then I suggest you take leave of this office immediately! Do I make myself clear, gentlemen?"

With that said, order is restored and so Andrew takes this opportunity to speak next. "What I want to know is… how bad it is and how bad it's going to get? Does anyone have a handle on that?"

Doug Lafferty jumps in "If I may...the latest information we have gathered indicates a tremendous amount of seismic activity all around the globe. I'm not just talking about two or three areas, here; I'm talking about close to a hundred, at last count. There have been unconfirmed reports of at least half that many tsunamis and twenty-five volcanic eruptions! This is *exactly* what has been prophesized...it's Armageddon!"

"Let's not get editorial, or hysterical, gentleman. Things are dramatic enough. Continue..." the president instructs.

"Madame President..." Jonathan Coakley interjects, "What have you heard from Germany, London, France, or any of the other world leaders? Is this cataclysm being felt as severely in their counties as we're experiencing here?"

The president responds, "Actually, Japan was the first to send out data about an abnormally high amount of seismic activity coupled with an increase of severe storms. Within minutes, we began getting reports from Australia, Hawaii and Canada, then Moscow, London and Lithuania, about similar simultaneous catastrophic events taking place. Then of course, as you now know, officials from around the country began reporting unfathomable identical cataclysms, which continue to increase by the minute!"

"Madame President" Andrew interrupts "I've spent the better part of two decades going before Senate and Congressional subcommittee after subcommittee warning our government of these exact potential cataclysms that have continually been ignored. With all due respect, the cause of these events, whether by this mysterious object or by some other source, almost seems irrelevant at this juncture, wouldn't you say? What needs our immediate attention is comprehensive – first, we need to keep what viable systems we have left in operation and determine as best we can, how to remain in communication with not only our own scientific and geologic communities but those around the world, as these events seem to be spreading like a ripple from a pebble in the water. Excuse me, bad analogy...more like a mega tsunami washing over country after country."

President Summers agrees, "Andrew is correct. We need to implement a cohesive plan of action. Hate to rush you, gentlemen, but I'm due to meet with General Whitfield and his chiefs of staff in a few minutes. Let me recap that you're all expected to reconvene at 2:30 p.m., just two short hours from now, in the Roosevelt Room for what may prove to be the biggest gathering of military, government and scientific minds in U.S. history. In the name of God, I hope everyone checks their egos at the door so we can have a useful and more importantly, a successful resolution to this urgent dilemma."

Just then, the door to the Oval Office opens and in enters Lieutenant Colonel Marshal Fletcher, acting White House liaison for the United States Air Force. He apologizes profusely for the interruption but has some urgent news that he must share with Madame President. She advises him that she's already late for another meeting, but Lt. Fletcher is quite insistent that she hear what he has to say. The two figures step aside, backs toward the others, head to head, and after a brief whispered exchange the president's voice raises "This is ALL we need…"

Turning about face, President Summers stares at the floor for a brief moment, takes in a long deep breath, raises her eyes to meet those of her contemporaries and declares "Gentlemen, I have just been informed by Lt. Fletcher that an apparent failed Russian operation that was intended to seize benefit from the calamitous weather anomalies for the purpose of military advantage, went horribly wrong; and so in response HAARP activated *their* systems, only to discover that they had lost control of their intended mark and are now unable to stop the wheels they've put in motion. In other words, they're adding to …no let me restate … appear to be *directly* responsible for contributing to the already compromised stability of the ionosphere, resulting in human manufactured catastrophic weather events, earthquakes, tornados…*you name it.*"

A collective gasp, followed by sudden silence overtakes the

room, and then one by one, the assembly considers the ominous consequences before them...before humanity!

With nothing more to be said, President Summers gathers herself together and so adjourns the meeting; heading off as promised, to yet another urgent conference. With the president's permission the five men remain in the Oval Office to conjoin individual data and ready their unparalleled proposals for what will go down in history as the most important meeting of their careers, more aptly put... their lives!

Troubled Waters

I don't mind telling you, I was worried – not just about what was happening around the planet, although wasn't that enough? There was something else…something more…something so big that it sent chills up my spine, but what was it?

I even took off my hat in the hope that whatever it was would make itself known to me, but with all that was going on - no such luck. I was overrun with too much data and couldn't decipher one thing from the other. I would just have to wait, I guess…

So for the time being, my dad, Uncle Brad and I were to head toward the higher ground of the Grand Canyon, as instructed, so we could obtain our next directive from the Federation, which became a monumental challenge, trying to avoid all the flooding that was inundating the lower valley. Even parts of Sedona were under siege. I needed to sleep – hadn't slept much at all, lately. Just wanted to close my eyes and shut everything out – at least for a little while. Just put on my hat to escape…

(*Flashback*)

Brad's jeep lurches forward and whines as it valiantly traverses its way through the off-road terrain. The main roads are now awash with rusty torrents of water from the once dry creek beds, whose liquid overruns the swollen banks. The sound of scraping tree branches on the jeep's tender canvas roof brings uncontrollable gasps from its passengers inside.

"Man!" Brad yells "I sure hope this roof holds or else we're gonna be three very wet puppies!"

Stephan turns from his position in the front passenger seat to check on Krystal. "You okay, sweetie?" he asks with a half laugh, trying to be cavalier about their predicament. Krystal doesn't answer right away, as she's distracted - trying to *tune in* to something that has bothered her since the moment they got into the jeep.

"Krystal?" Stephan prods. "Um...sorry Dad. What did you say? Oh, yeah...I'm fine..." her voice trails off as she grabs the back of Stephan's seat for stability, as they bounce uncontrollably from unseen road obstacles.

"Sorry folks!" Brad apologizes; knowing full well that he's doing the best he can to maneuver the jeep over and through the thick brush and rocky turf.

"I don't know this area as well as you do Brad, but aren't we still inside the reservation?" Stephan asks. "Yeah, I'm with you on that one, Stephan..." Brad answers. Their unspoken dialog acknowledges how dire their situation is and, more than ever, how they need a plan of action and fast, to get them out of this mess. *If we can just make our way to the Grand Canyon that's on higher ground...*

Brad tries desperately to get his bearings. After all, he's never had to work his way through this stretch of thicketed woods, off-road, in a jeep, during one of the worst rainstorms in Arizona's recorded history; never mind having to use his best driving dexterity to avoid getting stuck in the red clay muck – or worse!

Given they're forced to travel at a turtle's pace, Brad figures they still have a long way to go. Looking into his rearview mirror, Brad notices Krystal's weariness and suggests she try to close her eyes for a bit and rest. *Rest? Good luck! She probably feels like she's riding a bucking bronco back there. Rest...ha!*

Stephan fights to steady himself, as he cranes his neck to look over his shoulder, hoping to lock eyes with Krystal and offers, "Lie down, honey. You won't bounce around quite as much."

Time stands still as Krystal's gaze meets that of her father's. Hybrid or not, she's grateful for the momentary feeling of comfort and safety only her father's eyes can bolster. But it's more than that...intuitively, she's holding onto this moment, wishing she could freeze it in time, for she knows once this reverie is over, she'll be thrust back into their frenzied reality... and the *something else* she's so troubled about.

"Okay, Dad" Krystal's voice quivers, as they continue to be tossed about the jeep's interior like popcorn cornels on high heat. Stephan gives his daughter a wink then resumes his forward facing position, all the while bracing himself on any solid surface within his grasp.

Krystal reaches for her hat as she lowers and elongates her small frame onto the backseat. *Don't need any interruptions right now*...then whispers "Love you, Dad." Brad shoots a look at Stephan, who keeps his eyes forward then whispers back, "Love you too, baby."

To her surprise, Krystal finds herself drifting into a calm, serene slumber in no time at all. She floats unencumbered by gravity or the weight of her physical body and yet, has a strange sense of form. Colors - beautiful colors fill her vision as wisps of cobalt blue, vibrant yellow, aqua marine and indigo – all gliding by in a choreography of brilliant hues in ambiguous forms. Then, she detects a low vibration of undeterminable sound. *Is it music?* Not exactly - although it does have tone - a non-specific melody. Deeper and deeper she travels into this tranquil domain, leaving behind all fear and concern. The colors spiral together to the point of undistinguished recognition...then suddenly - to black. So peaceful...silent. For the time being, Krystal escapes into blissful repose, while Brad and Stephan remain in actuality, where life and death hang in the balance.

Then, without warning, Brad slams both feet onto the brakes, bringing the jeep to an abrupt halt, as before them lay a ragging torrent of water, blocking their path. Brad and Stephan study their situation with intense scrutiny, all the while exchanging telepathic options to one another.

Looks impassable…

Can't go back, water is rising…

We're so close…can we make it?

Without so much as a confirming glance, a mutual decision has been reached. Brad slowly puts his left foot full on the clutch, while his right hand reaches for the gear shift and edges it, ever so slowly, into first gear. The strain of the engine revs, all the while the once confidant driver second guesses the unspoken decision.

Stealth fully, Brad begins releasing the clutch, while applying just the right amount of pressure on his right foot that controls the gas pedal and, at a snail's pace, gradually activates their forward motion. *Not too late to turn back…*

Initially, the jeep responds well to Brad's mechanical asking, as they traverse the stony waterway. For but a moment, the jeep's traction fails, forcing it to slide sideways, but Brad remains cool and quickly regains full command of his vehicle. Inch by inch the jeep, with its precious cargo, makes its way further into the ever deepening creek. About halfway across – *the point of no return* – Brad lets out a gasp, as he spies what appears to be a large, uprooted tree that's raging directly toward them. With no other choice, Brad places both hands squarely on the steering wheel and yells "HANG ON!" Forcefully jolted out of her reverie, Krystal bolts upright, her protective hat falling to the floor of the jeep, and shouts "DAD!"

Brad quickly releases the clutch while giving his right foot the mental command *FULL GAS!* At first, the jeep slips and then, as if a gift from the heavens, regains its traction, but it's too late. The fallen tree catches the back bumper of the jeep, dragging it sideways as it rushes out of control downstream. No time for words or crying; the trio's suspended in time as their destiny teeters in uncertain peril.

Unexpectedly, the jeep breaks free of the tree's capture but the force caused by the release flips the jeep, dumping its riders into the frigid torrent. Suspended underwater, Krystal fights to find her way to the surface. She's tossed around like clothing in a spinning washing machine while floating debris bumps and scratches at her body. All of a sudden, a large bolder sits in the path of her uncontrollable course that holds the potential to cause her serious harm.

Before tragedy strikes, a strong arm grabs her by the waist, hoisting her tiny frame up to the surface, where she chokes and gasps for blessed breath. Her rescuer deftly drags Krystal and himself to the muddied embankment and temporary safe haven. When she's finally able to clear her vision, Krystal peers up to see her Uncle Brad lying on his side next to her, vomiting and coughing the extraneous water from his own aching lungs.

Quickly regaining her faculties, Krystal screams "DAD!" - all the while frantically searching the choppy water and debris laden creek banks for any sign of him. Brad struggles to clear consciousness and joins Krystal in the desperate search to locate Stephan. Although dramatically unsteady, both Krystal and Brad wobble to their feet, holding on to one another for support - in more ways than one. Not knowing if they should look upstream or down, it's Krystal who spots him first, clinging to a large rock on the opposite side of the embankment from where she and Brad stand. "Stephan!"- "Dad!" - "Hang on - we're coming!" they shout in unison.

Dazed, Stephan can hear his name being called but isn't looking in the direction of Brad and Krystal. Instead, his gaze falls upon a ghostly figure as it approaches; while the lower half of his body lies afloat in the raging water. Then he recognizes her - it's his beloved Liz who is smiling broadly, moving ever closer to her husband. He smiles back.

From across the way, Brad and Krystal are frozen to

where they stand as they watch Stephan's face turn from one of anxiousness to peace and they silently question - *Is he smiling?* Their answer comes swiftly as they realize that he is, indeed, but not at the prospect of being rescued.

And then, from out of the thickets comes a lone wolf, ever so slowly working its way toward the unaided Stephan. Just as Brad is about to shout out a warning to Stephan, Krystal touches his arm and says softly "It's alright…it's Lupo"

Understanding Lupo's guardianship for Stephan should provide them with a feeling of relief, but in its stead an odd sense of foreboding washes over them both at the same time. Confused, they wonder why they're filled with a sudden sadness. As Liz emerges into full form, Krystal whispers a barely audible, "Mom? *Mom!*…" her voice trails off as their question is about to be answered.

Aftermath

*S*o there it was…the answer to my question…that "something else" that was about to happen that would change my life, yet again, had occurred; only this time I was able to witness the event as it unfolded, in real time, before my very eyes. Dad's transcendence back into nonphysical was gifted by the presence of Mom and Lupo who were there to assist with his return home. Comforting, sure, but why wasn't I able to tune into this before it happened? Why was this particular information unavailable to me…me, who has all this precognitive forte? I had no answers.

Strange as it may seem, at that point in time, I found it hard to grieve. My Uncle Brad was great. He knew that I would choose my moment to acknowledge Dad's passing, just not then. There was nothing more that we could do. When the water receded, we'd head back to retrieve the vehicle that housed my father's amazing spirit for five and a half decades and find a proper place to put it to rest. While in my heart I knew his spirit lives on, still…it would be difficult to look upon his sleeping face. My challenges continued…

(Flashback)

Krystal and Brad stand stoically in reverent silence as Stephan's spirit ascends from his physical form that still lies by the water's edge. Taking his rightful place by his wife's side with Lupo close at hand, Stephen glances back one last time to look upon his Krystal. With momentary hesitation, Stephan pauses, struggling with the knowledge that he is leaving her...leaving his cherished Krystal to find her way and complete her task without him. Liz places her hand lovingly upon her husband's cheek in reassurance that their daughter will be well cared for and protected. For he now possess the same vantage point as Liz and he'll soon discover new ways to be of support and guidance as she journeys forward.

No tears flow from Krystal's eyes, which only betray her genuine inner struggle. Equally, hybrid and human sides are dealing with a monumental loss. *How can this be?*, she asks an invisible Power. She torments inwardly about life without him, her beloved father - her *Dad*; the man who raised her almost single handedly. This spiritual giant of a man who has blazed new trails, not only as a galactic advocate, seeker of truth and humanitarian warrior who took on the United States government and the Black Op, but in conjunction with having to raise an exceptional human-hybrid child without the benefit of other such parenting guideposts, for these special children come – *Instructions Not Included.*

Ready or not, Krystal has no choice but to acknowledge and deal with her continually increasing, ever present emotional human side, that she perhaps has deliberately kept at bay, and with good reason, for now, Krystal actually *knows* what a broken heart feels like and she detests the pain that overrides all else. This overwhelming, almost debilitating emotion, that gives her great pause and makes her wonder why anyone would chose to experience this mode of living with all its challenges. In spite of this, she keeps replaying her father's words ... "We signed up for this gig..." and knows that she must continue on, if only in his honor.

She has enjoyed the many conversations with her Uncle Brad who, despite his outward tough demeanor, has openly declared his immense fondness for Stephan and the unexpected soft spot that developed in his otherwise walled up heart; as they grew to be so much more than allies in this galactic fight, but soul brethren. Krystal knew that Brad would suffer in silence rather than add to her already unwelcome mourning.

She gratefully reflects on the recent birthday gift her father gave, that provided her with the opportunity to *feel* and experience the events surrounding her mother's passing some twelve years ago at Cathedral Rock and can't help but wonder if that was a preordained preparation for -yet another.

Knowing that nightfall will be coming soon, Brad takes full assessment of their situation, realizing that they must find shelter for the night, first and foremost. Without warning, Brad begins to cough uncontrollably in an effort to clear his lungs from the water he has swallowed while submerged beneath the raging current. When the spasm is over, he clears his throat, then speaks "Krystal, there's nothing more we can do. We need to gather whatever supplies we can salvage and find shelter. Hopefully, we'll be able to find some dry clothes ..." Krystal nods in agreement and then, in a quivering voice offers "Yes, I know. I'm very cold, Uncle Brad. Let's look around and see what we can find." Just as Brad begins to form a verbal acknowledgment, his cough returns in earnest, forcing him to drop to his knees, head bent over close to the ground as he spews copious amounts of liquid expelling from his lungs.

Shocked by what she's witnessing, Krystal rushes to his side and asks if he's alright. Momentarily weak from this violent episode, Brad waves his hand in the air signaling that he just needs a minute and then draws his trembling hand across his mouth, clearing any remaining spit. "I'm okay, honey, just swallowed more of that danged creek than I realized. Help me up, will ya?…let's start looking around…"

Remaining in close proximity of one another, they begin their vital search, stumbling over broken branches, occasionally losing their footing as they trudge through the muddied terrain. The rain has stopped, leaving in its wake plummeting temperatures, making it all the more imperative that they find dry clothing and, just as essential, dry matches so they can build a fire.

"Uncle Brad, look! Aren't those our backpacks?" Krystal shouts. She points a trembling finger towards the objects in question which are nested inside some broken tree branches, fortunately lying upon a dry portion of the creek bed. Ever so carefully, they make way toward their target, all the while silently praying that these objects hold the treasures they desperately seek.

"Yep, that's them!' Brad conveys with relief. "Stay here, Krystal…They're too close to the water. I'll climb in through that mess and then I'll toss 'em to you." Krystal nods in agreement, as her body is so cold she can no longer acknowledge verbally.

Awkwardly, Brad navigates the slippery creek bank, doing his best to avoid falling into the raging river. With few missteps, he is at last at his destination. One by one he lobs three backpacks onto higher, dryer ground. Gingerly, Krystal makes her way to where the backpacks lay in wait for their retrieval. They are in luck…the backpacks are intact and bone dry as are the contents within, which includes three flashlights and several books of matches. Without delay, they begin removing their wet clothes, Brad turning his back so as to offer Krystal modest privacy. It feels good to have dry clothes on once again and they are gratified for the viable clothing options which will provide crucial layering.

Just then, Krystal spots a crate floating down the creek that looks similar to the one they packed their food supplies into.

Brad spies it as well and although he's only half dressed, jumps into action, making a Herculean attempt to retrieve the cache, but it's out of reach, well into the middle of the watery torrent. Feeling defeated and completely frustrated, Brad lets out a string of profanities, then mumbles his apologizes as he resumes placing the remaining items of dry clothing about his frigid body- his cough continues to persist.

Rummaging through the backpacks, Krystal discovers several protein bars and some bottled water that Stephan must have placed in there. Clutching them close to her chest, Krystal whispers in blessing *"Thank you, Dad"* acknowledging her father's foresight. Hearing her words of thanks, Brad adds "Yeah, thanks man. Come on, Krystal, it's getting dark - we need to find some protection for the night. Storm or no storm, critters will be roaming around looking for food."

Wading through broken branches and other debris caused by the wind and rain, Brad and Krystal painstakingly work their way deeper into the woods in search of their haven. All the while, Brad checks in with his internal GPS in the hopes of maintaining some semblance of their position. At last they come upon a group of rocks that form a semi-circle with one large rock hovering overhead providing the perfect protection from the elements.

Weary and worn, Brad and Krystal plop down upon dry ground courtesy of the rock's overhang. Brad begins gathering whatever dried leaves and twigs can be found inside this natural cave and begins constructing a makeshift fire, just enough outside the enclosure to ensure the smoke doesn't come back at them, yet protected from the outside dampened ground.

Reaching into one of the backpacks, Brad pulls out a protein bar and offers half of it to Krystal. "No thanks, Uncle Brad. I can't eat." "Krystal, honey, you've got to eat something…at least take a bite" he offers just as you would any young child refusing to eat. Still, she waves him off, but accepts some bottled water.

"Let's get some sleep and first thing in the morning, we'll get a better bearing of where we are and then head back towards the reservation." Krystal silently nods in agreement and reaches for her backpack to use as a pillow, but first unzips one of the larger pockets and retrieves a hat which is a birthday gift from her Uncle Brad and then places it securely on her head. But before attempting sleep, Krystal has one last burning question "Uncle Brad, what about our planned meeting with the Federation? What do we do now? Do you think they even know what's happened to my dad?" Without hesitation, Brad answers swiftly "It'll all be worked out. They know what's happened, honey. Believe me... they know."

Watching Krystal as she performs her protective ritual, Brad slumps and hangs his head, and then places his face in his hands, fighting to stifle not only his cough, but the emotion that begins to overwhelm him. Both now in repose, they watch the fire's crackling blaze and pray that tomorrow they'll find their way back to the safety of the reservation and the comfort of William's and Daniel's presence, but not before retrieving Stephan's remains.

As Krystal drifts off into a fitful sleep, hat or no hat, visions of the day's traumatic events swirl around in her head, until finally peaceful slumber arrives with the lucid image of her father's smile.

Home, Home at Last

Home, Home at Last
Peace and rest at length have come
All the day's long toil is past,
And each heart is whispering,
"Home, Home at last."

~Thomas Hood (1799-1845)

The night was filled with fitful sleep and dreams that even my hat couldn't keep away. Uncle Brad coughed and choked most of the night and so I knew we needed to get back to the reservation sooner than later. Intuitively, I was very concerned and rightfully so. Whether a blessing or a curse, I have the ability to conduct body scans on any living thing and can "see" when the body is out of balance or in serious jeopardy due to injury or critical disease. Without his permission, I performed such a scan and quickly determined the latter diagnosis was the case. No time to waste.

How does that saying go? "I knew he knew, I knew..." and so he didn't put up much resistance to my taking charge. I let him rest while I packed up the few belongings we had and then asked for his guidance in determining which direction we needed to head in that would get us back to the reservation as quickly as possible. But first we needed to find my dad again, retrieve his body and figure a way to bring him back with us for proper burial. There was no way, I was going to leave him here...just no way...

(Flashback)

The morning sunlight didn't bring much in the way of emotional relief for the ordeal Brad and Krystal were about to endure. It was clear that Brad was very ill and needed medical attention but a pressing need to locate Stephan's body so that they could bring it back to the reservation took precedence.

Their own bodies stiff and aching from sleeping on the cold, hard ground only adds to their already compromised mobility. And now, they face the monumental task of transporting Stephan back to William's village for proper burial. In silence, they both pray that they have an energetic reserve and can summon up enough stamina for the long journey back.

Their stomachs growl in hunger which implore relief and so once again Brad offers Krystal half of a protein bar for which she accepts reluctantly. Nibbling their paltry breakfast, Brad double checks to ensure the fire is completely extinguished, lest they add forest fire to their already long list of calamities. Convinced it is, indeed, out, they gather up the backpacks and hoist them overhead and onto their aching shoulders, positive some fiendish entity must have mischievously placed some rocks inside, as they feel so much heavier this morning.

Brad gives Krystal a knowing wink then asks "Okay? Let's go" to which Krystal somberly responds "Yeah, I'm alright. I just want to find my dad and get you both back to William's. Which way do we go?" With feet spread wide apart to maintain his balance, Brad looks around, first to the left and then to the right; he gazes skyward to estimate the sun's rising position and declares "We need to head east first, towards the creek, then after that, southeast towards the reservation."

Implicitly trusting Brad's calculations, Krystal takes the

lead, stepping carefully over the wooded debris caused by the high winds and torrential rainfall from yesterday's storm. As they methodically make their way through the forest, Krystal removes her hat, hoping that her guides will provide assistance in honing in on Stephan's exact location.

For the first time since they left the reservation, Krystal asks Brad to check his watch and mark the time. When Brad complies, he's not at all surprised to find it has ceased functioning. "Damn!" Not sure as to why this was so important, Brad questions Krystal's reasoning to which she respond "If we can figure out how long it takes us to reach the creek, then we can estimate the distance of the reservation relative to our position. True?" Brad lets out a slight chuckle "Yep, you're right! Driving so slowly yesterday would be equivalent to our walking on foot, so we can gage how long it would take to get back to William's. Good girl!" and with that, Brad begins to cough, but this time it sounds deep and painful.

Time passes and the travelers are growing weak, but they press on. When they come to a clearing, they stop to look around and question which way they should go next. Brad is clearly getting sicker and Krystal is sure he has a fever so his usual lucid judgment is now clouded and unreliable. "I...I think...we should go...that way...I think..." Brad fumbles.

Just then Krystal receives - *No, he's wrong Krystal! Follow the path to the right. It will lead you to the creek. It will lead you to me! That's where I am!* Krystal asks telepathically *Dad? Dad, is that you?* Stephan answers, *Yes, my darling daughter. It's me. Just do as I tell you...*

Krystal knows that her Uncle Brad possess telepathic abilities himself, but because he is so ill, he can't tap into the conversation and so she stoically commands that they need to go to the right and follow the path that she believes will lead them to the creek and Stephan. Unable or unwilling to challenge her decisiveness, Brad complies and within moments, fatigue is replaced with optimism as they can hear the rushing water off in the distance.

Their energy renewed, they're able to increase their pace and at long last are standing at the water's edge. They're thankful that the once ragging river has receded to nothing more than a fast moving creek, making it possible to maneuver across to the other side by way of piled rocks and tree stumps that form a natural dam. Tentatively, they work their way across this naturally formed bridge to the safety of the creek's embankment on the other side. Krystal offers a steady hand to assist Brad as he stumbles on the last few steps.

Now safely across, they look up and down stream with the hope of spying Stephan. Krystal decides it's time for more help and asks *Dad...we're here! Where are you?* Brad becomes aware that Krystal is communicating with *someone* and so remains silent. Stephan answers, *Here Krystal! Walk downstream to where the tree trunk jets out into the creek bed. You'll find me there...waiting.* Krystal speaks aloud "We need to move downstream, Uncle Brad. Are you okay? Can you go on?" Brad gestures *okay* with one hand, while the other covers his mouth as he struggles to contain his ever deepening cough.

Making their way downstream becomes laborious as debris from fallen trees and anything else that got in the way of the violent flow, obscure an easy path. And then, they spot him! Krystal orders her limbs swiftly into action, but to no avail. While her spirit urges her forward, her body betrays her need and propels her in slow motion toward her father's remains.

When at last by his side, Krystal and Brad pause as they consider the depth of their situation. Brad falls to his knees, not so much in exhaustion, but coming to terms with the reality of what lies before him is overwhelming and so he weeps openly. Krystal makes a great physical effort to not follow suit as it would serve no purpose. Should they both emotionally succumb to the moment, their fate might have a different outcome.

"Uncle Brad, we need to figure out how we're going to transport Dad back with us" Krystal offers in an attempt to divert his attention from his sorrow. Wiping the tears from his reddened eyes, he thinks for a moment then replies "Yeah, sure. Um...let's see what we've got to work with. Lots of strong tree branches, that's for sure. Maybe we could construct a makeshift carrier..." Without any further discussion, both begin to scout the area for broken limbs that are strong enough to endure the journey.

Brad makes a valiant attempt to free some viable branches, but is too weak. Krystal suggests he sit and rest upon a dry flat boulder that's positioned well away from the water's edge while she utilizes not only her young physical body but her exceptional telekinetic skills to accomplish the task. Brad studies his niece in wonderment and feels such pride in her presence.

One by one, the branches do her bidding while in the meantime Brad's eyes scan the area for any suitable vines strong enough to be utilized to tie the branches firmly in place. "Wait! What about the material in my hat? It's strong, strong as anything else we've got available." Brad knows she's right and without any further discussion, Krystal reaches into her backpack and pulls out her new birthday hat, a gift from her Uncle. "Sorry, Uncle Brad. I really love the hat, but it has another vital purpose right now..." Together, they begin ripping small strips of material, long enough to be able to tie the branches securely together.

Feeling a bit stronger, Brad begins arranging the branches in a specific pattern; the two longest parallel branches to one another, about three feet apart and then a large one across the top, one in the middle and the final one at the bottom. Working in silence, they tie the branches as tightly as they can and then doubly secure them with some durable climbing vine they ripped away from a large nearby tree. Now it was time for Stephan.

This was the hardest part of all. Having to retrieve his body that was cold and bloated from the water's hold and then place it upon the makeshift gurney for their trek home. There they stood, daughter and best friend, combating an enormous grief as they tried to emotionally detach from the daunting undertaking of having to come into contact with a lifeless body that once housed such an astonishing being.

Just as they conjure up the courage to begin, they're distracted by some sounds coming from another part of the woods. They stop to listen as the sounds appear to be coming ever closer. The sun is high in the desert sky so it's not likely to be any animal, unless it's a bear, bob cat or mountain lion who's roaming the area. But it sounds bigger.

Closer and closer the sounds approach causing Krystal and Brad to momentarily move away from Stephan's body and seek protection under low hanging tree branches. And then they see it...first one, then two, then three horses bearing riders. Peeking out from within the safety of the tree leaves, it's Krystal who first identifies the riders. It's William, Daniel, and another man from the village who've come in search of their friends!

Krystal bursts out from behind the tree branches frantically waving her arms and shouts "Over here! We're over here!" The riders quickly turn their steeds in the direction of the pleading voice and race to her side. Once there, William and Daniel jump off their horses as they pass the reins to the third man in their rescue party.

Krystal runs straight into William's arms, while Brad weakly emerges from beneath the trees protective limbs. It takes no time for all to size up that something dire has happened. And it's not until all eyes fall upon Stephan's remains that the full impact of this tragedy is undeniably clear.

William cradles Krystal's head close into his chest as his emotion swells and whispers "I'm so sorry, Krystal..." Daniel rushes to aid Brad and somberly offers comfort to he and Krystal.

In his native tongue, the third man quietly utters something to which Daniel quickly responds and goes to one of the saddle bags to retrieve a hand woven blanket and then walks slowly toward where Stephan lies and covers his body in reverence.

First Krystal and then Brad are hoisted upon William and Daniel's horses respectively and are then joined by their owners. Placing her arms tightly about William's waist, her face now buried into the back of his woolen jacket she begins to quietly weep "Please William, we can't leave him here..." To which William replies, "No, little one. We won't leave him. He's coming home with us." And with that, William signals to the third rider, who will hang back to secure Stephan on his own horse and together they'll begin his final journey home.

Connecting the Dots

*U*ncle Brad's cough was getting worse. While he was pretty good at pretending it was no big deal and often joked that it probably was time he quit smoking (he never smoked a day in his life), I knew differently, so did William.

Besides being troubled about Uncle Brad, something strange was happening - I felt a shift since my dad passed. It was as if I now possessed a different kind of knowing - one that had lain dormant in me for such a long time. Adakor spoke of an "amnesia" that accompanied emergence into this physical reality, so maybe...just maybe I was beginning to "remember". Remember what? I'm not sure, just yet.

At first, I attributed this anomaly to the fact that I had basically become an orphan but it went far beyond that. I was feeling things I'd never felt before. I was consumed with all kinds of emotions and I don't mind telling you that in addition to these feelings being foreign to me, some were down-right overwhelming.

I'd counseled with Uncle Brad about it all, which I'm sure was more than uncomfortable for him being that he's a confirmed bachelor and never had kids of his own, let alone a hormonal pre-teen female; and while logically I understood the biochemical changes that were taking place in my human vehicle, I was totally unprepared for the range, intensity and frequency of these emotions.

You have to remember, that as a hybrid I've never found much need, let alone any intellectual capacity for the value of having all these *emotions in the first place, for they only seemed to gum things up and so I chose not to cultivate them, much to my dad's frustration.*

But what I could feel completely, was love, for it was the overpowering emotion that greeted me when I emerged into this physical experience, continually surrounded my every moment and was provided to me without conditions, boundaries or limitations. So, I embraced this emotion, this LOVE, easily and without intellectual evaluation.

Now, here I am, being bombarded with all these other emotions all at once! I sure wish my mom was here to help me through this…

It's funny, despite my psychic specialties, the only thing that inhibits my abilities these days, besides putting on my hat, are these powerful new feelings. I'll be honest, it scares me, for when these feelings take over I'm forced to question, more often than not, my normally crystal clear discernment and judgment. But lately, I'd been unable to "see" what's about to happen, as I could before and that was unsettling.

I was beginning to experience a lot of trepidation about what might happen next.

(Flashback)

Brad's cough had worsened. Even he couldn't stave off the concern of the others with his usual sarcasm and humor over his obvious declining health. He promises Krystal and William that as soon as the roads become passable again, he'll journey to the nearest medical facility in Flagstaff to get checked out. This seems to pacify everyone for the time being, everyone that is, except William, who remains cautious of Brad's condition.

The night after their return from the tragic event, Brad declares that he's feeling a lot stronger and so decides to take a short walk around William's acreage to get some fresh air and clear his head. Not everyone is in agreement that his decision is wise, given his weakened condition however, after promising not to journey too far, Brad grabs his winter jacket and off he goes alone, despite William and Daniel's offer to keep him company.

Not far into his trek, fatigue unexpectedly demands his body rest for a while. Spying an inviting perch atop a small mesa, Brad musters just enough reserve to reach its summit. Once there, he lowers himself upon a smooth boulder and then inhales deeply, taking in the magnificence of the flaming red-orange and yellow sun as it slips silently below the horizon. His reverie is suddenly interrupted by a snapping of a twig, indicating something or someone is approaching from behind. Assuming it's probably a desert critter beginning its nightly sojourn, he's a bit surprised to see William approach instead.

"*Beautiful*, isn't it?" William speaks in soft reverent tones. "I've watched many a sunset from this exact spot and I'm still awed by its magnificence" he continues. Brad swallows hard, clears his throat, and then turns his head as he wipes a tear from his eye hopping this betrayal of his emotions escapes Williams notice. It does not.

"Brad," William begins and gets right to the point, "Is there time?" Brad takes but a moment to answer, lowers his head and inhales deeply which only exacerbates his cough. Once the coughing subsides, Brad turns to meet William's gaze "I'm afraid not, my friend…'fraid not." The two friends sit and stare silently at one another in suspended time, their dialog non-verbal, yet powerful. It is Brad who breaks the silence, turning his focus upward toward the stars, as one by one, their twinkling illuminations emerge from the darkening desert sky. "William, you know the mystical rites of the ancients – I'd be honored if you'd help me prepare for the next phase of my journey."

Again, without speaking, William lifts his arm and then places it around Brad's shoulder applying gentle, loving pressure confirming to his friend, his brethren, that he accepts this honor. With nothing more to be said, these special friends, literally from different worlds sit in the night's stillness for a while, grateful for what has been and hopeful for what is to be.

With the rising of the next day's sun and without fanfare, a number of elite tribal members begin constructing a special tent in which Brad will inhabit for his remaining days. In ancient Navajo mythology, only the most highly respected ritual practitioners are allowed to prepare for this journey and so they go about their tasks in solemn silence.

When Stephan made his transition into spirit by the banks of the raging waters, Brad and Krystal had little choice but to perform their own ad hock tribute. They knew deep in their hearts that they'd find a proper time to grieve once they found safe haven on the Navajo reservation with William, Daniel and the others and could commit Stephen to his final resting place. It was a simple, yet eloquent ceremony, honoring a devoted and cherished father, an amazing friend and a dedicated advocate for cosmic truth. His presence will be sorely missed.

Now, here they were again, only this time readying for Brad's imminent departure. Regardless of her superior genetic makeup, Krystal has suffered a great loss and will again, very soon. It is clear to all that she'll be in need of loving care and attention in the days to follow.

William asks Daniel to keep close watch on Krystal while he and the others go about their duties in preparation for Brad's departure. Daniel welcomes having Krystal as his charge for he has grown quite fond of this quirky pre-teen, four years his junior and feels an affinity for what lies before her.

Now that the torrential rains have abated for a bit, Daniel suggests to Krystal that they go for a ride on horseback, as he wants to show her a special place that no one else knows about - not even William. Assuring her that Brad is in good hands and convincing her how she could use a diversion from all that's going on in the village, she reluctantly agrees. With little precious time left, Krystal has much to say to her Uncle and plans on spending time with him upon her return.

Although Krystal's been wearing one of her hats more often than not, ironically, its prior power no longer staves off the voices and becomes ineffective to hold back the persistent data that relentlessly pervades her consciousness. She's keenly aware that all too soon the "voices' will override her attempts to block them out and she'll need to confront the information head on and act appropriately. But for now, she welcomes Daniel's temporary distraction.

Once astride the horses, Krystal and Daniel find the way muddy and slippery but their steady steeds proceed sure-footedly, taking these riders to their destination without incident. High atop a rocky slope, Krystal and Daniel dismount and tie their horses to a large piece of deadwood that lies across the plateau, then stand in awe of the panorama before them. From this vantage point the young explorers can see for miles across the desert terrain, spotted with low brush and occasional White Birch and Ponderosa Pine, all the while menacing grey-black clouds loom above threatening yet another round of storms.

While taking in the beauty of the tundra below, the sun begins to emerge through ominous clouds, infusing glistening light into the late morning sky. The temperature rises quickly causing the two young friends to remove their heavy jackets. They struggle to comprehend how at this *very* moment, cataclysmic events continue to rage throughout the planet. The last report they heard on William's transistor radio was barely discernable, due to the tremendous amount of static. What they were able to hear was that volcanoes continued to erupt, earthquakes and massive flooding are widespread and how mega hurricane force winds were pelting all the United States coastal regions.

"Krystal, did you happen to hear William and the others talking about how the constellations have moved? How they're not where they normally are in the night sky?" Krystal sighs and adds "Yes, I heard them. But that's not all, Daniel…" Hesitating for but a moment Krystal continues before Daniel can urge her on to explain. "Daniel, I'm scared. What's happening around the planet is getting out of control and I don't know how to stop it!"

"Stop it? What do you mean stop it? How is a twelve-year

old, excuse me…a twelve-year old HYBRID supposed to have such power as to stop all this? That's crazy!" Daniel yells, now on his feet, hands outstretched in exasperation.

Daniel's outburst brings about an unexpected response from Krystal. Gathering his composure, Daniel sits down beside Krystal who is now fighting back tears. "Well, that's refreshing, at least" he quips as he takes his hand to wipe a solitary tear that inches it way down Krystal's cheek. "Nice to see that you *can* cry." "Yeah, surprise, surprise, Super Girl has emotions!" she flips back at him.

Realizing that he may have sounded a bit insensitive, Daniel quickly changes the subject and tells her he has a surprise for her. Daniel rises and walks over to his horse, reaches into one of the time-worn leather saddle bags and pulls out a small package wrapped in a red, white and black printed bandana.

"I know you had a birthday recently, but this was something I planned on giving you anyway" and with that Daniel extends his arm with gift in hand. Krystal wipes away a remaining tear and lets out a chuckle as she accepts the package but can't resist taking a stab at some humor and states, "I suppose the next time we fight, you'll have to bring me flowers or something."

Krystal's sanguine moment is quickly over once she unfolds the bandana to reveal a most beautiful, handcrafted headband made from smoked brain-tanned deer hide, adorned with white, teal, gold, brown and turquoise beading laid out in a most intricate design accented by two scared eagle feathers that adorn each side.

As Krystal slowly removes her hat, Daniel ceremoniously places the headband around her forehead, ties it in the back then begins, "Krystal, this is more than a pretty headband…it's special…just like you. This headband has been passed down for generations and is only given to *Tiponi,* Child of Importance, like you."

Krystal begins to interrupt and asks "Daniel, how do you know about Tip…"

"Because I too, am *Tiponi*. Remember how William told of taking me into his home after my mother died? Well, what he left out was that my mother, who married William's son, was Hopi, not Navajo. At first William and the others were very upset and outraged at the union of my mother and father, as they were not of the same tribe and belief. In fact, for many centuries, the Navajo and Hopi lived as enemies as they competed for the land and lived different philosophies.

"My father was considered an outcast until my mother became pregnant with me. I am told there was a meeting between the Elders of both tribes in an effort to decide how to deal with this matter and to declare if I was to be brought up Hopi or Navajo, as having both cultures in my education would be forbidden. But then my mother got very ill and when a tribal Shaman tried to figure out what was wrong with her, they discovered something that changed the outcome. It was determined that as a result of this union between my Hopi mother and Navajo father, I would be *Tiponi*, Child of Importance and that my emergence came from the Holy People and that these separate family groups should live in the condition of *Hozoji*, be in harmony with the supernatural powers, which is the single most important idea sought by my father's people, the Navajos.

"Sadly, my father was killed by a drunk driver two months before I was born. Apparently, he had driven to Flagstaff to purchase some things my mother would need when I arrived, but never made it home. She was heartbroken. I'm told that she never spoke again until the day I was born. When I emerged and was laid across her chest, she kissed my cheek and whispered *"Daniel, he shall be called Daniel."* When my mother died shortly thereafter, officially as a result of complications after childbirth, the others knew better, they knew she really died from a broken heart.

"My mother's family was so distraught over her passing, they thought it best for William, a respected Navajo Elder, to take me as his charge with the condition that he'd educate me equally in the ancient ways of both cultures, along with the ways of the modern world.

"Despite her immense grief, my Hopi grandmother stoically presented the time-honored headband to William with explicit instructions that when I was older, I would intuitively know who should wear it, for it had special powers of discernment to the wearer and would act as absolute counsel when worn. This honor bestowed on me was of the highest degree, passed down through generations of my Hopi ancestry by my great, great grandmother, Chumana, *Snake Maiden* of the Hopi tribe…"

Before Daniel can speak another word, Krystal jumps to her feet and shouts "Oh my God, Daniel, I know of Chumana! I *just* learned that her spirit foretold of my coming, assisted in my difficult birth and then guided my Earth mother back into non-physical!"

Krystal pauses for but a moment then ponders aloud "How is it that I didn't know this? How is it that I couldn't 'see' who you were? What's wrong with me lately? I don't understand why I didn't …"

Now, it is Daniel's turn to interrupt, "Whoa! Settle down Super Girl, settle down. Quite honestly Krystal, I knew you were different but I just chocked it up to your being a weird kid, or something but now…well, I guess this kind of connects the dots for us, doesn't it?"

Laughing Krystal replies "Looks like we've both been charged with a pretty big mission, I'd say" and then timidly continues "Daniel, I need to ask something of you…" Daniel turns towards his young friend and smiles, signaling for her to go on. "Daniel…I'd like to perform a mind meld with you…that is, if you're okay with it? There's some things I…we…need to know."

Immediately and without hesitation, Daniel turns his body to fully face Krystal and adds "Yeah, Krystal. I, too want… need to know what lies ahead for us both, so-o-o…" With that, Krystal and Daniel move awkwardly closer to one another and then nervously lean forward, forehead touching forehead, eyes looking down all the while fighting to control the muffled giggles that express their youthful anxiety. Then, the mood quickly shifts, as each one positions their individual left hand's index and middle fingers onto one another's temple, breathing deeply and then slowly closing their eyes in ritual preparation.

Instantly, the young Tiponis are joined as one in spirit as they begin their virtual journey into the future, their future...together. There before them, questions have found their answers. For now they are privy to the possibilities that lay ahead for them and the roles they will fulfill with one another in this space, time continuum. *This is part of the remembering Adakor told me would unfold* Krystal thinks to herself, however, since they are in mind meld, Daniel can hear her every thought and tells her so.

With questions answered and their curiosity satiated, slowly they re-emerge back into their third-dimension reality with a renewed purpose. They share an innocent smile and find great comfort in knowing that their journey together has, in fact, just begun and welcome its unfolding.

Time has gotten away from them both and before they realize it, the weakening sun is setting low in the sky."Guess we should head back before it rains again and so I can see Uncle Brad before nightfall. Oh, I almost forgot...Daniel, would you do me another big favor? I still need to get to the meeting place in the Grand Canyon and..." Daniel stops Krystal in mid-sentence and answers "I'd be honored to escort you there."

One last question...how will I know when to put this on?" Krystal inquires in earnest, referring to the headband Daniel has just given her. In a whisper he responds, "When all else fails, I guess...when all else fails."

Celebrate Me Home

I'm beginning to understand now. How could I have missed such an obviously clear intended lesson? A vital part of this human experience, especially for a hybrid, is to find the value and the necessity to feel and deal with a wide range of emotions, like love, compassion, anger and now, loss. I guess you could say that I've been given an accelerated course in my twelve short years and am about to receive my Masters in loss. I've had to process my mother's passing immediately after my birth, the unexpected departure of my beloved dad, and now having to prepare for Uncle Brad's imminent journey home. I've never felt so alone and confused.

Oh, I've tried to put all these unasked for emotions out of my experience and focus fully on my special mission, whose time-line had accelerated greatly, due to planetary urgency. But you know what... in all honesty... I'm pretty tired of being so special

(Flashback)

When Krystal and Daniel arrive back at the village, dusk is fast approaching and there's a palpable chill in the air, but it's not due to the setting sun. They are greeted by William who helps Krystal off her horse and then hands the reins to Daniel as he motions for him to bring the horses back to the stables. Reading the seriousness in William's face, Daniel nods in agreement and then turns the horses in unison towards the barn, glancing over his shoulder to watch Krystal's reaction to the words his grandfather is about to speak. "Krystal" William solemnly begins, "the time of transition is close at hand. Go to him, as he has much to share with you."

To her surprise, Krystal's legs betray her command to move and so falter as she attempts to make her way towards the tent where her uncle lies in wait for her arrival. William stands by the tent's entrance, opens the flap, gesturing for Krystal to enter, and then backs away so as to provide private audience between the two of them.

Once inside, Krystal drops to her knees and then takes her uncle's hand in hers. *Cold*, she thinks to herself, in spite of the warm fire that burns in close proximity. Before speaking, Brad gestures for her to look about the interior of the tent to take in and appreciate the artwork and symbolism that is hand painted onto the tent walls. For it tells a story of a man preparing to journey to the Holy Land where he is joyfully welcomed and becomes, once again, part of *All That Is.*

Krystal smiles as she absorbs the artwork and then turns back around toward her uncle. Reaching into her sweatshirt pocket she pulls out the red, white and black bandana that contains the gift Daniel bestowed upon her earlier that day. Holding it before him, she delights for but a moment as he wearily produces one of his million dollar smiles in approval of this magnificent gift.

"Daniel gave it to me. Isn't it beautiful?" her voice unexpectedly quivers. "Put it on, Krystal. I'd love to see it on you." Brad requests. Krystal happily complies and begins to chatter on about its ancestral history and significance, but is interrupted, "I know all about it Krystal, for William has spoken of his challenge accepting the union of his son with a Hopi woman, the tragedy that followed with his son's passing and the honor bestowed upon Daniel, who is also a *Tiponi.* So, you see,

I'm up to date" Brad states, more in the interest of saving time and his energy, for he has much to share with her.

"Krystal, my Krystal…one so wise, yet still so young. I'm so sorry, honey…sorry to have to leave you so soon after Stephan's… your dad's departure and just when you're beginning to come into the fulfillment of your own mission. But, even we hybrids are subject to the untimely breakdown of our human vehicles." Krystal's eyes begin to swell with emotion, knowing full well that this will mostly likely be their last dialog.

"Uncle Brad, I have so many questions and not enough time to get the answers. I'm scared, Uncle Brad…"

Brad's words and intonation are no longer coming through in sarcasm, but in intelligible, profound statements. "I'm sure you are, but know this – it is no mistake that we were brought here, at this time, in this manner to be among William, Daniel and the others. The Navajo Nation, along with all the other Native American cultures are the true stewards of the Earth and have great wisdom to share. You will become one of them and learn the ways of the Ancients. In exchange, you will teach them much about modern science and technologies, some of which the like has never been seen before by men of any nation. You are about to inherit Universal knowledge and will show them the galactic future of their people and of this planet, for you are guided by those in spirit and in full support of the Galactic Federation of which your parents and I belong."

Tearfully, Krystal responds, "I fear I'm not ready, Uncle Brad and that I won't be able to focus on what I'm here to do. I have all these emotions I still don't know what to do with and they are interfering with my thought process."

Brad laughs, then lets out a series of disturbing coughs. Regaining his composure he continues, "Krystal, these emotions are but a part of who you are. For most of your young life, you've been allowed to push these feelings down, not always in your best interest, but now you have no other choice but to deal with them. In every life form a balance must be struck. In the animal kingdom, there is a proliferation of life to counter the need for food. In the plant world, insects are paramount to the pollenization so as to propagate the species. And so it is with humans and hybrids. Humans tend to take advantage of their planetary environment and carelessly place their ecosystems in perilous jeopardy; while hybrids honor and protect their surroundings and utilize their highly advance technologies to stabilize their planets and moons. It is by Universal deliberateness that these two species, hybrids and humans are co-mingling on such a large mass consciousness scale and will continue, hopefully, for decades to come; for without these checks and balances life on Earth, at least, would cease to exist."

Krystal listens with great intent, then asks "Uncle Brad, the planet is suffering great natural invasions and destruction right now. Some of the greatest scientific minds in the world are gathering, at this very moment in an attempt to respond to and hopefully find a way to quell these cataclysmic disasters. What can I, a twelve- year old, hybrid do? Will they even listen to whatever sage advice or direction is passed down through me from the Federation?"

"You underestimate yourself, Krystal and those who will stand alongside as you steady the Earth and its inhabitants. For you are one of many. A whole generation of Tiponis have been born and now inhabit this planet, each with their own specific skills and purpose, whose main objective is to bring all who dwell on Earth to ascend to their next evolutionary state, which until now has eluded Earth's people for many millenniums.

"Each one has a special talent, and yours will be one of sage counsel for the headband you were gifted with today from Daniel's ancestors was destined to be yours. When worn, it will give you complete access to the guardians of the Universe, the Galactic Federation and Council of Lightworkers and other beings of superior anarchy whose only purpose is to stabilize the galaxy, while staving off those of negative and suspect intention in their quest to rule.

"You have been fortunate to have the love and support of many, as did your father and mother. Those individuals and groups are now part of your armory and will prove to be honorable and valuable allies in the days to come.

"As far as you mastering your emotions, it is a wise to allow nature to find the balance for you. If you try to eliminate or push them down, you'll find they have a life of their own and will work against you, not with you. There is no shame in feeling, Krystal. In fact, it's not our intelligence that defines us, it's how we *feel* and exhibit our passion that leaves our true life's legacy."

From the depths of her being, emotion finally overtakes Krystal, who beings to weep openly as she bends over to embrace her uncle whose life ebbs before her very eyes. Not wishing to leave for fear that she may never see him again, Krystal lies down in the crook of her uncle's arm, needing the comfort of the man she has adored and considered family since her birth.

"I'm kinda tired now, sweetie, but I want to tell you something that's important for you to hear. I've never been married, came close a couple of times, but for whatever reason just didn't. But I always wanted children and believe it or not, I always wanted a daughter. Well...I've been blessed with that one...I've been blessed by having you.." With that Brad slips into a peaceful slumber, his respirations barely visible, but nonetheless still there.

Krystal slowly follows suit and dreams of happier days with her Mom, Dad and Uncle Brad all together again. Music echoes through her dream with words of comfort that bring her to a familiar place of knowing:

I soar with the eagles,
I float on the wind,
I play with all nature, for it is my friend
I am ALL THAT IS, all that will ever be
I am the Source of creativity
I blend with the earth and the heavens above
I come to this physical place to bear witness of LOVE
When my journey is over and I'm at last home,
Let my essence remain with those I have known.

Epilogue

The time for remembering is at hand

~Adakor,

Magistrate to the Galactic Federation

As the desert sun descends below the great monoliths of the Grand Canyon, Krystal sits poised overlooking its great expanse, feeling dwarfed by its grandeur. Tilting her head skyward, she closes her eyes as she takes in a deep breath that signals her intent to begin the process of ritual telepathic communication with those who have guided her thus far.

Deeper and deeper Krystal goes into that place where linear time no longer dictates and dimensions fuse together. Once fully emerged into nothingness, Krystal reaches for her sacred headband she has carefully transported to this site in a handmade cowhide sleeve that William has lovely made for her and then slowly places it upon her forehead, allowing the soft eagle feathers strung together by turquoise beading to gently fall upon her skin. This sacred head piece, which allows only those of the highest vibration to reach her consciousness.

For this is the moment...more than any other... the time has come for revelation. In some respect she has dreaded this moment and yet knew it was destined to happen. Her next breath betrays her accomplished control as a shiver accompanies its release from her lungs. Oblivious to the darkening evening sky and the plummeting temperatures, Krystal remains detached from the outside world as she reaches her intended realm of multi-dimensional beings whose wisdom and ancestral teachings have protected her and now guide the way.

Okay, this is it. This is why I came here she reminds herself, all the while silently wishing her mother and father's presence would appear to comfort her ever increasing nervous anticipation. Then it begins...*Ohmm, Ohmm, OHmm, OHmm* – louder and louder the vibration rises to almost deafening decibels. *OHMMM, OHMMM, OHMMM* and then... silence.

The only sound is her pounding heart which painfully roars in her ears. Just when Krystal thinks she can't stand it any longer - all sounds cease. Then softly, almost as if in the distance she hears her name being spoken...*Krystal...Krystal...open your eyes, my child.*

Following the voice's instructions isn't all that easy, for she has been holding her eyes shut so very tightly; however with determined effort, Krystal's furiously blinking eyes finally open to reveal she has, indeed, arrived at her destination.

I don't believe I've ever been here before she thinks to herself, taking in the magnificence of this place that's filled with vibrant hues, some of which she has no known language to describe. Then, the voice responds to her thought: *Yes, you have, my child... for this is your home, your place of creation. For it is here, in this place that you vowed to fulfill your cosmic mission and take an active role in the evolutionary paradigm shift that was prophesized to occur on the planet that is referred to as EARTH.*

While Krystal has many questions, she instinctively knows that it is wise to let the voice continue. Again reading her thoughts, the telepathic conversation continues:

> *We have much to share with you, so it is our intention to communicate until we are complete. It is anticipated that you will have questions of your own and so it is that we will tend to those at the appropriate moment.*

It is relevant at this point, to caution you that your human consciousness will struggle with some matters, while attempting to comprehend our statements and remember what you have temporarily forgotten. It is by deliberate intention that certain elements of your etiology and reasons for your human… let us say…adventure have been erased, for if you were to fully recall your mission and purpose, the results would have varied greatly and not had the desired outcome.

Let us begin. You are a Star Child of the 5th world. Your Earth parents, Stephan and Elizabeth were summoned by the Galactic Federation as mere Star Seeds themselves and initiated into the program. Stephan came to us from the star system Sirius, while your mother's home planet is of a far away galaxy called Triton. They petitioned vigorously for placement in this experiment and so it was with your galactic family to offer you, to which you agreed, for each soul has the right to participation or refusal. That is your birth right.

You, Stephan and Elizabeth were a harmonic match of epic proportions and so it was deemed that together you would provide the ultimate hybrid/human unit. While in the Galactic nursery, you became part of an experiment with a highly evolved human child with unique psychic skills named Bethany, who was recruited in vitro to teach young hybrids how to interact with other humans and learn their behavioral patterns. This proved to be a superior opportunity to expand our experiment further and so it was decided that you would emerge into physical form as the offspring of hybrids Stephan and Elizabeth.

Unfortunately, Bethany succumbed to the pressures of her non-awakened parents and those around her that misunderstood her skills and so she self-terminated her participation in the program. This proved to be a paramount challenge for you, as we had counted on Bethany's assistance to mentor and help cultivate your human emotional side.

While this presented an unexpected obstacle, your father sought other resolutions to hasten your progression. Your mother's emergence back into non-physical was destined to occur in the way that it did as her participation was complete. As in most cases, spirit is allowed to continue their interaction with Earth bound souls and so it has been and will remain. The same allowances will be honored in regard to your father, Stephan and the spirit you refer to as "Uncle Brad".

In Earth years you are chronologically still a child, while cosmically you possess much wisdom and knowledge that now must be shared with those who seek such information. Now, it is time to remember much more...what you have been experiencing on this Earth plane is not, in fact, happening, by that I mean, it is not in the NOW but of the past. I will give you a moment to absorb what I have said...(pause)

I shall continue – while it is true that linear time inhabits 3rd dimension time space reality, reality being the operative word, you are, in fact, not of that time, but of the future... (again pause) for you are what is termed a "Time Traveler". You came to be part of this program, this Earth school to study, examine, evaluate and learn of your human/hybrid species evolutionary process.

The educators in the future devised a unique process for students, such as yourself, to experience the past, a sort of interactive virtual classroom where you could take part in your spiritual growth and perhaps influence its outcome. In the Earth science known as quantum physics, all things are possible and so it is with this exceptional classroom...you can actually "live" the past and chose to change the future of this planet Earth.

I assume that this concept is foreign to you as my words are interpreted, but think, Krystal...think...does any of this resonate with you?

At this point, Krystal struggles to wrap her human brain

around what has been revealed to her. She has not yet reached the place of full remembering and yet stands unflappable as she attempts to absorb this information. The voice scans Krystal's unified energetic field to evaluate her physical response to all that has been said and notes that while her heart rate is racing, all other systems remain within normal range.

The voice speaks:

Krystal, it is now appropriate to begin your questioning…

Krystal hesitates for but a moment, then asks:

Are you telling me that this has all been nothing more than a galactic game I've been playing? That my life's mission and that of my parents, Uncle Brad and all the others have no validation or true purpose?

Voice: I know not of the expression you refer to as "game" so instead will offer the word "experiment". In our realm, to experiment provides not only essential knowledge but great satisfaction while in process…I believe the appropriate corresponding Earth word is "joy".
As to the mater of validation and purpose, it is accurate to state that there is tremendous rationale for each individual mission, confirming the participatory commitment of the Star Seed. Being chosen and accepting is not suitable for all Star Children. It is reserved for those of higher vibration who willingly enroll into the program and are tutored how to utilize their accelerated abilities for the good of the program.

Krystal: You say that I am…we are….all Time Travelers from the future. How is this so?

Voice: When you entered into the program, you were told how your memory would be erased or temporarily inaccessible so as not to interfere with the process, which it surely would. To know you are far more advanced than your ancestors would inhibit your interaction immensely. Let me rephrase by utilizing an Earth expression, "we needed to level the playing field" so as to maintain a viable balance between the species, lest you be considered gods, as was the error in more ancient civilizations.

Krystal: *What specifically were we sent here to do, if not save the Earth and its people?*

Voice: *Wasn't that enough? You had the opportunity to travel back in linear time to witness the way things were, evaluate and disseminate how you would alter certain actions so as to bring about a different result. Each hybrid could calculate an outcome and then put into action their theories, then watch the results.*

I need to express how there is no correct action or answer, only variable results. That is the purpose of the program. Humanity was encoded with something termed "Free Will" and so it was decided that given many choices, which one would be chosen? Having to live out the results of that choice is what the program really is about.

Krystal: *So, what you're telling me is that while I'm working on my own mission...er...experiment...all the other hybrids are doing the same, at the same time? Wouldn't that produce chaotic results and conflict of action?*

Voice: *Not at all. What you have yet to realize is that as you each perform your individual experiment, the others are merely holographic replications to follow your bidding. To put it more simply, those you interact with are not real, but avatars of the true Star Being.*

Now Krystal is truly confused and hysterically questions: *Are you telling me that my parents, Uncle Brad, William, Daniel and all the others weren't real?*

Voice: *They are as real as you imagined them to be. It is not unlike being in a virtual dream state where sights, sounds, smells and touch are viable. The significant difference here is that while those known to you as your parents seemed to be present in your reality, they were indeed present in many realities at the same time.*

The same holds true for you. The reason you are not cognizant of this fact is that you have chosen to be physically focused on this time space continuum but whenever you change that focus you are able to traverse into any other dimension of your choosing. That is how you and Bethany were able to transport back and forth as young children. That was one of your first lessons.

The interaction with human children was two- fold; they were to teach young hybrids, such as yourself, how to interact with other humans while you were to remind them of their natural telepathic communication abilities which had been cloaked for millennium.

Krystal: *What about the catastrophes that are...um I mean... were occurring on Earth back then in 2012? Were they real? And by the way, what year am I from?*

Voice:. *First things first. The galactic threats of that time were real however, humanity had a more diabolical threat on their home planet. There were other humans who learned of our existence and that of those of lower vibration who promised them great power and wealth if they cooperated and did their bidding. Their agenda was not intended to be in the best interest of the masses and so an alliance was formed and has continued for all this time.*

In their distorted processing, they negated their loyalties to humanity and the planet, disregarding what dire consequence might follow their thoughtless actions.

It had become necessary for the Galactic Federation and other sovereign worlds to intercede and join forces as the results of such negative actions were far reaching into their proximity.

To answer your query about your position in the future, you are from 3025.

Even as Krystal attempts to process all that has been shared, a familiarity begins to rise within her being. It's as if she's awakening from a dead sleep and fights to clear the massive cob webs that permeate her human brain.

The Voice continues: *Krystal, we are aware of your struggle to remember. It is not paramount for you to assimilate it into focus right away. It will take some time...*

Krystal: *Do I HAVE time or is the...um...experiment over? And what do I do now?*

Voice: *No, Krystal...the experiment is not over – and it shall continue. You will have time to finish your mission, your part in the program and so it is appropriate for you to return to your Earth realm now to complete what you have just begun.*

Krystal: *One last question...does humanity survive and take its next evolutionary place into the galactic neighborhood?*

Voice: *What do YOU think?*

The Final Word

W hen I first sat down to write this book, I decided, due to the subject matter at hand, the reader would accept the events as they unfolded more easily if the book was deemed a work of fiction rather than if it had been written in a different genre.

After all, we are still processing and absorbing the plethora of materials that are available to us in so many formats, i.e., television, movies, books, Internet, and seminars relative to the existence of UFOs and E.T.'s.

Upon the book's completion, I was then struck with the quandary of whether or not to divulge even more information for the reader to consider relative to the plausibility of these events actually occurring, or should it remain the product of this author's wild imagination attempting to debunk the government's denial of the existence of these entities and their intended interaction with humanity?

Once I revisited the question, the answer was undeniable.

I needed to share with you, the reader, that many of the events portrayed in this book were, indeed, artistic recreations of actual happenings, and that the main character Stephan is loosely fashioned after a real person I knew who shared his amazing beginnings with me.

We were first introduced at his place of business in Florida right after my move from Boston, Massachusetts, in 1993. I found him to be a well-grounded individual, a respected businessman in his community, and a devoted family man.

Our casual conversations ultimately revealed a shared profound interest in "other" intangible things, such as angels, E.T.'s and UFOs. As time passed, he became more aware of my sincere exploration of the UFO and E.T. phenomena, and eventually felt comfortable enough to confide in me about his true identity and his own close encounters. His judgment was sound, as I remained open and accepting of the possibilities which piqued his desire to share even more amazing details of his Earth life. So intriguing was his story that I commented on how his would make a terrific book of fiction, and I would like to be the one to write it.

Having already shared some of my previous writing efforts with him, he expressed his admiration concerning my literary integrity and so, with his permission and encouragement, agreed to let me weave an imaginary tale with the stipulation that I honor his request to keep his identity a secret. So it was that we began our weekly Sunday afternoon meetings where I took copious notes and was allowed to tape his dialogues to assist me in formulating a viable story, with the hope of producing an epic impact upon the reader.

What impressed me most was this man's matter-of-fact recounting of his early life detailing events and encounters that were anything but normal by anyone's perspective. He was not seeking notoriety, nor was it his intention to shock me. He trusted me enough to unveil his unusual human life experiences while still a young boy, perhaps with a prophetic knowledge that I would one day write about all of this.

We both hoped the rise in mass consciousness had finally reached a level of elevation so that people would accept the possibility of a character, such as Stephan, as one of many who have walked among us since the beginning of time.

It was my intention to put a non-threatening, three-dimensional, humanoid face to those star beings living among us, in an effort to quantify their universal mission and focus, and for us to take care in our interaction with other species so as not to upset the balance of a, so far, peaceful coexistence.

Regrettably, I lost contact with this amazing being, and so took poetic license to conclude the possibilities.

I hope that one day he'll have the opportunity to read this story — and we will find ourselves, once again, in each other's experience, so that he can fill me in on his latest adventures. Sequel? Perhaps...

Afterword from Sheldan Nidle

T he whole concept of First Contact and what it means to humanity is a topic that is often ignored or misrepresented by most contemporary literature. My life's work has been committed to bringing this topic out and away from the obscurity in which it has dwelled for far too long.

At present, we are in the midst of a profound change in our consciousness. This change is bringing about not only a shift in our concepts of reality, but it is also a time where we find ourselves being bombarded with a host of physical and spiritual changes that are altering our environment forever.

At the heart of this transformation is the question of extraterrestrial life and how it is impacting our present existence and what affect it will bring to us in the very near future. This process of interaction is something that is not only very important to me but is, in my opinion, the most crucial set of events in the whole of recorded human history! For out of this is to come the ideas and the reasoning for what will shape how we view each other as well as the vast Universe that surrounds us.

This time of contact is nothing new and has actually been ongoing since our earliest beginnings on Mother Earth. Yet, this too has been swept under the proverbial rug, largely by our historians and especially by those who fear the challenge to purvey to the public what is now considered to be the

427

"conventional wisdom" of how you judge the nature of what constitutes this physical reality.

In short, humanity has reached a point where what is to be believed is no longer the all-powerful final arbiter for what is *real* and even for what is to be *believed*. Simply stated, there is a whole list of yet to be "main stream" alternatives percolating beneath the surface. At the top of this "Alternatives List" is a growing mass of literature about the UFOnauts and what beliefs and knowledge they have imparted to those "Earthlings" they have contacted.

Since I am one of those contactees, I feel particularly honored by my long association and interaction with them. My group which is from the Star *Sirius B*, has taught me much about the origins of Earth's humanity and continues to carry on this long teaching cycle with me that began when I was a very small child and even continues to this very day.

Along the way, all of the political, social and philosophic issues that I have alluded to were discussed with me in great detail and I in turn, imparted these teachings through my books, lectures and DVDs.

One of the things that I have observed along this amazing journey is that a great dichotomy continues to exist between what I call the "Accepters" and the "Skeptics". What is needed is to create a forum in which all parties can freely and with great openness discuss all the numerous controversial subjects that surround what the Sirians and the organization for the Light they belong to (The Galactic Federation) have raised with me, as well as a great number of other contactees.

In "HYBRID–The Trilogy" Louise Aveni addresses these and other vital subjects quite well during the course of this pleasingly quick and marvelously exciting read! I *highly* recommend it.

It is my hope that "HYBRID" will serve as one of those amazing books that can open up new and important vistas for those who venture within its wonderful pages. Maybe this book will insight the reader to question the nature of *this* reality and start them on a whole new life changing adventure.

Most of all, "HYBRID" introduces the reader to some basic aspects of the world that I, personally have lived since early childhood. For me, the time is well overdue for humanity to think openly about and to explore more fully the messages given to this world by the Sirians and their companions in the Galactic Federation of Light.

So, enjoy this work, as did I and use it as a catalyst to think more deeply about what is being brought forth within these inspirational pages.

May it serve as an *awakening* to new possibilities and especially bring clarity to a subject that is quite dear to my heart - First Contact with the Galactic Federation of Light!

With Love,

Sheldan Nidle
www.paoweb.com

About the Author

A native of Boston, Massachusetts, Louise Rose Aveni has dabbled in fictional writing for many years.

It wasn't until her bout with cancer in the mid 80's that she found her true literary voice. Simultaneously, as her spirit awakened, a long time curiosity with the idea of life on other planets and inter-dimentional realms gave rise to a renewed passion to explore the possibilities in earnest.

No longer concerned with how she would be perceived in her pursuit to obtain answers to her own core questions, Louise Rose penned her first novel titled LUPO-Conversations with an E.T.", which is the first of a trilogy series with HYBRID-The Conversation Continues" and finally "KRYSTAL 2012-A New Beginning", completing the saga.

"My intention for writing this trilogy was to put a non-threatening, benevolent face to those Star beings who have walked among us since the beginning and in preparation for their inevitable global contact, albeit to the contrary of the governments's continual denial of their very existence."

Louise Rose travels around the country with other authors providing conferences and interacting speaking engagements for those of like mind who are open to explore the infinite possibilities.

Being the former host of her own radio talk show "Now That's What I'm Talking About!" via Sedona Talk Radio, provided an audio vehicle to interview prominent researches, advocates, men and women of science as well as esteemed authors who shared their immense knowledge and experience relative to the subject of UFOs and the E.T.s.

Currently a resident of Sarasota, Florida, Louise Rose works as a freelance Ghostwriter, Editor, and Marketing Consultant. She continues her frequent travels to her "other" home in Sedona, Arizona to partake of its unprecedented beauty and commiserate with the abundance of other free thinkers.

Louise Rose invites you to visit her web sites at:

www.sedonaangels.com
www.myspace.com/louiseroseaveni

Louise Rose's books can also be found at: **www.amazon.com** as well as **Borders** and **Barnes & Noble.**

www.ingramcontent.com/pod-product-compliance
Lightning Source LLC
Chambersburg PA
CBHW031939260626
47157CB00016B/90